MIDNIGHT FIRE

WHITE HAVEN HUNTERS BOOK FIVE

TJ GREEN

Midnight Fire

Mountolive Publishing

Copyright ©2022 TJ Green

eBook ISBN: 978-1-99-004752-7

Paperback ISBN: 978-1-99-004753-4

Hardback ISBN: 978-1-991313-15-7

Cover Design by Fiona Jayde Media

Editing by Missed Period Editing

Contents

One

Harlan Beckett settled behind his desk with a cup of strong espresso and looked at the files that Eloise, Mason Jacobs's new secretary, had placed on his desk.

He sighed, hoping there was something more interesting in them than the current jobs he was working on. *Although, why was he complaining?* The last few weeks had been a welcome respite from the earlier turmoil.

It was a Wednesday in late August, Black Cronos had vanished, and the information on their possible whereabouts had dried up. Jackson Strange was researching files diligently, while Harlan focussed on his job with The Orphic Guild. He hated to say this, but while the jobs had been easy—he had needed to find a few alchemical manuscripts, old maps, and an unusual mirror—they were also boring. Nahum and Ash, the Nephilim, had helped him out with a few cases, and Gabe and Shadow with another, but he hadn't seen anything of them for a couple of weeks.

Restless, he headed to the window and looked down onto Eaton Place, which was lined with expensive and therefore exclusive properties, sipping his drink while he did so. He opened the window, and the sound of traffic carried inside on a wave of heat. London was hot, and it was making him claustrophobic. He had a sudden urge to get out of the city, and he returned to his desk, eager to see what new jobs he may have.

There were only a handful of files, all containing job requests from known clients, and he searched through them quickly, growing increasingly frustrated. More old documents to bid on in auctions, one grimoire to find for an out-of-town witch, and a charmed, bronze statue. He frowned at the last one. That sounded more interesting, but only just. He pinched the bridge of his nose. Dealing with Black Cronos seemed to have turned him into an adrenaline junkie.

While he was deciding on a plan of action for the day, his phone rang, the vibrations carrying it across the desk. The barking greeting of an old client made him wince.

"Morning, Theo. I'm not deaf."

"Sorry, old boy, I'm excited. I have a job for you. It's urgent."

Harlan rolled his eyes. All of Theo's jobs were *urgent* in his eyes. Theobald Henry James Carmichael was in his late seventies and rich, with a castle in Kent, a townhouse in London, a house in Provence, one in Madrid, and no doubt many others. He also had a very young wife, a few ex-wives, and half a dozen children. He had made his money by trading in stocks, and now was obsessed with antiques of an unusual provenance. He was The Orphic Guild's dream client.

"All your jobs are urgent, Theo," Harlan remonstrated with him gently.

"Ha! I know. The hazards of old age. I might die before you find my latest must-have."

"You're fitter than I am. You've got a good few years left in you yet. Go on, then. What do you need now?"

"You know, I don't really want to talk about this over the phone. It's sensitive."

Immediately suspicious, Harlan asked, "Sensitive how? Does it involve stealing?"

Theo snorted. "Nothing so sordid. Any chance you can pop in for a chat?"

"Are you in London?"

"In this heat? Are you mad? No, I'm at my estate in Temple Moreton. Can you pop in?"

Harlan suppressed a laugh. You could hardly pop into Theo's estate. It was nestled in the High Weald of Kent and a good two hours' drive, but it did provide Harlan with an excuse to get out of London.

"No problem. I can be there late morning."

"Perfect. You're going to like this job, Harlan. I can feel it in my bones. This is going to be my greatest acquisition yet."

Theo hung up abruptly, as usual, and Harlan pocketed his phone, musing on what Theo wanted him to find. Suddenly energised, he turned his attention to the files on his desk, noting down the objects he needed to locate and where he should start looking for them when he returned, and then decided to find Olivia before he left the office.

Knocking on her door down the corridor from his own, he stuck his head in. "Is this a good time?"

She looked up at him and smiled. "Always time for you." Olivia James was sun-kissed, her hair gleaming gold in the light from the window, her strappy sundress revealing toned shoulders and arms.

"You're chirpy," he observed as he crossed the room and perched on her desk. "Good night last night?"

"Nice pay check this morning. Moorland paid, and I've got my commission."

"Ah! I sense more Louboutins are on the way."

She slapped his leg playfully. "Cheeky. No, actually. I'm going on holiday. I've booked a villa in Italy, and I can't wait."

He checked his watch. "It's only half-past nine. That was quick."

"Idiot. No, I did it yesterday, knowing my commission was imminent."

"Is there room for two?" He gave her his most charming smile.

"No. I'm going with my best friend. No men allowed. Well, until, of course, we start meeting handsome Italian men."

"And I'll be stuck here, coping with Mason, alone."

Olivia sniggered. "You're hardly alone. I think Eloise seems to have mastered his moods." Her expression softened. "He seems a changed man the last couple of weeks. I think he's finally put his grief over Smythe aside."

Harlan nodded. "You're right, which is good. He's also stopped harassing me about Black Cronos." He eased off the desk and into a seat. "I'm sure it won't last, but it's a welcome respite."

"And JD?"

"Suspiciously quiet. Holed up in his dungeon, I think, experimenting."

"Don't you mean his lab?"

"It feels and looks like a dungeon! You'd think the same if you saw it."

Olivia leaned forward, eyes sharp. "Has he made progress with the whole enhanced-humans thing?"

"I'm not sure." Harlan thought about their last phone call and how cagey JD had been. "I don't think so, which is why he's quiet. I think he'd be broadcasting any success. He's finding it hard."

"Not surprising. What about his work on making weapons disappear?"

He'd told Olivia about JD's alchemical wheel and its correspondences, and how he'd made Shadow's knife resonate with her energy, and then one that worked with him. Harlan shrugged. "No word on that, either. I must admit, I didn't like the way that made me feel. If I'm honest, I've kept away, and fortunately, JD hasn't demanded my presence."

"That's fair enough." Olivia rested her chin on her long, elegant fingers. "With Black Cronos quiet, it gives him time to work, anyway."

"But it's unnerving. Where have they gone?"

"I'd like to say they're licking their wounds, but I doubt it."

"I doubt it, too," Harlan said with a sigh as he rose to his feet. "Anyway, I must go. I'm heading to Kent to see Theo. I'm hoping he has a juicy job. What have you got going on?"

"I'm tracking down a very tricky, supposedly magical reliquary. The search is becoming more convoluted by the day." Her eyes narrowed. "I was debating whether to involve Shadow and the Nephilim."

"I'm sure they'll be happy to help, although I know Barak is assisting Jackson with Black Cronos. I have no idea what the rest of them are up to. I'm sure at least one of them could help you, though."

She nodded, clearly already distracted by the idea. "Okay. I'll see how it goes."

Harlan left her to her thoughts, called Eloise to tell her where he was going, not wanting to talk to Mason, and headed out into the sunshine. *Time to see Theo and give his car a spin.*

Shadow pulled her bow string back, feeling the power and strength in it, before releasing the arrow. She watched it thump into the distant target at the edge of the field, and smiled with satisfaction as she hit the bullseye.

"Perfect," she declared. In seconds, she had shot a flurry of arrows at the target, all finding their mark, and she lowered the bow before turning to Gabe. "It's better than I hoped."

"Better than your fey-made one?"

She snorted. "Don't be an idiot! Of course not."

Gabe laughed, his teeth flashing white against his dark tan. "You are so easy to wind up." His skin was darker than normal, a result of the good weather they'd been having throughout August. His jaw was skimmed with stubble, but his warm brown eyes were hidden by his sunglasses.

She narrowed her eyes as she gave him a sidelong glance. "I am not. I am merely correcting you. Nothing made here will ever beat a fey-made weapon." She ran her hand across the carved wooden bow that was almost as tall as she was. "However, I will concede, this is excellent. It will be even better when El has strengthened it with magic."

Ever since her bow had broken when she fought against Black Cronos in France, she'd felt its loss. Her bow was an extension of her, even more than her sword. She had taken her time finding someone to make her a new one. It had to be right, and this was. She had found a craftsman in Devon to make it for her, and had chosen yew, a common wood for a long bow because of its high-tensile strength. However, the other advantage of yew was its magical properties. The tree symbolized immortality, rebirth, and protection, its connected elements were earth and water, and it was considered a guardian of the Otherworld. It was also strongly connected with the Goddess. As an added enhancement, protection runes had been carved into it.

"What material did you choose for the bowstring?" Gabe asked, taking it from her hands to examine it.

"I bowed to modernity and used Dacron. It seemed sensible. It will last longer, and it's lightweight." She shrugged. "I wanted the best bow possible. He made me some arrows, too. They're good, but I prefer my own." She sometimes spent hours making them herself, but she found it satisfying, and with her earth magic, it made it easier. "I'm going hunting tonight, when it's cooler." She lowered her sunglasses over her eyes to block out the glare of the mid-morning sun. "It's too hot now. I'll see El instead."

Gabe nodded. "Why don't I come with you? We can have a pub lunch in The Wayward Son. There's not much else to do around here."

"That's a great idea."

They strolled across the field next to the farmhouse above White Haven, heading through the side door and into the cool kitchen, where Niel was already prepping meat for the barbeque that evening.

Niel looked up as they entered, his hands covered in some kind of sauce. "Jackson has phoned Barak. He's talking to him now."

Shadow rested her bow against the wall as Gabe asked, "Black Cronos?"

"I reckon."

Barak, like Niel, was no longer working for Caspian Faversham, and he'd been eager to pick up more responsibility with their own business. Gabe had nominated him as Jackson's contact in the hunt for the shadowy organisation and their mysterious leader, who they suspected to be the immortal *Comte de Saint-Germain*. A few weeks previously, Barak and Estelle Faversham had visited The Retreat, the Paranormal Division's new headquarters, and now he and Jackson kept in regular contact. Shadow had long resigned herself to Estelle's constant presence. She would have to later, too, when she came to their barbeque. Her relationship with Barak was growing stronger every day, which was great for Barak, but painful for everyone else. At least Estelle was softening, slightly. She was like a rusty knife now, rather than a sharp one.

Before they could question Niel further, Barak bounded in, a satisfied smile on his face. "We think we have a lead!"

"Really?" Shadow asked, heading to the fridge and grabbing some beers for all of them. "You said that last time, and it went nowhere."

"And the time before that," Gabe added.

Barak shrugged, his huge shoulders rising and his chest muscles rippling beneath his t-shirt. "They're good at hiding. I suspected it would take a while. I'm actually enjoying the hunt. Besides, I'm getting to see new places with the beautiful Estelle. That's even better than finding them." He winked at Shadow, knowing it made her cranky. "Estelle is a woman with hidden depths."

"Like Loch Ness. We all know what's down there."

Barak's enthusiasm would not be subdued, and he blew her a kiss. "Tetchy madam."

"Piss off."

Gabe intervened, shooting Shadow a warning glance that she ignored. "Where are you heading?"

"Avignon. Apparently, there's another old *château* there that the *Comte* once stayed in."

"Who owns it now?" Shadow asked.

"The same people who built it centuries ago—the du Buade family. Jackson wonders if they have affiliations to Black Cronos."

Shadow leaned against the counter. "Why? Is there something suspicious about them?"

"They own a couple of businesses that Jackson thinks are dodgy. He's leaving no stone unturned."

"That's part of the problem," Gabe said, sitting at the kitchen table and raking his hand through his hair. "I think he's spreading his net too wide."

"But with no clues at all," Barak argued, "what's the alternative? We have to chase down every possible lead in the hope of a breakthrough."

Niel washed his hands, his food preparation finished, as he said, "At least Jackson is paying."

"Exactly!" Barak grinned. "And I get to see the world."

"When do you leave?" Shadow asked.

"In a couple of hours. I'll be there for three or four days, probably. It depends on what we find." He looked at the stack of meat that Niel was marinating, lips twisting with disappointment. "Unfortunately, I'll miss the barbeque."

Gabe studied him. "Don't hesitate to call for backup if you think you've found something."

Barak nodded as he put a number into his phone and headed out of the room. "Sure thing. I'll let Estelle know our plans."

Shadow patted Gabe's hand. "He'll be fine. It's like you said—they're chasing everything right now."

"But at some point they'll get lucky, and there's only two of them."

"At which time he'll call us." Shadow inwardly sighed. Gabe always worried about the others. He couldn't help it. It was even worse when he didn't have anything else to worry about, which they didn't right now.

"Come on. Time to see El, and then pub." She turned to Niel. "Want to join us?"

"Nah. I'm going to the barn to spar with Nahum. He's already warming up." He flexed his arms and rolled his shoulders as he gave them a wicked grin. "I'm already feeling victorious."

Shadow tutted. "Overconfidence will cost you."

"Says the woman who is constantly overconfident!"

"It's justified. I am fey!" she proclaimed, wide-eyed, and then dodged out of the kitchen before he could retaliate, giggling as Niel swore behind her. "Come on, Gabe. Places to be!"

Two

Jackson paced his office after finishing making all the arrangements for Barak and Estelle's trip, hoping that something useful would come of the latest intel.

He always knew that this would take a long time, but he was already getting impatient. He took a deep breath, reminding himself that this search had been going on for a long time, and that they were making more progress than they had in years. *Patience.* He itched to be going with Barak, but he would be of more use here. He had more leads to follow up, and that included liaising with JD.

His gaze swept around his organised office. He'd been working at The Retreat for weeks now, and his room was arranged perfectly. There were lots of shelves stacked with books on all sorts of subjects, filing cabinets for old paperwork, a polished wooden desk and comfortable chair, plus a computer and phone. In the corner was a coffee table with armchairs for guests and relaxing, where he did much of his reading, as well as a drinks cabinet and a kettle and mugs. It was self-sufficient. He'd recently acquired a long, low sofa, perfect for sleeping on if he needed to. Although he hadn't yet, he was preparing for the fact that he may have to hole up down here if he ever felt he was being followed.

However, after his latest conversation with Waylen Adams, the Director of the Paranormal Division, it seemed that he was already addressing that particular issue. There were many unused rooms and side corridors in The Retreat, and he had decided to utilise them. Some were being converted into bedrooms, others were storage rooms, and one had become a large kitchen and staffroom that was much improved on the old one. The labs were at the far end of the complex in much larger spaces, and they were now finally up and running. Not surprisingly, they had taken the longest time to organise with all of the equipment they needed. Layla Gould's office was close by, next to Russell Blake's, the Assistant Director of the PD.

Suddenly curious as to what was happening elsewhere in the headquarters, and needing to stretch his legs, Jackson pocketed his mobile phone and headed down the corridor to find the room the analysts were based in. He liked to check the paranormal activity occurring over the UK, just in case there was something that could be traced to Black Cronos.

Petra and Austin, the two young analysts, were deep in conversation when he entered their office, but they paused and greeted him, both of them wearing a worried frown.

"Everything okay?" he asked, immediately worried, too.

"Just the usual," Petra replied. "We both seem to be having spirit trouble, and we're not sure why."

Austin barked out a laugh. "Maybe the hot weather unsettles ghosts."

Petra rolled her eyes and threw a paperclip at him. "Idiot."

He laughed, unmoved by the teasing insult. "Well, something is stirring them up. Don't worry, Jackson. It's nothing we haven't experienced before. I'm sure it will settle down."

Jackson nodded and sat in a spare chair. "Nothing to do with Black Cronos?"

"No sign of anything that could be attributed to them." Petra gave him a half smile. "Sorry, but not sorry. I'm glad they've vanished."

"Well, me too, I guess. We can all do without destruction on an epic scale," Jackson confessed. "But still, a glimpse of them would be nice. Nothing from overseas?" He had asked them to keep in touch with their foreign colleagues.

Austin shook his head. "Nothing."

"Okay." Jackson sighed and rose to his feet. "I'll drop in on Layla, see if any more post-mortem results have come in. And see if maybe the lab has had a breakthrough."

Petra smiled at him sympathetically. "Regretting taking the job?"

"Not at all. Just regretting the slow progress." He shrugged. "Nothing I didn't expect. See you later."

Harlan gaped at Temple Keep, unable to hide his shock at how impressive the beautiful stone-built building was.

As far as castles went, it wasn't that big really, but it had a lot of charm. It was set in beautiful grounds that he'd caught tantalising glimpses of as he wound along the woodland-edged drive. He'd also caught sight of the moat that encompassed half the building, before the drive switched back, bringing him to the entrance. *Wow. Theo must be loaded.*

Harlan presumed Theo was looking out for him, because he bounded out of the front door and almost ran to greet him. He was a tall, bald man, with shrewd eyes, an extravagant, grey moustache, and a beard that stretched down to his chest. He looked the epitome of a country squire, wearing tweed trousers, shirt, and waistcoat.

"Nice car, Harlan," he said, casting his gaze along it as he shook his hand. "Must have cost you a pretty packet. Worth it, though."

"It didn't cost as much as this!" Harlan gestured to the house.

Theo winked. "It's only little, but it satisfies my need to pretend I'm royalty. My house in France is bigger. Anyway, enough of such vulgar topics. I can't wait to share what I want you to find."

"Why the secrecy?" Harlan asked, his intrigue growing by the second. "I can't help thinking you have me searching for something underhanded."

"Not at all. Just old, with a very *interesting* story attached. Plus, everyone's away, and I'm on my own. I'm going slightly mad with no one to talk to. Old Chivers and his wife don't really count. They're older than I am."

"Chivers?"

"The butler and his wife, my housekeeper. They're in the kitchen at the moment, preparing a late morning tea. It will be up in a moment."

Fortunately, Theo was ahead of him, striding across the entrance hall and up the curving staircase to the next floor, so he didn't see Harlan's clenched jaw. *He'd been brought here because Theo was bored?* He took a deep breath, exhaling slowly. *It was a job.* Plus, he *had* wanted to get out of the office.

Theo, talking all the while as he pointed out rooms, oil paintings, and furnishings, led him to a comfortable sitting room that overlooked the back of the house. It was furnished with a mixture of armchairs, a squishy sofa, and a table under the window. The old, leaded-paned windows were thrown open, and the view of the moat and the grounds was dazzling. Theo, however, ignored it, leading Harlan to the table where a small, slim, book lay open, its pages yellowed with age and slightly dogeared. Next to it was an antique dagger with what looked like a bone hilt engraved with symbols.

"This is the bugger." His finger jabbed at the knife.

"A dagger? May I?"

"Of course."

Harlan picked it up, examining it closely. Some of the symbols were familiar. "What's so special about this?"

Theo gave him an almost maniacal grin. "It belonged to William de la More, the last Master of England who served the Knights Templar."

Harlan groaned. "Oh, no. I sense a long and diabolical tale." He dropped into a chair with a finely woven tapestry base, wondering if he was sitting on a small fortune.

"Harlan! You have an overactive imagination. It's not diabolical, but it is interesting. It's rumoured to lead to treasure..." He trailed off, raising an eyebrow as he studied Harlan's face.

"Everything with the Templars is supposed to lead to secrets and wealth, and it rarely does. They are all dead ends. What's so different about this one?"

Theo gestured around him with a theatrical air. "This castle once belonged to him."

"I remember you telling me." Harlan looked around with renewed interest. "Is that why you bought it?"

"Sort of." Theo dropped into a chair opposite Harlan. "I bought this place because it was beautiful, close to London, private, and very old. As you know, I love history and ancient buildings, and when this came on the market years ago, I snapped it up. Obviously, I knew about the Templar connection. The name says it all, but I hadn't realised until the estate agent told me that it actually belonged to William's family! The tower was built in the twelfth century, and then bits have been added over the years." He broke off as an ancient man shuffled into the room pushing a wheeled trolly on which was laid a morning tea service, resplendent with small cakes, scones, and pots of tea and coffee. "Thanks, Chivers. You can have a few hours rest, now."

Chivers nodded and retreated, shutting the door behind him.

"Shouldn't he be retired?"

"I tried. He looked horrified when I suggested it, so I keep them both on. I have a couple of youngsters doing most of the work now, but he likes to feel useful."

"Is he?"

"His wife's cooking is divine, so yes. Help yourself to some cakes. Coffee or tea?"

"Coffee, please." Harlan inhaled the rich scents and he realised how hungry and thirsty he was after his drive.

Theo poured the drinks, choosing tea for himself, and after loading his own plate with cakes, resumed his tale. "As I was saying, this place belonged to the de la More family. Normans, obviously, landed gentry. The men had a history of joining the Templars, once they had a son to pass the estate on to. William was no different. Of course, by the time he joined, there were no Crusades, but there were plenty of lands to administer. They were still a powerful organisation, even in the late thirteenth century. He was the Grand Commander of England from 1298 to 1307, when they were arrested. Because this castle was owned by his son, who wasn't a Templar, it was never seized, as so many Templar properties were."

Harlan sensed this could go on and on, and he could do without a complicated history lesson. "Where did you find the knife?"

"Right here! Since the day I owned this place, I've been renovating. It's a never-ending job, as you can imagine. I've updated plumbing, electrics, plaster, the roof." He rolled his eyes. "Everything. Anyway, I arranged to have part of the cellars cleared out recently. My wife wants a home cinema, and it seems the perfect spot. It's damp down there, so they've been pulling out walls, plastering, waterproofing, and they found this!"

"In the wall?"

"Yes. Bricked up and wrapped in oilskin cloth."

Harlan leaned forward, interest piqued. "Anything else in there?"

"No. Just that. I made sure that they proceeded carefully after that, and kept a close eye on things. The discovery coincided with me dropping one or two other jobs. I decided that I needed to slow down. I was a member of a few company boards, and to be honest, it was all getting very tedious. All these young men and women with their energetic ideas." He huffed.

"Tiresome. So, I needed a hobby, and decided to research the castle and that knife. My wife more or less ordered me to do *something*, actually. I think I was getting under her feet." He took a bite of a fluffy scone and groaned. "Delicious. Anyway, I started doing research, quickly got bogged down, and then asked Owen, the assistant gardener to help. He's very good with the internet, and gave me a few tips. After that I headed to the local library and did a bit more research, and the lady there directed me to a whole section on the area. Fascinating!" Theo drew a breath while he had more cake, and then launched into a potted history of the castle that Harlan could barely keep track of. He finally said, "But other than a slight reference to the knife, I can find out nothing else." He looked sheepish. "I've been a bit possessed."

While Theo had been talking, Harlan studied the hilt, and recognised a couple of symbols as being Templar in origin. "Have you had it valued?"

"God, no! I didn't want anyone to get wind of it until I knew what it was—if it meant anything!"

"And does it?"

"I think it does. I think it leads to some of the Templar treasure." He picked up the old book. "This details some of the trials, and refers to a symbolic blade that was mentioned in William de la More's interrogation. He was asked about it and denied its existence. He said the one the authorities had already seized was the only ceremonial blade they used. Did you know that the Templars had hardly any weapons when they searched their holdings?"

"No. But then again, I don't know many details at all of anything Templar-related. It's a huge subject."

"You're not wrong there! Anyway, someone talked. Maybe under torture. The crown knew of this blade's existence, and were of course greedy for the order's land and money. William merely said many weapons had passed through Templar hands. How could he possibly know about all of them?"

Harlan was baffled. "That was like seven hundred years ago. Can you really read those records?"

"Yes! Well, *I* can't. Historians can, and do. They're extensive. I've read summaries. Anyway, I already had the knife, and when I read this—well, I assumed..."

Harlan nodded. "You thought this was *the* knife. It looks the part. It has emeralds on it, too. It must be valuable, especially considering the provenance. But I'm guessing you don't want to auction it?"

"No! Any treasure we find will be worth more than the knife!"

"I guess it makes sense that the final grand master would have had a part in hiding any treasure—or that it had already been hidden for safe keeping."

"Oh, yes. There were many commanders through the years, as there were in Portugal, France, Germany, Hungary, Croatia, the Holy Land, and others. They all played their part." Theo frowned. "You must know your Templar history. You're a collector!"

"I know the basics, obviously, but it's a big, convoluted subject, and I've had other things to occupy my time."

"You haven't searched for Templar treasure before?"

Harlan shook his head, amused at Theo's surprise. "There are plenty of others out there who've done that. Besides, I tend to stick to more occult subjects." He held his hand up to forestall Theo's arguments. "Yes, I know about the Holy Grail and all that, but that's not my field."

Theo leaned forward, his eyes sparkling. "But this could be lots of treasure! Gold, silver, precious gems...who knows what type of reliquaries or other fascinating things. Maybe written histories. What we find could be phenomenal."

"You really believe this?"

"I'm not discounting the possibility. Why are you?"

"Because it's the Knights Templar! They have been dissected and analysed, and still no one has found anything."

"Read it before you poo-poo it." Theo gestured at the text. "It's easier than me explaining."

"Where did you find this book?"

"It's a reprint of a book written by a local historian in the eighteenth century. I found it in the local library, squashed in the stacks. According to the author—a man called James Goodberry—the dagger, *my* dagger, had been listed as English commanders' property, and had been used in ceremonies. A knife was confiscated when they arrested William, but as I said earlier, it didn't match this description."

"1307 was when the Templars fell?"

Theo nodded. "In Europe. The Pope ordered their arrest on October 13th in France. He ordered the other countries that housed the Templars to comply. In England, the king delayed for a couple of months. He basically said the charges didn't hold up—he was right—but the pope prevailed eventually. When he did finally arrest them in December of that year, it was a loose affair. They would have had time to hide everything. Including this."

Harlan still wasn't convinced. "That means there might have been plenty of time to hide treasure, but also pass on instructions. The family probably dug the whole place up looking for it, and then either found it and spent it, or it was never there to begin with!"

"Or never found it at all!" Theo clearly wasn't going to let this go. "And we're not just talking about William's family. We're talking about the remains of the order. Please. Read the text. Humour me." He gave Harlan a toothy grin.

Harlan picked up a small, honeyed cake and chewed it thoughtfully as he scanned the page. Goodberry described the last few months before the English order fell, in what Harlan thought was a dubious leap of imagination as far as personal details went. However, he did talk about how William was a prisoner at a Templar manor, and then moved to other castles and kept in a reasonably good state, having been granted respect due to his position. He still was able to talk to other members of the order, and no doubt the few remaining members had gathered together in England to discuss strategies. That wasn't surprising though, considering they would have known what was happening on the continent. Goodberry, however, summarised other source documents that said the dagger was a family heirloom, not a Templar knife, but had recently been engraved by a local loyal to the family. The knife was then passed to a family friend, who hid it. The dagger then resurfaced years later, and Goodberry suggested it was then returned to Temple Keep, where it was hidden.

Harlan huffed as he leaned back and looked at Theo. "I grant you, it's intriguing, and considering you found the knife here, it seems Goodberry was accurate. It suggests nothing of what it may lead to, though."

"But there are connections—lots of them. And I own this place now. I put it at your disposal!"

"Surely the treasure won't be here. It would have been madness to hide it in a place that was about to be confiscated!"

"But that's the point. It *wasn't* about to be confiscated. It didn't belong to the Templars. The king couldn't legally grab it. They were only able to seize actual Templar property. If the knife is here, the treasure could be, too!" As Harlan paused, thinking about how long this could drag out, Theo added, "I'll pay well, and I'm prepared to let you look for a good while."

Harlan rubbed his jaw as his interest in finding lost treasure overcame his scepticism. Besides, he knew Mason would go nuts if he turned this down. He also knew Shadow loved treasure hunting, too. "I haven't got the time to devote to this, but I know someone—well, a few people, actually—who will be interested. As long as you don't mind them ducking in and out if more pressing needs arise." He wanted to hedge his bets, just in case Black Cronos turned up.

Theo whooped, which was unexpected from someone in his seventies, and his face creased into wrinkles. "Excellent. Who are they, and when can they start?"

Three

G abe chatted to El Robinson and Reuben Jackson, two of the White Haven witches, while Shadow took a call from Harlan. They were seated around a table in the courtyard of The Wayward Son pub, finishing their pints after a pub lunch, and discussing the latest news on Black Cronos.

The witches were looking tanned and relaxed, both blonder than normal, and Gabe presumed the sun had lightened their hair. El had escaped from her shop after she'd enhanced Shadow's bow with magic, leaving her employee, Zoey, to manage it. Reuben, on the other hand, seemed to always have very loose hours as far as his business went. Not that Gabe could complain. They were the same. In fact, he was enjoying their days off after their harried time chasing Black Cronos and a few other easy jobs they'd done for Harlan. He was also trying not to worry about Barak and Estelle.

"I still can't believe Barak and Estelle are together," El said, face wrinkling with a mixture of horror and bewilderment. "She's a nightmare!"

"Estelle needs a firm hand, that's all," Reuben said, breezily. "Most women do. I like to think I've been a steadying hand with you and your wild ways."

Gabe almost choked on his pint. "Herne's horns, Reuben. You do like to take your life in your hands."

Reuben winked at him, a goofy expression on his face. He looked very pleased with himself—for a second, anyway, before El used magic to boil his remaining beer. He watched it steaming with an anguished expression. "Woman! Look what you've done!"

"You shouldn't test me, Reuben Jackson. Tame my wild ways, indeed."

With an almost imperceptible motion, Reuben cast another spell, cooling his beer down so quickly that the glass turned frosty. "I take it all back! Just don't touch my beer again." He turned his attention back to Gabe. "Seriously, though. Why Estelle?"

Gabe sighed. "It's something we've all wondered about. I guess it takes all sorts. She does actually seem happier, with less of a..." He hesitated to say the phrase, but El said it for him.

"Resting bitch face? Or should I say resting *witch* face?" She sniggered. "That will be the day. I thought that was her only expression."

Gabe could see Shadow in the corner of the courtyard turning back to them, as if her conversation with Harlan was coming to an end. "Please change the subject. I have to listen to Shadow moaning all the time about her. She'll go off again if she hears this."

Reuben smirked and whispered, "Firm hand, Gabe, firm hand."

Fortunately, before El could boil his beer again, Shadow returned to the table with a flurry of goodbyes and sat in her chair again. Barely drawing breath, she said, "We've got a job."

Gabe felt himself bristle, partly in resentment at having to give up his leisure time, and partly because they should be discussing jobs before taking them. He was aware of Reuben's wide-eyed, questioning expression as if baiting him to challenge Shadow. He met his gaze and turned back to Shadow with pursed lips. *Challenge accepted.* "Darling, I thought we wanted a break."

She lifted her chin, her eyes steely. "Darling, I thought we wanted to make money."

"We have money. We've had several lucrative months."

"There is never such a thing as *too much money*."

"There is if it means we're exhausted and vulnerable to attack by Black Cronos."

"We'll be fine, and you know it. Besides, we get to stay in a castle."

"We've stayed in a castle. A big one, in Wales."

"This is another one in Kent. Wherever that is." She arched an eyebrow, her violet eyes pinning him beneath her intense stare. "Don't you want to know what the job is?"

Reuben and El were watching in rapt silence as Gabe said, "It better be good."

She smiled triumphantly. "We're searching for treasure. Templar treasure."

"And what the hell are the Templars?"

Shadow shrugged. "Some kind of knights, I gather, who had lots of money."

"You've just accepted the job! Why didn't you ask more questions?"

"It was long-winded. I ran out of patience once I heard *big treasure*! Besides, Harlan said the man who has hired us would explain more himself."

Not caring that they had witnesses to their argument, Gabe slapped his forehead with his hand. "What if we've agreed to something with a mad man?"

"I haven't signed anything yet. It was a phone call!"

Reuben bellowed with laughter. "Seriously? You have no idea who the Knights Templar are? You two are just priceless! I love you guys, really, I do."

Gabe glared at him. "Don't start, Jackson. I have to put up with enough from Shadow."

"Me? I'm adorable!" she exclaimed, while Reuben laughed some more.

"Why would they know?" El said, remonstrating Reuben, although Gabe noted she was desperately trying not to laugh, too. "They're not from here! Honestly, Reuben, you're like a naughty child."

Reuben ignored her jibe, rubbed his hands together, and settled more comfortably in his chair. "Let me enlighten you about the Knights Templar. It's a long and tragic tale, and yes, there's lots of treasure—supposedly."

Nahum joined Ash at the long, wooden table situated at the side of the farmhouse under a veranda they had recently built, wondering what progress he'd made on researching the Templars. He reached for a glass of water, hesitating to disturb him, as Ash was studying the laptop in front of him intently. Instead, Nahum leaned back, enjoying the new space they had created.

Since they had returned from their overseas travels, especially France, where they'd enjoyed dining on the long table beneath the vine-clad pergola, the Nephilim and Shadow had wanted to repeat the experience at their home. Once they'd returned from Mardin in Turkey, they'd started work on constructing a large veranda at the side of the house, alongside the door by the kitchen that provided easy access. The area also offered a breath-taking view across the fields and moors that surrounded them, with the sea shimmering beyond.

They had used thick, wooden beams to create the structure, and to support the climbing perennials they'd planted around the edges. Fortunately, with so many of them working together, the work had been completed quickly. They'd spread a fine white gravel on the ground, and it made the whole area seem light and airy. The one thing that had threatened to take much longer was, of course, the maturity of the plants. However, Shadow had taken charge of that, and with her own and Briar's magic, the plants had grown far quicker than normal, enough to soften the hard edges of the wood and add some shade. A wooden table and an eclectic selection of chairs had completed the space, with a barbeque grill placed at the end.

Nahum sighed with satisfaction, feeling his muscles start to unwind after his fighting practice with Niel earlier that day, and the sigh disturbed Ash, who finally looked up, blinking with surprise at Nahum's presence.

"Nahum! Sorry, I was engrossed."

"It's fine. I was enjoying the peace and quiet." He nodded at the laptop. "Find anything useful?"

Ash leaned back, pushing his hair from his eyes. "Herne's balls, it's a minefield! So much information, my head is spinning. But I can understand why so many people are obsessed with the Templars."

"Does this mean you will be?"

He laughed. "Interested, yes. Obsessed? Not yet."

"*Yet.* That's what's worrying me."

"Brother, I have too many other things that interest me to become obsessed with just one thing. Plus, quite honestly, I could be reading all of this non-stop for months, probably years. There is so much information and speculation about them. Their history, the myths and rumours. Fascinating."

Nahum already knew a little bit about the Templars from what Shadow and Gabe had told them after returning from the pub. He'd searched the internet, and after reading a few basic posts had left the rest to Ash. "Exhausting, from the little I read."

"That, too."

"So, what about the new job? Likely to be successful, or not?"

"Impossible to say right now. Whatever information this Theo man has will be more than I can likely find on the net." Ash's face creased with curiosity as he stared at the laptop.

Nahum smiled. "You want to go with them."

"I think I do."

The sound of voices disturbed them as Gabe and Shadow strolled around the side of the house from the barn, and Niel entered the veranda from behind them, placing a tray of beers on the table with a gruff, "I hope you're hungry. I have a mountain of meat to cook."

Ash nodded at him. "Always. Need any help?"

"No. All in hand."

He headed to light the barbeque while Gabe and Shadow joined them at the table. Both looked flushed, with sweat coating their faces and arms. They'd been sparring in the barn, and maybe a little something else, Nahum guessed, hiding a grin. They both looked sneaky and satisfied.

Gabe reached for the beers, cracking each one open and passing them around the table, as he asked, "What do you think, Ash?"

"I've just been telling Nahum how complicated their whole history is. It's hard to say about your particular job, as the details of it won't be anywhere on the internet, I'm sure."

"We like knotty histories," Shadow declared after sipping her beer. "The last couple of jobs were easy but unsatisfying. I'd like something to get my teeth into."

Nahum understood what she meant, but easy was welcome after Black Cronos, and their dealings with them were far from over.

"You might be biting off more than you can chew," Ash warned her as Niel joined them at the table, carrying the scent of burning charcoal with him. "What are your plans?"

"We'll head to Kent tomorrow morning," Gabe said. "Temple Keep is close to a place called Temple Moreton. The original owners were the de la Mores—William was the last English Master of the Templars. Theo will show us the evidence, and we'll go from there."

Niel grunted. "From what you said earlier, there doesn't sound like much evidence."

Shadow cast him a withering glance. "There's enough to start. What do you want? A dot to dot?"

"Just saying, sister. Don't get cranky."

The trouble, Nahum reflected, was that the downtime meant they were getting under each other's feet. This job, and Barak's, would be a good thing. He asked a question before the exchange escalated. "Why does the English master sound French?"

"Because he was Norman, who were French," Ash explained, "and descended from Vikings. They had invaded England years before, ruling the country for a good while. They still owned land and held positions of power. From my initial reading, it seems by the time the Templars were arrested, the members in England were few, and most of their masters were French. But, looking at other bases, they were there, too. Maybe that's why the arrests started in France."

"I haven't had a chance to read anything," Niel said, looking confused. "Who the hell were they, and why were they arrested?"

Ash leaned back in his chair, his hand loosely clasping his beer bottle that rested on the table. "Would you like me to give a very brief summary of them?"

"I would," Gabe told him. "I'd like to know exactly what we're letting ourselves in for." He cast Shadow a sidelong glance, which she acknowledged with a sly grin.

"Essentially, the Knights Templar were a religious organisation designed to carry the Christian faith into Jerusalem and the Holy Land—which in current terms is roughly Palestine, Israel, parts of Jordan, Lebanon, and Syria. The area was Muslim, and the Christians wanted to regain control of the land, particularly Jerusalem."

Nahum shook his head. "Not so different to the wars fought over that place today."

"Unfortunately, not," Ash said with a sigh.

No one said what Nahum was sure that they were all thinking. That the old God—their God—had been responsible for some of this. He brushed it aside, knowing it was something they could do nothing about.

Ash continued. "They formed after the first Crusade, which put Jerusalem into Christian hands. After that, Christians wanted to travel there on pilgrimage. The Knights Templar protected travellers, and allowed them safe passage through Muslim areas."

"Escorts, then," Gabe said. "That's sort of what Reuben said."

"Much more than that. The Templars were strict, and their knights were expected to give up all land and possessions. This meant they usually donated large chunks of their money to the order, which was kept for their exclusive use. This made them rich. It supported their battles, and later, funded building all over Europe and the east. They were also a formidable fighting force, and their numbers grew—as did their wealth. That made them enemies that eventually led to their downfall. But I'm getting ahead of myself. The organisation essentially became the first bank. Because of their reach and strength, people trusted them with money, and they also offered loans. They traded all sorts of things, which made lots more money, and they also owned fleets of ships and land. And," Ash grinned, "they were treasure hunters."

"Really?" Niel leaned forward, eyes wide. "Hunting for what?"

"Religious artifacts. Big ones. They searched for the Ark of the Covenant, among other things."

Gabe emitted a low whistle. "Did they find it?"

"Not sure. They dug beneath what was Solomon's palace and the First Temple in Jerusalem. No one knows what they found or where it went. Although, other histories suggest that the Ark had been in Ethiopia for years. The Templars carried out lots of excavations, and found lost scrolls, too."

Nahum nodded, remembering their rudimentary knowledge of Solomon—a powerful king, who existed after their time.

"Anyway," Ash continued after sipping his beer, "kings began to worry. The Templars were essentially a well-funded, private army."

"But I thought," Niel said, "that the church—Catholic, I presume—approved of them."

"It did. But the more powerful they became, the less the pope trusted them. Rumours surfaced of their mysterious rites, and eventually they were accused of heresy."

"What kind of rites?" Shadow asked.

Ash leaned forward to read the internet page on the laptop. "Worshipping an idol, sodomy, worshipping Baphomet, who many interpreted to be a devil, but was actually a symbol of balance in many occult and gnostic organisations. However," he turned the screen so that everyone could see the image, "he does have horns and goat's feet. You can see why religious leaders would have interpreted it that way."

"The charges were made up?" Nahum asked.

"Sounds like it. By the early fourteenth century, the pope was looking for a way to disband them. He was scared of their power, and jealous of their wealth. On Friday the thirteenth in October 1307, several countries moved to arrest them. That's one of the reasons why Friday the thirteenth is considered to mean bad luck." He grimaced. "It was not a good end. They were tortured, and many were burnt at the stake. It was like an early forerunner of the witch trials. They were tortured until they confessed."

"What happened to the treasure?" Niel asked.

"No one ever found it. Rumours are that a fleet of Templar ships left France loaded with treasure the night before the arrests, but no one saw the fleet again. It's been suggested that they landed in Scotland, and even Canada, but nothing was confirmed."

Shadow's violet eyes were glowing with excitement. "So, their treasure is out there, somewhere, and this clue that Theo has could really lead to some?"

"In theory, yes. But countless people across the world have been tracking down clues for years. It's every treasure hunter and conspiracy theorist's dream."

"Which means," Gabe said, "that if it does exist, the treasure could have been found long ago."

"Perhaps, yes." Ash gave his characteristic shrug, always understated. "I should also warn you that the English king at the time did not leap to torture his captives as quickly as the Europeans did. Like during the witch trials, the English were not known for their love of torture. And the king liked the Templars. They served under house arrest for quite a while, which might mean they did spread any treasure they possessed far and wide."

Nahum was impressed. "You found out a lot in a short time."

Ash turned his golden eyes on him. "I have merely scratched the surface. I confess, I plan to buy some more books on the subject. It's interesting, for the political and religious twists alone, never mind everything else." He turned back to Gabe. "I'd like to help."

"Good," Gabe said, standing and stretching. "I'd like you to look at the paperwork and dagger and help analyse them. We'll leave early tomorrow. Right now, however, I need a shower."

"Me too," Shadow said, draining her beer. She started to walk to her room, housed in the outbuilding around the courtyard. "How long until the food's ready, Niel?"

"An hour or two yet."

"Great, see you later."

She disappeared around the side of the house, and Gabe watched her leave, his lips twisting with unspoken annoyance.

Nahum smiled, knowing Gabe was still peeved that she'd accepted the job, and that Harlan had called her first. "Something on your mind, Gabe?"

"Nope. I'm just fine," he said striding around the table and through the door into the house.

Ash sighed with amusement. "Trouble in paradise!"

Niel snorted. "Unlikely. They smelt of sex. Ugh. The only sex I like to smell is my own."

"You wish," Nahum teased him. "By the time the others leave, there'll only be me, you, Zee, and Eli. The place will feel quiet."

"Let's hope it stays that way," Niel said, rising to his feet and heading to check the barbeque, unperturbed by Nahum's comment on his lack of a love life.

"He'll be bored in two days without Shadow to annoy him," Ash observed.

"And you'll have the pleasure instead."

Ash laughed. "I'll have research to keep me busy."

"I hope, for your sake, that's true. Plus, staying in a castle has got to be good! I feel I'm missing out."

"I'm sure you'll get your chance. Besides, you used to live in one."

"Several, in fact," Nahum said, his memories suddenly full of his old palaces surrounded by high walls, and his water-filled courtyards, lush with plants. "But that was a long time ago. Maybe I should build some water features here while I have the chance."

However, even as Nahum was saying it, he had a feeling that wouldn't happen. Barak could well find some clue to the whereabouts of Black Cronos in France, and who knows what Gabe might discover in Kent.

<hr />

The sun was setting as Barak surveyed the *château* situated on the rise of the hill, a vast grove of olive trees blanketing the space around it. The light caught the silvery leaves, and the building's huge stone blocks glowed a warm bronze as the sun tipped below the horizon. It was breathtakingly beautiful.

Estelle stood next to him, echoing his thoughts. "Wow. That's stunning. It's hard to think it might provide cover for Black Cronos."

"Part of me hopes that Jackson is wrong," Barak confessed, frowning at the idyllic scene. "However, we badly need a lead, and I'd like to think this is it."

Their flight had landed only a couple of hours ago, and they had picked up their hire car and driven to the hotel in the city centre. Jackson, ever the gentlemen, had booked two rooms, not presuming on the state of their relationship, but Barak hoped they wouldn't need the second room. They had slept together, several times, and yet he still sensed a reserve within Estelle that he desperately wished would go. However, patience had worked so far, and he was determined to crack whatever reservations Estelle still held regarding him.

"We should take the tour tomorrow," she suggested, disturbing his thoughts, and brushing her thick dark hair back from her face. "We can't stake out the place all night from here."

He nodded, thinking on their earlier discussion. The *château* was also a working farm, producing olive oil, a modest selection of wine, as well as preserves and cheeses. From the description on the website, a farm shop was in the grounds, and you could stroll a limited section of the gardens, as well as sign up for a tour of the olive press.

"I agree. The gardens open at ten o'clock, right?"

"Right, and the tour is at eleven." Estelle frowned at him. "You don't exactly blend in. If anyone is looking out for us, you'll stand out a mile away."

He laughed. "You think I'm on a 'most wanted' list?"

"It's very possible. I could be, too. We have all caused them lots of problems. Fortunately," she grinned, "I blend in much better than you do."

"It's a chance we'll have to take. Like Jackson said, the links could be purely historical."

"I still don't get it. The *château's* main business is the olive grove and farm. What's so suspicious about that?"

Barak realised he hadn't told Estelle his entire conversation with Jackson. They'd been too distracted with each other. "The count stayed in this place a long time ago, and according to records, was a good friend of the owner. However, it's still owned by the same family, and if he is immortal, and knew them well enough, they might still be connected. Also, during the war, there were rumours that the family was sympathetic to the Nazis."

Estelle sat on the bonnet of their rental car, a small Citroën that felt like a shoebox to Barak, nodding as she thought through the implications. "That may have offered them and Black Cronos freedom to move during the Second World War. But surely the Nazis wouldn't have wanted another group interfering in the war."

"I agree. But perhaps they didn't know." He fell silent while he considered the potential scenarios. "If this *château* and the family *was* sympathetic to the Nazis, they would have been free to continue to do their own business, which would have given cover to Black Cronos and their activities."

"But the Germans took over places like this. Turned them into their own headquarters."

"Maybe not this one, if they were compliant. That might have been the payoff. We support you, you leave us alone."

Estelle's dark eyes turned stormy. "Awful. They were monsters to support them."

"Maybe they were scared, too. Many were." Barak had read about the atrocities of that war. Despite the centuries between this time and his own, nothing really changed. "The Nazis were too big and terrifying for many to say no to."

"But if Black Cronos were here, then they were monsters twice over."

Barak followed Estelle's gaze, studying the charming *château* in the distance, and wondered what dark secrets it could hold. He hoped they were wrong.

"Come on. Enough speculation. I need food."

Four

Shadow thought that Theo Carmichael was proving to be a very affable host, especially as he plied them with excellent coffee in the first floor sitting room.

They had made good time on their journey on Thursday morning, and had arrived close to lunch. After showing them to their rooms to freshen up, they hadn't wasted time. Theo, as enthusiastic as a teenager, had spread out the research, comprising of a couple of books and handwritten notes, before them. Shadow was examining the dagger, Ash was reading the notes, and Gabe was studying Theo himself.

Shadow dragged her attention away from the knife and looked at Gabe as he said, "I want to be completely honest with you, Theo. This could all come to nothing."

"I know that. I'm no fool, Gabe, although I may seem like a babbling idiot right now." Theo's smile disappeared. "I'm well aware of the history of the Templars, and how convoluted it is. But I truly believe that the dagger leads to the treasure, and it's here somewhere. If not on these grounds, then at least close by."

Ash turned over another page, and looked up. "I'm hoping there's more than just this to help us. This is a very useful summary of the family and events at the time, but I need details. Source materials, or as close to that as possible. And a map of the grounds and the castle, if you've got one? Something to compare references to."

Theo nodded. "There are more documents in Bodiam Village Library. The librarian refused to let me photocopy all of it. Said it wasn't allowed, and you can't remove them from the library. I made a few notes." He gestured at the small notebook on the side.

"I prefer to see them myself," Ash told him. "The originals provide context. Sometimes you need to read between the lines."

Shadow knew bringing Ash would be a good idea. He was logical and organised when it came to research. Methodical.

Theo nodded, but he looked worried. "Not a problem. I can take you there. The only thing is, some of the documents are in French—old French. Some are in Latin. Only a few are translated. I have to admit, I've been reluctant to hire someone to get them translated. People can be unscrupulous. They may not translate them correctly, or could keep information back from me. Or even pass it on elsewhere."

Ash brightened. "That's not a problem. I can translate them. I am fluent in many languages. We both are." He gestured to Gabe.

"Are you? Brilliant!" He beamed at all of them.

"Hold on." Gabe held a hand up, puzzled. "You didn't tell Harlan this? Because he didn't mention we'd need to translate. Like Ash says, it's not a problem, but if you want your best success, translation is the key. It's just lucky we can help. Not everyone could."

Theo's eyes widened, and he stumbled over his words. "I'd hoped you would manage with what I have. And I thought if we could decipher the symbols on the dagger, that would also help. But yes, this is great news!"

Ash shrugged. "No harm done. I'd like to finish reading this first, and then head to the library as soon as possible. Is it close?"

"Just a few miles down the road." Theo beamed. "I'll give you a tour of the castle and grounds, we'll have a late lunch, and then I can take you. The librarian knows me, and that should make it easier." He turned to Gabe and Shadow. "What will you two do?"

"Study the map of the castle and look around," Shadow said immediately. "I want to know every inch of this place."

"Not a problem." Theo reached for a large roll of paper that was on an armchair. "There are a few blueprints in here."

Ash moved the papers aside, allowing room for Theo to unroll the large sheets of paper. The outer one looked modern, but rolled within it were older versions. He spread them out, pointing to a floor plan that was worn thin with age. "This one is not the original. That has long vanished. This is from the sixteenth century, when additions were made. The west wing, predominantly, and the lodge in the woods."

"Lodge?" Gabe lifted his head, staring at Theo.

"Hunting lodge. The grounds used to be much bigger, and there were deer here. The place is habitable, but it needs more work."

"So that wasn't here during William's time?"

"No. But it does have some fascinating symbols in there. I think it might even have been a Masonic lodge at some point. They are supposedly linked to the Templars—though a later organisation."

Shadow had been studying the symbols on the bone-handled dagger, unable to make much sense of them. "Do any of the symbols match the ones on the hilt?"

Theo looked startled. "I'm not sure!"

Shadow tried not to roll her eyes in front of the man employing them, but seriously?

Gabe shot her a look that told her to shut up, and instead nodded, satisfied. "Thanks, Theo. We can check that. There is plenty to keep us going. I do want to reiterate that this could take a while, and we still might find nothing."

"I know. I'm prepared for the fact that this could take weeks."

"Or months," Shadow said. "And we may not be able to spare that much time." In fact, she knew she'd go loopy if she had to search that long with no result. She'd rather be fighting Black Cronos.

"I understand. I'll leave you to it, and go to make lunch arrangements. Then we'll tour the grounds." He gave them beaming smiles. "It's excellent that you could come so quickly."

Ash looked at him, puzzled. "You're very generous to let us stay here to search. It will expedite things, hopefully. But what will you do while we're here?"

"Help, of course! We're in this together!"

Shadow stifled a groan, but Ash leapt in. "Perfect, thank you. Your help will be much appreciated."

With a quick nod, Theo left the room and Gabe exhaled. "Bollocks. I suspected he'd stick around, but I hoped he'd leave us to it. I don't want him crowding us."

Ash rolled his eyes. "Gabe. He would hardly leave us in his castle unattended. Plus, he's retired. This is his baby."

"Then you can babysit him," Shadow said. The man seemed pleasant enough, but he was old, and would no doubt fuss over things and hold them up.

"He's paying us, Shadow. This is his house, his search, his dagger, and maybe his treasure. We play by his rules."

Gabe just smirked at her. "I told you to ask more questions. If there's any justice, you'll be babysitting him more than anyone."

Shadow considered a retort, and decided silence was the best option. Shooting him a scathing glance, she studied the plans instead.

Jackson was trying to concentrate on his research about *Château du Buade*, going over the details about the du Buade family in case he had missed something significant, but his mind kept drifting to Barak and Estelle.

They were there now, hopefully on the guided tour, if their plans had come to fruition. Jackson didn't know why he was so worried. A ridiculously oversized Nephilim and a powerful witch didn't need his protection, yet he couldn't help but feel he'd sent them into the lion's den. Plus, it was broad daylight in August, and the place would be packed with visitors, so of course, nothing would happen to them.

However, what was playing on his mind was the fact that the family had been collaborators, and it was the area where his grandfather had been sent during the war. A place he had never returned from. *Was he just transmitting his fears and anger about his grandfather onto the current situation? Probably.* As his eyes strayed back to the documents in front of him, though, he imagined the horrors of that time. The uncertainty, the shootings, the torture.

He had also found the original communication sent from France at the time that had led to Jackson's grandfather going in the first place. It was part of a series of communications that detailed the Resistance's efforts, and their setbacks. The one that interested him most talked about the disappearance of a half dozen fighters, all of whom had vanished over the preceding months, and none of them had been found. Normally, captured Resistance fighters were paraded in the towns' squares—both the small villages and larger cities—so that no one was spared knowing the fate of those who dared to cross the Germans. But these four men and two women had not been made an example of. They hadn't appeared in the small villages or in Avignon itself, the largest town.

The Resistance had waited and watched, hoping the fighters themselves were in hiding and would reappear when it was safe, but eventually they had to assume they would not. They had wondered if they were dead, but their bodies were never found, either. And then one man returned—looking like a ghost. He was gaunt, hollow-eyed, and almost incomprehensible. Strange tattoos decorated his arms and chest. He talked about devils who walked among men, but that was all. Within hours he had died without being able to fully describe where he'd been.

When the English authorities were contacted, the news was passed on to the Paranormal Division, who were looking into links to the occult and the Nazis, and the news of another unknown group. They made a tentative connection between them, and that sealed Jackson's grandfather's fate. He parachuted into the area north of Avignon in March 1943. Within three days he'd vanished, along with his three companions.

When the phone rang on his desk, Jackson almost jumped out of his skin. He answered it quickly, anxious that his office should return to contemplative silence. "Jackson here."

"I have news," Layla Gould said, the PD's doctor. "Come on down to the lab."

The tour guide's droning voice was making Estelle sleepy, and she took a deep breath, trying not to yawn.

Of course, the long-winded tour wasn't the only reason for her tiredness. The previous night spent with Barak had done that. There'd been very little time for sleep. Her gaze slid to him now, and he flashed her a grin as if he knew exactly what she was thinking, his appreciative glance sliding down her toned figure. She nudged him to pay attention, deliberately staring at the man leading their group. With luck, the almost two-hour tour was coming to an end.

The group was large, a couple of dozen people, Estelle estimated, a mixture of ages and nationalities, and she and Barak had hung at the back, nodding as they listened, but they studied their surroundings carefully, both looking for a way to explore any private places without being easily spotted.

There was no doubt that the du Buade's castle was a beautiful place, but unfortunately the tour did not include the interior. Instead, they had been shown the gardens with a section for the bee hives, strolled through the olive groves, visited the squat stone building that housed the olive press, admired the vineyards and the huge vats stored in vaulted chambers, and now they were being shepherded to the ubiquitous gift shop with a café attached. With a final flurry, the tour guide smiled, nodded, and left them to it, and she drew Barak aside.

"So far so good. It all seems very respectable. But," she paused, looking across the grounds to the olive press in the distance. "I think I'd like to head back there. The door we spotted."

He nodded, eyes following her gaze. "With the electronic panel. It did seem jarring in such a rustic place. Of course, it could just be security for their stores. The building was big, and we only saw a part of it."

"But worth checking out." She looked up at him. "Considering the age of this place, there'll be extensive cellars, possibly connecting all of the outbuildings, and potentially the main building, as well. If we access one of them, we might find a way into the house."

"Agreed. Hopefully, the olive store will still be busy, and they won't notice us. It's worth a shot." Barak nodded towards the wine tasting rooms across the grounds, where for an extra charge you could sample their produce. "There will be cellars under there too, but too hard to access for us."

They had been shown inside, but there were a lot of staff there, and the doors to other rooms were behind the long counter.

"Maybe it's just paranoia," Estelle said uneasily, "but there is something unsettling about this place. Maybe it's just because I know its history." She tried to shake off her misgivings, but her magical abilities gave her more awareness than most, and she knew better than to ignore those feelings. "If it's tricky, we can come back tonight. At least we know the lay of the place now."

Barak looked longingly at the café, from which delicious, garlic-rich smells were emanating. "It almost seems a shame to miss that place, though."

"Later! Your appetite is astonishing...for many things!"

He grinned. "There were no complaints last night, though."

Knowing she had no comeback to that, she grabbed his hand and pulled him away from the café towards the far building that shimmered in the heat. A few other groups were heading that way, and they trailed behind them, happy to blend in.

The centuries-old building was split into sections. The olive press and associated equipment was in a cordoned off area, but was fully visible for the tour. There was also a small shop, and plenty of displays detailing the place's history, and once inside, they edged to the cool, shadowed recesses and the door that was almost hidden from sight. With Barak playing lookout, Estelle used her magic to disable the electronic lock and open the door, and within seconds, they had both slipped inside.

The room on the other side was large with high ceilings, rafters stretching above them. It had a couple of long, narrow windows, wooden double doors that opened to the rear, and a long counter that ran down one side. The main space was filled with crates containing bottles of olive oil, jarred olives, and stock for the shop. But set into one wall at the far end was another door with another key-coded electronic panel. Wordlessly, they crossed the room quickly, giving a cursory check in the crates that confirmed they were all olive-related products.

Fearful that someone would catch them snooping, Estelle once again used her magic to bypass security, and they slipped through the door, the brief flash of daylight illuminating a small stone landing with steps leading down into darkness.

"Excellent," Barak murmured. "Let's hope this isn't a dead end."

Estelle threw a witch-light ahead of them, and Barak led the way down the long stone staircase, his footfalls silent despite his size. When they reached the bottom, another room opened up, and Barak located the light switch and flicked it on.

The light showed another big, stone-walled room, but this one was much dustier than the one above. It had a few old crates in it, straw all over the floor, and some rickety shelving against one wall. "Damn it. Dead end," Barak murmured. "Why put an electronic lock on this?"

"There has to be something else here."

They both started looking around, Estelle focussing on the ground and the potential for a trap door, Barak tapping the walls. When he came to the shelves, he eased them aside, and gave a whoop of success. She hurried to his side, and saw a thick, wooden door set into the wall with another electronic key code panel next to it.

"At least there aren't security cameras, as well," Estelle noted as she studied the panel. She placed her hand on the door and focussed her magic, trying to discern what could be on the other side. She ran her hand across the walls before returning to the door. "A passage I think." She looked up at Barak, uncertain. "The further we go in, the harder it might be to get out."

"Second thoughts?"

"Just a consideration."

"Good. Let's do this."

Five

As promised, Ash was escorted by Theo to Bodiam Library after a delicious lunch. It was situated on one of the narrow village lanes, and was a popular place.

It had a good selection of new and old titles, browsed by a cross-section of society, but Theo bypassed the main room, taking him to the librarian behind the counter. After a polite chat, she escorted them to a series of rooms that were actually much bigger than the main, public area.

Ash looked at her, confused, and then back at the shelves. "This is more than I expected."

The librarian, Lily, gave him a beaming smile. "This place houses the documents from lots of historical houses in the area. Some hang on to their old libraries, but others have no idea what to do with their collections, so they come here."

"The books aren't sold to private buyers?"

"This place is private, sort of."

Theo chuckled. "In the 1970s, Roger Downes, who once owned Shellbrook Manor, decided to clear out his huge library, but rather than sell it all off and let the books leave the area or go to a big central library, he decided to endow Bodiam Library with the important items. He used his persuasive powers on other landowners in the area, and this place was created! A few of us, myself included, donate money regularly to maintain it. Some of the books from what was Temple Keep's library are here, too."

Lily smiled her thanks to Theo. "The usual rules apply when storing important documents. The rooms must be kept at the correct temperature, and the documents handled carefully. You also have to sign in and out. It's actually very exciting to be able to look after such an amazing collection. All sorts of people come to visit. They're not that valuable, of course. Only for local historical reasons." She gestured to a table. "Now, what was it you wanted, Theo?"

"There is the diary of Madeleine Montgomery, wife of a local landowner, a couple of local histories, and records for land that the Templars had owned in the area, and who had originally owned it." He pulled a list from his pocket. "Just a few things I'd like my friend to look over."

"Of course. Take a seat, and I'll get Adam to bring you the documents. Some of the later ones are originals, but the earlier ones are copies. The originals are too delicate for frequent inspection."

Ash frowned. "Where are they kept?"

"In the basement. I'm afraid no one touches them except experts."

Ash suppressed his annoyance. He would much rather see the originals, but the only way that would happen would be to break in. It was doable, of course, but he'd rather not. Hopefully the copies would be fine. He was itching to be able to browse the shelves, but sat where he was told, watching as Adam, an older librarian, accessed some books from a section to the rear of the room, and then placed them in front of Ash and Theo.

"These are the history books and the private diary, detailing some old searches in the eighteenth century. There was interest at the time in Templar treasure, but it never amounted to anything."

Theo nodded enthusiastically. "These are the ones I took notes from."

"Great, thanks." Ash pulled the books towards him.

Adam, however, didn't move, instead looking at Ash with open curiosity. "Are you Greek? Sorry, I heard you talking to Lily."

"I am, but I haven't lived there for a long time."

"Ah, I thought so. Are you related to the gentleman who came the other day?"

Ash found himself momentarily speechless, so it was Theo who answered, his face contorting with surprise. "Someone else has requested these documents?"

"Yes. Only a couple of days ago. He said he was a Templar scholar."

Ash felt the first stirring of unease. "No, I don't believe I'm related. What did he look like?"

"Forties perhaps, tanned, handsome. Darker haired than you."

Shit. That sounded like Nicoli. Ash made sure he still appeared calm before he spoke. Theo was purple with annoyance. "I suppose you have had quite a bit of interest in William de la More, due to his Templar links?"

"Sometimes. It seems to come in waves. Writers and students access the records the most." He shrugged, unconcerned. "Everyone's fascinated with the Templars. Of course," he glanced at Theo and laughed, "not everyone lives in a castle owned by one. I'm sure Theo has told you, however, that Temple Keep was never actually owned by the Templars."

"He did. It was private, right?"

"Yes. But other land around here was managed by them. They owned estates right across the country, but the other records you've requested list the local ones."

Ash nodded. "Great, thank you. Did the Greek visitor leave a name?"

"Of course. He was required to sign in, but I can't reveal his identity. Sorry."

"Just curious." Ash shrugged, eager that the man should leave them to it, and he pulled the old, leather-bound books towards him.

Adam continued, "I'll return soon with the copies of the land records."

Ash nodded and turned to Theo, who was looking decidedly worried. "Is there any reason someone else should be looking at these documents now, Theo?"

Theo blustered, but there was panic behind his eyes. "No, but as Adam said, many people are interested in the Templars."

"Who else have you discussed this with? Have you employed someone else?" Ash was trying to be calm, but failing. "We don't appreciate being made to compete."

"No! I haven't employed anyone else!"

Ash was not going to argue now. He needed to focus on the diary. However, he was sure Theo had said something to someone, and maybe they were searching for the treasure, too. Ash had a horrible feeling The Order of Lilith were involved, and that could make life very tricky indeed.

Before Ash could comment further, Adam returned, looking flustered. "I'm so sorry, Theo, I can't find the land records. Let me speak to Lily, in case they've been moved."

Ash watched Lily and Adam, heads bent together, frowns creasing their faces, before both of them headed to where the copies should be. Another flurry of activity and hushed conversation seemed to confirm the worst. Lily disappeared in one direction, while Adam returned to them.

"I'm so sorry, it seems they have disappeared. Perhaps they have been miscatalogued. Of course, we can always arrange for more copies. Just bear with us."

"But how can you have lost them?" Theo asked, agitated. "They were here the other day!"

"Please, Theo, just let us look." He scurried away without another word.

Ash turned to Theo again. "This is bad news, Theo. I suspect they'll find that the originals have vanished, too. Stolen."

By now their hushed voices were drawing attention, and Ash wanted Theo out of the way. "I need you to phone Gabe and let him know—just in case."

"Just in case of what?"

"Anything."

⤐⬦❖⬦⤏

The body laid out on the mortuary table made Jackson's skin crawl.

"Did you have to bring me here?" he asked Layla.

"Yes. You want answers about Black Cronos, don't you?"

"Of course!" He stared at the frozen features of the corpse with the large, ragged hole where one eye should have been. It was further deformed by evidence of the autopsy. He took a deep breath to quell his rising bile, trying not to inhale through his nose. "I thought you said that you hadn't found anything of use, though. That the tattoos had vanished. And I also thought," he added, looking around the chill room that he'd barely had time to inspect because Layla had hustled him right to the body, "that you weren't going to have a mortuary here."

"I changed my mind." She gestured around her. "The Retreat is huge, with lots of unoccupied rooms. Why not make use of them? I was sick of going back and forth to the main mortuary. At the moment, this still needs work, but it will suffice for now."

Happily diverted from the corpse revealed by the sheet drawn back to his navel, Jackson studied the room. It was tiled from floor to ceiling, but some areas looked unfinished. "Was this a bathroom?"

"Yes, a large one. It was the easiest place to convert. It's tiled, there's a water supply, and has plenty of room for cupboards and storage. Waylen arranged the work, and as you can see, it's been stripped out and the rest of the construction will commence soon. In the meantime, I manage."

"Where do you store the bodies?"

"The room next door. I'll only need a couple of fridges, though. This place will be for those bodies I need to study in depth. This poor man is it for now."

Jackson turned to the large, muscular man, wondering who he used to be before he became a weapon for Black Cronos. "Have you identified him?"

"I have, but I'll come on to that later." Layla's bright eyes were veiled, troubled, but she pointed at the corpse. "His body is finally revealing some secrets."

"Really? How?"

"As you can see, I've performed the autopsy. He was killed by an arrow shot to the head. Instant death."

"That would be Shadow. She's deadly accurate."

"I can see, which is fortunate for me. The reason I kept this body is because there were no other major wounds. On examination, his organs were normal, as was his brain—well, what was left of it." She said this matter-of-factly, but Jackson's stomach churned. Layla continued, oblivious. "The unusual black eyes your team described have gone, leaving just his normal appearance behind. Difficult to tell now, of course. But I was curious about the tattoos you mentioned, and the strange skin some of the warriors had—the metallic skin."

Jackson nodded. "I can't forget the tattoos. They were covered in them. The general consensus was that they were imbued with magic for strength and protection. But then they vanished after death. Their metallic skin I remember vaguely, but I wasn't fighting them."

"Fortunately for you." Layla ran an appraising glance down his body. "You're not built for fighting."

Jackson glanced down at his lean form, clad in his usual old jeans and worn trainers, slightly insulted. "I brought Barnaby in, didn't I?"

"You did, but you know what I mean."

He gave a sheepish grin. "Yes. I know my limitations. But get on with it. I'm bursting with impatience!"

Layla didn't answer him. Instead she crossed to the counter and retrieved a long, hand-held lamp, before turning the lights off. She shone the light on the body, and immediately tattoos on his skin glowed in the light.

"Holy crap! Black light?" Jackson exclaimed.

"Yes. I was so frustrated that I decided to try a few different lights—they all vary—and this one worked. Tattoos normally don't just disappear. I'm annoyed I didn't try this sooner."

"There were lots of bodies, and many of them were a bloody mess. A lot to process. At least you've found them now."

"The thing is, most of the bodies have now been cremated. We couldn't possibly keep them all."

"Of course not. But what have you found out about these tattoos? The symbols?" Despite Jackson's revulsion at the body before him, he stepped closer to study the sigils. "They're complex."

"I'm afraid I don't know much about them at all, but we can take photos, study them, and I'll look at the skin around them more closely. I can take some micro samples." She strode over to the main light and flicked it back on, making Jackson squint with the brightness. "I'll have to rig up better lighting, and I've decided to call in an expert. I think it's about time JD saw this."

"That's a great idea—if you can handle his nit-picking."

"He's in my lab, so he'll do as I say!"

Layla may be an older, slender woman, but she was razor-sharp and no pushover. Jackson wouldn't dare cross her, but he knew JD would try. However, they knew each other well, and had worked together in the past.

He nodded at the corpse, recalling her earlier statement. "You said you had an ID."

"Ah, yes." Layla fell silent as she returned the light to the counter, then leaned against it to face him, arms crossed. "I confess, it's not what we expected to find, but running out of ideas, I was prepared to try anything. When DNA tests failed, I ran his fingerprints. That failed, too, until I compared them to some old records. This will come as a bit of a shock."

Jackson's chest tightened. "Go on."

"This man is James Arbuthnot. He was part of your grandfather's team that was sent into France during World War Two."

Six

G abe crossed the castle grounds in the afternoon sunshine, tension radiating through him as he studied his surroundings.

"Someone could be watching us right now!" he complained to Shadow.

"Maybe." Dark sunglasses obscured her eyes. "We'll search after nightfall. We'll have the advantage then."

"Will we? We have no idea who stole those documents."

"Besides Nicoli, you mean? His team is nothing like Black Cronos."

Gabe paused in the shade beneath a spreading oak tree on their way to the hunting lodge. Theo had given them a tour earlier, but hadn't brought them this far. "We don't know who is on his team anymore. Half of them died in Raziel's temple. He'll have recruited more...and potentially, let's face it, probably already had more team members we've never met." He leaned against the tree trunk, staring back at the castle shimmering in the heat. "I'm more curious to know who hired *him*."

"If anyone did." Shadow slid her sunglasses onto her head, turning her violet eyes on him. "He may have found out about this potential treasure all on his own. He might even have a buyer lined up."

Gabe sighed as he considered her words, rolling his tense shoulders. "Damn it. You could be right."

"And unless we can get copies of the stolen documents, we're already behind. I hate that. At least we have permission to be here!"

"That might not be to our advantage if we're searching in the wrong place." Gabe pushed away from the tree, anxious to continue. "Come on. Let's get to the lodge."

They continued across the lush grass, maintained by a series of sprinklers, and soon entered a wooded area, a glimpse of the old lodge visible through the trees.

"This is impressive," Shadow said, when they finally stood before it. "Needs work, obviously."

"That's an understatement." The two storey lodge was constructed of brick and wood, with huge beams on the outside, but the whole place was dilapidated. The wooden trim was cracked and warped, the roof sagged, and weeds were springing up in the paving around it.

Theo had given them a huge, old iron key, and Gabe twisted it in the lock, forcing the door open to get inside. The smell of mildew hit him immediately.

"Watch your step, Shadow. The floor will be rotten."

"Herne's horns. It's a mess."

Apart from a few old pieces of heavy wooden furniture, the place was empty. A staircase swept up into gloom, and a cavernous fireplace dominated most of one wall.

"I honestly think this place will have nothing to do with the treasure or the knife," Gabe said thoughtfully. "It was built well after the Templar's time."

"We shouldn't rule out anything at this stage." Shadow headed to the fireplace, standing within the empty grate and looking up the chimney.

Gabe turned away, looking for the carvings that Theo had mentioned. They weren't hard to find. Unusual symbols had been carved into the wooden panelling. Occult symbols. As his eyes adjusted to the gloom, he realised there were lots of them on the coving, the ceiling rose, and the banisters. He swung around to study the chimney, watching as Shadow pushed and pulled at the stone mouldings there.

This place was more than just a hunting lodge. It had occult overtones.

And then he heard a distinct click and Shadow yelled, "Run!" just before a huge explosion blasted him across the room.

⚬◈◈⚬

Barak did not like this passageway beneath the *Château du Buade* one bit.

It was narrow and winding, with a few passages sloping off it, some up, some down, and others running level. They had stuck to the main tunnel, which was wider than the others. He had a good sense of direction, but even he was getting confused as to where they were headed. The air, however, was fresh, and the passages relatively dust free, which meant an air supply was getting down here, and people used it frequently.

"I think we're heading to the *château*," he whispered to Estelle, wary of his voice carrying. He pulled a compass out of his pocket, trying to envisage the grounds above him as he studied the map they had picked up on the tour. It was basic, but would suffice for their needs. "I think the tasting room and vineyards are that way." He pointed to his left. "The *château* should be straight ahead."

"There's not much to suggest Black Cronos, though, is there?"

"Not yet." He had a sudden recollection of the traps spread beneath Arklet Abbey. "Do you think this is booby trapped?"

Estelle shook her head. "With so many people above us? I doubt it. Plus, if people regularly use this, they wouldn't risk it. Arklet Abbey was evacuated. It was a last resort."

"I agree." He hurried onward, reassured, until he saw another door and another keypad set in the wall.

They crept closer and heard voices beyond it. Barak froze. There was a camera set in the door, almost imperceptible from a distance.

He started to pull Estelle back, hissing, "Get rid of your witch-light."

But it was too late. A solid metal gate slid out of the stone behind them, clanging to the floor.

They were trapped.

Ash took a deep breath, inhaling the scents of the old books, and pulled the small stack towards him. He may as well do something useful while they waited for word on the original records.

Theo had pulled up a chair next to him, plainly rattled, but he soldiered on. "The top book is written by an English scholar, and it has a large section on the English Templars. He talks about the commanders, and mentions Guillaume de la More—William, in English—and he speculates about the treasure. I liked it because it was pretty comprehensive. And he was local."

"The author?" Ash asked, thumbing through the book.

"Yes, he lived in Millcorner, a few miles away. The other book is a history of the Templars, and very interesting, but has less of a local flavour." He sighed. "I'm no scholar, so I have no idea how accurate these books are. I've read all sorts over the last few months, but as I told Harlan, it makes my head hurt. The diary is interesting, though. Madeleine Montgomery was the wife of a local landowner, and she wrote about many things. Dinners, guests, weekends, household trivia—a fascinating snapshot of the landed gentry. But she also mentions Temple Keep, and the dig on the grounds."

Ash looked at Theo, shocked. "You didn't mention that earlier!"

"But it came to nothing! I thought you might want to look at it, though."

"Absolutely." He picked up the first history book. "These are the ones you have a few photocopies of?"

"Yes—the passages that I thought were most relevant." Theo took the book from Ash and flicked through it, and then stopped, mouth open.

"What?"

"The pages have been cut out!"

Ash grabbed the book from his hand. Theo was right. A few pages had been sliced out of the book, cut close to the edge, and virtually impossible to see when the book was closed.

Bollocks.

"Someone else is also searching for this treasure, Theo, and destroying any evidence as they go." Ash quickly searched the other books and found them damaged, too. "Who have you been talking to?"

"No one! Well, my wife of course, but no details. She wouldn't be interested." His eyes widened at Ash's stare. "She's my wife! I trust her."

Ash wasn't so sure. When it came to treasure and untold wealth, allegiances sometimes vanished. "Theo, think! Why the sudden interest in this now? These books have been here for years! When were you last here?"

"Just last week, and they were intact then."

"You must have said something to someone about your recent activities."

"Just my assistant gardener!"

Ash groaned. "You have to be kidding me!"

"No!" Theo was glaring at him, eyes narrowed. "He helped me with some of the research. He's been working for me for years."

"You deal in stock and shares! You can't be that gullible."

"I'm not! I asked for some general assistance."

Ash took a deep breath, trying to calm down. "You are unfamiliar with the internet, then?"

"My dealing in stocks and shares was years ago! I had staff! I've been on boards since then—no internet necessary." Theo's lips were tight, but there was uncertainty now behind his eyes, and Ash felt suddenly sorry for him.

"I think you've underestimated the interest in all this. Perhaps you didn't say much to your gardener, but he might have looked into it further—done research of his own. He may even have employed someone to search on his behalf." *Nicoli, for example, but he kept that thought to himself.*

"Is he working today?"

"Owen? Er, probably."

"We need to talk to him when we get back." And keep Shadow and her sharp knives away from him.

Before Theo could respond, Adam returned, Lily at his side, both wearing pinched expressions. This was not going to be good news.

"The originals have gone, haven't they?" Ash asked before they could speak.

Lily nodded. "I don't know how! This place is secure."

"There's no sign of a break-in?"

"None! We have alarms, cameras, key codes!" Lily was almost spluttering with indignation.

Theo was thunderous as he stood up. "This is outrageous! I demand to see the area. There might be evidence!"

"We have already called the police," Lily said, trying to calm Theo down. "We will do everything we can..."

Theo cut her off. "I demand to see it myself." He leaned in, lowering his voice. "I donate to this place. I think you owe me this much."

Lily glanced around at the inquisitive glances of other library users, unwilling to be the centre of so much attention. Ash was impressed. Theo's relaxed nature obviously hid a core of steel. And maybe he was also motivated by his own failure in judgement.

Lily, however, was no pushover. "The police said not to touch anything!"

"I won't. I just want to look!"

Ash laid a hand on Theo's arm, knowing they wouldn't find a thing. Not *now*, anyway. "It's okay, Theo. Let the police do their job and we'll do ours. We have books to study." *What was left of them.* They could report the damage later.

Theo shot him an impatient look, but at Ash's intense stare, he finally acquiesced, and Lily bobbed away, shooting Ash a grateful glance.

Without another word, Ash pulled his pen and notepad out. There was probably nothing left in the books in front of him to help their search, or they would already have been stolen, but there may be a snippet of information that would help them.

Then tonight, they could break-in themselves and investigate fully.

Seven

S hadow crashed into the curving staircase, wood shattering as she ploughed straight through it and landed, winded, on the rotten floorboards on the other side.

She landed with such force that the floorboards cracked beneath her, and she fell through the hole and onto the foundation. For a few seconds, she couldn't think straight, or see beyond the darkness compounded by her narrowed vision, and her ears were ringing.

Herne's blistering balls. What had just happened?

Then she smelled smoke, and realised she could see a billowing, black cloud above her. A roaring noise supplanted the ringing in her ears.

Her memory returned with a rush. She'd triggered a bomb, and now there was a fire, and somewhere above her was Gabe.

She staggered to her feet, every muscle in her body aching, and with shock saw that her clothes were smouldering. She patted herself down, and yelled, "Gabe!"

There was no answer, and she scrambled up the shattered planks and back to the ground floor.

A scene of horror spread before her. One entire side of the house was on fire, flames curling across the ceiling. Black, choking smoke filled the space, obscuring her vision. Gabe had been behind her, well away from the blast. "Gabe!"

She started searching, pulling her t-shirt over her mouth as she zigzagged across the floor. Finally, a groan reached her, and then a fallen table was up-ended as Gabe emerged from beneath it, a cut across his forehead bleeding profusely.

He glared at her. "Shadow! What the hell have you done now?"

"Me?" Her relief at seeing him turned to outrage. "This explosion is nothing to do with me, you big, winged idiot!"

An ominous crash had them both looking upwards, just in time to see a huge, flaming beam fall down on the staircase, and that burst into flames, too.

"I suggest," she yelled, "that we get out of here!"

She turned to the door, but unfortunately the entrance was blocked by another fallen beam, and the flames licked higher, trapping them inside. The windows were their only way out, and they were boarded up, but Gabe was already sprinting to one furthest from the flames, and she followed him.

Gabe ripped the boards away, using one of them to punch through the glass and smash the jagged edges. With a whoosh, the flames roared across the ceiling, fuelled by the new supply of oxygen. Gabe grabbed Shadow and pushed her through the opening, and in seconds they were both outside and sprinting from the burning building.

Only at the edge of the tree line did they stop and look back. The entire building was now burning, flames already curling out of the roof, fuelled by the tinder-dry, rotten wood.

"Well," Gabe said, wiping the blood from his forehead, and trying to stem the bleeding, "someone didn't want us looking in there." He looked up and down her body, searching for injuries. "Are you okay?"

Shadow patted herself down. "Just sore. Fortunately, I was already running when the blast caught me. Which, by the way, was *not* my fault."

He grinned, pulling her to him for a kiss. "I know. But you did trigger it, somehow."

"Accidentally!"

"You're so easy to tease!"

"Piss off!" She reached her hand to the deep cut on his forehead. "Is this your only injury?"

He nodded, his laugh disappearing. "Just this and a very sore shoulder where the damn table hit me. We were bloody lucky, Shadow. That blast was meant to kill. I doubt Theo could have got away if he'd been the one to trigger it."

"Which means he's right. There *is* something to this treasure."

He nodded, and pulled his phone from his pocket. "I'd better call the fire brigade before the whole wood is set alight. Then you can tell me what happened."

Shadow studied the lodge, wincing as the roof collapsed inwards. "Herne's hairy bollocks! There'll be nothing left of that by the time they arrive."

She waited silently while Gabe made the call, trying to recall the design of the moulding that had triggered the blast, and wondering if there was any way she could have averted it.

"Go on," Gabe said when he finished the call. "What happened?"

"I noticed there were a lot of symbols around the fireplace. Some were in the wood, others in the stone."

"I noticed that, too—all around the room, including the staircase. Theo never said there were so many."

"The outer fire-surround was enormous, solid wood, but there was a huge stone lintel underneath, and obviously at the back of the fireplace. There was a relief right in the centre, but smaller ones around the edge. One of them looked to be an eye in a triangle, and others, well, I'm not sure.

Anyway," she shrugged, hoping the intricacies of the shapes would come back to her later, "I was feeling around a couple of them, and noticed one stood prouder than most. I pushed it, then pulled it, and saw wires. That's when I ran and shouted at you. I'd barely gone half a dozen paces when the explosion threw me across the room."

"What if they booby trapped the library?"

"Sounds like they've just stolen the documents, from what Theo says."

"I'd better phone Ash next."

"And I'll go and find the fire brigade," Shadow said, setting off across the grounds to direct them.

* * *

Estelle summoned her magic, power balling at the ends of her fingertips as the barrier dropped into place behind her.

Barak waited next to her, watching the door at the end of the corridor as voices grew louder. "They're coming. We either fight it out, or flee. Can you damage the camera from here? It's at the top of the door."

She saw it and hurled a blast of power at the target, reinforcing it with a spell, and with a satisfying crack, the camera shattered. The patter of footsteps slowed. "If it's Black Cronos on the other side, it will be a tough fight."

"But it's an opportunity to see what they're guarding. A risk I'm prepared to take." He levelled his dark eyes at her, uncompromising in this light.

"I agree. I'll use a spell on them—one to confuse them."

The door edged open before they could discuss it further. A flash bloomed as something shot down the passage towards them. Estelle threw a protective shield around them as she and Barak dived to the floor. Simultaneously, she hurled a fireball at the door, blasting it off its hinges and taking whoever was behind out with it.

Beyond the smouldering door frame, a man clambered to his feet in the centre of the room, something glinting in his palms. It looked suspiciously like the weapon that the Silencer of Souls had used on Shadow. Presuming the worst, Estelle aimed a blast of power at him, throwing him into the wall. She followed it up with a binding spell that wrapped his limbs to his body and sealed his mouth shut.

Neither waited to see what else would happen, opting instead to attack. They leapt to their feet and raced to the room's entrance, backs pressed flat against the wall for a brief moment as they peered inside.

One man lay insensible beneath the heavy wooden door in the middle of the room, as another groaned against the far wall. No one else was in sight, and there were no shouts or pounding feet, either.

Barak nodded in appreciation as he edged inside. "Nice work, Estelle. Fast, efficient, and effective, just as I like it. Well, not for *everything*, obviously."

He winked at her and she felt a flush creep up her cheeks like she was a schoolgirl with a crush. "Even now, that's where your mind goes?"

"Of course. However, I suppose I should focus on our immediate issue."

"Like where the hell are we and what just happened?"

The room had a bank of monitors on the wall that flickered with different scenes. A couple of doors were set in the far wall, both shut. A glass panel looked into what seemed to be a security checkpoint, with a door on either end. A low grill was set into it.

"It seems to be some kind of guard room." Estelle headed to a row of IDs and swipe cards on the wall, some of the hooks empty. "Is this just *château* security?"

Barak snorted. "Down here? I don't think so." He ignored the screens and strode over to the man immobilised by the binding spell. Grabbing him by the throat, he lifted him off his feet and seated him on an office chair.

He lowered his face so he was on eye level with the man. "He doesn't look like an enhanced human. His eyes are fine."

"No tattoos, either," Estelle noted as she studied his bare arms exposed by a short-sleeved shirt. She estimated he was in his late thirties, and was wearing a uniform of smart shirt, tie, and trousers. He looked like a security guard. He glared at her, a mixture of fear and frustration in his eyes. His jaw moved, but his lips remain sealed by her spell. She remembered her own fury when Caspian cast the same spell on her. It was horrible, but the man had just tried to kill them.

"I need to question him," Barak said.

"Let me check the cameras first."

Most of the screens showed rooms rather than outdoor areas, and a few showed corridors. A couple looked to be labs that had a handful of people working in them, some appeared to be cells, and one had been recently occupied, with an unmade bed. One room looked like a theatre, and a man was lying on a trolley as people moved around him. Her unease intensified. "By the Goddess, Barak. There's a man strapped to a trolley. He might be a prisoner. There are cells here somewhere!"

Barak grabbed the man's collar again, pulling him close as he growled, "What is this place?"

Estelle said a spell to muffle sound before releasing the binding on his tongue. The man, however, refused to speak.

"I asked you a question," Barak repeated. "If you want to keep your tongue, I suggest you use it." He repeated the question in French.

The man laughed derisively and replied in heavily-accented English. "I don't need you to translate, fool."

"Then answer the question."

"My life won't be worth living."

"It isn't anyway."

Barak dragged him to his feet, hauling him in front of the cameras. He pointed at the operating room. "Who is that and why is he here?"

"I don't know. I'm just security."

"Exactly. So, you see everything."

The security guard snorted. "There are rooms here that have no cameras." He stared at Barak impassive. "There are things they don't want you to see."

Estelle repressed a shudder. "Fancy *châteaus* don't normally have hidden lairs and prisoners. We know this has to do with Black Cronos. Is the *Comte* here?"

The guard looked genuinely shocked. "Who? I have never heard of that name."

A flicker of movement caught Estelle's eye, and she looked at the screens. One of them showed two guards walking down a corridor, and she heard footsteps outside. So did the guard, and he opened his mouth to scream. She sealed it shut again and he stared at her, horrified.

"We've got company, Barak. Change of shift, I bet. We've got a couple of minutes at most."

Barak's face wrinkled with annoyance, and he punched the guard, knocking him out cold, and then stowed him under a desk in the corner. "We'll let them in, incapacitate them, and find the prisoner. Bind this guy, too, just in case." He quickly picked up the other unconscious man and threw him through the blasted doorway, and then lifted the door and put it back in position. "That will have to do."

They positioned themselves on either side of the door, and heard the click as the door opened. The guards stepped inside, chatting and laughing, distracted enough that they didn't see the other guards weren't there until the door swung shut behind them. In seconds it was all over, and both lay incapacitated on the floor.

"Right," Estelle said, satisfied. "Let's find a floor plan. Time to rescue a prisoner."

"We aren't exactly equipped to pull off a rescue mission," Barak pointed out. "And it's broad daylight."

Estelle grinned, relishing the fact that she was working with the Nephilim—especially Barak. This was just what her life had been lacking. "Then we improvise!"

Eight

A sh stared at the ruins of the lodge, horrified. It was a smoking, waterlogged mess, merely a shell of a building. A small fire crew were still onsite, one man consulting with Theo.

Gabe and Shadow stood next to Ash, both singed, stinking of smoke, and covered in sooty smears. They were sheltering under the trees that had fortunately been saved as they were well away from the smouldering ruin, able to talk quietly. "You two were lucky. That blast must have been huge."

"It was designed to kill, that's for sure," Gabe said. "Meant to cover all traces of what might be found in there. I'm sure that building was more than just a hunting lodge."

"Whoever planted that bomb must be responsible for the theft of the papers, too," Ash said thoughtfully. "Why not just burn the place down?"

Shadow shrugged, and then winced. "To create maximum damage, I guess. Risky, though. The explosion might never have been triggered."

"Unless several things were booby trapped," Ash suggested.

"Of course! Which would explain the other explosions, after we escaped," Shadow said, nodding. "I hadn't considered that."

Gabe gestured towards Theo. "I think his life is at risk."

"And Owen, the assistant gardener, must have something to do with it." Ash related his conversation with Theo. "We need to find him. Question him."

"Ha!" Shadow snorted. "After this? He'll be long gone."

"We could be jumping to conclusions," Gabe pointed out.

"Come on." Ash turned away, striding back towards the main grounds. "Theo will be tied up there for a while. Let's see what we can find out about Owen. Have they interviewed you?"

Gabe nodded. "Just the fire brigade, not the police—yet. And they checked us for injuries. We were lucky not to be carted off to hospital. What about you? Have you found out anything useful?"

"Background stuff only, but someone doctored the books—cut out the salient pages. I need to examine Theo's copies. It was lucky he took them, and made notes." He pulled up short. "We still have his stuff, right? And the knife?"

"He put everything in his safe," Shadow said, "before he left with you."

They emerged from the woods, and the castle glowed in the late afternoon sunshine. It looked peaceful in its bucolic setting. Ash hoped it was peaceful inside, too, and that Chivers and his wife were okay.

A sudden urgency quickened his pace. "I should check."

"Then we'll head to the potting sheds to find the gardener," Gabe said, turning towards the long, brick-built buildings with low roofs behind the main house. "Call us if you need us."

Jackson felt sick, stunned with Layla's news, and for a moment, he couldn't speak.

"I'm sorry." Layla pulled a stool from under the bench, and made him sit on it. "There was no easy way to tell you. I'm shocked too, but I've had some time to get used to it."

"There's no mistake?" Jackson's tongue felt thick in his mouth as he stared at the body. "He was on my grandfather's team. You're sure?"

"I'm sure." Layla pulled out another stool and sat next to him. "Bastards, aren't they?"

The implications were horrific, but he had to ask. "The other bodies, could one of them have been my grandfather? Or even the rest of his team?"

"It's possible. Unfortunately, they've been cremated now, so we'll never know, but it's unlikely." She squeezed his hand. "The odds are ridiculous. It's more likely that your grandfather died, along with the rest of the team."

"*He* didn't. James."

"But you know what they were subjected to."

Bile rose in Jackson's throat, quickly followed by fury, and he rocketed to his feet, upending the stool. The noise of it hitting the floor echoed around the room. "Fuck them. I hate Black Cronos! They're monsters." He stared at James Arbuthnot's body. "They would have suffered. Horribly."

"Perhaps. We don't know that, though. We still have no idea what they do to affect the changes. Alchemical experimentation might not be as painful as other ways of changing the body."

Jackson turned to her. Layla still looked elegant, despite the scrubs that clad her slender body, but the fine lines on her face were exaggerated now by her fierce concentration. "You don't have to lie to me."

"Of course I don't. You're an adult. I would never dream of it." Her tone was brisk as she stood, brushing her scrubs down. She headed to the cupboards, pulling out instruments, the sharp smell of formaldehyde filling his nostrils. "And now that I can see the tattoos, I'm going to take samples. Lots of them. I'm sure there are still more secrets to unlock. James may help his country, after all. You, however, need to leave me in peace. If you'd like to help me, call JD."

Jackson nodded and left the room, hurrying to his office where he poured himself a neat whiskey. He threw it back, savouring the warmth as it travelled down his throat. He poured another, hoping to ease the trembling in his hands. Adrenalin still flooded his system, and for a few minutes, all he did was pace his office, trying to subdue his fury, but he couldn't settle. He decided to call JD, as promised.

Anna, JD's housekeeper, or whatever she was—*gatekeeper was more apt*—answered the phone, her clipped, sharp tone restoring some of his equilibrium. However, she refused to put him through to JD. "He's too busy. He forbade me from disturbing him for at least another couple of hours."

"He'll want to hear this, Anna!"

"Call back later." She ended the call, and he swore loudly into his empty office.

He needed a distraction. Another drink, though one with some company. Time to call Harlan.

⸱⸱❧✦☙⸱⸱

Harlan had never seen Jackson look so desolate. He was slumped in the corner of The Swan pub at the edge of Hyde Park, a half-drunk pint of Guinness on the table in front of him, and another two empty glasses on the side, staring into the distance.

There were plenty of seats outside under umbrellas in the sunshine, but Jackson was instead sitting in the gloomy interior. Harlan could understand why after hearing his news, and wished he'd been able to join him earlier. "I'm sorry, Jackson. I wish I could do more than just sympathise."

"It's fine. Of course you can't do anything. I just wanted someone to get drunk with."

"That might not be the best plan."

"I don't care."

Harlan sipped his own pint, considering the best course of action. "It's interesting, though. How old did James look?"

"Mid-thirties, I'd guess."

"Frozen in time, then."

Jackson looked at him, startled. "Well, yes. Of course."

"So it means that whatever alchemy does to their bodies—the enhanced strength, the metallic skin that seems to act like armour—it preserves life, too. Perhaps makes them immortal. Like the *comte*. Bloody hell. Immortal super-soldiers."

"Not unlike the Nephilim."

Harlan eased back in his chair. "They're not immortal. Just long-lived. Like Shadow." He reconsidered his assessment. "Maybe Black Cronos are long-lived too, rather than immortal. Perhaps the count wouldn't actually want his soldiers to live as long as him."

"If it is the count behind all this."

"Perhaps," Harlan mused, "that's also why Layla hasn't been able to identify most of them. They might all be very old. There'd be no DNA or fingerprints to compare them to."

"I'm sure they're still recruiting, though, somehow."

"Of course." Harlan didn't doubt that. "Let's just hope the tattoos reveal something of worth. You say you couldn't speak to JD?"

Jackson rolled his eyes as he picked up his pint. "No, Anna refused to put me through. She's worse than a GP's receptionist. Anyone would think I was trying to get an appointment with God. Not that He exists, of course."

"JD is a God, in his own head!" Harlan laughed. "And maybe Anna's. I'd love to know how she came to work for him." He sobered, wondering what JD was up to. "I must admit, I haven't spoken to him for a while. Perhaps he'll make a breakthrough...or Layla's discovery will help him to. Still no news from Barak?" Jackson had told him where he and Estelle had gone.

"No, actually." Jackson checked his watch. "They were on the tour this morning. I was expecting to hear from them by now. I'd phone, but if they're in hiding, I'd hate to give away their position."

"You say the *château* has links to the count?"

"Centuries ago. And now they have some less than transparent business dealings, despite their wholesome image as a tourist attraction." Jackson fidgeted, picking up his phone and scrolling for messages. "Nothing. At what point do I get worried? It's unlike Barak not to be in contact."

"Give it 'til nightfall. They must be following a lead. Is there backup in place if something goes wrong?"

"Nothing local, just Niel and Nahum, I guess. No involvement from the PD except extraction, perhaps. Waylen would need to arrange that. To be honest, I hadn't considered it. This was supposed to just be about watching them."

"If they saw an opportunity..."

"Damn it. Now I'm worried."

"Patience. They know what they're doing."

Jackson nodded, but he was clearly distracted. "Tell me about your latest jobs. What's happening?"

Harlan quickly summarised Theo's discovery of the knife and the search for Templar gold. "I haven't heard from them, either, but that doesn't surprise me. They've only just started the search."

Jackson frowned, and sat up straighter, staring over Harlan's shoulder at the TV next to the bar. "Did you say they were in Kent?"

"Yes, Temple Keep. Why?" He twisted to see the screen behind, horrified to see a screenshot of fire engines at the country estate, the caption, *'Fire at historic castle in Temple Moreton'* scrolling across the bottom of the page. "Holy shit!"

Gabe entered the huge potting shed at the rear of the courtyard behind the castle, having studied the rustic building for a short while for signs of movement. Although, *shed* was not the word he would have used to describe the place. It was actually built of brick.

On their way across the grounds, they passed about half a dozen staff gathered on the lawn in front of the house, all watching the smoke in the woods with rapt fascination, and a fair degree of worry. They hadn't lingered though, only long enough to ascertain that Owen, the assistant gardener, wasn't there, nor the head gardener, Malcolm. A couple of other junior gardeners were present, shrugging as they directed them to the courtyard.

The potting shed was surprisingly well organised, a series of interconnected spaces, most with external doors. The smell of compost hung on the air, rich and welcoming. Rows of gleaming, well-maintained tools were stored in racks along the wall, as were row upon row of plant pots—a mix of clay pots and plastic, of a variety of sizes. Seed trays were stacked up, but some were positioned under long windows, tiny shoots coming through that Gabe presumed were salad leaves for the kitchen garden.

The sound of loud music drew them through a couple of rooms, passing larger machinery such as lawnmowers and hedge-trimmers, to the end room where a middle-aged man stood at a long sink washing out plant pots and singing to the radio.

Gabe knocked on the door frame and shouted, "I'm looking for Owen!"

The man looked around, startled, water splashing everywhere. "Bloody hell! Are you trying to give me a heart attack?" His eyes narrowed with suspicion as he took in their appearance. Gabe had forgotten he looked such a sight. He placed the pot on the side and grabbed a cloth to dry his hands, then turned down the volume. "Who are you?"

"My name's Gabe, and this is Shadow. Theo hired us to help him with a project. Sorry about our appearance—we got caught in the fire." Gabe crossed the room to shake his hand, but Shadow merely nodded and stayed in the doorway, eyes darting everywhere.

"Fire? What fire?"

Gabe looked at him, incredulous. "The lodge in the wood has just blown up. Didn't you hear the fire engines? The explosion?"

"Explosion? Bloody hell!" He ran to the window looking onto the courtyard, where a plume of smoke could still be seen eddying across the grounds. "Was Theo in there? Or anyone?"

"Just us, although Theo's there now."

The man exhaled heavily. "That's all right, then. I like my music loud—you probably noticed. It must have blocked everything out." He studied them again, carefully this time, as he leaned against the sink. "You were lucky. How did it happen?"

"Hard to say right now," Gabe answered, fudging the truth. "You are?"

"Sorry, I'm Malcolm, the head gardener." A knowing look crossed his face. "You're helping Theo look for his Templar treasure!"

Gabe suppressed a groan, exchanging an annoyed glance with Shadow. *Did everyone know?* "News travels fast. Theo seemed to think it was a secret."

Malcolm laughed. "He talked to Chivers, and that man loves to gossip over his evening sherry. News gets round." Gabe clenched his jaw with annoyance, but Malcolm continued. "And of course, everyone knows about this castle's link to the Templars. It's a source of great pride and gossip—even now. I don't think anyone actually thinks there's any treasure, though. Over the years, many have looked for it and found nothing."

"What about Owen?"

"He enlisted Owen's help, didn't he? Owen's always bragging about his computer skills." He rolled his eyes. "Did you say you were looking for him?"

"Yes. I have a couple of questions for him." Gabe didn't elaborate, and wondered if there was any point, considering Chivers's gossip. However, Owen would have been more involved, and might have more information to share.

"The last time I saw him, he was supervising the junior gardeners in the greenhouse."

"They're all on the lawn now, watching the action. Except for Owen."

Malcolm shrugged. "Maybe he's still there on his own, then."

Shadow asked a question from the doorway. "Does he seem okay? Is he edgy? Worried?"

Malcolm shifted to look at her. "A bit quieter than normal, but other than that, no." He frowned. "You don't think he's got anything to do with this?"

Gabe answered first. "We're checking everything. Lodges don't normally explode."

"And Owen is not a bomber!"

"Good." Gabe turned away, collecting Shadow on his way out the door. "If you see him, tell him I want to chat."

They found the huge greenhouse in the walled garden a short distance away, but it took only a short search to see that Owen wasn't in there, either.

"He's on the run," Shadow declared. "Sneaky shit."

"We don't know that." Gabe still wasn't convinced that Owen was the source of the issue. "Malcolm said everyone knew Theo's secret after Chivers had gossiped. Anyone could have blabbed. And besides, everyone also knew about the castle's history."

Shadow idly played with her knives as she studied the plants in the greenhouse, the hot air wrapping around them. "Well, obviously Theo's interest has made someone think there are new clues, and seeing as his search isn't being broadcast on the news, someone local must have said something."

"Come on. Let's get to the main house and see how Ash is getting on, and then we should get an address for Owen. If he doesn't reappear in the next few hours, we'll go to his home. Maybe he's sick." Even as he said it, Gabe knew he was kidding himself.

"Or he's dead," Shadow said, cutting to the chase. "And then we'll know who we are really up against."

Nine

Barak opened the electronic lock using the pass they'd found in the office, and sidled through the door ahead of Estelle. Once on the other side, they paused, searching the space in front of them.

They were in a changing room. The shelves were stacked with surgical scrubs and handwashing facilities—and fortunately, no people. A room with showers and a bathroom was off to the side, and at the far end of the room was a door, partly ajar, opening onto a corridor. But there were several groups of clothing hanging on pegs, and shoes on the floor.

Barak whispered, "Half a dozen clothes—must mean half a dozen people."

"A hospital?" Estelle asked.

"A chamber of horrors, more like. But let's hope they're all medical staff and unarmed."

Before they left the guard room, they had studied a very basic floorplan that was pinned to the wall marking fire exits, and it was clear that anyone who entered the underground area had to pass through the glass-walled room adjacent to the security room. An antechamber, where they could be scanned and issued their security passes. He and Estelle had obviously entered through the back door. After walking along a couple of short passages and down a long, dank flight of stone steps, they were now in the heart of the complex.

Barak voiced the concerns that had been playing on his mind. "Why aren't the guards here enhanced soldiers, and why aren't there more people around?"

"Maybe because this is a satellite base?"

"Then why is there a prisoner here? I don't like it. Something feels off."

"It feels off *because* there's a prisoner here...maybe more than one. Perhaps he's housed here, ready for transfer to another facility? Unless," she faltered, "he could be a willing participant, and this place is a kind of barracks."

"I guess we're about to find out."

After a cursory examination of the changing room, Estelle edged to the door and looked out. She mouthed, *Voices*, and pointed to the right.

Barak joined her. The passageway ran from left to right. To the left were more doors, all shut, a couple with grills set in the top. *Cells, perhaps.* But on their right were more rooms, many with their doors open, all blazing with light and the sound of chatter. The place smelt of disinfectant and something he couldn't quite place. It gave him the chills.

Barak drew Estelle back inside the changing room. "That man must be somewhere on the right. If he's a prisoner, we should try to rescue him. But if he's not..."

"Either way, we're heading for a fight. Or we could just back out and report what we've found. We've already come this far, though."

"And," he sighed, wondering if he was mad for suggesting the next option, "we could cause a lot of disruption here."

Estelle's dark eyes brightened. "Sabotage?"

"Big time."

"I like that option better."

"We could be trapped if we get this wrong—if someone seals this exit."

Estelle shook her head, clearly considering their options. "Those doors have grills in them. They're cells, not barracks. Which means there's another way out—a route to bring prisoners in. Not through the staff area. And probably not marked on the map. I'm willing to chance it, anyway."

"Good. We take the staff out as cleanly as possible."

Barak advanced down the corridor, his booted feet silent on the stone floor, the dagger he'd strapped to his leg in his hand. But he'd barely walked three paces when the muted chatter raised in volume, and a voice shouted, "Stop him!"

An ear-piercing shriek echoed down the corridor, followed by the sounds of crashing furniture.

A man emerged from a corridor, a surgical gown flapping around him, tattoos snaking down his arms. Blood was splashed across his chest, and his eyes were wild, terrified. Right behind him was a man struggling to grip a rifle, and within seconds another couple of staff followed, all splattered with blood, all yelling.

The prisoner spotted Barak and dived into a side room. At the same time, the man with the rifle managed to secure his grip and shot at their captive—and then he saw Barak and Estelle, too. For a split second he froze, and then adjusted his aim.

Barak and Estelle hurtled through the closest doorway, but Estelle was ready to strike. A ball of fire grew in her hands, and she hurled it down the corridor, following it up with a blast of pure energy. It knocked every single member of staff off their feet, and the rifle clattered across the floor.

Barak took advantage of the lull and barrelled down the corridor, sprinting for the gun. The man who'd fired it ran in a crouch towards it. Barak released his knife with deadly accuracy, hitting the man in the chest, and he fell, unmoving.

Other staff emerged from a side room, and as Barak dived for the gun, Estelle dealt with them. A wind swept over Barak, powerful enough to force the staff back into the room. Then she said a spell. Barak felt the words of power take effect. Suddenly, the staff were trapped behind a wall of flames, and they backed to the wall, eyes wide, some with fear, others with fury.

Barak grabbed the gun and returned to Estelle. "This is a tranquilliser gun. Hold them here, I'll check the prisoner."

But before she could answer, another staff member bolted from the end room they hadn't yet secured, and ran around the corner and down the corridor the prisoner had emerged from.

"Leave him to me!" Estelle said, already giving chase.

Barak turned back to the prisoner, who wasn't taking any chances on Barak or Estelle helping him. He'd seized his opportunity as they dealt with the staff, and was running to the exit, a scalpel in his hand. But his steps were slowing, blood pouring from a wound on his thigh, a feathered dart cast aside on the floor.

Barak knew he couldn't let him escape. They needed him. And, he might give them away. He tackled him from behind, and they both hit the floor hard. Barak saw the deadly blade flash, and smacked down hard on the man's arm, crunching it into the floor.

"I'm here to help you!"

The man grunted, his face planted into the ground. "It doesn't seem like it!"

"We are getting you out of here."

"I can do it alone." The man had a French accent, but his English was good.

"Not half-drugged you can't."

Up close, the prisoner looked feverish, his face covered in sweat. His eyes had a strange sheen to them, and Barak wondered if he was suffering from some kind of physical change—courtesy of the tattoos, no doubt, as some of them looked fresh. However, he didn't have the strength that a Black Cronos soldier normally had. Maybe that was because of whatever they had drugged him with.

Making sure the scalpel was well out of reach, Barak eased up and off him in a gesture of good will. "This is not the time to argue. We all need to get out of here."

The man sat up, rubbing his head where it had struck the floor, but he eyed the staff pinned in the side-room by the flames. "Not before we deal with those."

Barak nodded, thinking through their options, and distracted by Estelle's return. She was tight-lipped with fury and radiating magic, but otherwise unharmed. "You need to see something,"

Barak stood, pulling the man to his feet, and quickly patted him down to check for other weapons. All the fight, however, seemed to have left him, and he sagged against the wall, breathing heavily and looking increasingly glassy-eyed.

Barak turned to Estelle. "We need to move the staff, get into the room they were in, and check everywhere else. We need answers—anything!"

Estelle didn't hesitate. "I can spell them to sleep and we can drag them into the cells." She glanced over her shoulder at the locked rooms at the other end of the corridor. "If that's what they are. But what if the camera feeds down here go elsewhere? Others could already be on the way. They might have even triggered an alarm we can't hear."

Barak was damn sure they weren't running out there yet, not after all this. "Then we'd best be quick."

Ten

Ash was standing at the window, staring at the smoke that drifted over the wood, when Shadow and Gabe entered the first floor sitting room.

He turned to them, amused. They were still streaked in black soot, and still wearing fire-damaged clothing. "Your smoky stench preceded you. You need a shower."

"Tough," Shadow said, scowling at his clean jeans and t-shirt before looking around the neat room. "Everything okay here?"

"Seems to be." Ash nodded at a large picture of a deer in dappled shade on the wall. "The safe is behind that, and it's sealed shut. Hopefully everything is locked within it, unless someone knows the code. Chivers certainly didn't...or so he says. Any luck finding Owen?"

"No," Gabe answered, heading to the table that was strewn with the notes Ash had taken that morning. "He's not in the potting sheds or greenhouse, but was here this morning. The head gardener, Malcolm, clearly thinks he has nothing to do with the fire. He also said," he looked up at Ash, his lips curling with annoyance, "that Chivers is a gossip, and everyone knows about the dagger anyway."

Shadow crossed to the window, looking over the moat and lush lawns. "Malcolm is wrong. He might work with Owen, but that doesn't mean he knows him well. Owen is on the run." She looked restless, her eyes darting everywhere, wild energy radiating from her. Ash was used to that now, after all the months spent living and working with her. Shadow could barely sit still once she was rattled. It was what made her so good at hunting. A fight honed her senses even more. "We need his address *now*. If we're wrong about his involvement, then no harm done. We can start looking elsewhere. Someone other than Theo must have his address. Chivers, perhaps."

Ash nodded. "Makes sense. They'll have all the staffs' addresses. If you see Chivers, go easy on him. He looked pretty shook up."

"He should be. His tattling might have caused this." Shadow was already heading to the door. "I'll go and get it. The sooner we look, the better."

"Be careful," Gabe warned her. "Meet me back here!"

But she had already gone, the door slamming behind her.

"She'll be fine," Ash said, watching Gabe as he rifled through Ash's notes.

"It's not her safety I'm worried about." He shot Ash a wry smile.

Ash laughed, glad to see Gabe's mood settling. "You two were lucky. I keep thinking about the size of that bomb—or bombs. Whoever's behind this does not want competitors. We need to get ahead, quickly. Theo must have noticed something he hasn't yet said to us."

Gabe tapped Ash's notes. "I know you've barely begun to look at these, but any ideas?"

"Nothing that stands out. The diary could be interesting, though. From the brief read I had of Theo's copy, Madeleine talks about a search on these grounds by some kind of historical society. Knowing where they searched could help us eliminate places now."

Gabe settled on the edge of the table. "So, this was a stronghold?"

"It was, but not for the Templars. William de la More's family had built this in the twelfth century, and he inherited it as the eldest son. Once

William had a son, he joined the Templars as had his forefathers. It was a tradition. But the keep was always passed on to family. Only money was donated to the Templars. That was pretty common. He travelled in the Middle East for a while, and was later rewarded when he was made Master of England."

"A very grand title."

"For good reason. It came with a lot of power. The title didn't last long, though, for any individual. There were many masters, and the position seemed to change hands frequently...I have no idea why. Poor old William had the misfortune of being the final one. Something struck me, though. I suspect his family would have done what many wealthy landowners did at the time. They would have built a chapel on site. Or even maybe in the building."

"Good point." Gabe's gaze was distant as he thought through the implications. "Theo didn't mention one, or show us one on the tour."

"No. Perhaps it was destroyed during the reformation, or just disintegrated over time. Or was converted into something else."

"Or it never existed in the first place."

"Perhaps. But if there was one, maybe something was hidden there. I'll ask Theo." Ash stared over the grounds. "Do you think he's safe out there?"

"With the fire brigade there, yes, of course. Don't you?"

"He's been gone a while. Shouldn't he be back by now?"

Alarm sparked in Gabe's eyes, his jaw tightening and pulling at the cut on his forehead. It had stopped bleeding, the blood congealed into a thick line. "Don't say something else has happened. You stay here, find us something to go on." He turned, shoulders bunching with annoyance under his torn t-shirt. "I'm going to go and check. I'll find Shadow on the way."

His phone rang as he was crossing the room. He looked at the screen and ignored the call. "It's Harlan. Do me a favour and update him. I haven't got time to talk to him now. And maybe we should call in backup. Things are getting complicated."

"Sure."

"By the way," Gabe paused at the door. "Theo was right about those symbols. They were everywhere. Perhaps there's more to the Freemasons than he made out. Good hunting."

"You too, brother."

Ash's phone was already ringing as Gabe walked out. Harlan again. "Harlan," he said, answering quickly. "Brace yourself. Things have gone a little sidewards here."

━━◈✦◈━━

"Sidewards!" Harlan muttered, still fuming at the wheel of his car as he navigated the London roads thick with traffic. "Bloody Nephilim. Masters of understatement."

"But they are okay. That's something!" Jackson gripped the side of his seat as Harlan took a sharp corner. "That fire looked big."

"Because it was a damn explosion!" Harlan repeated with disbelief, seething with both annoyance and relief. Annoyance that Nicoli might be involved, and relief that his friends weren't hurt. He told Jackson what had happened, and desperate to do something, had decided to visit Nicoli's office. Jackson had insisted on joining him. "You know, you don't have to come. It could be dangerous."

"I doubt Nicoli would be foolish enough to attack us in his office. In fact, I doubt he's even there."

"Well, we'll soon find out." Harlan grimaced as he saw the crowded streets around Nicoli's office. It had taken long enough to crawl through the traffic. "Goddamn it! There's nowhere to park."

"Why don't I jump out and go in, and you circle around?" Jackson suggested.

"No. I want to do this. I want to look into his lying eyes and see what bullshit he comes up with. *Damn it.*" He smacked the steering wheel. "Where the hell can I park?"

"In that case, why don't you jump out, and I'll circle around?"

Harlan looked at Jackson suspiciously. "Are you sober?"

"More or less. I only had a couple of sodding pints before your bloody call of doom."

"This car is my baby." Harlan stared at Jackson, making sure his eyes looked clear. "If I allow you to get behind the wheel, you are to treat it gently!"

"You've just smacked the steering wheel and driven around London like a mad man."

"But I know how to drive it!"

"I'm not an imbecile, and it is just a car."

Harlan's need to find Nicoli overcame his concern over his car. "Just be careful with it."

Jackson grinned, and with a sinking feeling, Harlan pulled to the side, double parked, and exited his car. He didn't even watch Jackson change seats, instead racing into Nicoli's offices.

Nicoli's business was on the second floor of a converted warehouse in Camden. Harlan charged up the stairs, emerging onto a landing with several doors leading off it. He spotted Nicoli's name on the wall next to a heavy-set wooden door: *Andreas Nicoli, Consultant.* He subdued a snort. *Of course, he wouldn't put Order of Lilith on the wall. People would think he ran a cult.*

Harlan took a deep breath, preparing himself for who he might find inside, and pushed the door open. On the other side was a small reception area, richly carpeted, with art on the walls, plush seats for clients to wait on, and a desk with a computer on it and all the normal receptionist paraphernalia. There were two other doors, both shut.

A young woman sitting behind the desk looked up, startled. "Can I help you?"

"Nicoli. Where is he?"

Her eyes darted behind her to the far door, and then to the computer in front of her. "Have you got..."

"No." He marched to the door she had glanced at, throwing it open. "Andreas Nicoli. What the hell are you up to?"

Andreas was standing at the large window, a coffee cup in hand, elegantly clad in an expensive suit. He leaned against the frame, smirking at Harlan. "My, my. If it isn't my good friend, Harlan Beckett!" He gestured to the window. "I saw you arrive in your beautiful car. If only you were wearing a very nice suit to go with it, instead of..." His lips twisted with disdain as he took in Harlan's jeans and leather jacket. "*That*. You look...flustered. Coffee?"

Harlan slammed the door shut behind him. "Screw your coffee. You heard me. What were you doing in Bodiam, in Kent? And why did you plant a bomb? You could have killed someone!"

Nicoli shrugged. "That is the general idea of a bomb. But I must confess, I have no idea what you're talking about." He walked to his desk, sat down, and gestured for Harlan to do the same.

Nicoli was as well-manicured as always. His sleek brown hair was expertly cut, his face clean shaven, his tan immaculate, and his physique lean. But his eyes sparkled with malice as he smiled at Harlan.

Harlan eyed the seat warily, and then studied the room before he sat down, as if there might be a hidden trap. He had never been here before, although he had been aware of where the office was for months. The room was as well decorated as the reception area, taking advantage of the old warehouse's design features. Long, black metal-framed windows, high ceiling, sleek wood floors, bare brick walls. The warehouse conversion had been completed to a high standard. The walls were decorated with modern art, as well as older pieces. The desk was polished and a sleek laptop was open on it.

Conceding that nothing looked remotely like a trap, Harlan still refused to sit, instead pacing to the window and looking down on to the street. His car, with Jackson in it, had vanished. Nicoli twisted in his seat, watching him.

"So nervy, Harlan," he said smoothly, his Greek-accented voice like honey. "Tell me what's bothering you."

"You are, you sneaky son of a bitch." He decided to level with him. "A man matching your description was seen in Bodiam Library, shortly before the papers you were looking at disappeared." He leaned across the desk, taking in the pungent scent of Nicoli's aftershave. "You stole them."

Nicoli rolled his eyes. "I am not the only Greek man in the country, imbecile."

"Cut the crap, Nicoli. This is a rarefied field we work in, and I know many of the players. You were studying documents about the Templars, and now they're gone."

"About the Templars? Interesting. And what might I have found?"

Harlan dropped into the chair, glaring at him. "The more important question is, why are you trying to kill people? Specifically, *my* people."

"*Your* people! Ha. Whom have you got chasing Templar treasure?"

"The very people who dragged your sorry ass out of The Temple of the Trinity."

"Ah! The delightful Shadow and her companions." His lips pursed, a slight grimace of regret crossing his face before it swiftly vanished. "Unfortunate. She is an admirable creature. I trust she is all right?"

"No thanks to you! The important part is that I was employed to search for it." Harlan was over this ridiculous dance. "Why are you looking for it?"

"I believe it is a public library. I am allowed to look. Like you I am interested in many things."

"It's quite a coincidence though, isn't it? That you should be looking right now."

"Like you, I was also employed. Competition is something we have to deal with. *You* have to deal with. If I happen to find the treasure first, then so be it." Nicoli sipped his coffee, eyeing Harlan across the rim. "I have not planted any bombs."

Nicoli was slippery. Just because he hadn't done it, didn't mean he wasn't behind it. "Then you employed someone to do it. Someone could have died!" Harlan's fury returned, and he wanted to punch Nicoli. Instead, he opted for abusing his desk. He slammed it hard, pinning Nicoli in place between his desk and the chair. "This isn't funny. Theo is a good man. You've just destroyed his lodge, and nearly killed Gabe and Shadow."

Nicoli had managed to avoid spilling his coffee and he placed the cup down, eyes narrowing. "Much blood has been spilled over Templar gold. They themselves spilled oceans of it to get their treasure while pursuing their religious ideals. I am merely continuing the tradition." Nicoli gripped his desk and pushed it forcefully back, making Harlan scoot backwards. "At least we now have our cards on the table. The hunt is on. It is a hunt I intend to win."

⋯⊖⟡⊖⋯

Gabe spotted Theo with relief. He was staring at the smouldering remains of the lodge, arms crossed, watching the police tape off the area.

"Herne's bloody horns," Shadow muttered as they approached. "That's all we need—the bloody police poking around."

Gabe looked at her, exasperated. "There's been a bomb! Of course they're here."

She slowed, loitering beneath the trees. "This will delay us searching for Owen. I'm going to go alone."

"You're kidding me!"

"Nope." She was already stepping away from him, melting into the long shadows cast by the lowering sun, her fey magic helping her blend into the natural environment. "They can question me later. Right now, I need to find Owen."

He nodded, trusting her instincts. She was probably right. Owen's disappearance was ominous. "How are you going to get there? You can't drive!"

"I'll go with Ash."

"You need to learn. Ash has got other things to be doing."

She bristled at their familiar argument. "I will. I've been busy!"

"Just be careful."

"Always." She winked, and then vanished.

Gabe headed to Theo's side, thinking he was going to have to blackmail her into taking driving lessons soon. Or just leave her stranded, occasionally. That would work. "Are you all right?" he asked Theo, pushing his irritation with Shadow aside.

Theo looked like he'd aged ten years. His mouth was set in a grim line and his shoulders sagged. Even his moustache seemed to have wilted. "Not really. Look at it. It's just waterlogged beams and bits of wall now!" His eyes swept over Gabe. "And look at you! You're injured, and no doubt covered in bruises. When I started this search, I had no idea this would happen. Are you sure it wasn't an electrical fault? It was old, and desperately needed updating."

"I'm sure. Shadow saw wires set behind a relief carved around the fireplace. They had nothing to do with light fittings."

"Behind a relief? What does that mean?"

Gabe had briefly discussed it with Theo earlier, but figured the shock had made him forgetful. "We think it must have triggered something to open. A secret panel, perhaps? A hiding place." Gabe shrugged as he glanced at the smoking remains of the lodge. "Whatever it was or contained is gone now."

"Which means someone else found it first. Whatever *it* was."

"Potentially, yes."

Theo closed his eyes, fingers pressing into his brow. When he opened them again, he looked resolute, stubborn. "I will not be put off by this. This is my find—my house! If whoever's behind this thinks they're scaring me off, they don't know Theobald Henry James Carmichael." He swelled his chest out and stretched to his full height, but he was still several inches shorter than Gabe. "I have conquered the stock market, ruled over boardrooms, and made millions in my life. This just confirms what I've long suspected. Somewhere on these grounds there is Templar treasure."

"Or another clue to Templar treasure," Gabe pointed out, feeling that he needed to remind Theo of the reality of the situation.

"We will find it," Theo insisted, "or die trying!"

"Slow down, Theo!" Gabe was not happy that Theo seemed willing to risk his own life, and everyone else's. "While I admire the fact that you're not put off by this, let's not get too carried away. No one needs to die. Ash raised an interesting point earlier. William, the last English Master, would have been deeply religious, and came from a rich, religious family. It makes sense that when they built this keep, they would also have built a chapel on these grounds. Have you heard anything about one?"

A gleam filled Theo's eyes. "That's an excellent suggestion. I hadn't considered that, but as I said, I haven't got the original plans, and I haven't read everything. But..." He trailed off, deep in thought.

Gabe prompted him. "Any possibility of hidden rooms in the keep, or the remains of a building on the grounds?"

"Perhaps. There might be some reference in the records that I've missed."

"If it's there, Ash will find it."

A shout interrupted them, and a hard-eyed man wearing a suit reached their side, his eyes raking over Gabe. "DI Gibson. You're the gentleman involved in the incident?"

Gabe shook his hand. "Yes, Gabreel Malouf."

"I have a few questions for you."

Gabe forced a smile, expecting to be questioned for a long time, and suddenly glad that Shadow wasn't there to antagonise the situation. "Of course. Go right ahead."

Eleven

With every passing minute, Estelle became more nervous, wary for any noise that could indicate others were approaching.

She and Barak had secured the facility's staff in the cells along the corridor, separating as many as they could. They were all sleeping soundly, courtesy of a spell. They had found that one of the rooms they had thought was a cell was actually the entrance to another corridor, this one much broader than the others. A cursory inspection of it led to an underground garage with a van parked in it, and the wide corridor beyond suggested it ran away from the *château* and further into the grounds.

The prisoner who had tried to escape was resting on a narrow examination table in one of the medical rooms, and they'd cleared it of potential weapons. Not that the man appeared likely to attack them. He seemed exhausted, and the tranquilliser dart had taken care of the rest.

Leaving him sleeping, they had quickly examined the other rooms, working their way methodically along the corridor. Many appeared to be minor surgical rooms, but at the end corridor they also found what looked like a post-surgery recovery room, as well as an operating theatre with restraints attached to the table. However, as well as containing conventional surgical equipment, there was also an array of tattoo inks and jars containing ground metals.

Estelle picked one up, holding it under an overhead light, and then studied the mixture prepared on the side. "They're mixing the metals and ink together. I think they're tattooing with both!"

Barak was taking pictures with his phone across the room. "Stage one, perhaps, of making their skin a protective armour."

"Which would explain why some of the soldiers seem to have copper skin, and others bronze or silver. Weird. Ingenious, even." She slipped a couple of the bottles into her bag. "They must apply some kind of alchemy to the tattoos afterward."

"JD or the PD can figure that out." Barak took a few more photos. "That will have to do. There's no big lab down here, though. You know, how it sounds like JD has, and the PD."

Estelle nodded, remembering the two different labs at The Retreat: one modern, one old-fashioned, both full of alchemical paraphernalia. "This is a preparation area. Why isn't there a lab here? Seems odd."

"Perhaps this place is just to expedite local victims. They must be constantly recruiting and experimenting." A grimace of distaste flashed across Barak's face as he headed to the door. "Come on. Time to get out of here."

"There's one more room," Estelle said, cranky about what had happened in there earlier when she raced after the fleeing staff member. "But I'll destroy all of this first." Estelle stood in the doorway while Barak listened for any sign of approaching guards.

"We're good. Go on."

She cast a silence spell for good measure before she hurled ball after ball of powerful blasts of magic at the equipment. Glass jars full of ink and metals exploded, shattering their contents everywhere. She used a spell to warp the metal instruments, and earth magic to crack the ground open, swallowing part of the room. When she'd finished, the room was ruined, and with satisfaction she led Barak down the corridor, pausing at the entrance to the final room with its door blasted off its hinges. Unlike the other rooms, it wasn't a lab or a medical room. It was an office.

"This is where I chased that bloody man to. Unfortunately, he got in here before I could reach him." She paused, furious with herself. "I was only seconds behind him, but in that time, he'd smashed both computers. They're utterly ruined."

Barak squeezed her arm. "He was doing what he was trained to do. It's annoying, but we've caused a lot of trouble here today."

"But we could have got so much information from them!"

Barak examined a large cork board on the wall, bits of paper and notes all over it. He started snapping photos. "We still could yet. Look for lists, phone numbers, anything helpful."

Estelle had barely examined the room earlier. Having incapacitated the staff member, she dragged him to the corridor and left him in a binding spell on the floor before returning to Barak. Now she pulled out drawers, rifling through them for anything of interest. A list of names that made no sense was next to the phone, and she grabbed it, pushing it into her pack. Unfortunately, there were no paper patient files of any sort.

"Damn it, Barak. I fucked up. There would have been so much information on those computers."

"No, you didn't." He grabbed her hand, pulling her from the room. "Time to go. The clock's ticking."

They headed back along the corridor, destroying everything in their wake, until they arrived in the room with the prisoner. He was still unconscious on the narrow trolley bed.

"There's no way we can get him out of here," Estelle said, taking in his tall frame. "You can't carry him across the grounds like that. Too many people would spot us."

"I'm not leaving him here to become a Black Cronos soldier. Poor bastard. Besides, he could have valuable information. There must be somewhere we can hide until nightfall."

Estelle nodded, thinking through their options. "If we can get back to the store room at the olive oil place, we could hide there. I could potentially use magic, but a veiling spell is not effective in the day. If we wait until nightfall, we can get to the car park and our car."

"Which will be the only one on the car park by then, and may well have attracted attention. And if they have shift changes, they'll discover what has happened well before then. Plus, the medical staff must be due to go home soon." Barak shook his head, perplexed. "We need to use that far corridor, take the van, and hope the underground road leads somewhere private. If that's the way they bring prisoners in, it will be quiet."

"But could well have security at the other end."

"That's our only option, Estelle." He walked to her side, taking her hands and kissing them. "We can do this. We have to. I promise you, we will not become Black Cronos's next subjects."

The thought of it chilled her blood, and her magic welled up again. "No. We will not!" She wondered where they would end up, and if they would even escape. Potentially, the corridor could lead to the centre of a Black Cronos spider's web. "All right. Let's do it."

<hr />

Shadow studied the small, modern terraced house from the passenger seat of Gabe's SUV. There was no movement from it, or from any neighbouring homes. The whole road seemed to be basking in the early evening heat.

"Damn it. I wish I could go through the gardens."

Ash huffed in amusement. "I can smell barbeques. Back gardens will be full right now. You'll have to do this the old-fashioned way and knock on the front door."

"I knew bringing you was a mistake."

"I brought *you*," Ash reminded her. "And I'll probably stop you from being arrested. Come on. Now that I'm here, I'm going in, too."

He exited the car, and Shadow followed him, resolving that she *would* learn to drive soon. Then she wouldn't have to be escorted everywhere by annoying Nephilim. "I need someone to teach me."

Ash looked at her, confused for a moment. "Ah! To learn to drive." He grinned. "I will. But only if you'll listen."

"I always listen."

"Let me qualify that. Only if you listen, and then do as I say."

"I can do that!"

"You can, but rarely do. And seeing as I am probably the most patient of us all, I would make the better teacher. Niel would kill you."

She snorted. "He could try."

"And would." He continued, undaunted. "So would Eli. Zee would refuse outright. Barak would laugh at the suggestion. Nahum, however, would be a good second choice. You would bicker with Gabe constantly."

"You make it sound as if I will be hard to teach."

Ash turned his golden eyes on her, full of laughter. "You will be an absolute nightmare. But I am willing to rise to the occasion."

She stopped on the pavement, rounding on him. "I'm not stupid."

"I know. You're clever and resourceful, and will no doubt pick it up in no time. But you don't like rules or boring things, and driving requires concentration, and sometimes that's very boring."

"I have watched buildings for endless hours on stakeouts. And I spend hours sparring and refining my fighting skills."

"And those have a monetary reward. This gets you from A to B."

Shadow itched to wipe the smirk off Ash's face, but knew he was right. "Fine. When we get home."

"Challenge accepted, sister." He gave her a rakish grin before turning back to the house. As they approached the front door, his voice dropped.

"Do you think you can ask Owen questions without terrifying him? If he's there, of course."

"How dare you."

"I dare and double-dare."

She glared at Ash, and then rapped on the door, emitting a waft of fey glamour for good measure.

For a moment, they heard nothing, and Shadow was already deciding how best to break in without alerting suspicion, when footsteps sounded and the door opened a short way, revealing a rangy figure who looked to be in his thirties on the other side. His face was impassive, but his eyes were wary. "Yes?"

"Owen?" Shadow asked, surprised he was actually there. "My name is Shadow, and this is Ash. We're friends of Theo's, and need to chat."

"Theo Carmichael? My employer?"

Shadow immediately decided he was an idiot, but kept smiling. "Yes. He said he'd discussed a few things with you. That you'd helped him with internet searches. We have a few more questions."

He immediately tried to shut the door, and Shadow stepped forward, wedging it open. "That's not very nice, Owen. Let's talk inside."

She forced her way in, blade already in her hand, and Owen backed up the hall, arms raised.

"I have nothing here at all. Nothing worth stealing."

She glanced around dismissively, noting the poor-quality furnishing. "No, I can see that. But all I want to do is talk."

"Then why the knife?"

"Because I don't like having the door shut in my face."

"I don't like having a knife in my face, either." Owen looked behind her as Ash followed her in, his eyes widening at his size. "Is he your enforcer?"

"Don't be ridiculous. I don't need one." She put her knife away, strengthened her glamour, and with satisfaction, saw his eyes glaze. "Please, Owen, we'd just like to talk. This is important. Your life could be at risk."

His jaw tightened, but he didn't look surprised. "Because of Theo's Templar research?"

"Exactly." And she wanted to know why he'd left work, but that could wait.

He didn't answer, instead leading them through the living room and out into the garden. For a moment, Shadow stopped, attention caught by the rampant growth of plants that filled the narrow plot. The fences down either side were covered in climbing plants, but she could only see a short way, as Owen had compartmentalised his garden into rooms. Trellises broke the space up, but beyond the first one, festooned in greenery, a bustle of growth could be seen further in.

Shadow turned to him, her opinion of him softening, as it always did when faced with someone with true gardening skills. "Your garden is amazing."

He offered her a shy smile. "Thank you. I spend all of my spare time here." He gestured to a round table with a few chairs under a pergola. "Take a seat. This is about the fire, isn't it? Not just the dagger." Owen's open expression became haunted, and he stared at the table, fingers rubbing the grain.

Shadow couldn't tell if he was scared or guilty. "This conversation is about many things. You assisted Theo with his research. How much did you help him uncover?"

"Very little. All I did was teach Theo how to search the internet for Templar history. For all of his knowledge, he's not that skilled with a computer. To be honest, they were fairly basic searches. I just helped a little."

"But he told you about the knife?"

"Of course. I admit, that was news to me, but not the Templar link. Everyone knows the keep's history, and the links to William de la More." He smiled. "It's fun to think that somewhere in the area could be Templar treasure. The knife with the symbols, that's new—to me, at least."

"Who did you tell?"

"No one!" His eyes widened with surprise. "Well, no one outside of the estate."

"Did you sell your information to anyone? Employ someone to help you?"

"Look at my house! It's small. I can't afford that. I spend all of my money on plants. And I would never betray Theo. He's a good man."

Shadow exchanged a questioning glance with Ash. This was not what she'd expected from Owen. "So, who did you talk to on the estate?"

"Everyone! The gardening staff, the house staff...when I see them. We're a close-knit group. It's just chat. And Theo didn't tell me not to. And besides," he laughed, "Chivers is a gossip. He'd seen the knife before I had."

Ash interrupted him. "So, why did you leave work today? We know you know the lodge burned down. Did you have anything to do with that?"

"No! I'm not a bloody arsonist. Besides, the fire could have damaged the woods. I would never risk them."

"Then why leave?" Shadow asked. "Everyone else was standing around, watching the action."

"To be honest, something struck me about the knife and the lodge, and I wanted to come back and check it out."

"It couldn't wait until tonight?" Ash asked, incredulous.

"I thought I could sneak off and no one would know." He shrugged, apologetic. "I'll make up the work time."

Shadow was growing impatient. "What struck you that was so important?"

"The knife's bone hilt had Templar symbols on it, and what hit me when I saw the lodge in flames was that it was filled with similar symbols."

"You went in it?" Ash asked.

"I looked through the windows, between a gap in the boards. We worked in the woods, and I was curious. We all were—the gardening staff, that is."

Shadow nodded. "Yes, you're right. There were symbols everywhere." She decided not to mention the one that was wired with a bomb. "Theo mentioned the Masons, too. He said they were linked to the Templars."

"After its downfall, other organisations rose in its wake. It's believed by some people that the few remaining survivors of the Templars were behind the rise of the Masons. They were originally a group of guildsmen. Stonemasons, actually. But over the years, this group changed. It's complicated."

Ash groaned. "It always is. And what's your conclusion?"

"I think the hunting lodge was once a Masonic lodge, but I have no idea how it connects with the knife with the bone handle. They might not be connected at all. It is suspicious that it burned down now, though." He suddenly seemed to take in Shadow's appearance. "Were you there at the time?"

"Yes, and I can assure you that fire was not accidental." Shadow changed tack. "Was there anyone in the household that you spoke to who seemed more interested than others in the news of the knife?"

"I don't think so." Owen shrugged. "Sorry."

"What about the symbols?" Ash asked. "Any that particularly strike you? Or any you might have seen around the house?"

"I hardly go in the house, so no. But I can show you a few of the symbols I recognised. On my laptop. It's on the sofa."

Ash nodded. "Yes, please."

Owen stood up, and Shadow followed him. As much as she thought she'd been wrong about him, she still didn't entirely trust him. Until they were out of the house, she wasn't going to take her eyes off him.

But this might be a lead, and one they couldn't pass up.

Twelve

B arak accelerated the stolen van along the concrete-lined underground tunnel, lit by the occasional overhead light, wondering
where they would end up.

Estelle was next to him, keeping an eye on the unconscious man on
the back seat, while trying to get a phone signal. "Nothing yet. We're
too far underground."

Barak spotted a camera on the wall and groaned. "Shit. Take that
out, Estelle. We're screwed. I bet that's being monitored in the *château*.
Or even somewhere ahead of us," he added.

Estelle blasted the camera as they passed it. "If—*once*—we get out,
where to next?"

"We hide anywhere we can until we get hold of Jackson. An abandoned building, a *gîte*, stables, anything!"

He estimated they had travelled along the underground road at least
a couple of kilometres, and with relief saw that the corridor was rising
to the surface on a gradual incline, but Barak didn't slow down. That
camera feed had to have alerted someone.

As he reached the top of the rise, the electric lights cut out, plunging them into darkness, and he quickly flipped the full beam of the headlights on.

"Get ready," he said to Estelle. "And keep your head down."

Estelle cast a spell, and a blue light expanded around the whole vehicle. "Extra protection," she told him, wriggling down in her seat.

The corridor levelled off, and in the brief sweep of the headlights, Barak saw a high-roofed space that looked like an underground garage or warehouse. And then a brilliant bank of white lights lit up the space in front of them, temporarily blinding him as the boom of weapons shattered the silence.

Estelle's protection spell flared, but it held, and Barak accelerated towards the lights. It was impossible to see how many people there were, or what was beyond the lights, but he wasn't stopping now.

Estelle, however, was casting spells, and one after another, all of the lights ahead exploded, plunging them into darkness, except for the narrow swathe of light cast by their headlights.

They illuminated a huge man pointing a fire-tipped weapon, and Barak drove at him. But he wasn't fast enough to stop him from shooting at them, and something exploded under the van, catapulting them into the air.

Flames erupted around them.

"What the actual fuck is going on?" Barak roared, furious. He wrestled the steering wheel pointlessly as the van started to twist towards the ground.

Time seemed to slow as torch lights flared across the room below. Barak estimated there were half a dozen people scrambling for cover, but some were definitely aiming weapons at them.

The huge man immediately below them was angling his weapon towards them, but the van crashed to the ground, half-crushing him. Metal and glass splintered around them, and only their seatbelts prevented them from being propelled through the shattered windscreen.

Barak needed to fly. He glanced at Estelle, relieved to see that although she was twisted and bloodied in her seat, she was still conscious. He yelled to be heard across the shouts, "Kill the lights!"

In seconds, he wrenched the seat belt off him, kicked the door open, extended his wings, and soared into the air, just as the sizzle of magic exploded outwards.

Barak had no idea how she'd done it, and right now he didn't care, but the torchlights vanished. He needed to stop their attackers before any more arrived. It was now pitch-black, but Barak's excellent night vision meant that he could see everything perfectly.

They were in the middle of a huge space that had another couple of vehicles in it, an office along one side, a regular doorway, as well as a huge roller door for the vehicles. All of the exits were shut tight. Half a dozen men and women were struggling to their feet and firing furiously. Shots echoed across the space, splintering the remaining windows of the van, and thudding into metal. A couple of people were motionless on the ground, but the man the van had almost crushed was still moving.

Barak swept down on them, a silent assassin in the dark, killing the closest two with his blade. Random bullets strafed through his wings, shattering fine bones and grazing his skin, but he whirled in the air, and threw his dagger across the room with unerring accuracy. It struck the third soldier in the throat and he dropped to the ground, blood splattering.

Pain rocked through Barak's body as another bullet struck his shoulder, but he couldn't stop now. He attacked the next one from behind, breaking his neck swiftly with strong hands, the *crunch* of bones loud as the shouts vanished.

In seconds, their assailants were dead. Except for one.

The van rocked on to its side, trapping Estelle inside as the man finally shouldered it aside. He was badly injured, one arm crushed and limp, but fire blazed in his eyes as he staggered to his feet. Barak ran over before he found his balance, punched him, then grabbed one leg with his own uninjured arm, lifting them both into the air as he did so. The man wriggled like an eel as he twisted to reach Barak, but Barak swung him around and smacked him against the closest wall. The sound of cracking bone was sickening. Barak dropped him to the ground, and killed him with a swift twist of his neck.

Back to the wall, he waited, chest heaving as he scanned the room for any sign of movement. When nothing stirred, he headed to the office, peering through the reinforced glass, but there were no other guards.

Grateful for the reprieve, but knowing reinforcements could arrive at any moment, he ran to the van, shouting, "All clear!"

Estelle was already scrambling up and out of the driver's buckled door, throwing a witch-light above them. Blood poured down her arm from a cut. "The prisoner is in a bad way, Barak. He's covered in bruises after all that, and there's a big wound on his head. I've stemmed the blood flow as best as I can, but he needs medical attention."

He focussed only on her, offering her his hand as she struggled to the ground. "But are you all right?"

She gave him a rueful smile. "Battered, but I'll survive." She spotted the blood pouring from his shoulder. Her eyes widened with horror. "Barak! You've been shot!"

He winced. "Yeah, it's painful, but I'll heal." To be honest, it burned like his arm was on fire, and his wings felt awkward and sore from the damage they'd sustained. He tried to ignore it and eyed their destroyed van. "We need new transport. And we need to get this back on its wheels to get the prisoner out. Over there." He nodded to the other two vehicles. One was marked with the *château's* logo, the other was a plain black transit van. "We'll use the black one. Can you find the keys while I get the van upright?"

While she searched, Barak folded his wings away, grasped the side of the van and wrenched it down, feeling every single muscle strain as he did so. Sweat broke across his face, but he took deep breaths in an effort to quell his nausea. He quickly made himself a rudimentary bandage from the remains of his t-shirt, wrapping it firmly around his shoulder.

Estelle exited the office, two sets of keys in her hand. She wiggled them, metal clinking. "Just in case."

"Great. Help me move the prisoner. I can't manage him alone."

Between them, and with Estelle using magic, they lifted the injured man from the back seat. He was still out cold, and Barak wasn't sure if it was a result of the tranquilliser or the head injury. His face was smeared with blood, both from the cut and a broken nose. The rear of their next van was kitted out with benches and they positioned him carefully, securing him with tie downs, before facing the shuttered doors that promised them a way out. *But what was beyond them? Another compound? Or a road to freedom?* A round green button marked the mechanism to open it.

"Start her up," he instructed Estelle, "and get in front of the door. Any sign of more soldiers, floor it. I'll catch up."

While she maneuvered the van into position, Barak retrieved his knife and collected a couple of weapons from the dead guards. The first was one of the metal palm-held devices, typical of Black Cronos, the other was a shotgun. Pocketing the small device, he loaded the shotgun, and then pressed the green button.

With an agonising slowness, the metal door rolled upwards and evening sunshine pierced the gloom. Barak dropped to the ground to the side of the doorframe and studied the scene beyond. All he could see was a paved area surrounded by forest. He rolled through, leapt to his feet, and raised his weapon, scanning his immediate surroundings.

All around him was a dense wall of trees with a narrow road leading away from the compound. Behind him was a series of hills that the warehouse was set into. There was no evidence of a building within it at all, other than the doors. It was breathtakingly quiet. Only the evening chorus of birds disturbed the silence. That and the van's engine, as Estelle pulled up next to him.

She leaned through the open window. "All clear then, although we must still be on the *château's* grounds."

"A back road, I hope." He closed the roller door again, sealing the facility shut, before clambering into the passenger seat. "Eyes peeled now. I'll call Jackson, and then try and find us a place to shelter."

Jackson was returning to The Retreat with Harlan when he received the call from Barak. He listened with a mixture of dread and excitement, and nodded his agreement as Barak ended the call.

"They're safe—but only just. I was right. The *château* is a front for Black Cronos."

"Shit!" Harlan glanced over at him, hands gripping the wheel. He was still fuming from his encounter with Nicoli. "What happened? How do they even know that?"

"Because they've rescued a prisoner and had to fight their way out. I need to get them out of there." Jackson was racing through contingency plans. There was a team they could call on in France, but they were nowhere near Barak and Estelle. "This was supposed to be reconnaissance. It could take hours to get someone out to them. I need to call Waylen. He could arrange something quicker than I can." His fingers fumbled for the number. "What the fuck have I done, Harlan? I'm not prepared. I could get them killed! I shouldn't even have accepted this job."

"Slow down! Barak and Estelle are resourceful. That's why they found the guy in the first place. Although, frankly, I need more details, because I'm as curious as hell! Where are they now?"

"Escaping out of the *château* grounds in a stolen Black Cronos van. Heading west, well away from the main building." Waylen's phone line started to ring, and while Jackson waited for him to answer, he twisted to look at Harlan. "They had an underground lair with an operating theatre. Estelle destroyed it."

"Wow. Go Estelle! And a lair? Like it. Very Bond!"

"Very annoying—and so not cool! These guys are like bloody termites."

"At least there were no booby-trapped passages, like in Scotland."

Jackson nodded, remembering the stench of dogs and blood, and the warren beneath Arklet Abbey. "That was a nightmare." Waylen's voice mail kicked in and Jackson slammed his hand onto the dashboard with frustration as he left a basic message to return the call.

Harlan glared at him. "Watch my car!"

"Sorry. I'm flustered." Jackson huffed, and then frowned as he looked at their surroundings. "This isn't the way to The Retreat."

"No. We're heading to my flat instead. We're going to consult a map and I'll see if I can help. The Orphic Guild has contacts in France—with a base in Paris."

"Don't you have issues of your own to deal with?"

"Oh, I'll deal with them, don't you worry! In the meantime, I have favours I can call in."

Fifteen minutes later, Jackson and Harlan sat around Harlan's computer, a map of the *château* and the surrounding area on the screen. "It must be one of these roads they're on," Jackson said, his fingers hovering over several lanes on the map. "Barak said they travelled about a couple of kilometres underground—he checked the odometer just after they escaped. But he wasn't sure where the underground medical facility was. He thinks to the west of the *château*."

Harlan leaned in, enlarging the screen. "And you say they entered via the olive oil store?" He flicked to the *château*'s website, quickly scrolling through the photos until he found a rustic stone building. "That place." He flicked back to the map and pointed at the *château*'s grounds again. "Which must be this building, here."

Jackson spotted the line of low hills on the map. "That should be where they exited. Right on the edge of the grounds, in that area of woodland. Velleron is the closest town."

Harlan reached for his phone. "I'll call the Paris branch, see if they can help."

"I'll call Waylen again. And then I'll call Barak, and see if they've found anywhere to hide."

Thirteen

"At least we know who we're up against," Gabe said to Ash, Shadow, and Theo, who were now gathered in Theo's sitting room.

Gabe had finally enjoyed a shower and changed his clothes after a long interview with the police, and then a conversation with Harlan. Shadow was still in her fire-blackened clothing.

"But we don't know who the thief is," Shadow complained. She stood at the window, looking across the grounds that were quickly disappearing in the thickening twilight. "If Nicoli is in London, then he has someone down here."

"Maybe more than one person," Ash reasoned. "And they are familiar with bombs, too."

Theo leaned back in the chair, eyes vacantly staring at the book in front of him. "I can't believe it. This is a nightmare. How has the news leaked?"

Gabe couldn't hide his frustration. "It wasn't a secret, Theo! Your staff knew about it, and people talk. Chivers talked! It could have been a completely innocuous comment. Nicoli is very good at sniffing out opportunities."

Ash had his laptop open and he pointed at the screen. "These are common Masonic images. Do any of you recognise these?"

Gabe stood behind Ash and leaned over his shoulder. "I recognise the eye, and the compass, and the G-sign. The designs were in the finials on the wooden staircase, and in some of the plasterwork."

Shadow stood next to him. "I can't see the one I moved, though. The one with the bomb behind it."

Ash looked up at her. "Can you remember what it looks like? I've barely started the search."

"It looked like a bunch of flowers or something."

"This perhaps?" Ash scrolled to another image. "The Masonic Sheaf of Corn. It represents money earned or something like that."

"Yes! That's it!"

"But what does it mean?" Theo asked, annoyed. "Why put a bomb behind it?"

"I suspect it opened a secret compartment," Shadow said. "I've come across many things like that. Or it could have opened a door to a secret room, or a small place to hide an object, papers, or a map, even."

"Another clue that could be gone!" Theo's face was turning purple with annoyance.

Ash shrugged. "Perhaps. Or it could have been a ruse, and the bomb was just to scare you or anyone else off the trail. But you and Owen are right. It does appear that it was a Masonic lodge. The symbols all suggest it. Of course, it may have nothing to do with Templar treasure."

Shadow snorted. "I don't believe that for a moment."

"However, what I need to do," Ash continued, nodding at the dagger on the table next to him, "is examine that hilt. The symbols have to mean something useful, or else why hide it?"

Gabe lifted it, feeling its weight. "It's surprisingly heavy."

Shadow nodded. "I thought that, too. It's not balanced either, but I wondered if that's because it was ceremonial. The hilt is heavy."

"And ornate," Gabe noted. Silver and gold metals were inlaid into the bone, and the emeralds glinted along the base. However, the lodge continued to distract him. "Who built the lodge, Theo? You said it was constructed years after the keep was built. Was it a descendent of William, or someone else?"

"I can't remember, but the plans are in that collection." He gestured to the sofa where he'd placed the plans after removing them from the safe.

Gabe had perused them earlier that day, but could recollect no details, and had barely looked at the plans for the lodge. Placing the knife down, he unrolled the blueprints on the table, sifting through them until he found the one he wanted. It was a photocopy of the original document, and the spidery writing was hard to make out, as was the floor plan. "This is weird." He pointed to the tangle of schematics. Stairs were marked, as were rooms, doorways, and the huge fireplace and central hall was immediately obvious. "What is that section, there? It looks like a third level." He turned to Theo. "Was there attic space?"

"Yes, I went up there years ago. But it was a shallow pitch roof and nothing was up there. No rooms, certainly."

"I don't think that's attic space, Gabe," Ash said, frowning over the drawings. "I think it's a cellar."

"A cellar?" Theo frowned. "I'm pretty sure there wasn't one of those."

"Perhaps that's what the relief triggered," Shadow suggested, her excitement obvious. "A doorway. And if it's a cellar..."

"It could still be there!" Gabe said, already walking to the door. "The bomb may not have destroyed it. We need to check."

Theo rose to his feet. "Surely the fire brigade or the police will have found it?"

"Not necessarily. The remains of the building were smouldering, and still hot. Debris was all over the place. And it was unsafe. They've barely touched it," Gabe reminded him. "They're going back tomorrow to examine it in the light, when it's cooler."

Ash grabbed his backpack, stuffing the books, notes, and the plans inside it. "These are coming with us—just in case."

Gabe turned to Shadow, knowing that what he was about to ask her would not be received well. "Shadow, I want you to stay here with Theo."

She glared at him. "Like a guard dog?"

"Exactly. If someone is watching this place, they could wait until we've left and come in. Theo could be at risk—as could the whole household. That might have been the sole point of the bomb. To distract everyone and get in here."

Ash nodded. "That's true. There are a lot of people on the grounds now. They could blend in."

"I can't guard an entire castle!"

"You could from the roof!" Theo said, eager to help. "You have a 360-degree view from the tower—through the battlements."

Shadow's expression brightened as she eyed her bow and quiver full of arrows propped against the wall. "Now you're talking, Theo."

"And," Gabe added, "either Nahum or Niel are on the way right now. I trust that you can watch this place on your own in the meantime."

"Well, *now* I can." Her violet eyes gleamed. "Lead the way, Theo. And bring me some food when I'm settled. I'm starving."

Exhausted, Estelle completed the protection spell around the dilapidated barn they had found sanctuary in, and stood for a moment, looking down the only lane that led to their location.

It was virtually dusk now, and she could see lights from a small village twinkling in the distance, and the occasional flash of headlights as cars swept along the lanes. But the approach to the barn remained devoid of traffic, and she took a deep breath of relief.

They had found this place only fifteen minutes earlier, after Barak had directed her through convoluted back lanes, eager to lose any would-be pursuers and find an unassuming shelter. They had travelled steadily west, passing towns and villages, debating their best course of action. Had it been just Barak and Estelle, they could have found a room somewhere, but that was impossible with the prisoner. It would look far too suspicious.

Fortunately, Barak had spotted the building in the slanting rays of the setting sun, set low on a hillside surrounded by olive trees, and on a whim, they headed to it. The lane ended at a rutted track, allowing Estelle to ease their van right into the barn itself. It had huge wooden doors, but one had collapsed on the ground, and portions of the roof had also disintegrated. However, the other half offered shelter from any potential helicopters that could be looking for them. Neither of them could forget the helicopter that had whisked Professor Stefan Hope-Robbins away in Turkey.

Estelle headed inside the building, and found Barak in the back of the van, tending to the prisoner.

"Is he still unconscious?"

Barak nodded as he straightened up and joined her in the barn. "Yes, but his breathing appears easier, and it seems more like a natural sleep now. I hate to think what he's gone through."

Estelle studied the prone figure. He was still in the surgical gown, but they had stolen a selection of scrubs for him to change into. It wasn't ideal, but it was better than nothing. "I know we think some soldiers were willingly recruited, but I don't think he was. How do you even start to control someone who doesn't want to be part of Black Cronos?"

"Maybe some sort of mind control? An implant? Alchemy, or magic?" He shrugged and then winced, hand flying to his shoulder. "I don't like to think of what they might do."

"Me neither. But I know what I do want. Food. Then I'll try a healing spell on him—and you. You need a scrub top to wear, too. You can't walk around looking like that—as much as I like admiring your pecs." She reached across the driver's seat and grabbed the bag of food and drinks that she had bought on a very quick stop to put petrol in the van. Barak, with his bare chest, injured shoulder, and makeshift, blood-stained dressing, had stayed in the van. "I can't think straight I'm so hungry."

Barak grabbed the picnic blankets she'd bought at the same time. "Let's sit at the barn doors, just beneath the roof, and keep watch."

They positioned themselves carefully, and for good measure, Estelle shrouded them in the veiling spell, too. She bit into a baguette with relish. "This is good."

"A bit stale now, but better than nothing." For a few minutes they ate in companiable silence before Barak said, "Thanks for your help back there. You were incredible."

"Incredible? I like that. To be fair, so were you."

"You're always incredible, Estelle. Never forget that." His voice was soft, his brown eyes full of promise.

Estelle smiled, feeling herself blushing. So close to him, she was well aware of his heat, and his size, and she had an urge to keep touching him. She clutched her food instead. "You're too good to me."

"No, I'm not. I'm as good as anyone should be." He took another bite of food, watching her thoughtfully. She felt scrutinised by his studied gaze, and glanced away. But then he spoke again. "What happened that made you so guarded? So closed off to the world?"

Her head snapped around to him. "I'm not closed off!"

His voice, like his gaze, remained gentle. "Not to me. Not anymore. Or not all of the time, at least. Don't close off to me now."

Estelle felt tears well up and she looked at the rug, angry at herself. "I'm not closing myself to you. Not intentionally, anyway. It's like flexing a muscle. I do it instinctively." She forced herself to say what she'd been thinking for weeks. "I'm comfortable with you, Barak. More than I have been with anyone for a very long time. You make me feel safe. And I don't mean just physically."

"I know what you mean." He reached across and brushed her hair back from her shoulders, caressing her cheek as he did so. She leaned into his hand, savouring his warmth. "I won't abuse you, misuse you, or harm you in any way. What happened? Because I swear, if someone did something to you, I will find him and kill him. Or her, for that matter."

She caught his hand in hers and kissed it. "He's already dead. And besides, it wasn't just him. It was a series of events that taught me not to trust."

"Who's *he*? Your father?"

At the very mention of his name, her skin crawled. "Yes, him. He was never a father figure, though. Not a kind one, anyway. He may have been modern in the sense that he encouraged education and allowed me a place in the family business—well, *insisted* I have a place in the family business, actually. But he was always, always, criticising me. Not just me, either, to be fair. Caspian received it just as much. He was sharp with his own brother—my uncle—and my cousins, too. He was a miserable bastard. I hated him."

Barak nodded, eyes watchful as he considered his words. "And the events?"

"After a childhood of constantly feeling like I was never good enough, it made me sensitive. I withdrew. From everything. School, university, even work. I was constantly protecting myself, so much so that I was accused of being frigid by boyfriends. And they were probably right." She could feel herself trembling, and she looked away, unable to meet Barak's eyes. "I've missed out on so much, because I wouldn't let myself do anything in the end. What a waste of a life."

"I'm sorry you had to put up with all of that, but your behaviour makes sense. Why put yourself out there to be constantly found wanting? I get that. But he's dead now. You are a powerful witch and a clever woman, and very beautiful, too. And, you have *not* wasted your life. You've achieved so much!"

"Money, yes. Job, sure. And I admit, I'm proud of my magical abilities. It's the one thing that sustains me when everything else feels like a prison. But there's more to life than all of that. Caspian is now realising that, too."

A flash of guilt ripped through her as she thought of how her father had driven a wedge between her and Caspian. "I'm horrible to Caspian, and have said terrible things to him."

"He's already forgiven you. I can tell."

"He's still wary around me. Like most people."

"They'll change when they see *you* change. I don't understand why you hate the White Haven witches so much. They killed your father, but they did you a favour."

"I know." Her usual anger at even the mention of them didn't appear. Instead, she sighed. "They weren't intimidated by him, and I resented that—and their unwavering self-belief. And they're always so bloody happy!" She caught Barak's grin and started to laugh, too. "I know, I know! That's terrible, isn't it? I'm a monster!"

"You resented what you didn't have. It made you bitter. But that's all changing, right? You're living fully now! Maybe a little too fully!" He gestured around them. "We're sheltering in an abandoned barn, fleeing Black Cronos, with a prisoner in a van. And we're stuck."

"The thing is, though, I'm actually loving all of this! How weird is that? I'm terrified half the time, but also have never felt so alive. And I'm using my magic to its full capacity. Challenging myself constantly. It's addictive." She took a deep breath, savouring the warm evening air, the wide-open sky, and Barak, and voiced what she really felt. "I feel free."

"I'll share a secret." Barak leaned closer. "I love it, too. Most of the time, at least. I was born for it. It's in my blood."

Estelle kissed Barak, allowing herself to do so without fear of rejection or criticism, knowing that this man could be her answer to everything. This *Nephilim*. A magnificent creature of muscle and feather, of mystery and strength, and unbelievable gentleness.

For the first time in a very long time, Estelle allowed herself hope.

Fourteen

Ash stood next to Gabe at the edge of the ruined lodge, the air still thick with the stench of burnt wood, although the smoke had long vanished.

Although it was dark, the Nephilim's excellent night vision allowed him to see that portions of some walls, interior and exterior, still stood, but the roof had collapsed, leaving only the occasional beam jutting into the air. A portion of the stairs and upper floor remained, as did part of the stone fireplace, but the explosion had effectively destroyed everything else.

"Most of the floor is gone," Ash noted, peering between the joists to the earth beneath. "There's certainly no cellar in this part of the lodge."

"It's huge, though. There could be something at the back."

Ash sighed. "Look at that place! As mad as Theo's idea of this lost treasure seems, he has to be right, or this wouldn't have happened. We can't forget the theft in the library, either. I had hoped we were one step ahead, but now I feel we are way behind on this chase."

"We have the dagger. That's something."

"True." Ash felt annoyed with himself. "I've been caught up in background information when I should be analysing it. But if I'm honest, it's hard to know where to start, and getting some context on this whole situation is important. How do I know the importance of a symbol, otherwise?"

"Don't beat yourself up over it. We only arrived this morning. I know I said earlier that Nicoli only needed a bit of information to get involved, but now I think he must have been ahead of Theo, even. This bomb, the theft...that's a lot of planning."

"But he has a formidable organisation, plus money and resources. With all that behind him, it's easy to get ahead quickly. Theo was thinking that we had time, and so did Harlan. We were wrong." Ash studied his old friend's face as he turned towards him, a frown between his brows. "Right now, we just need to act, and figure it out as we go along. We've played catch-up before."

"True, but I feel there were valuable clues in there that we have now lost. But you're right, nothing we can do about that now except find the cellar."

"And the chapel, if it exists. Once we're done here, I'd like to study the grounds again—from the air. It's risky, but needs must."

Gabe pulled his t-shirt off, expanding his wings. "Agreed. It will be easier to fly at night. Hopefully, no one will see us."

Ash nodded his agreement, thankful that the police had restricted themselves to blocking the driveway, and stripped his t-shirt off and extended his wings, too. He flexed them, glad to feel the cool night air ruffling his feathers. He strapped the pack to his chest, not wanting to leave it unattended, and then soared into the air.

From above, it was easy to see the huge footprint of the lodge, but while Gabe studied the building, Ash took in their surroundings. The immediate woods stretched out around the lodge, and beyond it were the lawns and gardens, the moat glinting with lights from the keep above it. The tower where Shadow was positioned, blocked a portion of the night sky, but he couldn't see her. That wasn't surprising. No doubt she had hidden herself well. The lanes around the estate were quiet, and no one was approaching it. Not in a vehicle, at least. Ash focussed on their immediate area, searching for anyone that could be on foot, but other than the gentle stir of leaves in the breeze, nothing moved.

Gabe called to him from where he hovered above a small square of ground that looked darker than its surroundings, set close to an internal wall but partly covered by blackened beams. "I've found it. I can see steps going down, but we'll have to move the beams to get access."

Together they lifted a couple of beams aside, and folding their wings away, edged carefully down the stone stairs. The wall to one side fell away, revealing a small anteroom, beyond which was a larger room, stone-slabbed, with a vaulted stone ceiling and a series of archways overhead. The room had been protected from the fire by its position and stone structure, and Ash used his torch so he could see the details of it clearly. The beam illuminated an altar at the far side.

"Gabe! Look. From what I've read, the Masons would have had an altar. This must have been a hidden inner sanctum."

"And the same symbols that we saw above are down here." Gabe played his own torch along the walls and ceiling, picking out the reliefs. "Look. They're everywhere."

Ash couldn't help but be disappointed. "But there's nothing else here. It's been completed cleared out."

"But maybe there are hidden rooms or compartments...if we want to risk searching it. This place could be wired to a bomb, too." Gabe's lips were set in a thin line. "I think we have to look, though. We might not get another chance."

Ash nodded, and wordlessly, they started the search.

———⊰✦⊱———

Harlan paced his study, phone in one hand and bourbon in the other, nodding as he listened to Pierre at the other end. Satisfied, he said goodbye and ended the call.

"Well?" Jackson asked. He was sitting in front of the computer, cradling a glass of whiskey.

"There's an apartment above a small supermarket that we've used before, in Méthamis, and Barak and Estelle can use it. Pierre says the keys are in a lock box on the property. I have the code. You can send your extraction team there. It's up to Barak and Estelle as to whether they stay at the barn overnight, or head there now."

"From the last conversation I had with them, they're staying at the barn. It's isolated, and they feel safe there. Plus, they're exhausted." Jackson sipped his drink and smacked his lips. "I needed that. I still can't believe it. That they actually broke in to the *château*! It's incredible."

"They're resourceful. That's what's so good about them," Harlan said, easing into his seat again, and realising he was also exhausted. "But you have decisions to make now. What are you going to do about the *château* and the owners, now you've confirmed their involvement? And what are you going to do with your prisoner? Not that he's really *your* prisoner."

"Great questions! As far as the *château* goes, I'm torn. We could take this higher, get a team together to raid the place, but that will take time. I honestly wasn't anticipating this, and after Barak and Estelle swept through there, I imagine that they will be clearing everything out and destroying any evidence of what they were doing. Unfortunately, they'll likely be destroying *anything* that could link them to Black Cronos. It doesn't change what we know, though. Tomorrow I'll start an in-depth investigation into the family—their associates, money, assets...everything."

"You're right," Harlan conceded. "But you've identified a link in the chain, and it could inadvertently lead you to another."

"Let's hope so. In the meantime," Jackson sighed, a hand rubbing his eyes, "how do we keep the prisoner safe? Black Cronos will want him back, surely. He'll have secrets to share that we badly need."

Harlan shook his head. "I doubt he will. Not unless he's been privy to certain conversations. I think you'll find he can tell you nothing."

"But anything could help! Where he was abducted from, or if he was moved between facilities."

Harlan noted the grim determination on Jackson's face. "Please don't tell me you're thinking of going over there." They'd argued about that earlier, and worried about the team, Jackson had been prepared to fly in there single-handedly. Now, however, he just looked resigned.

"No. I'll meet them at the airport here instead. Waylen has arranged for a medic to be part of the extraction team, and they'll transport them to a private plane."

"At Avignon?"

"No, a private airport to the north of the city. They're on the way now."

"Good. Black Cronos might search the main airport. Hell, they might watch all of them." He considered his next words carefully. "You know, we might have rattled them too much. They might well come after us—harder, this time."

"I've considered that, but I don't think they will. With luck, they won't know who has infiltrated them—not for sure, anyway. For all we know, they've made lots of different enemies. As a consequence, I doubt they'll start an all-out war with us. It will bring them too much attention, and covert is their entire way of operating."

"What about picking us off, one by one?"

Jackson stared balefully at him. "It's possible."

"That settles it. I'm moving into the Mandarin Oriental again."

"Why are you so worried? You had nothing to do with this!"

"Because I'm associated with you and the Nephilim. You should move into The Retreat—just in case." Harlan had a better idea. "Actually, I know what I'm going to do. I'm going to Kent to stay with Theo. I think I should help with the search for Templar treasure." Harlan felt the stir of familiar excitement that appeared with all the most intriguing jobs, and this one, despite his earlier scoffing, was shaping up to be a beauty.

Jackson snorted. "So you're putting yourself in the path of a bomber and Nicoli? Yes, much safer!"

"Safer than Black Cronos!" Nicoli's smug face flashed into his brain. "Besides, that irritating bastard has annoyed the crap out of me. I do not intend to let him win. And that means I need to be in Kent."

"Or are you better off watching him? He's pulling strings from here."

"He'll be extra careful from now on. I could watch his office all week and still see nothing of relevance."

"I told you not to go charging in there."

"At least now I know for sure he's involved. I still can't believe he was behind the bomb, though."

"If I'm honest, neither can I." There was a deep crease between Jackson's brows as he raked his hands through his shaggy hair. "Nicoli is sneaky and underhanded, but very determined. Theft, assault, blackmail, subterfuge—all of those are Nicoli's calling cards. But a bomb? Did he really admit to that?"

Harlan scratched his jaw, and a prickle of discomfort ran down his spine as he considered their heated conversation. "Actually, not exactly. He said he hadn't planted it or something of the sort, and I accused him of hiring someone. You know how pedantic he is. He didn't deny that."

"I wonder if there's a third player in all this. Someone who really planted the bomb."

"Like who?"

"I don't know. Maybe I'm just paranoid. Tiredness does that to me." Jackson finished his drink, placed his glass on the table and stood. "I'm shattered, and I have a lot to process about Layla's news and everything else, so I'm going home. I need to be fresh in the morning. Although..." he hesitated, deep in thought.

"You're changing your mind, aren't you? About going to France."

Jackson nodded. "I feel I should meet them and escort them out of there. I head this investigation! I could still get a late flight and be part of the extraction team."

"Don't you trust your team?"

"Of course I do, but after Layla's news, I want answers."

"And you'll get them."

Jackson scowled as he wrestled with his emotions, but when he met Harlan's eyes, he looked resolute. "I'm going."

Despite his misgivings, Harlan knew Jackson wouldn't be dissuaded, and he understood why, too. Sitting here seemed...lazy. "Do you need a lift?"

"No, thanks. I'll walk or get the tube or something. I'll keep you informed, Harlan."

"Good luck."

Harlan topped up his drink and moved to the window, watching Jackson exit the building and lope down the street. Jackson's decision goaded him into action, too. *What if there was another dangerous group searching for Templar gold?* He knew he couldn't stay here, far from the action. He'd go to Theo's. *Right now.*

Shadow rested her cheek against the cool stone parapet as she watched the driveway below.

Theo was right. Up here offered the perfect place to survey the grounds. The parapets were high, offering plenty of space to shelter behind, with narrow gaps to aim her bow through. She could see all approaches to the keep, but the moon, a silvered crescent, provided a wealth of shadows. Complete darkness cloaked parts of the drive and areas of the grounds that were scattered with trees. The wood was dense and impenetrable from here, but she could see the break in the canopy, revealing where the lodge had been.

She studied the drive again, and then crept around the tower, surveying the lanes that bordered the grounds. Only the occasional car and its headlights provided illumination there. Moving again, she studied the string of courtyards below with their collection of out-buildings, and the greenhouse set inside the walled garden.

If she were a thief—which she was, on occasion—she wouldn't approach via the drive or anywhere near it. Plus, a patrol car was parked at the gate. She'd cross the grounds from the lane, sticking to the edges of the lawns and the huge, perennial borders that at this time of year were thick with flowers. Or she'd arrive in the day with the crowds of emergency personnel and hide somewhere, emerging only when no one expected it.

The sound of an approaching car disturbed her thoughts, and she swung around to the front of the house. She raised her bow, sighting the car along the arrow as it sped up the drive. There was no subtlety of approach here, and with a sigh of relief, she realised why. It was Nahum's car, and Niel was in the passenger seat. She smirked. It appeared that neither could decide who should come, and they both had. She waited until they stopped in front of the keep, and then released an arrow at Niel's feet as he exited the car.

He yelled and then scowled as he looked up, raising his middle finger in salute. The subtle moonlight gave his blond hair and beard a silvery glow. Shadow returned his one-fingered greeting, and dropped back with a grin, out of sight, continuing to survey her surroundings.

Within ten minutes, both had joined her up on the wide, round roof of the tower, Theo with them, and they clustered behind a thick pillar of stone.

Niel grimaced as he handed her the arrow. "You're funny, Shadow."

"I know. Your face was a picture."

"Now, now," Nahum chided, although he couldn't hide his amusement. "Please don't start already."

Theo looked confused, and nervously stroked his luxuriant moustache. "Is there a problem? You are acquainted? Gabe said..."

Nahum smiled. "Shadow just likes to tease Niel. Ignore them both."

Theo still looked uncertain. "I feel you should settle in. You've had a long journey."

Niel stopped him. "We're here to help, and Nahum almost killed us, he drove so quickly to get here. It would be a waste to rest. We're just fine, Theo."

"He's right." Shadow nodded to the doorway that led to the steps and the lower floors. "You can head back downstairs, Theo. Is the place locked up? Every door? Every window?"

Theo nodded. "Yes, and all the outbuildings too, just as you asked."

"Good. Head back down and keep searching those records." Shadow had learned that Theo needed to be kept busy to stay out of her way. "Particularly the symbols on the knife's hilt!"

Theo agreed and retreated, leaving them alone, and Shadow returned to her watch, Nahum and Niel following her, keeping well out of sight.

"You were risky, taking that shot," Niel observed. "You could have been spotted."

"Unlikely, from that angle. If anyone is coming tonight, they won't approach from that side. It will be from the grounds. There are places along the lane where you can get over the walls, or through the hedge. We also wondered if someone had sneaked in when there were a lot of emergency services here."

"Good point," Nahum said, nodding. "Nothing so far?"

"No. Although, your arrival might have put them off."

"Where's the lodge?" Niel asked, scanning the grounds.

Shadow pointed it out. "Gabe and Ash are there now."

Nahum settled himself into position. "We may as well watch with you for a while."

They fell silent for several minutes, focussing on the grounds below them, with only the sound of a distant barking dog to disturb the quiet.

Then Niel called softly. "I see something." In seconds Shadow was at his side, Nahum on her left. "Down there, in the shadow of the wall." Shadow raised her bow, focussing on the spot Niel had directed her to. His voice was low in her ear. "By the rhododendron."

"What the fuck is a rhododendron?"

"The big, bloody bush on the far, right corner!"

She waited, marginally distracted by Niel's gardening knowledge, and was finally rewarded as a creeping figure edged towards the house.

Nahum put his mouth to her ear on her other side. "Don't kill him. We need to talk to whoever it is."

"I'm not an idiot. I'll injure the intruder. Will you two shut up and let me focus?" *Why in the great Goddess's name had she let them watch with her?*

She waited for her eyes to adjust to the light, discerning what was plant from person. A leg injury would bleed a lot, but it would immobilise him. Unfortunately, the thick bushes were impeding her sight, unless she guessed at his position.

As she aimed her arrow, her finger ready to release, a blast rocked the grounds, and a plume of fire lit up the sky, directly where the lodge had been.

Fifteen

A groan summoned Barak from thoughtful contemplation. He was leaning against the rotten doorframe at the entrance to the barn, nursing his injured shoulder, and feeling grateful for Estelle's magic and his own healing abilities that had eased some of the pain. Already he could feel the flesh and bone knitting back together.

He looked around at the van, seeing movement within. Their prisoner was stirring, the blankets shifting off him as he struggled to sit up. The noise roused Estelle from her light slumber, too.

He took a moment before responding, not wanting to rush their guest, but also enjoying the view of Estelle stretching like a cat as she yawned, her eyes flickering open. They had talked a lot earlier that evening, and he was glad of it. Estelle had opened up to him properly for the first time in months. Despite their recent physical closeness, she had always kept something back. However, now he felt the change in her, and he'd watched her sleeping, easy in his heart at their newfound honesty. She blinked up at him, her eyes warm.

He squeezed her hand. "Our guest is awake. Stay here, and keep an eye on the road." Barak crossed the barn. "Easy," he said, stepping into the van and crouching at the man's side in an attempt to subdue the man's noticeable rising panic. "You were drugged."

The man groaned again, his voice rasping, making his French accent stronger. "Not for the first time." He tried to focus, eyes blinking rapidly. "*Merde*. Where am I?"

"Somewhere safe. We're hiding in a barn, well away from the *château*." Barak handed him a bottle of water. "Here. Drink up. It's just water."

The man sniffed at the bottle, then squinted at Barak. "I don't know if I can trust you!"

"You're alive, aren't you? And not tied up, either. You've been sleeping for hours. I could have killed you plenty of times by now."

He nodded and downed the water, finishing the bottle in one long drink, before wiping his mouth with the back of his hand. "I still feel dizzy."

"The after-effects of the drug. You need food, too." He pointed to the scrubs stacked at the side. "Get changed, and then come and join us."

Barak backed out and gave the man a moment of privacy, then watched him test his strength before exiting the van. He took a deep breath and looked around, his chest rising and falling. He flexed his fingers and stretched as he took his bearings. He was tall, around six feet, slimly built with a wiry, muscular frame. His head was shaved, although he had stubble across his jaw. He spotted Estelle sitting quietly by the door, and frowned. "Who's that?"

"My friend, Estelle. She was at the facility, remember? She helped you escape. I'm Barak." He extended his hand, and the man shook it with a firm grip.

"Lucien." Tension seeped out of him. "Yes. Sorry. My memory is hazy."

"Not surprising, all things considered. Come and join us." Barak was now sure that Lucien wasn't a threat. Even if he was, they should be able to handle him easily.

Barak sat next to Estelle on the rug, and they both gave Lucien plenty of room. He stood for a moment, looking down the lane, before finally sitting and introducing himself to Estelle.

Estelle handed him a pre-packed baguette. "Sorry. It's all we had time to buy."

"Anything right now is fine. Tell me what's going on."

They had already discussed how much to tell him when he finally woke up, both reluctant to disclose too much. Estelle started. "We work with an organisation investigating the paranormal. In recent months, we've discovered some individuals who have developed unusual physical enhancements. They seem to be associated with a powerful group who have few morals. Through various means, we found *Château du Buade*." She succinctly explained how they discovered Lucien at the facility, finally asking, "Do you know who captured you?"

"No, but I know why they did. I've been working at the *château* for the last few months—a temporary summer job." He shrugged at Barak's questioning expression. "I was looking for a change. Life has been tricky lately. The *château* seemed like a good place to try something new. Anyway, I was staying on site, in one of the workers' cottages, helping in the shops and café, and getting ready for the olive harvest later in the year. Then I saw something I shouldn't."

"Like what?" Barak asked.

"I don't sleep that well, so sometimes I explore the grounds at night. I found a large door set into a hill, and I saw vans coming and going. I went back a few times after that, thinking at first that it was supplies for the *château*, but it didn't make sense. Why not take vans to the front? I see delivery vans there all the time. And why deliver in the middle of the night? I knew this was something different." He shrugged. "I was careless. They spotted me. I think they shot at me. The next thing I know, I was in that underground lab being endlessly questioned. 'Who did I work for? Was someone else with me? Why was I there?'" His gaze became distant as he looked, unseeing, down the lane. "They didn't believe me at first. Then they asked about *me*. Where I was from. My family. My friends. When they realised that I had no one close in the area, that my life had...changed," he hesitated over the word, his eyes haunted, "they said they had a new job for me, helping them in their research. I refused." He huffed. "Turns out, they didn't like that. I didn't really have a choice."

"Then what?" Barak asked, as Lucien hesitated again.

"It was only a week or so ago, but I feel it's been months. They ran a whole load of tests on me, and," he glanced down at his arms, "they did this."

"Were there others with you at any point?"

"One man and one woman, but not for long. They disappeared within days of my arrival. I never spoke to them. They were careful to keep us separated." He finished his food, and brushed crumbs off his chest. "I need to go now. I can't stay here. They'll be looking for us. They won't stop. They made that *very* clear."

Barak held his hand out in a stop sign. "We have a plan to get out of here. Out of France. That includes you, too. But we'd like your help in exchange. There are things you must have heard in there. We suspect that the facility is one of many. We aim to shut them down, for good." He gestured at the tattoos. "Those, we think, are stage one of a kind of transformation."

"What sort of transformation?"

"Enhanced strength, speed, longevity. And potentially some kind of mind control. Something that would have made you compliant."

"The big man. The main doctor. He talked about stages in the process." Lucien's eyes clouded as he struggled to remember. "I was drugged at the time. These tattoos are everywhere. They took time to do." He lifted his shirt. "They cover my chest and my back, and they feel odd. They tingle, on occasion." He closed his eyes tightly, as if to block the memory. "They ran energy pulses over me. Over *them*."

"Like electrocution?" Estelle asked, eyes widening in alarm.

He flexed his arm muscles. "No, something different. I have no idea."
Barak leaned forward, now more certain than ever that this man
could help them. His captors were trying to activate or prime his
tattoos. But another thought struck him, something that should have
occurred to him far sooner. He glanced down the lane, expecting to hear
car engines and the screech of tires. "Did you have a tracker implanted
on you?"

"Who knows? Maybe?"

Estelle turned to Barak. "Potentially, if there is one, my spell will
disrupt it."

"Spell?" Lucien edged back. "What are you talking about?"

"Just something that protects us." Estelle's magic was already rising,
ready to subdue Lucien, but he was too exhausted to fight.

"I just want to get out of here."

Barak came to a quick decision. If Lucien did have a tracker implanted somewhere on his body, Black Cronos would have followed
them part of the way, even if Estelle's spell was blanketing it now. They
could be waiting somewhere on the lanes for them to move again, and
travelling at night would be better than daylight. "Let's get moving
now, just in case. We have a rendezvous anyway in a few hours. Can you
protect us while we travel, Estelle?"

"I can protect Lucien. No problem. The van, while we're moving, is
harder."

He nodded. "Do what you can. Anything to buy us more time will
be good."

─━◆◆◆━─

Nahum dived off the keep's tower, extending his wings and soaring towards the woods, not caring who saw him. His priority was his brothers.

Niel swooped next to him, but headed towards where they had seen the intruder. Shadow remained behind, still watching the grounds.

Another roar heralded a column of flames shooting up above the wood, and Nahum circled around it. The fire illuminated the sprawled figures of Gabe and Ash on the ground beyond the house. Nahum dropped to their side, calling their names.

"We're fine!" Gabe said, sitting up and rubbing his head. "It was a controlled explosion."

"Controlled? You're kidding, right? Your feathers are singed!"

Gabe reached over, quelling the red glow on his wing tips. "No. We used that!" He pointed at a long, wooden beam that was burning at one end. "That was our trigger."

Ash staggered to his feet. "It was still a big blast, though. And now we've destroyed the Inner Sanctum, too."

Nahum stared at them, exasperated. "What the hell are you two doing? You could have been killed! And what the hell is the Inner Sanctum?"

"It's a ruse. The whole place is! The explosion...everything!" Gabe groaned as he stood up. "We think this was meant to distract us from the real place we should be looking. The chapel."

Nahum had only received a garbled message earlier, and there was no mention of Inner Sanctums. "Keep explaining, please. I'm playing catch up here!"

The distant flashing of red and blue lights, accompanied by the whine of engines tearing down the lanes made them all stop.

Gabe led them into the woods. "This way."

"Shadow thinks you're dead."

Gabe winced, and pulled his phone out of his pocket. "Shit. Go ahead. I'll call her."

Ash took over the lead, weaving through the trees, away from the castle, setting a quick pace. He talked as he walked. "The knife that Theo found hidden in the walls of his cellar is marked with Templar symbols."

"Which started this whole thing off. I get that. How did he find it?"

"Constructing a cinema room."

"Nice!"

"I guess so. Anyway, he thinks that the symbols on its hilt are a coded message, a type of map."

"To treasure."

"Yes, because Temple Keep used to belong to the final English Commander."

"What if it's a fake?"

Ash shook his head. "I know weapons. It's old. I've studied the symbols a little, but so far, they make little sense. I'm trying to get my head around it all."

"Where does the exploding lodge come into this?"

Ash paused in a clearing, a shaft of moonlight illuminating his pinched expression. "The lodge was built centuries after the keep, but had lots of symbols carved into it. However, they are more Masonic in origin, an organisation believed to have formed from the ashes of the Knights Templar."

"And what are they? What did they do?"

"Not did. *Do*! They're still around. Originally, hundreds of years ago, they were a guild of stonemasons. Men with businesses helping other men get ahead. It evolved over time. Became more secretive. They had rituals and secret handshakes." Ash rolled his eyes. "Nothing new, really."

Nahum laughed. "No. Secret organisations have been around for millennia. What's the link with the dagger?"

"It's murky. When the Templars were rounded up and tortured, their treasure disappeared. Maybe it was hidden in one place. Maybe it was separated. Anyway, the organisation's property was split up, their possessions shared out. Other organisations developed from it, and the Masons are thought to be one of them. The Knights Hospitaller benefitted most—I think. However, the treasure vanished, but there *were* survivors, as I mentioned before. Men who ran before the net closed and the Templars were arrested for heresy. It's believed that their knowledge was passed down, potentially knowledge about the missing treasure, maybe also their rituals. After discovering the knife with the carved hilt, Theo believes it's a new clue to the cache of English treasure that was hidden somewhere around here. It seems Theo's lodge, built well after the main castle, was probably a Masonic lodge."

"Which is why you were searching it."

"Yes." Ash plunged into the trees again, still talking. "It made sense to check it out. But when Gabe and Shadow investigated it, *boom!*" He quickly summarised how Shadow had found and activated the trigger. "But we reasoned it must be a trigger to something! A hidden room or hiding place. We examined the blueprint of the building and found a cellar in the foundation."

Nahum understood Ash's reasoning. "You thought the bomb had been planted to hide the cellar."

"Initially, yes. That's what Gabe and I were doing. Checking it out. But the room was empty, and footprints were visible on the ground. Someone had already been there. We knew that potentially if something was there, it had been removed, or it was a false trail. We spotted a carved relief that was slightly protruding from the wall behind the altar. It looked suspicious."

"Too suspicious?"

"Exactly! So, we prodded it with a big stick."

Nahum couldn't hide his surprise. "I thought you liked to preserve things. You didn't have to set it off. You could have avoided it!"

Ash stopped again as they reached the top of the rise and a break in the trees. He put his hands on his hips as he studied the surrounding gardens. He finally faced him, his eyes glittering with pleasure as Gabe joined them again. "We could have avoided it, of course. But someone is watching us. Or watching the castle, or Theo. We decided not to disappoint them."

Nahum knew that expression well. His brothers were hunting, and the chase was intriguing.

However, before he could ask more questions, Gabe interrupted their conversation. "I gather that Niel is here. He's given chase to the intruder."

"Intruder?" Ash's eyes widened as he stared at Nahum. "You kept *that* quiet."

"You were on a roll." He turned back to Gabe. "Has he found the suspect?"

"Not so far. Shadow virtually told me to get lost while she watched him. After giving me an earful of abuse for scaring her." He looked sheepish. "She was worried."

"We all were! Which brings me back to your insane idea to trigger the explosion. Please tell me you have a plan! Are you planning on pretending you're dead or something?"

"No! That would be far too inconvenient," Gabe said with a frown. "We will let Theo spread the word that we have given up. That all clues have been destroyed, and we fear there is no way forward now. Let the opposition relax."

"And in the meantime?" Nahum asked.

Ash pointed across the ground to a colonnaded folly with a domed roof surrounded by shrubbery and plants. "We investigate *that*."

"Why?"

He smiled. "Follow me."

※◆◇◆※

Niel had been planning on flying low over the walled garden in an attempt to spot their intruder, but the flash of lights and wail of sirens had made that impossible.

As soon as the bomb exploded, all three of them had lost track of the suspect as they turned to watch the flames tear up the night sky. Shadow swore as her aim went wide, and her arrow thudded into the wall. Similarly furious with himself, Niel focussed on the ground again, and made a split-second decision to pursue the figure while Nahum raced in the other direction.

He landed in the shadow of the wall, his back to the stone, folded his wings behind him, and waited. Nothing stirred. The intruder was stealthy and quick. Niel plucked Shadow's arrow out of the wall, and proceeded along the back of the wide border, the large perennials and climbing plants at the rear serving both to mask his movements and thwart his every step.

He finally reached the gate into the walled kitchen garden. He edged inside, waiting in the doorframe. A flicker of movement against the far wall caught his eye. He crouched and crept down the gravelled path, but no matter how hard he tried, every now and again the crunch of gravel gave him away. Abandoning all pretence, he ran instead, sprinting along the paths by the most direct route. Unfortunately, by the time he reached the spot, no one was there.

But a large tree was overhanging the garden wall.

Niel leapt up and grabbed a branch, hoping it wouldn't snap beneath his weight, and then clambered up and along it. On the other side of the wall was the park-like grounds, dotted with trees. He waited and watched again. While he studied the dappled shade, he reflected on the figure he'd seen, and the niggling suspicion of who he thought it might be.

It had been hard to judge from atop the tower, but on the ground, the brief glimpse of the figure had revealed they were slight of build and short. The suspect's movements had been deft, and had hardly caused any damage when progressing along the border. He recalled the almond eyes and petite build of the intruder at the farmhouse. *Mouse.* He was sure it was the same person.

But Mouse had been working for The Orphic Guild, recruited by Mason and JD to interfere with the hunt for the Dark Star Astrolabe. They wouldn't have recruited her this time. She was obviously a freelancer, which perhaps meant Nicoli had employed her. *Maybe she had broken into the library, too. But was she the bomber?*

Niel considered his conversation with her. *No.* If he was any judge of character, she wasn't a bomber. Although, maybe he just didn't want her to be one. He may have seen her only once, and briefly at that, but her eyes were imprinted in his thoughts. And if it was her, he wanted to catch her for several reasons.

Unfortunately, however, the longer he sat there searching the grounds, the more certain he was that she had escaped. He slipped from his perch and set off on foot, determined to find something.

Sixteen

Estelle spotted a dark van exit a side road and pull onto the lane behind them, barely a couple of miles from the barn.

"Barak!"

"I see it. I can't risk going any faster, or we'll crash."

Lucien leaned forward, head poking between the seats. "Is it them? What did you call them? Black Cronos?"

"Yep. And their trademark black van—just like the one we're in." Barak glanced at Estelle. "Your spell?"

"In place!" But the words *trademark black van* took ominous shape in her head. "They're tracking our van. They must be!"

Barak swore, but remained focussed on the road. Estelle consulted the map on her phone. It was still dark, hours away from dawn, and she wondered if they'd done the right thing by moving, but it was too late to debate that now.

"In another couple of miles, we'll be on the outskirts of a small town. Lots of winding roads. We might be able to lose them and swap cars."

Barak cocked an eye at her. "Are you suggesting we steal a car?"

"Do you have a better idea?"

"No."

Lucien stared at them. "Who the hell are you two? International spies?"

Estelle liked the sound of that. It was glamourous, if dangerous. She hedged. "Not exactly. Our job is varied. Right now, you're the priority. But I'd like to see Barak in a tuxedo at a casino. He'd look good as 007."

"And you wearing a floor-length evening gown, draped in diamonds? I could handle that."

"*Mon Dieu.* At least you love your work." Lucien seemed to have recovered from his earlier shock, despite the fact that he kept glancing nervously out of the tinted windows behind him. "I have no idea what I will do...if I survive. That van is getting closer."

"Love is a questionable word right now!" Barak braked hard to take the next turn before accelerating again. A break in the vineyards showed another lane on the left, another van travelling swiftly along it, ready to intercept them.

"Barak!" Estelle shouted. "Floor it!"

A boom shook the back of the van, and the rear wheels snaked across the road before Barak could wrest it back under control.

"What the hell was that?" Lucien asked, his voice rising with fear.

Estelle twisted in her seat, just about able to see the flash of a weapon in an outstretched hand coming out of the passenger-side window. "One of their weird weapons!"

Barak gave her a sidelong glance. "Any magic you can use to help us?"

"Lucien," she warned, "you may wish to look away."

Estelle wound down the window, and promptly blasted the hedge behind her. It erupted into flames, and with a grasping motion, she pulled part of the hedge out of the ground and flung the shrubs across the road. She magnified the fire, making a huge wall of flames. Not even seeing the van's response, she looked ahead. The other black van was racing to intercept them, and they were due to hit the intersection at the same time.

Estelle didn't have time for finesse, and while travelling in a moving vehicle, performing any kind of earth magic was hard. She also couldn't see the drivers, which made it difficult to cast any kind of spell on them. She liked to see who she was aiming at. She opted for the most straightforward plan of attack.

"Barak, open your window!"

"I'm driving!"

"Fine! I'll do it my way!"

When they reached the intersection, mere seconds ahead of the enemy van, she hurled a white-hot ball of energy just under Barak's nose. It shattered the driver's side window and hurtled through the other van's windshield, causing the van to veer through the hedge and into the vineyard, where it thudded to a stop in a plume of earth and splattering plants. Barak didn't stop, racing onwards down the dark lane towards the twinkle of street lights.

Lucien leaned forward again, staring at her. "What was that?"

She studied his expression. He wasn't scared. He was curious. "Magic. I'm a witch. A good one."

"Glad you're on my side."

"They have plenty of tricks up their sleeve. We're not out of it, yet."

"No, we're not." Lucien pointed to a van bouncing along a rutted track at the edge of a vineyard to their right. "There's another one."

"For fuck's sake," Barak said. "They'll reach the road ahead of us."

Estelle knew she didn't have the power to lift the whole van out of their way, and even if she blasted it, it would still block their path. "Stop the van."

"Are you insane?"

"No. Do it."

Barak screeched to a halt, and Estelle leapt out and ran in front of their van as Black Cronos crashed through a gate and onto the lane. A flash of a weapon gave her split-second warning, and she threw up a protective shield just as a fireball roared towards her. It stopped as if it had hit a wall only feet away.

The van swerved towards them, and Estelle braced herself. She had one chance to get this right, because she had no doubt that the van would block their way as the soldiers attacked them. She threw two balls of pure energy under the van, then lifted her hands and used the power she had just released and the vehicle's own momentum to lift it. She almost staggered from the concentration it required, but she couldn't stop now. The van lifted higher, but it was still on a collision course and not nearly high enough to clear their own vehicle.

It was going to crash right into them.

And then a flash of darkness to her left almost took her breath away.

Barak exploded from the driver's side of the van like a bullet, wings shooting outwards as he leapt beneath the van and lifted it himself. He flipped it aside, and it landed on its roof in the vineyard, glass shattering and metal groaning from the impact. Estelle followed it up with a blast of fire.

"Get in!" Lucien yelled. "I see more on the hill!"

On the narrow rise above them, headlights raced along an unseen lane.

Wordlessly, they both leapt back into the van, and Barak accelerated.

Estelle focussed on the road, heart hammering and hands shaking. "Head for the centre of town. We need a car park or something."

In a few more moments they were on the outskirts of the town, and unless Estelle was imagining it, curtains were twitching. The last attack had to have been audible from here. Barak slowed down in the town so as not to attract more attention. The roads were lined with shops, houses, and parked cars. He took a sharp turn down a narrow alley that cut between roads, and parked behind a row of shops so they were well out of sight. He pointed to a battered, silver four-door Citroen. "Everyone out. That one will do. Estelle?"

"It will be my pleasure."

She used magic to unlock the car, and after searching the van for anything that would give them away, they swapped vehicles. Seconds later, they were easing away from the alley. Once again, she secured the protection spell around Lucien.

For a few minutes, they were silent and watchful as Barak drove along the quiet streets. It was still dark, but a few other cars were around at this hour. Hopefully, they would blend in.

Estelle leaned back, sighing with relief. She'd never been so terrified or exhilarated in her life. "I think we're okay."

"So where to now?" Lucien asked.

"The safehouse. And our rescue, hopefully." She pulled her phone out again. "I'll pull up the directions."

***

For what felt like the hundredth time, Harlan explained who he was to the policeman at the end of Theo's drive.

"I'm a friend of Theo's. I've come to help!"

"At two in the morning?" The police officer looked sceptical.

"That's what friends do!"

With a stern frown and a sweeping glance of disapproval, the officer radioed through to a colleague. Harlan waited, his fingers drumming the steering wheel as he studied the blaze of light in the distance. He could only see the castle tower above the trees, illuminated with flashing red and blue lights.

After Jackson had left, Harlan had tipped his bourbon down the sink, packed a bag, and driven to Kent. He hoped Theo would be understanding at the hour of his arrival. He could also check in on JD from there, as he lived only a short distance away. He wanted to know what the wily old dog was up to. Right now, however, he wondered what was going on at the castle. He'd tried to ring Theo, and then Gabe, Ash, and Shadow, but no one answered. Dread settled in the pit of his stomach. He glared at the tight-lipped police officer again. However, with a curt nod, the officer pulled the police tape away, and Harlan was allowed to enter.

Theo was waiting for him outside the huge wooden doors. Everything about him sagged, from his moustache to the old cardigan he'd thrown on over a rumpled shirt. Regardless, he shook Harlan's hand vigorously. "I'm glad to see you. Things have taken a turn for the worse!"

"And then some!" Harlan marvelled at English understatement. "Is everyone okay? What's on fire?"

"There was another explosion at the lodge, but Gabe and Ash are fine. Gabe called Shadow."

"And where's she?"

Theo pointed upwards. "The tower roof. Their two colleagues have arrived." He frowned. "They're all so huge!"

Harlan spotted Nahum's car. "Nahum and Niel, I presume?"

Theo nodded. "Nahum is with Gabe and Ash, Niel is with Shadow. Come in. Get some tea."

"Anything stronger available?"

Theo barked a dry laugh as he herded Harlan inside, masking an almost maniacal desperation. "Of course. I'll join you."

As they reached the entrance hallway, lit only by lamps, Chivers appeared at the end of the hall looking like a spectral apparition, and Theo requested their drinks. "Bring them up to the sitting room, please." He led them up the staircase. "Are you planning on staying, Harlan?"

Harlan looked at him, feeling guilty. "I was hoping to. My bag is in the trunk of my car, but I can stay in the village. I guess you already have a full house. It was presumptuous of me, sorry. I acted on impulse."

"Not at all. The more the merrier. I have enough rooms here to accommodate an army. The way this search is going, I may have to."

He flung open the door of the sitting room, and Harlan gasped. The room was in darkness, but the curtains were wide open, revealing the flashing lights of the fire engines and police cars in the woods.

"Holy shit, Theo. That's a lot of people."

"It's not every day I have *two* bombs exploding on my property." He stood at the window, arms crossed and lips pressed tight. "I've started something I never expected."

"But it means you're right. You doubted yourself earlier. You can't anymore. The theft at the library, the bombed lodge, Nicoli's involvement, and possibly others." Harlan grinned at him, unable to hide his enthusiasm, despite the night's events.

Theo nodded, a twinkle returning to his eyes. "You're right, of course. I'm just tired."

"Shouldn't you be down there?"

"There's nothing I can do. I saw enough this afternoon. Actually, yesterday afternoon."

"Where have Gabe and the others gone now?"

"To the pavilion. I don't know why. Ash had an idea, apparently."

Harlan nodded, gazing across the grounds. *What were they looking for now?*

<hr />

Gabe stood at the entrance to the pavilion, finally understanding what Ash had seen earlier. "I see it now. The old marks on the ground. Looks like foundations. Tricky to make out from here, though."

Nahum was walking across the dry, sun-baked grass, brown and stubbly from the hot summer weather. "But what's the significance of them?" And then a knowing smile crossed his face. "The old chapel."

Ash nodded. "I think so. The hot weather has dried the ground so much that it's exposing the old foundation. It would be easier to see from above, but that's impossible in the day, and it certainly is right now." He nodded to the flashing lights of the emergency vehicles across the park. "They'll search the grounds soon. It's inevitable."

Gabe nodded, staring beyond them to Temple Keep. "The castle, too. Although, I doubt there'll be a bomb in there, not with all the staff around."

"It depends who planted the bombs and how determined they are. And what's at stake," Nahum reasoned. "So, what do we do with these foundations?"

Ash paced across the faint outline of the depression in the grass. "I wanted to see if perhaps there was something underground, that might now be under the pavilion."

"Like a crypt?" Nahum asked, looking doubtful.

"Possibly."

While his brothers investigated the old site marked on the grass, Gabe studied the inside of the pavilion. It had a huge porch entrance supported by pillars, and set within it were two wooden doors that were currently wedged open. Three of the walls had large windows set into them, offering views of the gardens and a pond, and the centre of the space was filled with wicker furniture and rugs. The perfect summer spot for relaxing. Maybe Ash was right, and the pavilion had been the chapel, a decent distance away from the house. *But why knock it down?*

He examined the floor. It was lined with huge stone tiles, and was elevated off the ground by about a foot. High foundations, which could hide all sorts of things. *But...* He stepped to the doorway again. "This is probably a concrete foundation, Ash. It's nuts. We can't destroy the pavilion just to get under it on a whim!"

Ash was already heading around the side, but he paused to answer Gabe. "I'm not saying we dig it up, but I am curious. I think we should eliminate it."

"Or find a good reason to dig it up," Nahum added. "You need more than a hunch, otherwise it's a gigantic waste of time. Did you even see a chapel on the maps of the grounds? This could have been anything. Maybe another old summerhouse that was knocked down to make way for this one."

Ash shook his head, looking more doubtful by the moment. Gabe knew he'd been excited about this possibility, but now... Glancing around the grounds again and seeing no one approaching, Gabe flew to the flat roof above. He crouched at the end and peered over the side.

"I can see the old foundations clearly from here. They *do* seem to disappear under this building."

"But," Nahum argued, "it could have been *anything*. You guys have gone mad. The bombs have addled your brain."

Gabe didn't answer. *Maybe they were going about this wrong.* They'd been here less than twenty-four hours, and in that time, he'd already been nearly killed twice. Although it was important to act quickly, they also needed to be smart about it. He stood up, surveying his surroundings. The summer house was to the rear of the grounds. Only a short distance away was the hamlet of Temple Moreton, named after the keep and the family who owned it. The cluster of rooftops huddled close together. If he remembered correctly, Theo had said that land had been sold from the estate years before. Perhaps the village had once been part of the grounds—owned by William de More and his descendants. Perhaps there was a chapel there, or something worth searching in one of the houses—if any of the original ones were still standing.

Seeing lights moving towards them from the woods, he ducked and dropped to the ground on the far side of the pavilion. "I've had another idea," he announced to his brothers.

"What idea?" Nahum asked suspiciously. "I'm knackered, and wasn't expecting to be digging up the grounds in the middle of the bloody night."

Gabe grinned as he slapped his shoulder, directing his brothers back towards the house. "There'll be no digging tonight! Don't worry, sleeping beauty, your bed awaits. This can wait until tomorrow."

Seventeen

J ackson studied Lucien Moreau, noting the man looked as exhausted as he felt. *Not surprising, really.* Both of them had been up most of the night trying to reach the safehouse, and he was struggling to keep his eyes open. *At least*, Jackson reflected, *he hadn't been shot at.*

It was just before seven on Friday morning, and they were in the living area of a small apartment in Méthamis. Jackson and a team of six armed men and women, one of them with medical training, had arrived only fifteen minutes earlier. Four of the team members were out on the street, looking inconspicuous as they surveyed the area. A couple were in the apartment. Estelle and Barak had summarised their story, surprised to see Jackson with the team. The medic checked over Lucien and dressed his head wound while they talked.

"Where are you taking me?" Lucien asked. "And can you keep me safe?"

"We have another safehouse in London," Jackson told him, trying to look like this was something he arranged every day. "It will also be guarded by a small team at all times, but you need to confirm that you'll comply. If you leave on your own—as in, sneak off—we can't guarantee your safety."

"I have no wish to die! Or be recaptured! But equally, I do not wish to be experimented on by you, either!" Lucien's French accent was strong, but his English was excellent. His pale brown eyes were sharp, and Jackson felt he was being assessed, as were the rest of the team. Under these circumstances, he would do the same.

But although Jackson could sympathise, he was also frustrated. "We're not monsters, but we do need to check you over. Try to understand what they were doing with those tattoos." The symbols and sigils were entwined so closely, it was hard to see where one ended and the other began. "However, in order to understand them properly, we'd like you to stay at our headquarters for a while. You won't see where it is, or how you enter, but you will be safe there. Secure."

"Another lab?"

Barak answered first. "Not like the facility you were in. I've been there, and I can vouch for Jackson. You'll have your own room, too."

Lucien looked at Barak and Estelle. "Is that where you were given your powers? Your wings?"

"You mean my magic?" Estelle looked shocked for a moment, and then her stance softened. "No, I was born with it. I doubt anything anyone could do to you would give you my powers."

"And nothing will give you my wings, either," Barak added.

Jackson could only imagine the conversation they'd had following their attack. The fact that they had both shown their paranormal abilities to Lucien indicated how much pressure they had been under. He was also getting nervous with all the explaining, but he knew that to force Lucien would be the wrong thing now. He wasn't a prisoner; he was an asset. A valuable one.

Jackson tried to be reasonable. "Look, Lucien, I desperately want you to come with us. Black Cronos are dangerous, and I have my own personal reasons for getting involved in searching for them. But at the end of the day, I'm not going to force you to comply. This is an extraction team—that's all.

We're taking you to safety. If you're not happy, you can walk out of that door right now. I won't stop you. I will, however, wish you luck, because Barak and Estelle will no longer be your body guards."

Lucien nodded, his eyes dropping to the floor for a brief moment before addressing Barak and Estelle again. "You two are coming, too?"

"Actually, no," Barak answered.

Jackson's head whipped around to stare at them. "You're not? Why?"

"Estelle and I have been thinking. We'd like to keep searching here. We've rattled them now. We might be able to find out more. And we have those notes we'd like to investigate."

"But they've seen you! They may even still be searching for you."

"They *might* have seen us. We knocked out all of their cameras, and were fighting mostly in the dark. It's a risk we're prepared to take." Estelle smiled. "Plus, we are better equipped than most to deal with them. And I have connections here. I've already sourced us somewhere secure to stay, and a car. I won't tell you where, though. Not yet."

Jackson studied their set expressions. He knew better than to try to talk them out of it. "I won't deny that I'm worried, but equally, anything else you can find out will be fantastic. Obviously, on our end, we'll keep investigating the family and their connections. You need to send me copies of what you found in the office, too."

Barak nodded. "Thanks, Jackson. After seeing that place, we are doubly motivated to keep going. We'll keep you informed, and you need to let us know how Lucien is doing, too. Do you need us to go with you to the airport?"

Jackson glanced around to the team leader, David Miller, standing behind him. Miller was ex-military. He had a sidearm under his jacket, but as Waylen had stressed, the team was there for protection only. They were not an assault team. He wasn't sure Miller would make the distinction, though. He made Jackson nervous just looking at him, even though he knew he was on his side. "Do we need extra help?" he asked him.

He shook his head. "We're just fine."

"In that case, bring the van around," Jackson instructed him.

While the man radioed his team, and his companion instructed Lucien as to their next steps, Jackson moved aside to speak to Barak and Estelle privately. "Are you sure you know what you're doing?"

Barak laughed. "That's a matter to debate, but we know *who* we're up against."

"What will you do next?"

"Go to Estelle's place, and get some sleep first." He pointed at his eyes, which to Jackson looked perfectly fine. "See these bags? I'm shattered! There's only so much excitement even a Nephilim can take. Then we'll work on our next move." He lowered his voice, shooting a glance at Lucien before continuing. "From what Lucien said to us earlier, I think that if you play this right, he'll join the cause."

"Why? What did he say?"

"He's running from something. Looking for a change. He seemed...excited by what we did. He even said he had no idea what he was going to do next."

Jackson looked over at Lucien, excitement stirring at the possibilities. "That would be useful, especially if we could activate those tattoos somehow. I'll need to investigate him first, though."

Estelle leaned in. "You're going to involve JD, I presume?"

"Once we've run our own tests. Although, I'm worried what JD will say—or do. I don't want to scare Lucien. But..."

Barak finished his sentence. "JD is your best shot. And he'll be way ahead of your team."

Jackson nodded, already planning his next step. The Retreat, background checks, blood tests, scans, everything health-related, then JD. *If* he could convince Lucien. He needed to play it right.

Shadow stretched luxuriously across Gabe's chest, listening to the steady thumping of his heart that was always so reassuring, even when he was snoring. And even when he smelled of smoke and fire, like he did now.

Not that she smelled much better. They had both showered before bed, sluicing off the black soot that had been ingrained on their skin and in their hair. It had infiltrated her nose and her ears, and she could still taste it.

She studied Gabe, noting the slightly singed edge of his thick, dark hair. It was lucky he and Ash had escaped from the second blast with so little damage. They had arrived back at the castle with a determined swagger to their stride, discussing their plans for the next day. Not that they could discuss them for long. The police had arrived, asking plenty of questions. Fortunately, Gabe and Ash had managed to shower first, and had successfully denied being anywhere near the second blast. The grounds would be teaming with people today. Apparently, a bomb disposal squad was going to sweep the castle. It was only because Theo was rich and influential that they were able to stay at the keep overnight. The police had warned them that they were there at their own risk until the morning.

And then there was the intruder. She had watched from the tower as Niel continued to search on foot, but the blast had allowed the would-be thief to vanish. He had told her of his theory, but as Shadow had never met Mouse, she had to trust his judgement. They hadn't told the police about the intruder. That was something *they* would deal with.

Shadow rolled onto her back and stared at the high ceiling, thinking they needed to get up. The trail was going cold. Just as she was about to roll out of bed, Gabe's hand snaked out and pinned her down.

"Where do you think you're going?" He nuzzled into her neck, stretching against her.

"I was going to have another shower, because I still stink of smoke. As do you."

"Good. We can both stink together." He opened one eye, squinting at her. "We can shower together, too."

"We have things to do! Lots of things. Like tracking down bombers and thieves, and discovering what the dagger's mysterious symbols mean. And finding gold, of course." She showered kisses along his neck as she said, "Lots...of...lovely...gold."

"Yes, but there'll be more bombs, and threats, and also the police. Lots of police." He kissed behind her ear. "Staying here is better."

She giggled. "Like all of that would put you off the hunt! Besides, if we don't get out of here quickly, the police will question us for hours."

"They've already questioned us for hours. How much more can they ask?"

Shadow may be new to this world of police and rules and bomb squads, but she knew enough to realise that this was serious, and despite the fact that Theo had employed them, they looked suspicious. "We arrived twenty-four hours ago, and there have been two bombs set off since then."

Gabe grunted, finally opening both eyes. "We were nearly killed. They can't possibly think we're to blame."

"But it looks bad! They were asking Theo all sorts of questions last night—especially about the Templar gold. It sounded like they thought he'd gone mad."

Gabe propped himself up on one elbow, looking down at her. "How do you know that?"

"I eavesdropped after the second bomb, which by the way—" she poked him hard in the chest, "scared the crap out of me! You could have called first!"

"Sorry." He leaned in and kissed her. "We were excited."

"Excited? You're madder than I am."

"And that's why we're perfect together." His eyes flamed with desire, but curiosity won over. "Go on."

"I watched the action from the tower for some time, wondering if anyone would appear to witness the destruction."

"The bomber, you mean?"

"Yes, or the mysterious intruder."

"They might have been one and the same."

"Perhaps. Unfortunately, all the emergency vehicles and police made that impossible. I noticed the village lights going on, and the casual pass-er-by in a car gawking from the lane, but nothing suspicious was happening. The intruder had vanished, and Niel was coming back to the keep. I went downstairs then. I was thinking I should listen to the staff gossip, but ended up overhearing Theo instead. And then I bumped into Harlan."

Harlan had gone to bed by the time Gabe had arrived back, and he said, "How's he doing?"

"He was worried about us, and furious with Nicoli. But he's fine. Just knackered. He had news about Barak, too."

"Barak?" Gabe tensed. "Is he okay?"

"Yes, but it's a long story."

"In that case," Gabe leaned in for another kiss, his hand sliding down her body, "you can tell me later. I've got other things on my mind right now."

She teased him a little. "You don't want to know about their encounter with Black Cronos?"

He tensed again. "But they're okay?"

"Yes."

"Then no. Later." And with that, he lowered his head, and she surrendered to the moment.

———⊳✦⊲———

Breakfast, Niel decided, felt more like a council of war. It was fortunate that the food was excellent, or he might have complained about the subject matter.

Harlan, Shadow, and his brothers were all dressed casually in either khakis or jeans, but Theo wore a shirt, trousers, and plaid waistcoat. They were sitting around a wooden table in an informal dining room on the ground floor of the castle that overlooked the moat. The windows were open wide to welcome in the warm breeze, and he could hear the gentle lap of the water against the stone walls.

Harlan was scowling at the other end of the table, having just described his encounter with Nicoli. "Unfortunately," he said, savagely buttering his toast, "I don't think that Nicoli did plant the bombs. Jackson was right. It's not his style."

"Any idea who might have?" Gabe asked. He looked calm and in control, despite the events of the previous few hours. Gabe did not rattle easily.

"Not yet. I'm running through potential rivals. Unfortunately, or perhaps fortunately, none of them are usually this overtly violent."

"A new player?" Nahum asked.

"Perhaps. Or an old one that is very motivated."

Theo was twirling his moustache, and despite his obvious worry, was looking more animated this morning. "I shall just be much happier when the police have searched the house today. The thought of there being a bomb in here is quite terrifying."

Niel stared at him, bacon halfway to his mouth. "And yet you didn't want to move out last night?"

"Absolutely not! I will not be driven from my home by these thugs!" He banged the table with his fist.

Niel had to give the old man credit. He was belligerent, and not easily intimidated. Not many would be willing to stick around after two bombs had exploded on his property.

"As much as I would like to investigate the possibility of hidden rooms in this house," Ash said, "I think that would be a bad idea until the whole place has been thoroughly investigated."

"You think something else is hidden here?" Shadow asked.

"It's possible. The blade was hidden here. I doubt the treasure will be, though."

Niel snorted. "No. That would be far too easy."

"There might be other clues to its whereabouts, though."

Theo's fingers drummed on the table. "But don't forget that I have refurbished much of this castle over the years. I found a priest hole in one of the bedrooms, but that would have been added much later. Most of the cellars were converted to the cinema room, and all have been damp-proofed." He grimaced. "The moat makes life difficult."

A thought struck Niel. "The moat is original, then?"

"Oh, yes. It was part of the original castle."

Niel peered out of the window at it. The water looked black in the shadow of the building, the sun still behind it at this hour. It looked low as a result of the recent dry weather, and he could see where the water level had been. The stones that were revealed were old and stained with lichen and mosses. "Has it ever been drained?"

"No, but I've had it cleaned occasionally."

"Thinking of having a swim?" Ash asked Niel, his eyes dancing with laughter.

Niel shrugged. "It just struck me that hiding something in the brickwork of the moat could be a possibility."

Shadow's nose wrinkled with dislike. "It looks dirty! You wouldn't be able to see a thing down there."

"And it's big," Harlan added. "That would take a long time to search."

"Unless you drained it," Nahum suggested.

"Drain my moat?" Theo looked outraged. "That would be a nightmare! And expensive. Not to mention messy. No!"

Niel could feel outrage flowing from Theo, but mainly amusement and incredulity from everyone else, and he held up his hand for calm. "Chill out, people. I just thought I'd throw it into the mix. Besides, some moats can be constructed of dirt, too. Parts of this one could be." He stared down into the water again, wishing he'd never mentioned it. Certainly no one was going to volunteer to swim in it, and he didn't want to, either. "Forget it! Just a question."

Gabe eyed him speculatively, and Niel waited for the inevitable, but then he just shrugged and poured himself more coffee. "Which is why I want to focus on the village, Temple Moreton. Theo, in the records you've read, there are a lot of details about the Templars and their contacts. Is there anything about who William de la More would have trusted?"

"Well, there were other knights, of course, and sergeants. I can refresh my memory. And his son and family, naturally."

"Good. What about servants?"

"Perhaps, but I doubt their names would have been recorded. They wouldn't have been considered important enough. Why?"

"The hamlet was once on these lands, right? Part of the feudal system that existed then?"

Theo nodded. "And still does, although not quite in the same way. Many grand estates still own vast tracts of lands and villages, and those who live there are tenants."

Harlan huffed with astonishment. "You think something is hidden in the village? In a house?"

"Perhaps," Gabe reasoned. "I could be completely wrong, but some of the houses might be as old as this castle. A church, perhaps."

Theo brightened. "There is a church there, of course. I'm not sure of its age, but I think it's as old as the castle. I'm not a religious man, but have been in there once when I first bought the estate."

Ash nodded, leaning forward. "I thought there might once have been a chapel on the grounds. There are old foundations out by the pavilion, and the only reason we can see them now is because of the weeks of sunshine that has dried the ground. But Gabe thinks it's unlikely, and he could be right. The other option is that we look at William's associates. Other manor houses in the area, perhaps. We were talking last night, and wondered if the bombs were meant to kill us, scare us, or just make us think we are too late."

"What if we *are* too late?" Harlan asked. "Say someone has other clues that have given them a way forward."

"But we have the dagger," Theo protested.

"Yes, we do," Niel said, spearing a forkful of scrambled eggs. It wasn't as delicious as one of his breakfasts, but it was pretty good. "And we wouldn't have had an intruder trying to break in last night if it was unimportant."

"Of course. I'd forgotten about the intruder," Harlan said.

"Which brings me to my observation," Niel said, staring at Harlan. "From the admittedly brief glance I had of the potential thief last night, it looked suspiciously like Mouse."

"Mouse!" Harlan crashed his mug on the table. "But we use her!"

"That's what I thought. But she's freelance, right?"

Theo was looking between them, bewildered. "A mouse?"

"Not *a* mouse. Mouse." Niel held his hand up. "About yay big, petite, stealthy—almond eyes."

Shadow grinned. "Memorable, were they?"

"Actually, yes!"

Before she could make any further comment, Harlan sighed. "She's one of the best in the business. We have to be careful if you're right and it is her."

"It will be my pleasure to keep watch," Niel said, smiling broadly at Shadow's smirk.

"Which means," Ash said, "that the dagger has to be my focus today. I also need to look at those notes I made yesterday, check Theo's information, and cross-reference everything we have."

"In which case," Gabe said, "the rest of us need to get out of the house; let the police do their thing. We'll head to the village."

Anxious to search for signs of Mouse, Niel said, "I was going to check the grounds in the daylight. I might learn something new. Try to confirm it was Mouse."

"Why don't we help search the village first, and then I'll join you later?" Nahum suggested. "Two of us will make light work of it."

"Fair enough," Niel said, pushing his plate away. "Harlan, did you say that Nicoli is the one who stole those papers from the library? Do we need to steal them back?"

Ash intervened. "Not yet. See how I fare today."

"Well, I'm aiming to help you guys, but I need to see JD first," Harlan said, finishing his coffee and looking wistfully at the empty cafetière. "I have other things to discuss."

Niel knew what he was cryptically referring to. He had managed to speak to Barak before breakfast, and was reassured to hear that he and Estelle were both unharmed. Unfortunately, Barak had given him only the briefest rundown of what had happened, and said he'd be in touch when they were settled elsewhere and had rested.

Theo stood. "I'll leave you all to it. I realise you have things you may wish to talk about privately. I'll be in my study looking for those names, if anyone wants me."

Ash nodded. "I'll join you soon."

As soon as Theo left the room, everyone turned to Harlan, but Nahum asked the question that they all wanted to know. "What's happening with the prisoner?"

"Jackson has collected him this morning, and they are on their way back to London." He checked his watch. "The flight is due to leave soon. I'm just hoping Black Cronos hasn't tracked them down again. But he's not *our* prisoner."

"Well, no," Shadow agreed, "but he's hardly likely to be safe walking the streets."

"He'll have to learn to hide from them," Gabe mused. "Disguise himself, somehow. Or be prepared to fight them."

"Or join them," Nahum suggested, clearly distrustful of the man already.

"Or join *us*," Niel added. "Barak mentioned that he could be interested in joining the PD—if approached correctly."

Harlan nodded. "Jackson mentioned something similar, but our conversation was brief."

"And JD?" Nahum asked. "What will he do in all this?"

"That's exactly what I want to find out!" Harlan stood, his chair scraping back. "Wish me luck, and let's hope he doesn't piss me off as much as he usually does."

Eighteen

Harlan was surprised to find that JD wasn't in his lab, but in the glass-walled room at the top of his house.

It was very hot, despite the open windows and lowered blinds. JD was wearing an informal shirt with huge, billowing sleeves that made him look like a renaissance artist, his glasses perched on the end of his nose as he studied a star chart.

"Looking for something in particular, JD?" Harlan asked, standing next to him.

"I'm working on a formula that you wouldn't understand, something that needs a certain planetary alignment. I need to time it perfectly."

Harlan was glad he hadn't bothered to describe the details. "Fair enough. How are the weapon experiments going?"

JD snorted. "They're going, that's about as much as I can say. I take two steps forward and one step back all the time. Some progress, at least." He scribbled some notes on a pad, placed his glasses into his top pocket, and finally focussed on Harlan. "You look pensive. Is there an issue?"

"Sort of. I have news." He relayed Barak and Estelle's success.

"*Château du Buade*! I remember that place during the war. Second one, that is. We had the owner under surveillance, but found nothing to link him to Black Cronos. Collaborators, though." JD's eyes clouded with memories.

"So I gather."

"Many were. Unpleasant, but people did what they needed to do to survive. Horrible news from Layla, though." JD led him to a table where Anna had left them iced water laced with sliced lemons, and poured two glasses, handing Harlan one. "I gather Jackson is upset."

"Very. Which is why he's so pleased by Barak's success." He hadn't yet told him the biggest news, and he watched JD closely. "They found a prisoner, and took him with them. Jackson is taking him to London." He outlined what had happened.

"Good God." JD started pacing. "This could change everything! I want him here."

"I think Jackson would rather you go there. And he has to consent!"

"I know that. I'm not a bloody fool!"

"He's covered in tattoos. Barak thinks it was the start of their process of transformation. He said they had a kind of operating theatre. Estelle found pots of ground metals they mixed with inks."

"Intriguing. I wonder what Layla will find when she analyses the skin around the tattoos on James's body. Good to know they haven't completely vanished after all. Did they find anything alchemical in the facility?"

"I don't think so, but they're forwarding a few things on to Jackson. There was an office there, with a list of what looked like codenames."

"Intriguing. I'd like that list, too. But it will be no good me going to The Retreat. Their equipment is juvenile compared to mine. Lucien needs to come here."

"Well, you might want to rethink that approach, considering we don't know anything about him, but that's between you and Jackson." Harlan was more than happy to stay out of that argument. "Look, I can't stay long.

This Templar business is sucking up my time. It's taken an ugly turn. But, is there anything I can do for you before I go?" *Please don't take me to the lab.*

To his utter relief, JD shook his head. "No. What kind of Templar business? What ugly turn?"

"Sorry, I presumed Mason would have told you."

"We don't live in each other's pockets, you imbecile!"

Harlan clenched his fists. This man was infuriating. He took a deep breath and related their latest job.

JD stared at Harlan, frozen in shock. "He found the dagger? In the keep?"

"*The* dagger? Yes. You knew about it?"

"Of course! I searched for it back in the 1800s. Dug half the damn grounds up and found nothing!"

Harlan could feel his mouth gaping open, both of them staring at each other in a ridiculous tableau. "You did? Why?"

"I was part of the search party." JD frowned and rubbed his head. "I can't remember the exact circumstances, but I'll give it some thought. I've been caught up in a few Templar-related treasure hunts. None of them ever yielded anything. They're sneaky buggers."

Why the hell hadn't he thought to ask JD sooner? As far as treasure and religious artefacts were concerned, of course JD would have been interested. "JD, anything you can remember will be immensely helpful. Ruling things out is imperative if we're to get ahead of the competition. We think Nicoli has contracted Mouse to steal the dagger. And, well, I'm sure you've heard about the explosions."

"That was Theo's place?"

"Yes. They blew up his hunting lodge."

"That bloody Masonic monstrosity? Good. But no, it wouldn't have been there. I was a member of a secret society for a while, you know. Well, a couple actually, at different times. Got tired of it. All that ritual, secret nonsense."

Harlan was struggling to find his words. "Unbelievable."

"Everyone of import seemed to be in one at some point, and probably still are. Powerful men get kicks out of secret knowledge. There's a certain crossover with alchemy, you know. Symbols, a hierarchy of knowledge, internal levels of initiation. Much like The Order of the Golden Dawn and The Order of the Midnight Sun."

"What was the group called?"

"The one I was in at the time of the treasure hunt was called The Order of Illumination."

"Are you for real?"

"Of course!"

"Are they still around?"

"Not that I know of. Our mission was the acquisition of knowledge, obviously, particularly pertaining to Templar wealth. But we combined it with religious knowledge—I was still trying to communicate with angels at that point. Of course, I had a completely different name."

Harlan sank down onto the closest chair. *That made perfect sense.* All the links between the organisations and aspirations of higher knowledge, and power. "Surely the freemasons and the Templars were about monetary acquisitions, though."

"Not always. Why do you think they coveted certain religious artifacts? Esoteric knowledge was important to them, and us. Although, obviously the Templars were before my time, they continued in one form or another."

"Including the Order of Illumination?"

"Oh, no. That was no old order. It was started by a member of the aristocracy in 1789."

Harlan wished he could read JD's mind. *On second thought, maybe not.* "What aren't you telling me?"

"Something is percolating at the back of my mind."

"Are you well-versed in Masonic and Templar symbology?"

"I was. I'd need a refresher."

"I'm sure Ash will work it out."

"Ah, yes. The Greek scholar." JD's eyes narrowed. "Who do you think the bomber is?"

"We don't know, but we doubt it's Nicoli."

"No. Too inelegant for that viper." JD ran his fingers across his lower lip. "I need to think on this. I'll call you if anything strikes me."

His eyes were clouded as he turned to the window, and effectively dismissed, Harlan left him to his thoughts.

It had taken approximately half an hour to walk around the village, and Nahum leaned on the lychgate that led into the churchyard, waiting for the chapel to be opened up. They had already strolled all around the graveyard after leaving Shadow and Gabe to investigate the inn, and Nahum and Niel were awaiting the arrival of the vicar after seeing a timetable on the main door.

"Well, it's slim pickings here," Nahum observed.

Niel grunted, shifting his weight against the stone pillar that was part of the lychgate, shadows from the plant-wrapped archway falling across his face. "When Theo said the village was small, he wasn't kidding. He's right about the church, too." He nodded at the old stone building at the end of the path. "It looks the same age as the castle. It's bigger than I expected, too."

"As befitting an English commander." Nahum studied the roofline. "It will have been refurbished. That looks like a new roof. I have trouble thinking anything could be hidden in that." Movement to his right caught his eye, and he saw the vicar cross the graveyard from another lane to the side. "There he is. Let's see if we can get in."

The vicar was making his way to the side entrance, and Nahum and Niel quickened their pace to reach him, arriving just in time to see him pushing his way through the heavy door. He was a trim man of medium height with a thatch of thick grey hair, who looked to be in his sixties. His eyes widened with alarm as his gaze swept over them. "Can I help you?"

Nahum extended his hand. "I'm Nahum, this is Niel. We're friends of Theo's from Temple Keep."

He visibly relaxed as he shook their hands. "Colin Roberts. Vicar of Temple Church, and a few of the surrounding churches, actually. Terrible business with the fire. Is Theo okay?"

"He's fine," Nahum reassured him. "But busy with the police and the fire investigation team. It was quite a shock—for all of us." Nahum looked down the side path and out to the lane, wondering if there was a vicarage they'd missed. "Do you live in the village?"

"No. In Bodiam. We rotate our services through the surrounding villages, however, and this Sunday the service will be here. I'm checking to make sure everything is in order." He grimaced. "Good timing, I think. The parishioners will be in need of support after the recent events."

"Indeed, they will." Niel nodded to the corridor beyond the open door. "We were hoping we could come in, Father. We're interested in the church's architecture."

"Really? You're men of God?"

Nahum nodded. "Of a sort. It's been a while since we've offered our respects. Being caught up in the events at Theo's has prompted our wish to be here today." *Not exactly a lie.*

"Of course. The Lord's house will always offer sanctuary and respite in troubled times. If you head to the main door, I'll open it up for you." He bobbed his head and smiled before heading inside.

Niel snorted as they walked to the main entrance. "Offer our respects! I hope you don't think I'll be doing *that*."

"Just be polite, at least!"

"Of course. Colin seems a perfectly nice man. Misguided, obviously, but I won't disillusion him."

"Good." Niel seemed more belligerent than usual. "What's got your goat?"

"Just the feeling that we're barking up the wrong tree. From what Theo has said, this area must have been researched a million times as regards to lost treasure. We're covering old ground."

"But with fresh eyes! And besides, we need to get an objective view of everything to move forward." Nahum lowered his voice. "Two bombs, Niel! Theo is on to something."

The door to the church opened before Niel could respond, and Colin welcomed them in, wedging the door open and allowing the sunshine to pour into the vestibule. "Welcome to Temple Church. It's a fine old building. A struggle to maintain, obviously, although Theo is a charitable donor." Colin led them inside, his arms thrown wide. "Isn't it beautiful?"

Nahum took in the rows of wooden pews, the soaring columns leading to a vaulted roof, the elaborate pulpit, and the ornate, stained glass windows. A large altar was at the far end, a towering cross above it, a choir area behind, and a small chapel to either side. A door to the right led to a private area, where Nahum assumed the side entrance was.

"We were saying outside," Nahum said, obviously impressed, "that it's bigger than we expected for a small village."

Colin smiled. "But it's a small village with a big history! The name says it all."

"Do you know much about the Templars?" Niel asked.

"The basics, just like everyone else, I guess. This was constructed by the de la More family at the same time as the keep, but it was added to in later years. Made more elaborate." He shrugged. "All of the men joined the Templars, you know, after they had produced a male heir."

Niel shook his head. "I didn't know that."

Colin nodded enthusiastically, walking down the nave, and they followed him. "The Templars only really wanted older soldiers who had already been married and were prepared to dedicate their life to the order, and poverty. William de la More was typical in that sense. He was a wealthy man, born into nobility, and followed the family tradition. The hamlet and this church were on the grounds for hundreds of years."

Nahum was confused. "So, William was older when he joined, which means he wasn't a Templar long. How did he get to be the master?"

"Oh no, he was with them for years. His wife died young, and he left the children in the care of his sister. All his lands were left to his oldest son. It meant that men like him had no distractions, were mature, and dedicated to the cause. Although, of course by the time William joined them, they were an order known less for the Crusades than their banking. William added to this place, too, you know, once he became the Grand Master."

Nahum looked at the church with renewed interest. "Really? What did he add?"

"The pulpit used to be simpler. He wanted something larger. And the altar was made bigger, too."

"Interesting." Did that mean he had concealed something?

"But you said he made a vow of poverty?" Niel asked.

"They all did. It was a condition of them joining. It was common that many Templars donated large amounts of money or land to the order, some even their entire property; other knights donated smaller amounts and passed on their wealth and property to family. Of course, this made the Templars as an organisation very rich, even though the individual knights were poor. On top of that, they banked other peoples' money and charged *rent*." Colin laughed. "Which meant interest, although they couldn't call it that. William was master for nine years. From 1298 to 1307. This building was added to in 1300." Colin turned and led the way to a small side chapel. There were half a dozen pews and a modest altar at the front. "This was the de la Mores' private chapel." He raised his eyebrows conspiratorially. "Not many know that, actually. We don't advertise it. It seems irrelevant. Catholic, of course, at the time. All of it was."

Nahum tried to quell his rising excitement. *Surely this new information meant something.* "Is it different in any way from the main church?"

"Not particularly. Simpler, of course, but intimate." He pointed to the heavy wooden door. "The family could shut out everything for private worship, although obviously would have joined the main congregation at Sunday Mass. William added the stained-glass window, too. It wasn't the original." The design was of a knight kneeling at the side of a horse, the Templar cross unfurling on a flag, a huge cross dominated the scene. "Simple, but beautiful."

"He did all this, despite his vow of poverty?" Niel repeated, clearly as confused as Nahum.

Colin shrugged. "Perhaps it was deemed Templar business. Or maybe it was done under the auspices of his family. His son was an adult by then, so it didn't reflect on William directly. You have to understand that records are scant to non-existent. However," he pointed up to the vaulted ceiling. "If you look closely, you will see Templar symbols are carved into the stonework."

Something else struck Nahum. "Was the entire village, keep, and church renamed, or was it always called Temple Moreton and Temple Keep?"

"Good question, Nahum! Yes, it was renamed, in honour of William. This hamlet was originally Moreton—'ton' actually means farm or hamlet—and the keep was Moreton Keep."

"Let me guess," Niel said dryly. "The Church was called Moreton Church."

"Our Lady of Moreton Chapel, actually. Then Our Lady of Temple Church. With the dissolution of the monasteries and all things Catholic being banned, it became just Temple Church. 'Our Lady' has strong Catholic overtones."

Nahum studied the church as Colin led them back into the main nave. Such division from Catholicism to the Church of England, and it all came down to divorce, power, and money. Money was never far from any decision. *But was there significance in the renaming and additions to the church, and was it anything to do with treasure?*

"Of course," Colin continued, "The Templars had many buildings and places named after them. Anything with the name 'Temple' in is undoubtedly linked to the Templars. We are certainly not unique."

Niel said, "We walked around the graveyard, but didn't see any graves that might have belonged to the family."

"Oh no, you won't." Colin laughed, his finger running along his white clerical collar. "They were landed gentry." He tapped the ground with his foot. "They are buried below us, in the crypt."

Nahum blinked with surprise, and tried to keep the excitement out of his voice. "There's a crypt? Is the whole family there?"

"I believe so. I confess, I haven't examined the place in detail. It gets cleaned a few times a year." As if anticipating their next question, he said, "We keep it locked, and do not allow the public to go down there. I'm not sure the stonework is that safe, really." Colin checked his watch. "If you don't mind, I really need to check on a few things for Sunday."

"Of course, but one more question," Nahum said quickly. "William de la More died in the Tower of London. Is he down there?"

"No, unfortunately. Only his predecessors and descendants. I can't quite recall when the last one was interred there, though." Colin's eyes narrowed. "This is no casual interest, is it? Is this about Templar treasure?"

"It's a recent interest of Theo's, that's all."

"And the fire? Is that related to this new interest?"

"Perhaps. A bomb was planted in Theo's lodge. Two, actually. He didn't make any secret of his new search. Not locally, anyway."

Colin's joviality vanished, his eyes hardening. "So, others are involved?"

"It seems so."

"I wonder..." For a moment, Colin didn't speak, and he stood in front of the main altar, staring up at the image of Christ on the cross, as if wrestling with something. Nahum exchanged another worried glance with Niel, but they waited silently. Something was troubling the vicar. After a few moments of silent contemplation, he turned back to them. "I think someone broke in here the other week."

"Why?" Niel asked. "Damaged locks? Something stolen?"

"Nothing. That's the thing, so I didn't report it. But things were misplaced. I popped in to pick up some vestments I had left here. The door to the vestry had been left open, and I always shut everything. There was also an unusual air to the place. Something different. I decided that perhaps the cleaner hadn't been as meticulous as usual, but then I found out she hadn't been in. She'd been sick. Never mind. I'm being paranoid."

Nahum had a sudden vision of the bomber sneaking around the church looking for the most likely spot to plant something. "Or perhaps not." He placed his hand on Colin's shoulder, turning him gently towards the door. "I think we should leave. *Now.*"

Nineteen

Barak studied the list they had printed out, a headache settling between his eyes. "This is gibberish."

"It's a code!" Estelle leaned over and kissed his cheek. "We'll work it out."

"We need a key for that, and we haven't got one."

"Yet!"

"You're enjoying this, aren't you?"

"It's a puzzle. I like puzzles."

"I'd rather be naked with you." He kissed her again.

"And you will be," she eventually answered when he released her. "But we need to get somewhere with this. It dictates where we go next!"

"Bed sounds good."

"You have a one-track mind."

"Only with you, Estelle." She smelled delicious. *Apples and honey. Like a pie.* He wanted to eat her up.

She pointed at the list, laughing. "Focus!"

They were in a small *gîte* south of Avignon that belonged to a business friend of Estelle's, and although it was nowhere near as grand as the *château* they had first stayed in, it was beautifully decorated in a rustic French fashion, and very intimate. It was also nestled deep within an olive grove, and while Barak would have preferred something with a view for safety purposes, the flipside was that it was hidden away. Fortunately, it was well supplied with a computer and printer, and they had printed off all the photos they had taken of the facility's office.

They had left the safehouse without any difficulties, and used a taxi to return to their hotel in Avignon. They had retrieved their belongings, left immediately in another taxi, and were dropped off to collect a new rental car from a different company. They hadn't dared risk retrieving the other one at the *château*, and Barak had phoned the company with a terrible excuse as to why they'd had to abandon the car.

"The trouble is," Barak said with a sigh, his attention returning reluctantly to their current problems, "is that whoever, or wherever these places are, they will have been alerted by now."

"Perhaps. But if these are big facilities, then they won't be able to shut down so easily. They'll just increase their security instead."

"Great! Even better!"

She poked him in the ribs. "Or, they will feel sufficiently safe with their code names and current security that they might not feel threatened at all."

"True. They haven't survived this long without being smart and taking precautions. But perhaps we're approaching this the wrong way. If we *are* right, and this is about old connections to the count, then we should cross-reference known places with these names. See if we can identify a link."

Estelle nodded thoughtfully. "That makes sense. Sort of reverse engineer it. It's worth trying."

"But have we brought anything about the count with us? I know I haven't. I travelled light."

"Me, too. But we have the internet. And Jackson. He can send us a list of what he's found so far, and we can start with that."

Barak checked his watch. "It will probably be a few hours before he can speak to us. He'll be busy with Lucien. We can buy a few books, though. I could do with familiarising myself with the count properly. I feel I need to sink into his mind, try to get a feel for the man we're pursuing. And it might distract me from worrying about my brothers, too."

His phone call with Niel had disturbed him. His brothers were well able to look after themselves, but it sounded as if they had run into another powerful enemy.

Estelle squeezed his thigh in an attempt to reassure him. "They'll be okay. Let's focus on our problems. You can always phone them again later."

He sighed, knowing she was right. And besides, he was too far away to help them. Instead, he looked to the bright sunshine outside, and the seating area beneath the trees. "That looks like the perfect spot."

"Coffee and croissants?"

"Even better."

He watched her easy sway of hips as she headed to the kitchen, and felt extremely content. He could get used to this. He just hoped that she could, too.

<hr />

Gabe stretched his long legs out in front of him, and studied the winding lanes surrounding The Knight's Rest, the inn in Temple Moreton, reflecting on the fact that you'd have to be an idiot not to know this place was connected to the Templars.

He lifted the coffee cup to his lips and sipped it. At least they made good coffee, not that he should be surprised. This might be a small village, but the inn had a reputation as a gastro pub, and there was a large car park to accommodate its visitors. Today, bathed in late August sunshine, it already had a fair number of people drinking coffee in its courtyard area.

The pub had originally had a stable block, and although it had been converted and built on over the years, parts of the building still looked like stables, with its long, low roof that had skylight windows built into it. Gabe was partial to good food and wondered if he should book a table there for him and Shadow. It would be nice to ditch his brothers for a few hours and spend some time alone with her. As big as the castle was, it was starting to feel crowded. He looked around, wondering if she'd managed to see anything interesting after she'd volunteered to scout the place out.

He spotted her sauntering around the side of the building, and within moments she was sitting next to him, a disgruntled look on her face as she reached for her coffee.

"No luck, I take it?" he asked her.

"Not really. There aren't any unusual symbols etched into beams, stonework, or anything else! The main dining area is deserted at this hour, but I passed through it on the way to the toilets and loitered. There's an old stone fireplace in there, but there are no tempting symbols at all."

"Not surprising, really. This place has been renovated to within an inch of its life. Nicely done, but anything original will have been extensively investigated years ago."

"And that's the trouble with this whole thing, isn't it?" Shadow sipped her coffee, her eyes sweeping the courtyard and customers. "Anything that has strong links with the Templars has been investigated by treasure hunters several times over, and no one has ever found *anything*."

"Not that's been publicly acknowledged. Who's to say it hasn't already been found, and is now in some very secure vault somewhere? But I don't actually believe that."

Shadow cocked her head at him. "Why not?"

"If treasure hunters had found it, they would have shouted about it."

"Would they? I wouldn't. I would have kept quiet and sold it off, bits at a time, on the black market. Or kept it in my own secure vault to admire at leisure."

He laughed. "Would you have rolled around in it?"

"Maybe. Probably naked. All that gold and jewels on my bare skin." She gave him an impish grin.

Images flooded his mind and ended in his jeans. "Behave. I'm in public." All she did was laugh, and he focussed on other things. "I've been trying to imagine what kind of treasure it is, though. They were, understandably for a religious order, obsessed with religious artifacts. What if they really did find the Ark of the Covenant or the Holy Grail? Or lost scrolls? Or magical books..." He trailed off, trying to imagine what else they may have found.

"Tell me again what the significance of the Ark of the Covenant is?"

"It contains God's ten commandments, written down by Moses on two stone tablets and encased in a wooden box, covered in gold."

"And was that in your time?"

"Yes. But I never saw them, or had anything to do with them. I was busy elsewhere." *Fighting.* He didn't need to say it. They both knew his history. "The Ark also contained Aaron's Rod, which is a walking stick with mythical properties, and *manna*—a food that can sustain someone over long periods. Now I did try that, and it was impressive. Designed by angels."

Shadow shrugged. "The gold part sounds interesting. Stone tablets, not so much."

"But if you were religious, and deeply devout, that would be quite something, right?"

"I guess so."

Gabe subdued a grin. *At least Shadow was refreshingly honest.* "But there are lots of relics from that time that the Templars might have looked for. Powerful weapons that we carried, for example, or books of power such as that which Raziel made. I mean, honestly, it's endless. They spent years in the Middle East, in all of those places where we lived, loved, and waged war."

"But like you said before, so much would be dust."

"But powerful objects have ways of hiding themselves and remaining annoyingly intact to wreak havoc later on. And gold doesn't disappear, or jewels."

"Thank Herne for that."

Gabe's brain ached with the possibilities. No wonder the Templar history and their fabled treasure had fascinated people for over seven hundred years. He was starting to see why. And powerful organisations didn't just disappear overnight. They just changed and adapted. However, before he could muse on it further, a fire engine and police car sped past them, and his phone pealed on the table.

Nahum.

Ash turned the knife over again, feeling the age in it, and wondered how he could unlock its secrets. He tried to banish all his pre-conceptions, and studied it with cold, analytical eyes.

A Damascus steel blade, double-edged, dull, and its edge blunt. Ceremonial then, not a weapon as such. The bone hilt was yellowed with age, but felt as hard as iron. It was inlaid with a selection of metals in a curling design that framed the symbols, with a row of small emeralds edging the base where it met the blade.

The symbols on the hilt had been burned into it. He could swear he scented the burnt odour of bone from its inscription, but knew that after all this time, he must be imagining it. The largest symbol was the image of two knights on one horse, a typical Templar image, but without writing around it. There was also the de la More family crest, the Star of David, and the cross and the crown. Nothing that remotely suggested where he should go next. Maybe this *was* just a ceremonial knife. It was certainly interesting, but perhaps that was all it was. He had tentatively pushed and prodded some of the symbols, but that was pointless. They were just engravings.

Theo called over from across the room where he sat in a shaft of sunlight. "I have a magnifying glass, if that helps."

"I'm worried I'll break it." He studied it again, turning it over in his hands, the bone warming beneath his touch. "The blade is Damascus steel, you know. That makes it one of the earliest examples. It must have cost a lot at the time. Never mind the emeralds and precious metals set into it."

Theo stood, rummaged in a drawer, and then handed him a small magnifying glass. "All it's worth to me is the information it contains. Why hide a ceremonial knife? I feel sure it means something."

Ash bent his head over it again, and then jerked in shock. "There *is* writing around the two men on a horse image. Herne's balls! It's tiny. I thought it was just an abstract pattern."

"You know what has just struck me," Theo said, almost breathlessly as he sank into the chair next to him. "The two knights on a horse symbol was never used as a seal in England. Only France. The Grand Masters here used the *Agnus Dei*. The lamb of God. Other countries had other seals."

Ash jerked up in shock, staring at Theo, the writing momentarily forgotten. "Is that right? Are you sure?"

"Very. It's what I've just been reading about. All the Grand Masters, or Grand Commanders, as they were also called, had a seal. They used the same seal always—no matter who was the commander. There might have been slight variations, but always *Agnus Dei* in England."

"So, the English commanders, no matter who it was, should have always used the *Agnus Dei*?"

"Yes." Theo rose from his chair, grabbed his book, and handed it to Ash as he sat again. "See? A lamb with a crossed foreleg and the cross. It has the cross of St George on it, too."

"Holy shit." Ash handed the book back and picked up the knife again. "Then this is significant. A sign. Either this isn't William's knife, and it has something to do with the French order, or the seal is a clue. But the fact that the family crest is there... The two men on a horse emblem denotes poverty, is that right?"

"Yes. It developed very early on in Templar history. It essentially demonstrates that the knights were so poor that they had to share a horse. I guess it also shows brotherly loyalty. However, one of the many Templar rules forbade two men on the same horse. They were, in actual fact, also allowed to own up to three. The image is just symbolic and does not reflect the truth."

Ash sat back, filtering through the information before finally looking at Theo. "We're on to something, Theo." He lifted the hilt and the magnifying glass again and moved to the window where the light was brighter.

Theo followed him, clasping his hands together almost in prayer. "Can you read it?"

"Not yet." Ash bent over the handle, hardly daring to breathe. Then the words floated into focus, and he realised they were Latin. "Two brothers, united under God." *What the hell did that mean? Two knights? A knight and his sergeant? Two masters?* He bent his head again, and noticed a deeper indentation around the seal than the other marks, and also down an inlaid metallic wavy line running along the length of the hilt, skilfully hidden within the other elaborate designs. He stared at Theo. "I'm going to try something. Something risky."

"Perhaps we should take photos first?"

"Yes, excellent plan."

Ash waited impatiently while Theo took photos, and then picked up Theo's fine-bladed letter opener. He ran it around the edge of the seal, clearing out centuries' old dirt, and exposing the seam even more. With great care, he pushed the seal down. When nothing happened, he hit it harder. Still nothing happened.

"Just whack it!" Theo said, equally impatient next to him.

"Wait!" Ash wanted to do this cleanly.

Earlier, Ash had used an oiled cloth to polish the hilt and blade, and he picked up the bottle of oil and dribbled some around the seal and along what appeared to be a seam. After waiting a few moments for it to soak in, he picked up a pen from the table, fitting the head of the pen neatly over the seal, and used the end of the magnifying glass like a hammer. He cracked it downward, and the seal clicked down. The curving seam that ran the length of the hilt along the silver and gold metalwork split open by mere millimetres.

Theo squealed like a child. "You did it!"

Hardly daring to speak, Ash inserted the fine blade of the letter opener into the seam and eased it open, exposing an ornate key beneath the bone hilt. It was carved from iron, and screwed to the blade.

"I've done *something*, Theo. But what does it open?"

Twenty

J ackson watched a security guard run another metal detector over Lucien's body, and then usher him through the scanner that looked like something you'd find in an airport.

It was a recent installation at The Retreat, and although Jackson resented having to pass through it every day, he had to admit that it made him feel safer.

Lucien lifted his arms obediently and spread his legs wide, and then stepped through at a nod from the guard. "All clear, Jackson."

"You know this is the fourth time I've been scanned," Lucien complained to everyone.

Jackson sighed as he led him down the corridor, four members of the extraction team marching behind them. "I was there every time. I know. But I told you it would happen. At least you're not blindfolded anymore."

Jackson finally felt himself relax, his shoulders loosening from the knots that seemed welded into place from his neck downwards. It had been a tense trip from France to The Retreat, all of them on alert for signs of attack. However, no one had followed them from the safehouse, and they had carefully travelled along main roads with lots of traffic to take them to the private airport. At that point, Lucien had been blindfolded until they stepped into The Retreat's corridors.

Now he looked around, curious at his surroundings. "This is impressive. Your base?"

"Yes, and your home for a while."

"And these men? They're staying, too?"

"For now."

"But you said I wasn't a prisoner."

"They're here to protect this place and those who work in it from you." Jackson's eyes swept over him. Lucien was still wearing the baggy green scrubs and Crocs from the facility, the short sleeves revealing the full range of tattoos on his skin. His sharp face and keen eyes gave him a dangerous air, and Jackson still wasn't sure how much to trust him. He was considering all options, including the possibility that he could be a plant who was activated by Barak and Estelle's unexpected arrival and suddenly put into action. On the journey, Jackson had mulled on the fact that his attempted escape had been suspiciously well-timed, and Jackson was wary of such things. But perhaps the Gods were smiling on them, for once.

A cynical curl of Lucien's lip preceded a snort. "Semantics."

"This is our headquarters. What do you expect? I want to trust you, but there's too much I don't know about you. Would you behave any differently?"

"Perhaps not." Lucien's expression was guarded, but his eyes still flitted everywhere, and Jackson suddenly had misgivings at ever bringing him here. But where else could he go? Not another safehouse...not yet, at least.

"Why are you wearing scrubs?"

"Barak stole them for me. I was in a surgical gown when I tried to escape."

Jackson nodded. Something else to check with Barak and Estelle. He should have asked more questions when he had the time, but everything was so unexpected.

Jackson turned down a side corridor that led to the labs and morgue, and opening a door, gestured him inside a room with a reinforced glass window, an observation room on the other side. "I won't be long."

The guards remained with Lucien while Jackson continued to Layla's medical suite.

She was already in her examination room, her equipment ready—camera, sample kits, and other things Jackson didn't recognise—and was wearing a white lab coat over her clothes. "He's here?"

"In the holding room. Look, I'm worried he might be a plant. I may be paranoid, but..."

"That's okay. I'll keep the guards handy and run lots of tests. I'll take samples of his tattoos too, compare them to the ones I took from James. What's your gut telling you?"

"That he's genuine, but I'm worried to trust my instincts right now. I don't know whether I'm coming or going. Barak and Estelle are convinced he's trustworthy. Said he was shot with a tranquilliser gun and out cold for hours."

"That's good to know. I'll run tox reports." Layla squeezed his arm reassuringly. "I'll chat with him while I work. I have a surprisingly good bedside manner. I'll get some background on him, too."

Jackson smiled and took a deep breath. "Thanks. I have the basics. Last known address, date of birth, full name. I'll see what I can find and let you know. I asked him about conversations he might have heard, but he denied hearing anything, really."

"I'll try again. He's been stressed, as well as drugged. It plays havoc with memory. How long are we keeping him here?"

"Great question. If we think he's untrustworthy in any way, then not long at all. But he could be a valuable asset. A way in. I guess we play it by ear."

"I want you to go home, Jackson. Sleep. Rest. You'll function better afterward. You have also had a big shock in the past day or so."

Jackson nodded, knowing she was right, but time was against him. "There's too much to do first."

"It can wait a couple of hours."

"I'm not sure it can. Be careful."

Jackson's steps quickened as he reached his office, but as he passed Waylen's open door, he heard a shout. "Jackson! You're back."

Jackson leaned on the doorframe, unwilling to step inside and be delayed even more. "Back, but shattered, and with plenty to check up on."

"I can see you're tired." Waylen was wearing his familiar suit and white shirt, and stood and rounded his desk, perching on the edge. "You did well, though."

"Let's hope so."

"You're not convinced?"

"I'm worried he's a plant." He outlined his fears, and then stifled a yawn. "I'm going to run background checks now."

"When was the last time you slept?"

"Maybe the night before last?"

"Then go home and sleep first."

"It will take too long. Barak and Estelle are out there, searching and going through code stuff—which they have hopefully sent to me by now. They risked their lives for this. I can't just sleep. And going home will take too long!"

"That settles it." Waylen headed back around the desk, rummaged in his drawer, then handed Jackson a key. "We're a small team. We work together. I may have put you in charge of this thing, but that doesn't mean I'm about to abandon you. Head down the west corridor, through another locked door. You'll find new sleeping quarters there. Grab the room you like; it's yours from now on—not that I expect you to use it often! List?" He held his hand out expectantly.

Jackson dug into the deep pockets of his long mac, finding sweet wrappers, bits of paper, and sticks of gum, before finally landing on his little pocket book. He pulled it out and ripped out Lucien's details. "These all need checking."

"Good. I'll do it now. Now go. Everything's fine here."

Jackson turned away, feeling his burden lifted. But a new heaviness now dogged his steps. Were Black Cronos searching for them? Was his home still a safe place to be? And worse, would he be living in The Retreat forever?

Twenty-One

It was a raucous dinner that night at Temple Keep, everyone interrupting each other's conversations, and Harlan could barely think straight.

All four Nephilim, Shadow, Theo, and himself, were seated in the informal dining room overlooking the moat, the sun low on the horizon. The atmosphere was a result of the elation of Ash's discovery, and the fact that they'd found another bomb.

"Seriously, guys," he remonstrated, shouting to be heard above the din, "can we all stop yelling? I can't hear a thing except Niel bellowing about bombs! We have a lead! What are we doing with it?"

Niel continued to grumble. "There's a lunatic bomber out there who could have wired a bomb to *anything*. I have every reason to moan! I like all of my limbs exactly where they are. And my ruggedly handsome face needs to stay that way."

Shadow spit her drink out, a spray of wine landing across the remnants of food on her plate. "Did you say that you were *ruggedly handsome*? Have you been reading soft porn or something?"

"I have a mirror, and women stare. A lot."

"Deluded women."

"The lady doth protest too much, methinks."

Gabe glared at him. "Which means what, Niel?"

"Which means that while she may have eyes only for you, she cannot be blind to this!" His hand swept around his face, as if presenting a work of art.

"I most certainly can be, you giant oaf," Shadow protested. "Talk to your hand, why don't you? Perhaps while you're thinking of Mouse!"

Did she mean what Harlan thought she meant?

Now Gabe glared at Shadow. "Seriously? Again? We're in company!"

Theo looked amused. "Don't mind me. I've heard worse around conference tables."

Nahum cocked his head at Niel, unable to hide a smirk. "At least we found the bomb before it went off this time. And I told you not to linger!"

"I took photos! I thought it was important!" Niel was belligerent.

"And," Gabe added, wagging his fork at Niel, "the whole house has been swept. There are no bombs in here."

Harlan massaged his forehead, feeling the tension behind his eyes. He'd grabbed a couple of hours sleep that afternoon after returning from JD's house, but it didn't seem to be helping. "Where was the bomb in the church?"

"In the pulpit," Nahum told him. "Wired to the top step."

"Shit. They meant to kill the vicar? That seems harsh!"

"Apparently," Niel said, rolling his eyes, "it wasn't a big bomb. Enough for a little scare. Like, oh, that's just my leg missing. I'll survive. Do you get my concern now?"

"I doubt it was meant for the vicar," Shadow said. She was twirling her dinner knife with the same dexterity as she twirled her daggers, and Theo was watching, mesmerised. "It was meant for us—or Theo. It was obvious we would have searched the church. I don't like being one step behind."

"At least it gives us a timeframe for the bombs," Harlan said. "It crossed my mind that they could have been planted a while ago, but if the vicar comes here every month, then that can't be the case."

Nahum nodded. "Excellent point, which suggests Theo finding the dagger has triggered everything."

"And now we have the chance to be ahead," Ash told them. "We just have to work out what the key opens."

The dagger was on the table, now in three pieces—the hilt, the blade, and the key that had been unscrewed from a slim metal shaft atop the blade.

"Yes, so easy." Shadow gave him a side-long glare.

Ash continued regardless, but he looked edgy. "We just have to be smart. I've been thinking on those symbols all afternoon, and I have a theory. It's a leap, but possible."

"Do you want a drumroll?" Niel asked.

Ash ignored him. "The symbols are the key. The family crest clearly links the knife to William de la More. But here at Temple Keep? Or at an older family estate—which is where? Does it even exist anymore? Where was he buried? Is that even useful?"

"He wasn't buried at the local church," Nahum said. "But as I mentioned earlier, there is a crypt containing other family members. I'm not sure how many, though. The vicar said it was unsafe, and the public weren't allowed down there. Something to investigate later, perhaps."

"I confess, I never knew about that," Theo said, looking vexed.

"Clearly it's something they don't wish to advertise," Gabe mused.

Ash jotted a note down. "I'll think on that. Which brings me to my next point. The writing around the seal: 'Two brothers united under God'. I thought it might be like a brotherhood, meaning two knights. But it could mean two actual brothers. Did William have a brother? Or did he have two sons?"

"We can check in the family crypt," Theo said.

"Exactly. But more intriguing is why is the Star of David, a Jewish symbol, on the knife hilt?"

Gabe shrugged. "Would it be something to do with Jerusalem, and the Temple Mount where the Templars stayed for a while?"

"Perhaps, but that was well before William's time. But I've had another idea. You won't like it. The Star of David is also the alchemical sign meaning 'as above, so below'."

Harlan was so shocked that he fumbled his fork and it clattered against his plate. "Goddamn it, Ash! That's not funny."

"It's not meant to be." Ash's golden-brown eyes were deadly serious. "What if that's another clue to what the key leads to? Something alchemical. The Templars were all over the Middle East, north Africa, Europe. They were avaricious in their search for powerful objects—usually religious, but not always. The other clue is the emeralds around the base of the hilt." He stared around the table meaningfully.

Gabe groaned, dropping his head on the table, and Theo looked at him and then the rest of them in shock. "What?"

It took Harlan a moment to catch on and then his eyes widened. "You think it's the Emerald Tablet of Hermes Trismegistus. The actual *original* tablet?"

"It's possible, right?" Ash said.

Nahum frowned. "But everyone knows what it says! Translations are available, and have been for years."

"But they aren't the original tablet." Ash pushed his plate aside and pulled his notebook towards him. "The text is available in multiple languages, both shortened and longer versions. It's cryptic and odd. But the phrase, 'That which is above is like to that which is below, and that which is below is like to that which is above,' comes from that document. From my admittedly limited understanding, it underpins all alchemical principles." He picked up the hilt, which opened like a book on tiny hidden hinges. "It has emeralds on it. Why emeralds, out of all the gems you could pick?

It's a sign. The original document is thought to be inscribed on actual emerald—hence the name. It could contain all sorts of coded messages."

A horrible fear settled in Harlan's stomach, and from the grim look on Ash's face, he hadn't shared all of his thoughts. Harlan huffed, thinking of JD's news that he had yet to disclose. "You think other alchemists are after this? Is this Black Cronos again? The count?"

"Oh, fuck! Don't tell me it's *them* again!" Niel was red-faced and furious. "I came here for a treasure hunt, not to fight some bomb-wielding Black Cronos mercenary!"

"Let them come!" Shadow said. "I relish it."

"Slow down!" Ash held his hand up. "I have been reviewing a few things this afternoon. The Count of St Germain was known to be involved in many things. We believe he is behind Black Cronos, but we don't know for sure. Barak and Estelle's progress suggests that yes, it looks more likely. But the count was also linked with several secret societies. The Freemasons, the Templars, the Rosicrucians, the Illuminati, and more. Rumours? Perhaps. Can we discount them? No." His fingers drummed the table. "A lot is made of the Templar trials, and with good reason. Many were arrested, tortured, and tried. Some were burned at the stake. But the majority of knights, sergeants, and others were absorbed into other orders, or their orders changed names. Their knowledge would have been passed down. Maybe the count was in an order that was once the Templars. In Portugal, a place he was suspected to be a native of, the organisation literally just changed names. What if the count diversified, and has several groups running?"

Nahum had a resigned expression on his face as he leaned his chin into his left hand, his right resting on his wine glass. "I reluctantly admit, there is a certain logic to that. He has his experimental, alchemical branch and a treasure-seeking branch."

"No way!" Harlan looked around at the mix of expressions—resignation, excitement, belligerence, wariness, and just plain baffled. He was well aware he needed to share JD's news, but couldn't with Theo there. They'd probably said too much already. "We're paranoid—for good reason—but not everything comes back to our old friend. However, Ash, you could well be right about another Templar organisation that still keeps watch for news of lost treasure. They would be very motivated to reclaim what they would see as theirs."

"But," Shadow countered, "if it was theirs, wouldn't they know where it was anyway?"

"Not necessarily." Ash leaned forward, warming to his subject. "In France there was a finite amount of time to hide gold and treasure. England, Portugal, and Spain had a little longer. But they all had to move quickly. Suddenly, kings they'd had good relationships with for years were put in precarious positions by the pope and King Philip the Fourth of France. They had an agenda. They wanted Templar money and their power. So, the Templars put plans into place, and treasure and money were hidden. But we all know how things get lost, or clues get convoluted over time. Wars interfere, changes of governments, popes—you name it. The dissolution of the monasteries here in England, perhaps. Especially if the treasure was split up. All these years later, maybe the descendants of the Templars are as confused as everyone else. Prepared to follow up every lead—and this is a good one."

"They're our bombers," Gabe said with a grim certainty.

"I would put money on it."

Theo took a large sip of wine, and his hand seemed to shake, but seemingly more from excitement than worry. Harlan had seen that look on his face before. "My God. An actual secret Templar organisation is here, in Temple Moreton, searching for *that*!" He pointed at the key.

"No." Shadow shook her head. "They are looking for what that opens—or what's on the other side of what that opens. And let's face it. They like bombs. Who says they need a key?"

"If they want what is beyond it to be intact, they won't use a bomb," Ash reasoned.

Gabe reached for the wine bottle and topped up his drink, as if preparing for a long discussion. "Then we need to make a decision. Where do we go next?" He glanced over at Niel and Nahum. "The church?"

"Unlikely, despite the bomb," Niel said. "But we could go back after dark and check it out properly. Colin, the vicar, pointed out some Templar designs carved into the stonework close to the roof."

Gabe nodded. "That's a good idea. Despite Colin's doubts, we shouldn't rule it out."

"The other ideas I want to explore," Ash said, "are why use the seal of the two knights on horseback. I feel sure there's a message concealed in there. And it's a Damascus steel blade. Could that be a clue?"

"But the key is made from iron, right?" Niel asked.

"Yes."

"I can help follow up some things," Theo said, eager to help. "I can look at William's family and associate knights. Try to work out what 'Two brothers under God' could reference."

Ash smiled at him. "That would be really useful. Thanks, Theo."

"I have something to share," Harlan said, topping his own glass up. He looked at Theo apologetically. "I'm afraid it's a bit sensitive, Theo, and this feels really rude, but..."

Theo held his hand up. "I understand, although I admit to feeling a little aggrieved. I'll head back to my study and continue my research."

"Thank you." Harlan felt horrible. He had imposed himself on Theo, and now thrown him out of the discussion, but his news was important. He waited until the door had shut behind him and Theo's footsteps had faded down the corridor. "I had an intriguing discussion with JD earlier. He said he was a member of a secret society in the 1800s, before he got sick of it all. He was part of the group that searched these grounds back then. The same search outlined in the diary by Lady Madeleine Montgomery."

A stunned silence fell around the table, before Ash finally spoke. "JD was part of that search? Why didn't we know this before?"

"He didn't know what was happening here. He only vaguely knew about the bomb. He lives in his own world, you know."

Gabe muttered something unintelligible under his breath, his jaw clenching. "Has he any useful insights?"

"Not so far. Just that they searched everything and found nothing." Harlan grimaced as he apologised. "I guess it was a long time ago. He also says he's rusty on Templar symbology."

"Well, that just proves what a shit search they did," Niel pointed out. "They missed the dagger!"

Nahum shook his head, amused. "Well, this just gets weirder by the minute. I guess if JD can offer some useful insights, then great, but essentially we now have a clue—a big one—that they didn't. We need to follow that and not get distracted by anything else."

"Exactly," Shadow agreed. "I've experienced more than one treasure hunt that became confusing because of too many details. We have to remain focussed. Forget the bombs and previous searches, and all of that tedious information about Templar politics."

"We can't forget *everything*," Gabe reminded her. "We have an unknown thief who was on the grounds last night, and a bomber who may well be part of an old Templar organisation who is prepared to kill to get their way."

"But who they are," she argued, "doesn't matter. We just need to be better than them."

Gabe turned to Harlan. "What was the name of JD's secret society?"

"The Order of Illumination." He glanced around the table. "Does that ring a bell with anyone?" There was a general shaking of heads. "Okay. So, what now? What can I do to help?"

"We split up and follow what little clues we have," Gabe said decisively. "Niel, I think you should keep watch for our intruder. If it's Mouse, you seem to have a connection."

Niel mock saluted. "On it. I'll set up where I think she came in last night. Nahum and I searched the grounds again this afternoon, and found a likely spot where she climbed over the wall. I'll find a place to hole up."

"Good. Nahum, are you okay to search Temple Church? I think those symbols are worth investigating, as well as the crypt. Harlan, want to go with him?"

"Sure. I *love* crypts." He turned to Nahum. "Okay with you?"

"Happy to have help."

"Shadow," Gabe said, "you're with me. We'll search the old potting sheds here. According to the plans, they would have been the old stable block. I'm wondering if that seal with the two knights and the horse could have another meaning."

"It's worth exploring. I," Ash said, rising to his feet, "will join Theo for yet more research."

Shadow stood, too. "Should any of us be searching for errant knights with bombs?"

"Maybe that's something we should all do," Gabe said, as chairs scraped back and everyone prepared to leave. "I guess they must be here, somewhere. Watching and waiting. We need to be careful."

As Harlan joined Nahum, he wondered if staying in London might have been his safest option.

Twenty-Two

E stelle stretched out on the rug and gazed at the stars that were just beginning to appear. The sun had dropped below the horizon, and twilight was thickening, especially at the *gîte*, surrounded by olive groves.

Barak was next to her, hands behind his head as he too looked at the sky. They had both been struck by apathy and despondency, caused by their lack of progress and the events of the day before that were catching up with them.

Barak rolled onto his side, head propped on one hand to look at her. "What are we going to do? None of this list makes any sense to us!"

"Yet." She turned to look at him. "They're not stupid. They wouldn't give obvious names that anyone would make a connection with, but I'm sure we'll work it out. Tiredness doesn't help us think. Besides, Jackson may have a breakthrough."

"I think my brain is stuck in a rut. All we do is circle the same old things."

Estelle nodded, staring at the stars again, and letting her thoughts drift. "We're not thinking like they are. Or like he is. The *comte*. We need to put ourselves in his shoes."

Barak huffed as he also settled on his back again, hands behind his head once more. "I don't think I can. Or want to."

"We have to. We need to focus on what the count wants. What he's trying to achieve."

"The perfect warrior, created with alchemy. Or the perfect enhanced human."

"But isn't it more than that?"

Estelle fell silent as the stars became brighter against the backdrop of the night sky. She stared at them, thinking of astrology, the planets and their correspondences, and how practitioners of alchemy and magic saw connections in everything. As a witch she experienced these connections every day, and almost took them for granted, they came so naturally to her. She could feel her connection with the unseen energy of the world even stronger now that she was spreadeagled on the earth, relishing the hum of ancient magic in the soil.

Earth, air, fire, water—the fundamentals of life and the profound connection with the psyche could not be separated. Water was in the air and the earth, it ran through humans, animals, and plants. Air carried water and the heat of the sun, and the sun's heat penetrated the earth and enabled everything to grow. Within the earth were precious metals and crystals, birthed by the planet's energies. She could feel it all, a web that couldn't be broken. Her strength was fire, but it didn't mean she wasn't connected to the other elements. It was impossible not to be connected. The psyche drew it all together, and for some, like Alex, the White Haven witch, they saw beyond this realm and into the next. Other worlds, where spirits and demons walked. And the Nephilim. That's where they had been for millennia. She glanced at Barak, who was lost in his own thoughts.

The elemental energies were all around her. It just took a moment to feel for them. It wasn't hard. What was hard was manipulating them. That needed power that only a few had. Like she'd told Lucien, she had been born with it. But it took practice to hone her skills and maintain them. For men like JD and the *Comte de Saint-Germain*, and many other men and women like them, they had no natural abilities. For them, it was decades of hard work. And they needed power to draw on for that. They desired to master the elements. Her thoughts focussed, penetrating beyond that. She and other witches wielded power, and manipulated it through spells and complex language. It was a type of creation. She was in a sense no different to alchemists. But, perhaps while she accepted magic and her ability to use it, it seemed that alchemists—or some of them, at least—tried to see beyond that. To find the language of creation.

"Barak," she said, turning to him again, propping her head on her hand. "You're a Nephilim, the son of a Fallen Angel. Do you believe that the language of a God or angels is written in our DNA or, I don't know, *everything*? I read about that somewhere."

"Herne's horns, Estelle! That's a big question!" He mirrored her actions and turned to face her again. "Why? Do you?"

"No, actually. Not like *the* God. Yours. I'm not a creationist. I firmly believe that magic is everywhere, and it has nothing to do with Gods. They're a part of it, not the cause of it."

"Interesting." His eyebrow lifted. "Why would I believe any different?"

"Because of who your father is. I'm trying to think how an alchemist does. Like JD, who studied the language of angels. They are seeking the language of creation. To become one with the universe. To see beyond the mechanics of it, I suppose. Is that possible?"

He grinned. "I love that you have just asked me that insanely big question! Like I'd know the answer!"

She prodded his chest and wished she hadn't. It was like pushing solid rock. "But your father was an angel—at the right hand of your God. You pursued the Book of Raziel, that was supposedly the foundational grimoire."

"*One* of them. And I didn't, actually. I was stuck at home—thankfully. Sounded like a bloody nightmare. But no, my father was no one's right hand. He was part of an army of angels. They exist on a different plane, and by the sound of it after what the Igigi said, they are stuck in it."

"But they aren't corporeal," she persisted.

"No, they are light and energy. But I guess it's fair to say that they tap into the fundamental elements of our existence. Don't ask me how, though. As you know, my father has healing skills, but was far more interested in destruction."

Barak rarely spoke of his father. He never appeared tense about him, just resigned, and somehow dismissive. "But Nahum said he could show remarkable kindness when he chose to heal."

"Probably for an ulterior motive, like them needing to keep fighting. But," Barak smiled, "maybe I'm being harsh. He wasn't a father figure...not how people expect one to be."

"Well, I guess we both share that experience."

"Where's this going, Estelle? Angels are just another paranormal creature, like we are—maybe with better connections. Some of us have more strength than others, or different strengths."

"I'm just trying to fathom the count's motives."

"I think it's simple, and it's something I've talked about a few times with my brothers. He—like JD—wants to harness the power of creation, to position himself as a God. He's trying to crack a formula. But you know what? It's too big. The formula is too great and varied, and ancient, powerful magic beyond what we can ever fathom, is behind it all. The Green Man conjured Ravens' Wood out of thin air!"

Estelle was baffled. "What are you talking about? Ravens' Wood in White Haven is ancient woodland, and has been there for millennia. I remember playing in it as a child."

Barak smiled enigmatically. "That's what he wants you to believe. But according to Shadow—poof! Came out of nowhere."

Estelle felt dizzy and confused, her mind at war with itself. "When?"

"At Imbolc. This year."

"Impossible."

"And yet, it happened. I remember it being here when I arrived. But it actually wasn't. So, my point is, the alchemists can all try as much as they want. They will only ever achieve a portion of what the Gods can do. They will never tap into ancient magic. *Never.*"

Estelle pushed aside the endless questions she had on Ravens' Wood, and focussed on the count. "But he's had success, of a sort."

"Of course he has."

"So, bear with me. Have you seen JD's lab?"

"No, why?"

"I just wondered about his grid of correspondences. You know, that enormous, complex wheel that Harlan and Shadow talked about."

"Where he manipulated weapons and tried to experiment on poor Harlan? I remember. No, I haven't seen it."

"So, as you've just said, JD is an alchemist, and so is the Count of St Germain. But they don't have real magic like witches, or the innate magic that you or Shadow have. They have to force nature to work for them. That's why the creation of a superior being is so hard."

"But we couldn't create an enhanced human, even with our natural magic. Mine is limited. Yes, I have wings and can speak any language, living or dead, but I can't wield the elements. Neither can Shadow. And *you* couldn't create a super being, either. Or could you?"

"No, actually, I couldn't. And wouldn't want to, either."

"But if you did," he asked, shuffling to get comfortable, "how would you do it?"

"I have no idea! I suppose I would have to create a spell to do it, but that would be incredibly complex. I wouldn't even know where to begin."

"Exactly. Because it's ancient, powerful magic beyond our ken, mixed with generations of adaption and change."

"But I guess," she reluctantly admitted, "that is partly what the count has done. Which brings me to my point. The metals ground into tattoo ink, for example, to create the metallic skin and weapons that seem to spring from nowhere. They must be activated somehow. The count must have a bigger alchemical correspondence wheel...or something of the sort."

Barak nodded. His expression, barely visible in the dim light, looked thoughtful. "So, it would need to be man-sized or something bigger. And," he added, his voice quickening with excitement, "he would need to power it somehow, like in the cave beyond Mithras Temple."

"The Dark Star Chamber. Yes. That had rudimentary batteries." Estelle shuddered at the thought. She could still feel the enormous power that she'd drawn on and that had almost killed her. The mere thought of it made the fine hair on her arms rise off her skin. "The power you broke before it consumed me. Did I ever thank you properly for that? You saved my life."

He leaned forward and kissed her. "And I would do it again in a heartbeat. I've read *Frankenstein*, you know. It was like Dr Frankenstein's lab. He animated the creature with lightning."

"You see, that's what I mean! I think he's based his giant wheel—if that's what he's got—at a centre of enormous power. Like a ley line or something!"

"That's an intriguing thought. But the lab we raided wasn't on one."

"Have we checked? Maybe it was! Or, maybe it didn't need to be. It seemed to be a preparation station." Estelle started to feel excited and sat up. "We think Black Cronos has a spider's web of places, but a spider's web has a centre. There can't be many places where they would complete whatever they do to make their superhumans. And maybe they do other things there!" She shrugged, putting aside questions about the existence of the universe and the powers of the Gods. "Whatever. The count needs power to draw on. Huge power. That's what we need to search for."

"Places where power gathers. Like stone circles and ley lines." Barak sat up, too. "That is definitely worth investigating. But the code names?"

"Maybe they will make more sense once we look into this." She stood and extended her hand. "Come on. Time to search the internet again."

Twenty-Three

T he shadows were long beneath the trees behind the walled garden when Niel started to search for a place to hide and watch
for their intruder.

This area was far more open than the wood, the trees placed further
apart. In fact, he realised as he strolled through them in the evening
gloaming, they were all fruit trees. A mixture of apple, pear, plum, and
cherry varieties. He hadn't noticed that when he was there earlier with
Nahum, after they had escaped the tedium of the bomb squad and
the encounter with the irate Detective Inspector. Then they had been
preoccupied with where the intruder had exited the grounds—and
where he or she might enter again.

Trust Theo to have his own orchard. Fruit was hanging ready, and come
September, he imagined the kitchen would be in a frenzy of storing for the
winter. He sighed. He used to have orchards. In the spring, the air would
be rich with the scent of blossoms, and if he narrowed his eyes, he could
imagine how this orchard would look, thick with pink and white flowers.
It made him slightly homesick, but he shook it off. He wasn't here to dwell

on the past. As his brothers had annoyingly pointed out, he was prone to it.

Instead, he focussed on his quarry. He was well aware that Mouse, if that's who it was, may not come back that night, or might even search for another place through which to enter Temple Keep's grounds. Sections of the wall had hedges alongside it, and large tree branches overhung some parts. He had climbed one earlier to view the country lane on the other side with a narrow verge full of wild flowers.

Now he paused, inhaling the rich, grassy scent that was magnified by the warmth of the evening, and searched for the part of the boundary wall they had spotted earlier. It was accessible because of the slightly bulging bricks at the base, distended by tree roots. Seeing it to his right, he headed to the closest tree with the thickest branches, and climbed high into the canopy. He scrambled around the central trunk until he found the perfect spot. A large branch, smothered in overhanging leaves, that offered a good place to see a large portion of the boundary.

As he eased his back against the trunk, his legs bracing against the branch, he considered Mouse's almond eyes. In their brief, but memorable, encounter, he'd shared a kinship. Maybe that word was too strong. *A connection.* He liked her. He'd imagined what she might look like without her black balaclava. Hopefully, in a few hours, he might not have to wonder anymore.

Even better, perhaps he could persuade her to work *with* them.

Shadow placed her hands on her hips as she stared at the potting sheds.

"I can't believe this is my Friday night! At least if it was still a stable, there'd be horses here." She was missing Kailen, and his familiar scent.

"Well, I was planning on wining and dining you at The Knight's Rest, and then thought, Shadow doesn't care about that! She'd love to search for Templar treasure instead!"

She turned to look at Gabe. His right eyebrow was raised, and his lips were twisted in an annoying smirk that she wanted to wipe right off his face. "I would be excited if I thought we'd actually find any. Instead, I'm going to stink of compost and old wellington boots."

"Sexy."

"Funny."

"I tell you what." He leaned in, nuzzling her neck, his hands sliding over her hips. "I'll help you wash every single bit of compost smell off you later. Deal?"

"Only if you let me run my hands through your deliciously thick feathers."

His eyes darkened to a stormy black and he almost growled. "Deal."

Teasing him, she pulled away, and sashayed to the main doors that were locked for the night. She turned back, pleased to see him watching her hips. "Come on, then. Our bath awaits."

Using the key Theo had provided them, she unlocked the door, progressed into the dark interior of the shed, and flicked the light on. It threw the shelves, work surfaces, and rows of gardening implements into stark relief. Interconnected rooms marched away on either side of them. Nothing looked remotely intriguing. "This is a seriously massive waste of time."

"We don't know that unless we check thoroughly. We barely glanced at the place when we were here earlier. According to the oldest plans Theo has, this building looks virtually unchanged—except for the interior layout, of course. The foundations are the same and could hide a tunnel or something. I mean, look at the ancient stonework." He walked over to the back wall mostly hidden by shelving and stacks of pots, and crouched to move them, exposing the base. "That is old, thick stone. Some of the walls look as if they have been repaired. These do not."

Shadow studied his vaguely hopeful expression. "You're not convincing me, or yourself."

"Shadow. Please. The two knights on horseback have to signify something. This was a stable block. It's also close enough to the house that they might be connected in some way." He pointed to either side. "The interior walls look more recent, but we have to check everything. Even the stone slabs on the floor. There could be symbols in the stonework."

"Did they sweep for bombs in here?"

"Yes. I checked and double checked."

She huffed. "All right. We may as well get this over with. I'll start at the other end, where we found Malcolm."

⚜

Nahum stood with his hands on hips in the middle of Temple Church's main nave. It was dark, with only a few stripes of light from a distant street light illuminating the interior.

"So, where do we start? The unstable crypt or the symbols?"

"Let's leave the most exciting part until last, shall we?" Harlan's drawl was unmistakably sarcastic. "Let's start with the symbols."

"Not thrilled at searching through old tombs?"

"The last time that happened, I was being pursued by zombies."

Nahum grinned. "Ah, yes. Old Haven Church. That was fun."

"So. Much. Fun. And the last time I was in a church, Jackson was hanging me upside down by my ankles over the pulpit."

"Well, the advantage of wings is that I can handle all of that."

"Good." Harlan flicked his torch on and aimed it down at the floor, shielding it with his hand. "Are you sure the door is locked behind us? I don't want a crazy, errant knight sneaking up on me."

"You could have stayed with Ash and Theo, you know. I can manage alone."

Harlan cocked his head at him. "Okay, I'll shut up and just get on with it. I'll start in the family chapel."

Nahum stretched out his wings, glad that the main nave of Temple Church was a good size. "In which case, you'll find me up there."

The vaulted stone roof comprised of a series of arches sweeping out of pillars. Templar symbols as well as traditional church carvings dotted the stonework, especially where the arches intersected with the pillars. Nahum spotted several Green Man carvings, not uncommon in churches, as well as a variety of Templar crosses, a couple of *Agnus Deis*, and a carving of two knights on horseback again.

He briefly considered whether he should touch any of the carvings, seeing as the bomb squad could hardly had examined up here, but that also meant it was unlikely their adversaries could have planted a bomb, either. Besides, these were grubby from centuries of grime and dust and clearly hadn't been tampered with. He worked his way methodically around the entire roof, pushing and pulling, but nothing budged.

Exhausting the roof, he joined Harlan, finding him on his hands and knees under the stained glass window in the private chapel. "Find anything?"

Harlan stood up, turned his torch off, and dusted off his knees and hands. "Actually, yes. I kept thinking about the fact that this stained glass image is the French seal." They both stared up at it, able to see it relatively clearly because of the streetlights outside. The colours were muted, but still visible. "I know it's a traditional Templar sign, but why not put the *Agnus Dei* into stained glass? Why this? It makes me think that like the symbol on the dagger's hilt, this must mean something."

Nahum nodded. "That actually makes a lot of sense. The image is different, though. Only one knight is on the horse, the other is kneeling."

"I know, right? Does that mean something, too?"

"I saw the two-knight image carved in the ceiling, but it was solid. They all were. Nothing budged, no matter how much I tried to move them. Why were you looking at the floor?"

"The stone slabs are a slightly different size under the window. They're bigger than the rest of the floor. Not obviously so, but..."

Nahum studied the ground, comparing the slabs as he paced across the floor. "Herne's balls. You're right. But, could it just be because they edge the outer wall?"

"Maybe. But the different image, and the stone slabs... It bothers me."

"Any other important symbols here?"

"Nope. I've poked around the altar, and inspected the slabs. There's nothing on them, either. Unless age has completely erased them, or the pews obscured them." He pointed upwards. "That's the only part I couldn't manage."

"I can do that," Nahum said, already flexing his wings. "After I've checked here, I'll move on to the other small chapel. Think you can check the ground floor of the main nave for me? I want to exhaust everything up here before we find the crypt. If there is something hidden in here, the trigger for it must be somewhere else." He scanned the family chapel again, a prickle of unease sliding down his spine. "Now that I'm here again, at night, in the dark, I feel the press of years here. Secrets. I dismissed this place earlier. Now, I'm not so sure."

Harlan slapped his shoulder. "I hope you're right, my friend. Frankly, if I'm going to spend hours of my life in here getting covered in dust and shit, I want it to be worth something."

And with that, he strode away, leaving Nahum to his thoughts.

Theo's voice jolted Ash out of his contemplative study, and he looked up, bringing himself out of the dusty Templar past with its secrets, murky politics, and betrayals, to the present.

"Two brothers. It could refer to William's two sons." Theo tapped the page. "I found a passing reference in one of these history books, and Lady Madeleine mentions them, too. Apparently, there was a lot of interest in the crypt below Temple Church when the Order of Illumination searched for the treasure."

"He had two sons?"

"The heir and the spare. And one daughter."

Ash leaned back in his chair, his own research temporarily forgotten. "And they're in the crypt?"

"Yes. But nothing remotely resembling treasure, or the clue to treasure, was found there."

"Damn it." Although he couldn't say as much to Theo, he felt sure JD would have been thorough. "I need to keep searching for clues to William's burial. He has to be somewhere. Even though he died in the Tower, he would have been respectfully laid to rest."

"Could he have been buried in the Tower grounds?"

"Perhaps. But from everything I have read, that was reserved for those who were killed there. He died of natural causes."

Theo headed to a side cabinet, pulled out two cutglass tumblers, and offered Ash a drink. "Whiskey?"

"Perfect. Are you sure you haven't missed any hidden rooms in the castle over the course of your renovations?"

Theo handed him the glass and stood at the leaded windows overlooking the grounds. The heavy damask curtains had been left slightly open, but in the lamplight, Ash could see nothing beyond their own reflections.

Theo shook his head. "I can't be one hundred percent sure, obviously, but I'm as sure as I can be. We stripped walls back, left some stonework on show, plastered over others. Other than the priest hole, which was obviously a later addition, and the compartment in the cellar wall, it has revealed only old fireplaces which were bricked up or made smaller. Oh, and the pantry off the kitchen had a false wall, but when we knocked that down, we found nothing exciting."

"It's accessible now?"

"Yes, of course. But we pulled up the old floor and laid a new one. There was nothing there."

"Not even in the old fire surrounds?"

"'Fraid not."

"Damn it!" Ash took a sip of the smooth malt whiskey, thinking of what Shadow had said earlier. "It's easy for Shadow to say we need to dismiss all the other history and conjecture, but it's not that simple. William had two knights who he stayed in close contact with, even after his arrest. What if the knights on horseback refers to them? They're two brothers of a different sort!"

Theo didn't answer, lost in his own thoughts, and Ash fell silent, too. It was easy to let his thoughts drift to the past in the ancient keep. As he sipped his whiskey, he imagined what the castle would be like when it was first built. The oldest part of the keep, the tower and the square building attached to it, had small windows throughout, including in this study, which was on the second floor of the tower. The light would have been dim, the candles and oil lamps providing scant light. Fires would have blazed for most of the year. Sweet-smelling rushes mixed with herbs would have covered the floors, and servants would have scurried everywhere. Trusted servants who would have been well paid, perhaps, to keep their silence in a castle owned by several generations of Templars. The moat would have sealed them all in, keeping them safe from attack. Except it couldn't really, because it was only on one side.

He circled back to the images on the hilt. The family crest. The two knights on horseback. The cross and the crown. The Star of David—or the alchemical symbol, as he thought of it now: *as above, so below.*

"Theo, what's beneath the oldest part of the keep? Is that where the cellar is?"

"No, that's under the east wing of the castle. The later addition. It was built over what was the other half of the moat."

"So the moat went all the way around, originally?"

"Yes, but it hasn't for hundreds of years. That's why the cellars are so deep under the east wing. They used the old moat. Then they refilled the remaining part that you can see now."

"So, what's under the keep and original hall?"

"A square, very dank hole of nothingness. You can access it through the laundry room."

"Nobody builds a dank hole of nothingness for no good reason, Theo." Ash drained his whiskey and stood up, grabbing the bone hilt and placing it in his pocket.

"Now?" Theo's moustache quivered with horror. "It's horrible down there. Probably flooded. I haven't been down there in years. The builders cemented the slabs in."

"Then we'll just have to break through them." Ash suppressed his impatience. "Do you want to find this treasure or not?"

"Yes."

"Then we have to search it." Not knowing what they might find, Ash strapped on his sword that was placed on a chair.

Theo had nervously glanced at it earlier, but ignored it. Now he clearly couldn't resist asking, "Why do you carry a sword?"

Ash laughed in an attempt to make light of it. "It comforts me. It's a family thing. I've had fencing lessons for years."

"That's hardly a foil." He cocked an eyebrow at him. "It's a full sword, and deadly sharp. I checked. Your team carry them, too. And that Shadow..." His eyes widened. "She manipulates her daggers like a professional."

"We *are* professionals. We work in security, as well as this kind of thing. Blades are our weapon of choice."

"Niel has an axe."

Ash scratched his neck, and decided honesty was best. "At least we're on your side, Theo."

Theo reluctantly got to his feet. "All right. Follow me. But trust me, it won't be pleasant."

— ❖ —

Niel saw the shadow slide over the wall and ease to the ground. If he hadn't been watching so closely, he'd have presumed that the shadow was caused by a cloud passing over the moon.

He let the intruder cross the stretch of grass below him, noting the petite form and deft movements that suggested a female, and smiled. *Mouse.* She passed beneath him and, wondering where she would go, decided to follow at a distance. He finally slipped to the ground, as stealthy as she had been, and pursued her on foot.

She kept to the shadows, but followed a more or less straight line to the walled garden, opened the gate, and passed through it. Niel couldn't even hear the snick of the gate as it shut. The walled garden was close to the house, the gate at the other side exited close to the drive and the stables. If she wasn't careful, Mouse would run into Gabe and Shadow. Actually, that was the last thing he wanted.

He ran across the grass and vaulted up the wall to crouch at the top. He saw her weave across the gravelled paths, again utterly silent, her footsteps sure and quick. Unless she was planning to swim, which was highly unlikely, she'd have to circle behind the keep, past the tower. Or go the long way around and intersect the drive.

But then she diverted her path, heading away from the gate. Instead, she headed to a section of wall that was closest to the keep, and thick with espaliered fruit trees. She effortlessly climbed them before reaching the top of the wall and dropping down to the other side. As soon as she was out of sight, he ran along the top of the wall to the corner. She had already reached the side of the moat. He was tempted to intercept her right then, but curious, he watched as she pulled a lightweight rope out of her pack that was fixed to a small device with a grappling hook on the end. She aimed for the top of the tower.

She was a good shot. With a tiny clink, it caught on the ramparts, and after tugging it a couple of times to make sure it was secure, she wound up the rope to shorten it, stepped back and took a running jump. She tucked her legs up and swung over the water, hit the wall, and steadied herself. Then she hit a button on her device, and within seconds, she was being pulled up the wall, walking up it like a monkey.

Niel could barely believe his eyes. She was good. Very good. And impressively silent and quick. But he wasn't there to admire her. *Well, not totally.* It was clear she was heading for the top of the keep. *Good.* He would meet her there. He stepped from his hiding place, extended his wings, and swooping around the back of the tower, landed softly beyond the parapet. Trying not to feel like an exultant stalker, he slipped inside the unlocked door built into the wall of the tower and waited at the top of the stairs for her arrival.

Twenty-Four

Harlan stood on the top step leading down to the crypt, the entrance in a concealed part of the choir that was well away from the nave where the public went, and hoped the roof wasn't about to fall in on them.

"There won't be zombies down there, you know," Nahum said, prodding him gently in the shoulder. "Get a move on."

"But the roof might fall on my head."

"If it was that dangerous, the whole church would be closed. Plus, the bomb squad was down here earlier. I saw Colin give them the keys and direct them where to go." He shook the keys he'd taken from the sacristy. "These ones. Shall I go first?"

"No." Harlan took the keys. "I'm good. It reminds me of my old treasure hunting days. They were nowhere near as dignified as my current jobs."

"There you go, then. A chance to relive your youth."

Harlan descended the dozen steps to a sturdy wooden door that sealed the crypt. With a deep breath, he placed the key in the lock, expecting it would be stiff from lack of use, but it turned easily, and he swung it open.

A musty, damp smell enveloped them, and he paused just inside the entrance to take his bearings. His flashlight showed a huge room that ran almost halfway under the nave, and was almost as wide. Pillars ran the length of the space, supporting a simple roof arranged in a series of squares. Beneath it were at least a dozen tombs, surrounded by a variety of metal grills.

"Holy shit. I didn't expect this." Harlan stepped further inside, reassured by the solidity of the space.

Nahum headed towards an oil lamp and a box of matches to the right of the entrance on a stone shelf, and lit the wick. A warm, orange glow dispelled the darkness, and also showed a series of lamps and candles around the room. As Harlan started to examine an eye-catching tomb on the second row, Nahum lit all of the lights, and soon the crypt felt far more welcoming that it had only moments before.

"Unbelievable," Harlan mumbled as he stared at the full-sized figure of a knight resting on the tomb in front of him. "This is amazing. I can see the detail on his chainmail. This is incredibly well preserved."

"I guess that's what happens in a private tomb. No grubby hands wearing the design away." Nahum looked unsettled for a moment, cocking his head as if straining to hear something.

"What's wrong?"

Nahum gave a slow smile. "The voices of the dead. I hear them murmuring."

Harlan gave an involuntary shudder as goose bumps erupted along his skin. He stared into the dark corners, as if something was stirring there. "Can you see spirits?"

"No. I can't even discern what they're saying." He shrugged it off. "It's a skill, for want of a better word, that I share with Gabe."

"They're not telling you where the treasure is? That would be nice!"

Nahum shook his head as he started to examine the tombs. "No, I'm afraid not."

Harlan's attention returned to the tomb in front of him, taking in the stone carving of the armour, the helmet, and the long sword resting between the knight's hands that ran the length of his body. "Robert de la More. Died 1278. He must have been a Knight Templar, too."

"William's father, perhaps? Or maybe an uncle?" Nahum moved away to investigate another tomb, this one much simpler with the family crest on it. "This is Henri de la More, who died in 1267." He hesitated, looking at Nahum. "Someone who wasn't a Templar, by the look of it."

"Hard to say. Presumably not all of them became Templars, or I guess they would all have knights on their tombs. I only have the names of the sons." Harlan pulled his notebook from his pocket, scanning the hasty notes he'd made before they left. "The oldest son was called Henri, and the youngest was Olivier."

They both started to explore, Nahum heading one way and Harlan the other. Nahum said, "Neither would have been knights, so their tombs should be simpler."

"Depends on your version of simple, I guess." Harlan used his torch to highlight details. Some had angels carved atop them, others ornate crosses mounted on a variety of plinths. Others had flowers carved around them, particularly those tombs belonging to women. He also realised, as he progressed through the crypt, that there were a series of recesses in the wall where yet more tombs lay, and he checked the dates. "There are several generations here. All the way up to the sixteenth century. I wonder what happened then."

"Perhaps the family moved, or they all died. No heirs at all." Nahum suddenly stopped. "Over here! I've found the brothers."

Harlan hurried to his side, his footfall echoing through the chamber, and for a moment he thought he heard footsteps above. He stopped abruptly to listen, but was greeted only by silence. Shaking off his nerves, he continued to Nahum's side. Both brothers' tombs were heavily carved with an inscription running down the tomb lid. Both also had crosses mounted at the head, and symbols of the Templars were also engraved into the lid and sides.

Harlan ran his fingers over the cold surface of Henri's tomb. "You're right. The dates and names fit." He started to push on the different symbols, hoping something would give. "Damn it. All these are solid."

Nahum was similarly engaged, and for minutes there was silence as they thoroughly investigated. Then Nahum stood, shoulders dropping. "Nothing. But…" he pointed upwards. "There are more symbols above."

Harlan had been so side-tracked by the tombs that he hadn't spent more than cursory moments inspecting the roof, but now he saw that Nahum was right. More Templar symbols were carved into certain points of the ceiling. "But Nahum, surely JD's team, the Order of Illumination, would have done all of this a few hundred years ago. What could we find that they didn't?"

"You know what they couldn't do then, but we can? Open the tombs."

"Are you nuts?"

"No. They would have been watched by the church, and probably wouldn't have had permission to open them. We can." He laughed at Harlan's expression. "I don't like it either, but they'll all be dust now. No bodies left at all. I'll check the ceiling just in case, and you can search Henri's tomb."

Harlan grumbled under his breath as he and Nahum heaved the lid to the side, twisting it to reveal the inside rather than removing it completely. Wincing at the scrape of stone that rumbled around them, Harlan was grateful that Nahum was with him. His strength made light work of it.

And then Harlan was aware of a change in the light as the candles flickered. Harlan and Nahum whipped around, just in time to see a small, round object bouncing towards them, and a huge hooded figure in the entrance of the crypt before it fled.

Their unknown assailant had thrown a grenade, and they had nowhere to go.

Gabe straightened up, and finally admitted defeat. There was nothing to suggest there was anything hidden in the old stable block.

He steeled himself as Shadow huffed next to him, hand on hips, leg tapping the floor and violet eyes wide. "Can we go now? This is pointless!"

"It is not pointless. We have ruled it out!"

"Yes, we most certainly have. Can we go to the church now?"

"You don't want to join Niel on intruder watch?"

She cocked her head at him. "And deny him his reunion? I don't think so."

"And what if it's a brutish male intruder with a face like a bulldog?"

"Then he'll still enjoy the fight. I want to search for treasure!"

Unable to suppress his own curiosity, Gabe extended his arm and gestured to the door. "Then let's go, my beloved."

In minutes they were striding across the grounds towards the pavilion, the shortest route Gabe estimated to the village.

"You know," he whispered, "we need to be quiet, just in case our intruder is still finding her way inside. We don't want to scare her off."

"In that case, we should fly. There's hardly any moon."

Gabe considered their options. They certainly didn't want to get caught in Niel's stakeout, and he was itching to get to the church. He quickly pulled his shirt off and extended his wings. "All right. Let's do it."

In seconds Shadow's lithe form was wrapped around his body, and he ascended to a good height before wheeling around and heading to the church. He studied the ground, wondering if there was something they might spot from up here that could give them a clue. However, everything was quiet. He could see the fluttering yellow tape around the bombed lodge, and the police car still parked at the entrance to the drive, but if there were any secrets hiding in the darkness, they weren't revealing themselves now.

Within minutes, the village of Temple Moreton was below them, the occasional light showing in the windows of the houses. The inn was closed at this hour, and Gabe realised they had been in the barn longer than he had anticipated. Shadow was facing him, her legs wrapped around his waist, her familiar scent enveloping him. She lifted her lips to his ear. "Gabe. I see figures below, in the graveyard. It's not Harlan or Nahum."

Startled, he twisted to stare below him. She was right. A couple of tall people stood just inside the lychgate, and... He waited, hovering, looking for signs of movement. Shuffling shadows revealed another couple standing at the entrance to the side path.

Within seconds he had perched on the bell tower and released Shadow, who whispered, "Bollocks. I've left my bow at the keep."

"They might not be our enemy. Best not to kill them—yet." Aware that Nahum and Harlan were inside the church, and worried for their safety, he studied the grounds again, finally spotting another couple of figures at the side entrance to the church. They had easy sight of the side gate. They were dressed in black, and appeared to be wearing long cloaks. "I see six in total. You?"

"Same, two at each gate, two at the side entrance. But who knows how many more are inside? They certainly aren't friends."

"Agreed. I'm going to drop down on the far side of the tower where no one can see us. If we take out the two at the church's side door, they won't spot whoever heads to the side gate."

"Fine." Shadow's blade was already in hand. "I'll take the side gate once we're done."

"Just don't kill them until we know who they are! Maybe try to take one alive."

Shooting him an impatient look, Shadow wrapped herself around him again. He swung over the tower's roof and glided to the ground. As soon as he landed, they rounded the corner together, weaving between the tombs so that the long grass masked their steps.

They dropped behind a huge tombstone as the side entrance came into view. The two guards were draped in long, sweeping cloaks, cowl hoods drawn up over their heads so that their faces were pools of darkness. Their backs were to the door, and they faced towards the graveyard. Their gloved hands gripped the hilt of huge swords, the points resting on the ground.

Modern day knights, and potentially their bombers.

Gabe knew these men would be skilled fighters. He glanced at Shadow, and she gestured to indicate that she would circle around. In seconds she had vanished like a wraith between the graves, and Gabe edged well to the side, trying to mask his approach. He only needed to give her a moment to get in position. Just as he was about to make his attack, a deep boom sounded within the church, and the ground shuddered beneath him.

Shit.

———⊰❖⊱———

Ash stared into the deep cellar that, to be honest, looked more like a pit of death beneath the keep's tower, and wrinkled his nose at the dank smell.

"Bloody hell, Theo. You weren't wrong about this."

"It's gross. But I think the water has dropped since the last time I looked. Probably because the dry weather has lowered the moat level."

Ash studied the ground, noting a pool of dark water that even his torch light didn't penetrate. "I need to get down there and check the floor. Let's position the ladder."

"Are you mad?" Theo looked at him, appalled. "It stinks down there."

Ash had been crouching to get a better view, but now he straightened up. "It's the oldest part of the castle, and according to you, there is no other cellar—not of this age, anyway. All of these castles usually had private exits that would allow someone to escape in the event they were surrounded. I'm sure this castle is no different. This is the only place you haven't renovated or explored. I think that down there must be an entrance to a passageway."

"But what has that to do with Templar treasure?"

"I don't know. Maybe nothing. But we're running out of options, and we need to check. If I'm wrong, fine. I'll just have a hot shower after. You stay here."

With obvious reluctance, Theo helped Ash position the ladder, and Ash quickly descended. The cellar was only about ten square feet, and the water was a foot deep and icy cold. Ash tentatively tested his footing, shining his torch into the water. It was brackish, and probably full of bugs. It was also slimy beneath, and the walls glistened with moisture.

Theo was right, though. There was clearly a line showing where the water level had been. Ash examined the walls with great care, but there were no doorways marked here. Not surprising. They were probably level with the moat. If there was a passage, it would run beneath it. Turning his attention to the floor, he gave up on trying to keep clean and instead ran his hands across the uneven floor. It seemed to be made of both earth and stone. Probably covered by a layer of silt. He wished he'd thought to bring a spade, but the only thing he had picked up was a crowbar. Testing and prodding the floor methodically, he finally had success. He was tapping the floor with the bar, when the sound changed to a slighter deeper, more hollow noise.

"Hey, Theo! I've found something!"

Tracing the edge of the stone, Ash identified the large stone slab. He wedged the crowbar into place and lifted. For long moments nothing happened, until finally, with a sucking sound, the huge stone slab lifted up a few millimetres. Ash doubled his efforts, until finally it lifted properly and the water gurgled through the gap to whatever was below. Wedging the crowbar in the gap, Ash lifted the edge with his bare hands and flipped the slab over. With luck, Theo would be so astonished at his find, he wouldn't question Ash's inhuman strength.

Theo was already descending the ladder. He hurried to his side and peered into the square hole. "I can't believe it! This was here all along!"

"Well, we don't know where it goes yet. Don't get your hopes up. It could be blocked, or flooded."

Ash stuck his head through the gap and shined his torch around. The hole led to the start of a narrow stone-lined passage that ran away from the castle towards the grounds and the village. The water that drained from the cellar had formed puddles below, but it wasn't completely flooded.

Ash swung down, landing gently on his feet. The passage was low, barely five feet high, but his light showed that although the passage was thick with spider webs and the odd fallen stone, it was otherwise intact. It snaked away beyond his light, the air stale and forbidding. He looked up at Theo. "I'm happy to go on my own. I'll tell you what I find."

"Are you mad? Of course I'm coming!"

Feeling sure he'd be quicker alone, Ash nevertheless helped Theo into the passageway and then set off carefully, checking around him with every step. The last thing they needed was for the roof to collapse on them. They'd managed to travel a reasonable distance when the ground shuddered. Ash paused, horrified.

He stared at the rounded roof, and saw a cascade of cracks splinter overhead, allowing a trickle of soil through. He was poised to run, but fortunately the trickle was all that came down. *But ahead?* He peered into the darkness. If there'd been a rockfall, he couldn't discern one from here.

"Not another bomb?" Theo asked, who like Ash, was frozen with horror.

Ash took in the old man's expression. He hadn't expected any of this. "It must be. Come on, let's get moving."

"*Towards* it? Are you mad?"

"You can turn back if you want, but my brother and Harlan are up ahead."

Hopefully still alive.

—◆◆◆—

Through the slight gap between the door and the frame, Niel watched the slender form of Mouse jump over the parapet. She quickly coiled the lightweight rope and placed it in her backpack. The grappling gun device remained fixed to her arm.

Once she was ready, which took seconds only, she ran to the door and tugged it open. As the door opened, he stepped forward.

She gasped and whirled around, running back to the wall. But Niel was on her in seconds, grasping her shoulders, and spinning her around.

"Mouse, I'd recognise those eyes anywhere!"

She squirmed and kicked him in the shin. Then, in a move that baffled Niel, she gripped his arms and used them to lever herself up and then kicked him in the stomach with both feet. She vaulted backwards at the same time he staggered back, landing on her feet before sprinting towards the ramparts.

Niel regained his footing quickly, and virtually throwing himself across the roof, tackled her to the floor, face-down. His sheer bulk pressed her flat, but she wriggled like an eel, and he was very grateful that his brothers weren't there to see him struggle with a woman who was barely half his weight and size.

"Mouse! I just want to talk!"

"Then why the hell am I pinned to the ground?"

"You were about to run!"

"That's what happens when I'm ambushed by an enormous man with an axe!" She twisted her head to stare at him. "As I do recall, you were a little less handsy last time."

"So you remember me, then?" He felt ridiculously pleased to hear that.

"Of course I do." He couldn't see her face, as she had a mask on again, but her almond eyes gleamed with annoyance, and something that might have been humour. "I should point out that I rarely get caught, so the occasion was memorable."

"Good. This one should be, too." He edged back just enough to allow her to twist around, and now she lay fully under him, back pressed to the floor, her backpack a few feet away. He kept an eye on her grappling device, his hand pinning that arm to the ground. The rope might not be attached, but the hook would cause a nasty wound. Aware he could crush her, he supported himself on his other arm, his elbow pressing her arm into her side, effectively pinning her in place.

"Well, this is all very nice," she said briskly, "but what now? Are we going to lie here all night?"

There was nothing Niel would like better. Her musky, spicy scent filled his nostrils like a dream, but he focussed on the job. "What are you here for, Mouse?"

"Oh, please! Let's not dance around this. I need the Templar blade, and I intend to get it."

"Unfortunately, you can't have it. You see, it actually belongs to Theo."

"Theo can't always have his own way."

"In this particular instance, he will. What I really want to know is, who has paid for your services? The sneaky Greek, Nicoli?"

"Classified."

"I know he did it. A Greek man matching his description was in the library the day the documents he was looking at were stolen. Your doing?"

"Maybe." She stared at him, defiant. "Theo is an idiot if he thought no one else would be interested in Templar treasure and William de la More's dagger."

"And the bombs? Were they you, too?"

"Do I look like a bomber?"

"Hard to say. I can't see your face, which seems unfair. You can see mine." He was itching to pull down the mask, but he felt that would somehow be a violation. Ridiculous, really, when he was pinning her to the ground.

"I can assure you, I am not the bomber. You've attracted the attention of the Knights of Truth and Justice."

Niel froze. "Who are they, and how do you know?"

"Your team hasn't done their homework well enough. They have been searching for the treasure for centuries."

"A remnant of the Knights Templar?"

"Hardly a remnant. They are ruthless, organised, and violent when necessary." She struggled again. "Let me go, Niel. Well done. You've caught me. I need to leave now. Unless you're going to call the police." Her eyes held a trace of fear.

"No. That wouldn't do either of us any favours." He sat, still clasping her grappling gun device, and in a few seconds, unbuckled it, finally releasing her arm.

In seconds, she leapt to her feet, eyes darting everywhere, but she was trapped and she knew it. He wanted to fly with her, feel her arms around him, but she didn't know he was a Nephilim, and he wasn't about to tell her. Of course, Nicoli might have, but he wouldn't take that risk while he didn't need to.

She rubbed her wrist where he'd restrained her. "You're ruining my perfect theft rate."

"I take that as a compliment. I'll be honest, I'm impressed. You're very...flexible."

A smile creased her eyes. "And then some. You, meanwhile, seem as inflexible as a plank of wood."

"But I have other attributes."

"I'm sure you have." Her eyes travelled over him.

Yes. He definitely counted that as flirting. Niel decided not to push it, and instead held his arm out in the direction of the door. "After you."

"Aren't you letting me go?"

"Unfortunately, I can't allow you to leave. My brothers want to chat. I suggest you consider telling us who hired you."

"I don't know who did, other than Nicoli. It's pointless keeping me here. I can't tell you anything else."

"You can think on that while I escort you to meet Theo and Ash. I promise that they're very civilised." Shooting him another hard stare, she rapidly descended the steps that hugged the tower walls before they reached the top floor landing. "Keep going," he instructed her. But when they reached Theo's study, neither he nor Ash was there. There was no sign of a struggle, but a few papers and the hilt and key were gone. "Down again. They must be in the main keep."

The tower felt eerily quiet. On the ground floor, he saw a light in the laundry room through a half-open door. He grabbed Mouse's elbow so she couldn't run, and then pushed the door open. The room was large and lined with shelves that were filled with towels, sheets, and other furnishings. Shelving units jutted into the floor space, blocking the back of the room from view. The smell of dampness and rot filled his nostrils.

"That smells like the moat," Mouse muttered, her free hand flying to block her nose. "Has someone come in that way?"

Niel's finger flew to his lips and he listened. None of the household staff were in view and it was silent. He weaved through the shelves, and at the far end of the room saw a hole in the floor. Peering downwards into an inky black cellar, he saw puddles on the ground. A metal ladder was propped against the side, wedged into the earth below, and there was another hole in the floor.

Either Ash and Theo were down there, or someone had broken in and was now somewhere in the keep. *It had to be Ash, or else where was he?* Either way, he had to investigate.

"Sorry, Mouse. You're coming with me."

"You have got to be kidding me!"

"I'm not leaving you alone, which means where I go, you go. After you."

She was halfway down the ladder when the ground shuddered, rocking the ladder. Niel grabbed it to stabilise it, and Mouse glared at him. "I suggest we think of a new plan."

Twenty-Five

As soon as Nahum saw the grenade rattle across the floor and land at his feet, he knew they had only seconds before it exploded.

"Take cover!" he yelled at Harlan. With lightning-fast reflexes, he grabbed the grenade and hurled it into Henri's tomb, and with strength enhanced by adrenalin, booted the lid partway back on before diving for cover behind the next tomb.

With a deafening roar the grenade exploded, cracking the enormous tomb, and sending dust and debris hurtling into the air. For a second, he could see and hear nothing at all. The candles flickered out, and a high-pitched whine filled his ears. He peered around the tomb he was sheltering behind, and through the whirling dust, saw a figure running towards them.

It looked like the angel of death, but it wasn't wings behind him; it was a billowing black cloak. The figure wasn't bothering to hide, thinking he was hidden by the dust cloud. *Wrong*.

Nahum pulled his throwing knives from where he'd strapped them to his legs and forearms and hurled one after the other at their attacker. With a grunt, their assailant fell, clutching his leg as one of Nahum's knives found its mark.

Nahum struggled to his feet, shaking his head to clear it, and then dropped to the ground again as he immediately saw another cloaked figure at the entrance to the crypt. *Shit.*

Fortunately, he and Harlan were well down the crypt, and in the darkness they would be hard to spot. He still had another couple of knives, but the figure was too far away at present, and he wasn't advancing, either. He must have seen his companion fall and had edged inside to wait and watch. Nahum estimated they had seconds only before he decided to act. With luck the assailant wouldn't risk another grenade, but he didn't want to assume that.

"Harlan," he whispered. "Are you okay?"

"I'm alive, but *okay* is a stretch." He was crouching a few feet away, back pressed to another tomb. "How many?"

"One wounded, another at the entrance. We're trapped." Nahum risked peering around the tomb again. The fallen man—at least he was pretty sure it was a male, from the size of him—was nowhere to be seen. Neither was the man at the entrance. He was potentially edging towards them right now.

Candlelight bloomed on the other side of the crypt. *Bollocks.* His main advantage was the darkness, and now that had gone, but at least he had a rough idea where one of the men was. Unless someone else had snuck in while he wasn't looking, there were still only two of them.

He eased his sword from his scabbard and indicated to Harlan to stay put. He was going to circle around and kill their assailants. Keeping low, he ran to the next tomb, intending to edge his way forward. There was no other way.

Just as he had advanced a few paces, the unpleasantly familiar rattle of another grenade bouncing across the floor had Nahum whirling around again. Their attacker's aim was good. The grenade stopped a few feet away.

There was no way he could get to it in time. He threw himself behind a tomb, using it to shield him from the blast.

But this time, there wasn't a huge boom of detonation. Instead, smoke hissed out, creating an impenetrable haze.

Excellent, the smoke would work to his advantage, too.

⟩⟨⟩⟨

As soon as the boom shook the ground, Shadow made her move.

The knight that was her mark had turned slightly to look at his companion, and taking advantage of his distraction, she plunged her sword into the side of his abdomen, angling upwards. Unfortunately, it struck armour that was hidden by the cloak, deflecting her blade.

He whipped around to face her, sword swinging towards her, and she immediately parried, swearing under her breath. She should have anticipated armour. Their blades clashed breathtakingly quickly as they fought around the tombs. The knight's cloak billowed behind him, and his cowl hood fell back, revealing a bearded man. She caught details as they fought. He wore fitted, black chest armour much like their own that she had left in the keep, but it also had the large Templar cross emblazoned on it in silver. Sturdy leather gloves covered his hands, but his arms were bare except for armguards. He was brawny and big, but she was used to fighting men of that build. His size gave him brute strength, but he lacked flexibility and her quickness.

From the corner of her eye, she spotted the guards on the side gate come running. The others from the main lychgate would be with them soon. Close by, Gabe was fighting for his life. The clash of their swords was loud, and if they didn't end this quickly, very soon someone would hear it and call the police. Fortunately, she had fey speed on her side.

As she fought her opponent, he lost his balance trying to catch her. She capitalised on it, slicing behind his knees as he spun around. He fell to the ground with an agonized cry that quickly became a gurgle as she slashed his throat.

She turned to face her next opponent. Fire surged through her; a wild adrenalin rush she hadn't experienced in weeks. She'd missed this.

Niel waited for the repercussive shudder to stop. It was coming from his right; the direction of the village, or maybe the centre of the grounds again.

He pulled Mouse back up the ladder. "I agree. Change of plan. That was either another bomb, or the tunnel has collapsed." Both were nightmarish scenarios.

They looked out of the window onto the courtyard of the keep, both silent. There were no other booming sounds, or the flare of flames.

"I think it must have been underground," Niel suggested. "With luck, no one will have called the police."

"But if it's underground, where is it?"

"It must be the village. That's where some of my team is."

"And if there are people in the tunnel below?"

Niel was torn with indecision. If he headed down the passage to check on who he thought was Ash and Theo, he may get stuck there. But if they were in trouble... *No. Ash could deal with it.* Niel needed to find out what was going on, and that meant heading to the church. Nahum thought it had been cleared of bombs, but if he was wrong, he could be badly injured, and so could Harlan.

"If it's Ash, I have to trust that he'll be okay." He grabbed Mouse's elbow and pulled her out of the exterior door and into the small courtyard, one of the many that made up the warren of buildings and spaces around the keep. "You're coming with me."

"I don't think so!" She looked both outraged and amused at the same time.

He pulled his t-shirt off as he spoke, ready to unfurl his wings. Right then, he didn't care whether she knew he was Nephilim or not. "I'm not leaving you here, alone, to plunder the castle. You're coming with me to check on my brothers."

"Oh, really! You're going to carry me there? Over your shoulder like a Neanderthal?"

"You're not a Neanderthal," he quipped.

"Not me, you idiot! *You!*"

He grinned broadly at her, and then spread his wings. They took up most of the small courtyard.

Mouse stepped back, eyes wide. "I thought Nicoli was just spinning tales about you."

"Nope." He gestured in. "Come here."

She backed away, but her eyes lingered a little too long on his bare chest. "I don't think so."

"Mouse! I don't often offer people a lift. Come on."

She backed up again, but the courtyard was small, and in seconds he'd gripped her around the waist and lifted them both into the air. She squealed in shock, before clinging on tightly, and Niel swept across the sky towards the church. He was glad to see there were no signs of police or fire engines, and the police car at the drive entrance was still in position. But as he neared the church, he saw the fight below, and without a second's thought, deposited Mouse on the edge of the graveyard, and ran to join Gabe and Shadow.

—⟨⊙⟩⟨⊙⟩—

Harlan was heartily sick of hiding behind a tomb and half choking to death on the smoke bomb. His ears still rang, and he wondered why he hadn't bothered to carry a weapon.

"Well, you weren't expecting the damn Knights Templar to jump out on you, Harlan," he muttered to himself. "You're an idiot! *Always* carry a weapon when working with Shadow and the Nephilim. They attract violence like a moth to flame."

The sound of a grunt and thud made him wince, and he hoped that was an injured knight, not Nahum. He wanted to help, but the memory of the long swords in the knights' hands made him reconsider. They would cut him in half just as soon as look at him. And then the sound of an uneven gait and a wheezing noise made him freeze. The wounded knight came into view as the smoke eddied. He was limping, his injured leg pouring blood as he headed towards the shattered tomb and whatever may be in it. He certainly wasn't looking for Harlan.

I don't think so, bud.

Seizing his chance, he grabbed a chunk of shattered stone, eased upright, and whacked the knight on the back of the head. He fell forward with a satisfying thump, landing half in the tomb. Harlan grabbed the back of the cloak at his neck, and dragged him backwards until he was on the floor.

Nahum staggered out of the smoke, winded and covered in blood. "I heard the noise! You're okay?"

"Better than you!" Harlan took in his bloodied state. "Are you injured?"

"All his blood, not mine." Nahum's hair was standing up in tufts, and he wiped the back of his hand across his face, smearing more blood over it. "I suspect they'll have reinforcements coming along soon. What's in the tomb?"

"Not sure. Was just about to check."

The lid of Henri's tomb had cracked into pieces. Half was on the floor, while the rest had tipped into the sarcophagus. Big cracks ran across the base, revealing a dark space beneath.

Harlan cocked his head at Nahum. "Something is under there." He sat on the edge of the tomb and supported his weight, before kicking the cracked slab. "It's not budging."

The sound of footsteps had them both whirling around, but it was Gabe and Shadow.

Harlan took in their bloodied appearance and slashed clothing. "I take it you found more knights?"

Shadow nodded. "Outside the church. Six of them. Niel arrived too, and he helped finish them off."

"All dead?" Harlan asked.

"Very," Shadow answered. She nudged the knight beyond the shattered tomb with her foot. "He isn't, though. Good. He might be able to answer some questions."

"You two had us worried after we heard that explosion," Gabe said, squeezing Nahum's shoulder. "Are you injured?"

"This isn't my blood," Nahum reassured him, wiping his bloodied sword on the knight's black cloak. "We had two to tackle down here. I presume Niel is keeping watch?"

"With Mouse." Gabe shrugged, amused. "Long story. What have you found? Please tell me you have something, because we found absolutely nothing in the old stables!" A frown creased his face. "Niel thinks Ash is in an underground passage." He quickly summarised Niel's findings.

Harlan was still perched on the edge of the tomb, and he pointed at the cracked base. "We definitely found something. There seems to be a hollow space beneath the sarcophagus. Maybe Ash has found another way to it." He indicated the irregular piece of stone he'd been trying to dislodge. "That looks to be the most likely piece to knock through."

Without another word, they all positioned themselves, and started to hammer on the stone with their feet. The jarring impact rocked through Harlan's body. The stone was wedged well into position, and it took several minutes before it finally dislodged and dropped into the space below. Harlan angled his flashlight downward, illuminating a chamber that looked about ten feet deep. And something was in there. Something blocky and tomb-shaped.

Shadow was pressing against him in an effort to see too, and she quickly said, "Me first!" Before Harlan could object, she wiggled over the edge and dropped inside.

Gabe called after her. "Be careful!"

Her muffled voice shouted back, "You're going to want to see this!"

Infected by Shadow's reckless enthusiasm, Harlan said, "I'm coming."

He wriggled down through the hole, fingers gripping the stone edge, and then dropped to the ground, narrowly missing landing on the huge tomb that dominated the space. He turned his flashlight on. "Well, at least we know why the two brothers on horseback was a clue. Something we got right!"

"But there's no treasure here!"

Shadow was right. The chamber was bare of ornamentation, but covered in fragments of rock and dust caused by the explosion above. A doorway in the wall led to another passageway. "There's another exit."

"I'll check it out in a minute," she said, preoccupied by the huge tomb.

The tomb itself was impressive. It was comprised of a series of stone bases, the lowest one wide and thick, stepping up by four levels to the sarcophagus itself that was on Harlan's eye level. The stone was richly carved with plants and swirling imagery, as well as Templar symbols. On top was another effigy, resting on his back, clad in full armour, a sword between gloved hands that ran the length of the tomb. Written at the base, below the knight's booted feet, was the epitaph bearing William de la More's name.

He called up to Nahum and Gabe. "We've found William's tomb!"

In seconds Nahum swung down to join them. "But no treasure?"

"Not unless it's in the tomb with him. Or down there." He indicated the narrow passage. "What do you think?"

Nahum rubbed his bloodied jaw. "If someone has gone to all the trouble to hide William's tomb, surely you would at least make one route inside, and that could be the way Ash will approach—if he's in the passage. Let's face it, that grenade did us a favour. We'd never have found this place otherwise."

"You don't know that," Harlan disagreed. "We'd barely started examining the brothers' tombs before we were attacked. There might well have been a mechanism to get in. And what about the key in the hilt? That must have a use." There were still too many questions. Too many variables.

"While you two are arguing," Shadow declared, "I'm moving on."

"*Wait*!" Gabe's voice boomed from above. In moments, he dropped down, too. "I've just checked with Niel. It's all quiet up there. No police, no more knights. He's dragged the bodies out of the way for now, but we need to be quick—just in case."

"Easier to say than do, brother," Nahum said, turning his attention back to the tomb. "Unless there's treasure down wherever that other passage leads, this tomb must tell us where to go next, or why hide it?"

Shadow was already at the start of the next tunnel. "Gabe. Time to go."

Gabe nodded. "I'm coming. You two stay here and examine every inch of that tomb."

He left with Shadow, and Harlan surveyed the tomb with pursed lips. "I wish I knew what we're looking for. A keyhole, perhaps? Another mechanism? The tomb is elaborate, which suggests there has to be something else here."

"I agree. I'm going to get some of those candles and lanterns from above. Let's light this place up."

Twenty-Six

A sh used his sword to hack into the tree roots that thrust through the sides of the passageway, hoping that the whole place wasn't about to cave in on their heads.

They had just passed through a particularly tricky section of the tunnel, where a thick root had dislodged part of the rock wall. They had slid past the rockfall and earth, relieved to find that the rest of the passageway was intact, but from there, it had been slow going. It was clear they were under the wooded section of Theo's land.

"Do you think it's much further?" Theo asked, his voice muffled from the shirt he had pulled over his mouth in an effort not to inhale dust and debris.

Ash tried to estimate the distance they had covered. "Hard to say. I'm a bit disorientated. We just have to keep moving."

However, within minutes the passageway inclined, and just as Ash started to feel hopeful that they were within reach of their destination—wherever that may be—they reached an intersection where three passages diverged. Onc path ran straight ahead, the others went left and right. All were of equal heights and widths, and nothing indicated where they might lead.

He turned to Theo. "We should have known this wouldn't be straight-forward."

"So which one do we choose?" Theo was filthy. Dirt was smeared across his face and clothes, and Ash knew he looked worse. His feet were still damp from where he'd waded through the filth of the moat beneath the tower.

"Got any matches? We could check for air flow. Or we could be method-ical. Start with the left-hand passage and then try the next."

"Perhaps. It would help if we knew where we were. I suspect we're close to the village now."

"Me, too. One could lead to the church, one perhaps to the old inn. They're the two oldest buildings in the village. But the other?"

"There would have been other old buildings," Theo reasoned. "They've just been knocked down over the years. Or one could lead to a cave. We have no idea how far these will run."

Ash considered the possibilities. "I can't help but feel we should keep going down the centre one. It's the one that calls to me."

"Then let's do that. And let's hope the paths don't diverge again." Theo lifted a bushy eyebrow. "Or we might find ourselves lost down here."

<hr />

Niel leaned against the side door of the church, surveying the graveyard, with Mouse next to him.

The bodies of the dead knights had been placed next to the wall, so that any casual passer-by couldn't see them. Not that there should be anyone passing by after midnight in a small village. The place was quiet, the inn closed, and the church was on the edge of the village anyway, providing some privacy.

The fight had sounded loud with the clashing of swords and grunts of engagement, but it was over relatively quickly once Niel arrived to help

Gabe and Shadow. To Niel's surprise, Mouse hadn't escaped. He watched her, wishing he could trust her, but knew he couldn't.

"I presume you're waiting to see what we find," he said to her.

"Of course." She leaned against the wall, her face still covered by the black mask that revealed only those beguiling eyes. "I was employed to find the treasure. I intend to do that."

"Who by?"

"Nicoli. You know that."

"But who employed Nicoli?"

Her eyes lifted in a smile. "I don't know. I'm just a contractor. I don't ask questions."

"You don't care who you work for? Whether you're on the side of right or wrong?"

She rolled her eyes. "Who's to say who is right or wrong? Should Theo get to find Templar treasure that isn't his? Or should the rightful heirs find it?"

"You think that's who those guys are? The rightful heirs?" He nodded at the half a dozen dead knights. It seemed a strange word to call them, but having inspected their bodies, it was only fair. They all wore heavy black cloaks of good quality wool, and donned modern body armour of black Kevlar. Their swords were also quality, but the hilts were relatively plain, the blade lacking engravings or any ornamentation. "The Knights of Truth and Justice."

"From the insignias on their chests, I would say they are, wouldn't you?"

"I guess so." The silver Templar cross marked on the breastplate was interwoven with an ornate *T* and *J*. Beyond that, there was nothing to identify them. At least they didn't have tattoos and strange, metallic skin.

"Yes," Mouse continued, "I do think they have a claim. The Templar treasure was put aside for the *Templars*. King Philip of France and the pope stole huge sweeps of land and property. Men are no different through time. They are motivated by greed. Theo too, perhaps."

"I think he's thrilled by the chase rather than the monetary value. He said he'll donate it to a museum."

"It's not his to donate. What about you? Do you feel guilty that you killed them?"

"Yes, a little," he admitted, turning to study her expression. "But they were determined to kill *us*. They left us little choice."

Something felt wrong. Mouse protested that she didn't know who had employed her, but she seemed knowledgeable about the knights, and sympathetic to their cause. And it wasn't just her attitude that worried him.

Where were the knights based? There were only half a dozen men outside, plus a couple inside, from what Gabe had told him. There must be more of them if they were so determined to find the treasure first. *And Mouse.* Was there another connection, or were there really several groups interested in the treasure? Some would be interested in pure monetary value, for others there might be religious significance. Or Ash might be right. There could be esoteric knowledge hidden here somewhere. Eighteen ships had disappeared. *It couldn't possibly all be here, could it?*

A prickle of unease ran down his spine as a noise beyond the graveyard broke the night's silence. He wasn't even sure what he'd heard. *The crack of a twig? A footfall?* He stepped forward to try to see onto the lane beyond the side gate, and felt Mouse reach his side. He assumed that she was also looking to see what was going on, until he felt something jab his skin.

Pain ripped through him as his body spasmed, and the world went dark.

⌁⟫⟪⌁

Gabe halted in the middle of the next chamber and stared in shock at the richly engraved walls all around him.

"What the hell are we supposed to do with this?"

"Maybe nothing?" Shadow looked as unconvinced as her voice sounded.

"No one goes to all this trouble for *nothing*!"

"Maybe the Templars and their descendants do. Sounds like they enjoyed a bit of pomp and ceremony."

The room they stood in was only a short distance from the tomb chamber, but it could not have been more different. As Gabe took stock of the place, his torch sweeping over the floor and the ceiling, he realised that not only were the walls carved, but the floor and ceiling was, too.

"I feel," Gabe said with a sinking suspicion, "like I'm standing in one of those Chinese puzzle boxes."

"What are they?"

"Don't you ever listen to anything? Ash was talking about them a month or so ago."

"Only when it sounds interesting. That obviously didn't. What about them?"

"They're intricate boxes that have things hidden in them. You have to work out what to press and move to open them up."

Shadow nodded as she prowled around the space. "I get it. The fey made similar pieces. Mystery boxes."

"Well, you know what I mean, then. Except we're on the inside. We need to figure out the right thing to press to reveal the prize—which is hopefully the treasure."

"And if we press the wrong thing?"

"Maybe you should stop walking, Shadow."

She halted, head cocked. "You think I'll trigger something?"

"This could be a test. Much like the Temple of Raziel. It's for the initiated." He hadn't moved from the spot in the centre, and now he wondered why he'd blundered inside. "We aren't even close to being initiated."

"But we have clues, and we're smart. Plus, we have a key."

"Not right now we don't." He groaned. "Bollocks. We should have waited outside."

Shadow's hands flew to her hips. "If you think I'm going to stand here like a terrified fawn, you don't know me at all, Gabe!"

"We need to be smart, Shadow. I know you're not terrified."

"We marched halfway across the floor and haven't triggered anything yet. You're just paranoid."

"Look around. We're surrounded by Templar imagery, as well as the Green Man, leaves, plants, heraldic symbols, and what appears to be a kind of history." A series of images caught his eye as he shone his torch around the room. It was hard to know what to focus on first. "And look. Ships on a river."

"Herne's horns." Shadow's voice rose in excitement. "This could be a map to all of the treasure. Perhaps that's what this place is! This isn't just a bit of it. This is the storehouse of knowledge!"

"You might be right. Maybe this is where Ash's key fits?"

Shadow pointed to another arched doorway opposite the one they had arrived through. "Ash must still be somewhere that way." She took a half pace forward and froze as something clicked beneath her foot. Immediately, a grating noise emanated around them. "Oops."

"Shadow! I told you not to move!"

"It was an accident!"

Gabe glanced at the open doorways wondering whether to run for it, but the doors were several paces away, and they might trigger something else on the way out. "Just don't move again. You must have opened something."

"But what?"

Both swept their torchlight around the room with increasing panic as the grating noise intensified.

"There! That stone!" Shadow's voice rose with excitement as her light showed a stone block moving backwards into the wall. As it dropped into position, everything fell silent. "Is that it? It's over?"

"Maybe?"

Then a whirring noise began, and with startling speed, doors slammed down into the only exits, and they were trapped inside.

─··◈··─

"I can't see a keyhole or anything!" Nahum declared, standing and stretching, his hands kneading his lower back.

"Neither can I." Harlan was still on his hands and knees as he examined the relief carved onto the lowest section of the tomb. "Intriguing, though. I think these reliefs tell a history. The words aren't Latin."

Nahum walked around to study the inscription. "No. Old French. They're all names. Probably the names of the English masters." The names made one big list around the lower level. All ornately carved in flowery script, and still reasonably crisp-edged.

"Wow. It's quite something, isn't it? To be looking at the final resting place of the last Commander of the English Templars. The end of a tragic piece of history."

"Why do you think their story has lasted so long?" Nahum asked.

Harlan stood and dusted off his knees. "Good question. I think it's the mystery of it all. Everyone loves missing treasure, don't they? And it was the swiftness of it. The shock. The fact that such a huge organisation could suddenly disappear in a matter of days."

"Although months is more realistic," Nahum pointed out.

"But still swift for such a powerful, far-reaching group. It's sort of a lesson, I think, that even the strongest and most powerful organisations are not immune to time, greed, and enemies. '*Look on my works, ye mighty, and despair! Nothing beside remains. Round the decay of that colossal wreck, boundless and bare, the lone and level sands stretch far away.*'" He cocked his head at Nahum. "Shelley."

Nahum smiled. "I've heard of him. I didn't take you for a poetry lover."

"I'm full of surprises. That was Ozymandias."

"Yeah, well. I'm living proof of those words." A wave of melancholy swept over Nahum. "Civilisations, organisations, dynasties, royal families...Gods. They all have their time, and then they're gone."

"The Igigi survived. And so have you."

"More by luck for us, and we are a fraction of the many Nephilim." Nahum shrugged off his mood. "No time for retrospection, Harlan. Perhaps we should go check on Gabe and Shad—" He didn't finish his sentence. A noise from above caught his attention and he froze, gesturing silence to Harlan.

A female voice with a hint of an accent, and a slight tease to her tone, called down to them. "So, that's where you are." Nahum leapt backwards, sword raised as she said, "Don't worry. No harm will come to you if you just do as we say."

Through the opening in the cracked slab, Nahum saw the veiled face of a woman, and clustered behind her, at least half a dozen knights. Ice filled his veins. "You must be Mouse. Where's Niel? I swear, if—"

"He's fine. More or less. And will remain so if you do exactly what I say."

"Are you bargaining with his life?"

"Yes. With all of your lives. Step back. We're coming down."

Nahum didn't move. "Prove he's alive first."

"When I'm down there. I can't do it from here."

Nahum knew he had no choice, not if Niel was in danger. He stepped back, Harlan retreating next to him, released the hilt of his sword, and held his hands high. "Fine."

The petite woman wriggled through the gap and dropped to the ground with the grace of a gymnast, quickly followed, with less grace, by three tall knights, clad in the familiar clothing of the Knights of Truth and Justice. All three swiftly bowed their heads and dropped to one knee before the tomb of William de la More before rising to their feet again.

"You trespass on hallowed ground, Nephilim," one of the knights said.

His shoulders looked broad, but that was deceptive. The cloak added width and bulk. His true build once the cloak was swept back showed he was wiry, his face thin, gaunt almost, marked perhaps with the fervour of a disciple.

"So do you," Nahum shot back.

The knight shook his head. "No. We belong here. The Dagger of Secrets was meant for us." *Dagger of Secrets?* He glanced around the tomb and then spotted the doorway. "Your companions are through there, I presume?" He gestured to his two associates who turned as if to leave.

Nahum stepped in front of them. "Show me proof that Niel is alive." He was prepared to fight to the death if Niel was dead. He wouldn't bargain.

The knight gestured impatiently to Mouse, and she held up her phone, showing Nahum a picture of Niel, unconscious, and trussed and bound outside the church. A knight stood over him. "There. He's okay, and will be released when this is over."

"But don't push me," the knight added, his voice gruff. "We have lost men because of you. I will not risk more if I can help it."

Nahum couldn't help himself. "You bombed Theo's grounds and threw grenades at us. Of course we retaliated!"

The knight clenched his jaw. "Enough. There will be no more bombs, but we *will* take the treasure."

Nahum glanced at Harlan, who nodded in agreement. "There's been enough bloodshed, Nahum. Let this play out."

Nahum hated being backed into a corner, but knew he had no choice. And all the talk of who was really deserving of the treasure made him consider their actions. Perhaps their team wasn't meant to find it. "Fine. Truce. But no more bloodshed or bombs, or that's all off."

The knight nodded, and his companions quickly exited the room, following Gabe and Shadow's path. As soon as they had left, he said, "Give me the dagger."

"We can't," Harlan answered. "Ash has it, and we don't know where he is. We think he's following a passage from under the keep."

"Ah, yes. Then we will capture him soon, too. Men are following them." He stepped past Nahum and began to inspect the tomb.

Nahum turned his attention to the woman, understanding why Neil was taken with her. She was slender, graceful, and had very pretty eyes. Unfortunately, those eyes currently held a steely reserve. "So, you're Mouse. We thought you were working for someone else, but you've been working with these people all along."

"It's just a job." She cast the knight a sidelong glance. "But I don't like bloodshed. I'm a thief. That's all. That's why your friend is still alive—because of me."

"Because of *me*," the knight retorted, eyes still on the tomb. "My decision."

Before she could respond, one of the knights returned, panic in his eyes. "Sire. The next room is sealed. There's no way inside."

Nahum and Harlan exchanged a panic-stricken glance, and regardless of Mouse and heavily armed knights, raced down the passage.

Twenty-Seven

As soon as the doors sealed shut, Shadow heard the sound of trickling water.

"Oh, that's not good." She spun around, looking for the source of the noise, and with horror saw water streaming in through the dislodged stone.

Gabe was furious. "Herne's steaming balls! Now we're going to drown in here! I told you not to move!"

"And I told you it was an accident!"

"Well un-accident it."

She glared at him. "That's not even a word!"

Gabe strode over to the hole in the wall, thrust his hand through the water, and grimaced. "The bloody stone is gone. And the water is freezing!"

"You expected to find a plug?"

"Will you please do something useful, Shadow!"

Biting back a retort, she studied the block beneath her feet that had triggered the mechanism. She placed her blade down the side in an attempt to manoeuvre it back out, but it was pointless. Her gaze swept the room. There had to be *something* to reverse it. *Another mechanism? Maybe related to the river carved on the wall.* She studied it with fierce intensity. The freezing water was already sloshing around her ankles.

"Gabe, we need to be logical."

"Yes, I know. But we're running short on time."

"We have time!" She glared at him. "This is a slow trickle."

"We'll freeze before we drown." He marched to the doorway they had entered through, retracing his steps. "I'm going to try brute force—and summon help. Nahum!"

Leaving Gabe to try and batter his way out, Shadow tried to focus on the carvings, but it was impossible. Her thoughts refused to settle. There were so many images that it was hard to say what was more important. There were carvings of men being burned at the stake, men being tortured...gruesome images that told of the horrible demise of the Templars. But there was also a huge map of Europe and the Middle East carved onto one wall. Various posts were marked. *Centres of power, perhaps? Places where treasure was hidden—or where treasure had been found?*

Shadow was still unfamiliar with most of Europe, but she recognized France, Spain, Portugal, and the United Kingdom. Despite the urgency of their situation, she found herself fascinated by the story told on the walls. One thing was clear, though. She was completely unequal to this task.

"Gabe, I think we're going to drown."

"Not funny, Shadow."

"I'm not trying to be funny. I can't work out what we're supposed to do!"

Suddenly the sound of running water changed and slowed, and with a sigh of relief, Shadow looked at the flow. "Oh good, it's slowing..." She faltered. The clear water wasn't clear anymore. It was increasingly murky. And then a thin stream of mud oozed through the opening instead. "Oh shit, Gabe. I think we'll suffocate in mud, instead."

"What?" He turned to her, fists bloodied from where he'd been trying to release the door, and his eyes fell to the flow of ooze. "Brilliant. Just brilliant!"

"It must be a lake or something that silted up." Her spirits brightened. "This will buy us time."

"A delay to our eventual suffocation. And it stinks!"

He was right. The smell of rot filled the air, and Shadow pulled her t-shirt over her mouth again. *Herne's horns.*

She turned back to the images. Focus. Death was not an option.

———◇◆◇———

Ash turned to Theo, head cocked. "Can you hear water?"

Theo stopped and listened, his face creased in concentration. "Yes. A weird gurgle. I think it's coming from the room ahead. '*The Chamber of Truth*'."

They had just arrived in a small, square room that was half filled with rockfall and earth. Just visible over the mound was a doorway of solid stone, covered in carved reliefs. It fitted snugly into an arched stone frame. Carved into the arch, in Latin, was the name of the room that Ash had just translated.

Ash eyed the mound of earth and the unstable roof above. The fall looked to be a mixture of old and fresh, perhaps the latest triggered by the rumble they felt earlier. Or maybe this *was* the rumble they'd felt. Hoping the roof would hold, he was about to start cautiously clambering over it when a muffled yell made him stop.

"Did you hear that?" He stared beyond Theo, down the receding passageway, but couldn't see a thing.

"That was ahead, not behind us," Theo said with certainty. "Someone's in there."

Abandoning caution, Ash scrambled over the rockfall, Theo next to him, and shouted, "Hello!"

A muffled shout called back, but he couldn't make out the words. However, the voice was familiar. "Bloody hell. I think that's Gabe. He's in trouble."

"Would our key help?"

"The key! Brilliant thinking, Theo." Ash fished the key from his pocket. "Any sign of a keyhole?"

Over half of the door was buried in soil, and while Theo used his hands to dig the bottom half of the door out, Ash examined the upper portion. Dust lay thick in the folds and curves of the carvings, and he started to scrub it with his bare hand, holding his torch steady with the other. It was pitch black, and the air was thick with the smell of decay. The more Theo dug and the more Ash cleaned the door, the more choking clouds of debris flew up. Through increasingly gritty eyes, Ash made slow progress as the yelling increased in volume.

What the hell was happening in there?

"I'm trying to be as quick as I can!" he shouted back, almost losing his footing as Theo moved more and more earth. "Theo!"

"Sorry! This stuff is caked in, Ash. There are huge rocks in it."

Shadow's voice sounded close to his ear. "I'm going to drown in mud! What are you doing?"

"What do you think I'm doing, you crazy fey madam?" *Shit. He shouldn't have said fey.* Hopefully, Theo would think it was an endearing insult.

Ash wrestled a huge rock from the base of the door and threw it to the other side of the room, allowing Theo to move the earth more easily, then turned his attention to the door again. He wished there was no ornamentation. He was sick of ornate reliefs; beautiful or not, they were giving him a headache. There was still no sign of a keyhole, and he wondered if he'd got it all wrong. *Was there a mechanism instead?*

"Shadow, is there anything on your side?"

"I'm not a complete idiot! Of course there bloody isn't."

Gabe yelled, "Ash, time is pressing!"

"We're being as quick as we can!" While he searched, he asked, "What happened?"

"Shadow released something, and it trapped us inside."

"Who's us?"

"Just us two. The others are elsewhere—Niel, too." Silence fell, and then Gabe shouted again. "The bloody knights are on the other side! Get us out!"

Ash froze.

"Knights?" Theo asked, halting too. "Here?"

"That must mean they have the others," Ash reasoned. "Hurry!"

They both redoubled their efforts. And then Ash spotted it. The keyhole was in the centre, a part previously covered by the earth from the collapsed roof, placed within a carving of an eye. It had been plugged with earth, but as he scrubbed away at the door, a portion had fallen free, revealing the outline. He scrabbled at it with the end of his finger, but only succeeded in jamming it further in. Then he tried the point of his knife, but that wasn't much better.

Gabe bellowed again. "Ash!"

"I've found it. Give me a moment!"

"Here!" Theo thrust a small penknife at him with a tiny blade. "Will this do?"

Relief flooded through him. "Theo. You're a genius! Shine the torch on it."

In a few seconds, Ash managed to scrape most of the earth out, and inserted the key. It slotted in, and with a few wiggles, he felt it drop into place. With a deep breath, he turned it.

Nothing happened.

"It's stuck." Sweat trickled down Ash's brow and into his eyes, and he swept it away with the back of his hand. "I need oil."

"Sorry, I don't carry that."

"I think I need a bucket of it."

Shadow yelled again. "Use brute force, you giant oaf!"

"Shut up, Shadow. This is your fault!" Ash shouted back.

Theo sniggered. "She's really quite funny."

Ash continued to twist and wriggle the key. "See how you like constantly being insulted."

"It's a sign of affection. It's quite charming, really."

"Good. She can live with you, then."

"I can hear you!" she yelled, her muffled voice outraged. "You'll regret that when I'm out."

"If you still want me to teach you to drive, please shut up!"

Ash finally felt the lock give and the key moved a quarter turn. He jiggled it again, and with incremental movements, it finally twisted through the full turn. A mechanism started grinding within the door, and it shuddered to the right a few inches before sticking again. It was enough for a gap to appear between the door and the frame, and a foul smelling, thick slushy liquid oozed out. Gabe and Shadow's face pressed to the gap, Shadow's below Gabe.

"It's stuck!" Ash told them. "You need to help."

Between them, many fingers wedged into the slim gap, they forced the door open, and the sludgy ooze turned into a deluge. Ash recoiled, a hand flying over his mouth, as he and Theo backed up onto the mound of earth.

"Were you in a sewer?" he asked, trying not to heave.

For a moment, neither Gabe nor Shadow spoke, both of them scooting out of the door, looking almost green. They had been waist-deep in the filthy, muddy liquid, and now both of them were caked in it. It was smeared over their arms and faces, and Ash couldn't help but snigger as relief swept over him.

Shadow glared at him. "It's not funny. I could have drowned in effluent. I still might."

She was right; the mud was now rising in the antechamber. It was blocked by the fall of earth and was seeping into it, creating an even greater, sludgy mix.

Gabe leaned back against the wall taking deep breaths, but the air in the small, collapsed chamber wasn't really that fresh, either. "It wasn't a sewer. It might have been an old lake that's dried up now or something. I hope. Maybe it was a cess pit."

"That's the way I'd torment anyone who was raiding my tomb," Theo said, nodding. "I like their style."

Gabe suddenly took in the half-collapsed chamber. "Oh, crap. I thought we'd escaped. Where are we now?"

"Don't worry, there is a way out," Ash reassured him. "Back that way. We have two other options, but have no idea where they come out, or whether they're in a worse state than this. Did you say that knights are here?"

Shadow answered as she clambered up the mound of earth and rocks. "Yes. They must have followed us into the church, which means...*Niel*!"

"Don't even think it, Shadow," Gabe warned. "We'll go around, some-how, and find him."

Ash had a million questions, but they would have to wait. He scrambled back to the passage, already feeling the earth start to collapse under him, weakened by the muddy mix. He'd only gone a few short feet back down the tunnel when he heard voices and saw the flash of a torch.

He turned his own off, shushing the others to silence. But it was too late. A booming voice yelled down the passage. "Halt! Surrender to the Knights of Truth and Justice, now!"

"Back up!" Ash yelled, trying not to fall over his retreating companions in the cramped space. He pointed up to the already unstable roof. "We either fight our way out, or block the way completely."

Shadow groaned. "But then we're stuck in the chamber of death!"

"Gabe?" Ash needed his opinion. "I don't know how many knights there are, and to be honest, there's not much room for fighting."

Gabe nodded. "Retreat. The main chamber is the answer. We just—" he glared at Shadow, "need to be smarter about working it out."

"And if we can't?" Theo asked, eyes widening with horror. "We're trapping ourselves in a tomb."

"There's another way out, remember?" Gabe said. "It just has knights on the other side of it, too."

Without another word, they scrambled back over the mound of earth. This time Gabe balanced himself on the top, and started pulling at the remaining brickwork on the ceiling closest to the passage, as Ash helped him.

Together they pulled several stone blocks free and hurled them down the passage, and with an ominous rumble, the roof collapsed.

Twenty-Eight

"You know," Barak said, "I could get used to this. But weirdly, I think I miss my brothers."

"What about Shadow?" Estelle asked, amused.

"Even her!" He grinned and kissed Estelle. "But regular holidays like this may be the way to go."

They were seated in the *gîte's* living room, where they had set up the laptop on the coffee table. Both of them were seated on cushions on the floor, the remains of cheese, crackers, and olives on the table. Barak was drinking beer, Estelle wine, and both were tired. It was after midnight, and they'd been researching for hours. Barak's eyes were gritty, and his brain felt like a big knot.

"I'm not sure I'd call this a holiday!" Estelle gestured at the list of sites they'd made after their internet search. "We need to narrow these down, and to be honest, the internet doesn't have nearly enough detail. We need books! Maps!"

"I agree." Barak felt they'd barely scratched the surface of what they needed to know. "And we might even be completely wrong."

"Possibly. But it feels right!" Estelle raked her hand through her hair, her frustration and tiredness clear. "And I can't help but think on what Ash last said to you about the Templars."

"Don't bring that up again," Barak groaned.

"It's important. This is another facet of the count that we can't afford to ignore. It could well be tied into all of this."

Barak contemplated his conversation with Ash earlier that evening. Their latest job was delivering more than just a treasure hunt. It had brought bombs and subterfuge, and a new, unknown enemy that they feared was linked with the shadowy figure of the count.

Barak finally looked at Estelle. "I feel we're mired in darkness and cobwebs. That nothing's real. It's like..." he struggled to describe it. "Like trying to hold water with my bare hands."

Estelle reached for her glass of wine. "We can't forget yesterday's success. Finding Lucien and that facility was concrete proof of what they do. I know we've encountered their soldiers many times, but I feel we achieved a tiny glimpse into their inner workings. This potential Templar link just adds a whole new level of intrigue."

"But also another thread to pick away at. That's a good thing. However," he hated what he was about to say, because he loved spending time with Estelle, "I think we should return to England, and see Jackson at The Retreat. Thinking we could crack things from here is nuts. Fun, but nuts nonetheless."

"I know, but I like it here."

"I confess, I suggested it really just to be with you." He kissed her hand, happy to see her blush with pleasure. "I've loved every second of it. But, I'm a bit worried about Lucien." An uneasy feeling had been growing in him all night. "I don't know why, but I just am."

"You don't trust him?"

"I think I do. Maybe I just don't trust what's been done to him. He could be a ticking time bomb—metaphorically speaking. I think I'm going to phone Jackson."

"Now?" Estelle checked her watch. "It's late."

Barak reached for his phone. "I don't care. I have to. Hopefully things are okay." He shrugged, trying to make light of it, but he just had a bad feeling he couldn't shake. "Maybe Ash's news has made me paranoid."

"Trust your instincts. I do. I'll search for flights and get us on the earliest one. And for the record, I've enjoyed every second, too."

⸱⸱❖⸱⸱

Jackson had been mired in a dream-filled sleep when his phone rang, and for a few moments he couldn't work out where he was, or what was happening.

Instinctively, he grabbed his phone, more to stop the noise than anything else. "Hello? Jackson speaking."

"It's Barak. Sorry. Did I wake you?"

Jackson groaned as he lay back on his pillow, staring into the darkness, and slightly dazzled by the light from his phone. There was no streetlight filtering into The Retreat, and the darkness was all consuming. "Yes, but it's a relief. I was having a horrible sleep. Is everything okay?"

"Just frustrated with our slow research, but we know we need to be realistic, and we can't justify spending weeks here. We're coming home tomorrow. But that's not why I called. I'm worried about Lucien."

Jackson sat up, his own fears rising again. "Why?"

"We don't know what they've done to him. I'm worried that something will trigger him. Something unexpected. Or *they* will. Something Lucien can't control...or won't want to."

"Like a sleeper agent?" Jackson couldn't keep the incredulity out of his voice.

Barak gave one of his deep, melodic laughs. "Something like that. I'm probably paranoid. I know I'm tired. I guess I just wanted to reassure myself that everything was okay."

Jackson rose from his bed, flicked the lamp on, and reached for his clothes. "He's in an observation room, and the team that extracted him is guarding him. It's not a cell, but we're being careful."

After a protracted argument earlier in the evening that Jackson lost, Lucien had been confined to the observation room rather than the bedroom that had been prepared for him. Miller, the team leader, had argued for caution. Waylen had agreed. Jackson had felt that every promise he'd made had been broken, but it was out of his control. Lucien had looked at him with barely concealed anger and disappointment, and maybe even fear. Fortunately, Layla had struck up a good relationship with him as she took samples and ran tests. Now they were just waiting for results.

"I'll get dressed," Jackson continued, "and I'll go and check on him. You get some sleep too, okay. You coming here tomorrow?"

"Yeah. I'll text you the time when I know it. Be careful, Jackson!"

"You too."

Jackson ended the call, and for a moment sat quietly, gathering his thoughts. The Retreat was utterly silent, but he was tucked down another side passage behind a locked door, and no one else was sleeping here. London could have exploded above him and he would never know. His room was large and comfortable, and like the rest of the headquarters, decorated in the Art Nouveau style.

Rubbing the sleep from his eyes, he got dressed, reached into the drawer for the service issued firearm he'd been trained to use, and strapped on his holster—just in case. Within minutes he reached the dimly lit corridor leading to the labs and the observation room, and heard shouts and thumping sounds from up ahead.

Shit.

He ran, and as he rounded the corner, he paused, horrified. The door to the observation room lay on the floor, light blazing from the room, and Lucien was standing atop it, the body of a guard on the ground at his feet. Lucien was clad only in his scrub bottoms. His feet and chest were bare, and his tattoos writhed in the light. His skin glowed like burnished copper, and as Jackson ran into view, Lucien turned unblinking, metallic eyes on him.

Jackson fumbled for his gun. The last thing he wanted to do was shoot Lucien, but there were no other guards in sight. *Where were they? Were they all dead?*

Lucien stepped off the door and over the guard's body, walking towards Jackson. He showed no sign of recognition.

Jackson's mouth was dry as he spoke. "Lucien! It's Jackson. I'm a friend. I'm here to help. Stop, or I'll shoot."

Lucien didn't stop, instead cocking his head at the gun before ignoring it. Jackson backed up, steadying his aim. If he shot at his leg, he wouldn't kill him, but that was a risky shot. He might miss.

"Lucien! I don't want to shoot, but I will. Stop *now!*"

He kept coming, and the only image that flashed into Jackson's head was the Terminator. Lucien wasn't going to stop until he was dead.

Jackson aimed for his legs, hoping the metallic skin didn't extend that far. Two shots missed and hit the wall, but the third found its mark—and didn't penetrate his skin or slow him down. Lucien blinked, and his eyes turned black before becoming metallic again.

Herne's balls. He had no Nephilim to save him now. He was screwed. Jackson raised his gun, aiming for Lucien's chest as he retreated down the corridor. His aim was true this time, but again, the bullets seemed to bounce off him. Jackson glanced to either side, wondering which was the best room he could shelter in, and he yelled for the guards on the main entrance. They were a distance away, but the sound should carry.

They needed an alarm system. If he survived this, he would insist on it.

Lucien's pace quickened, and Jackson fired again. He'd be out of bullets soon—not that they made the slightest difference. Just as he was about to turn and run, a figure crawled into view beyond Lucien and raised a weapon. At the same time, someone yelled from behind him. "Get down!"

Jackson turned and saw Miller with a rifle in his hands.

"Now, Jackson!"

Jackson threw himself to the floor and rolled to the side of the passage, just as Lucien broke into a sprint. Miller and the guard fired together, shots peppering Lucien from both directions. After a few faltering steps, Lucien dropped and thudded to the floor.

Miller raced to Lucien and stood over him, nudging his body with his toe. "He's out cold."

Jackson sat up, heart thumping. "Not dead?"

Miller grinned. "I wouldn't kill your prized asset, Jackson."

He stumbled over his words. "How? What?"

"Something the lab's been working on. Armour-piercing tranquilliser darts—especially designed for these guys. I wasn't sure they'd work, but I'm impressed. However, I'm not sure how long he'll be out for."

"Where are we going to put him? We haven't got any cells here!"

"We'll improvise."

Twenty-Nine

Niel's entire body ached, especially his jaw. In fact, it was clenched shut so tightly, his muscles felt locked in position.

For a second, he was utterly confused. Then his memory flooded back. He'd been attacked from behind. *By Mouse.*

Curse words littered his thoughts, but he didn't move or open his eyes, needing his captors to think he was still unconscious. He was lying face-down on the bare earth, soil and grit pressing into his skin. His hands were bound, and he heard breathing and felt the unmistakable presence of someone close by. A guard—most likely a knight.

He considered his options. His restraints were tight, and felt like rope, but Niel was supernaturally strong. However, he needed to be quick if he was to break free *and* overpower the guard. *But what had Mouse used on him?* The most likely option was a Taser or something similar. Ash had described his experience when he'd been captured by Black Cronos in the Igigi's cave, and it sounded the same.

It was a weakness, and Niel hated to be vulnerable. Had Mouse known about that, or was it just a lucky guess? A woman as small as she was needed to pack a powerful weapon. At least she didn't kill him. As he mused on that, his smouldering resentment became puzzlement. Why wasn't he dead? He must be a bargaining tool. Well, screw that.

He heard footsteps behind him and continued to pretend he was unconscious. A man joined his guard, and they both started to talk in hushed voices in a foreign language.

Portuguese. Interesting. Fortunately, Niel understood every word, and heard enough to know that Nahum and Harlan were also hostages, and that the others were stuck in another room.

In seconds, another voice joined them, and they all moved further away. The group was angry and frustrated. Their plans had been thwarted, and it sounded as if their other team members were in trouble. This was his moment to act, while their attention was elsewhere. Although his hands were bound behind him, his wings would not be impeded. He opened his eyes to slits, and saw he was a short distance from the church wall.

Niel flexed his shoulders and his wings expanded in one smooth, powerful movement. His wingspan was so great, he connected with a guard behind him, making him stumble. Using his wings as leverage, he bounded to his feet and ran, and seconds later was off the ground and flying to the bell tower at the top of the church. He ducked inside and sheltered within its thick walls.

His limbs still felt stiff, but he jerked his hands outwards, shredding the rope to free his arms. He didn't have any weapons except his bare hands, but they were good enough.

He dropped onto the church roof, ran across it, and peered over the side. One of the knights was searching the night sky for him, sword clenched in his hand. The other two had vanished. *To the tower perhaps?* With the other two nowhere in sight, Niel plunged over the far side of the church, ready to circle around and attack the knight. He'd been caught off guard once. He wouldn't be again.

Gabe took a deep breath. "Can we all focus, please!" He glared at Shadow, who was about to start arguing with Ash. "This is the place! The Chamber of Truth. Somewhere in here is a way to another room. Or a map. Or something."

So much for his motivational speech.

He continued, undaunted. "Now that we're in here again, we can't fuck it up. Concentrate."

"Is that aimed at me?" Shadow asked.

"Everyone."

"Well, if I can point out one important thing," Ash said in a low voice, "the mud has seeped into some rather interesting grooves."

They were all standing in the doorway, scared to set foot in the room again in case they triggered something, but Ash pointed to a series of grooves etched into the centre of the floor that weren't visible before.

Shadow grimaced. "Well, it's good to see that our brush with death wasn't all for nothing."

Ash ignored her tone. "What's through the other door?"

Gabe answered him. "Another antechamber, a short passage, and then de la More's tomb, right under the crypt."

"Anything in that?"

"We left Nahum and Harlan exploring it. The room itself was plain, the tomb huge. I have no idea if they found anything. They were attacked in the crypt, but won that fight."

"Okay." Ash nodded. "So this is called the Chamber of Truth. The dagger points the way to a treasure. We think. This room," he looked at it with trepidation, "is the answer. Look at how detailed it is. You already triggered one trap. We need to trigger the *right* mechanism."

"Another keyhole?" Theo asked, looking hopeful.

"Perhaps. We need to think like a Templar."

Shadow stared at him. "What do you think the grooves are?"

"They run along a set of slabs. I think they're a stairway." Ash pointed downward. "To another level. Let's face it—if there's another room, it's either accessed through the rear wall, or the front one. And that's where you triggered the stone that allowed the flood of mud, which has now mercifully stopped. There's already a room on that side and this side."

Shadow grinned, and in the torch light, and smeared with mud and blood, she looked like a demon. "I like it. You're right. You're good at this."

"It's just logical. We just need to work out what triggers it. Quickly." He nodded to the opposite door. "Before they find a way in. We also need something to bargain with."

Gabe wished they could fly. That would mean they wouldn't need to touch the floor at all. Unfortunately, the room wasn't big enough to allow any decent manoeuvrability. He studied the ground again, looking for patterns in the slabs, depressions, anything uneven. Ash was right. The remnants of the mud helped. It had coated the lower half of the walls, and still pooled in the corners, but it did highlight some of the reliefs.

"Ash, I think the key must have closed the flooding mechanism and allowed some of the mud to drain downwards, too." He pointed at the edge of some of the slabs that looked to have fine grills in them. "This place must have taken a long time to build."

"Well, the door jammed," Shadow pointed out, "so let's hope nothing else has failed over the years."

Ash stepped inside the room. "Follow me. I think the slabs marked with *Agnus Dei* symbols are safe. Can you see how they snake across the floor? They look the most stable of all of them. And there's more of them than any other."

"Well spotted," Gabe said, following him. The *Agnus Dei* slabs were clustered around both entrances, which had prevented them causing more problems earlier.

Theo pointed at one of the images in the wall. "That looks like the keep, and it's set within the grounds. And is that the village?"

"I think so." Ash stepped carefully on the designated slabs until he stood in front of it. "And there's the church. Is that a lake in the grounds?"

"Looks like it," Shadow said. "The one by the pavilion."

"But is it relevant?" Gabe asked. He was behind the others, as there wasn't room for him to get closer. He studied the church relief and compared it to the others spread across the wall. "The village is far more detailed than the rest of the carvings. You can see the individual headstones in the graveyard, the bell tower, the path—even the lych-gate."

Ash nodded. "Too much detail to be irrelevant."

"The church cross!" Theo's voice rose with excitement. "It's sitting slightly proud."

"Isn't that a bit obvious?" Shadow asked, her voice filled with doubt.

"But look at how many other crosses there are," Gabe pointed out. "They're on all kinds of buildings spread across the map of Europe and the Middle East." It was the one constant of the images. Crosses were everywhere, large and small. Some were plain, others were ornate. "In fact, a few of them look as if they are sitting proud of the rest. Perhaps we need to press them at the same time."

"I doubt that," Ash said, but he sounded uncertain. "It makes more sense that the village church would be the trigger."

"For death?" Shadow asked scathingly.

"But what about the cross on Temple Mount?" Theo asked. "Or the ones in France. Wouldn't one of true significance be the one to try?"

"Surely Temple Mount is too obvious," Gabe reasoned.

"I agree," Ash said. "It's tempting to assume that, of course, but we're beneath Temple Church, next to William's crypt. It's logical to choose this one."

Shadow huffed. "Maybe that's what they want you to think."

Gabe was getting a headache. Trying to second guess someone else's reasoning, especially when they wanted to set a trap, was a nightmare.

Ash took a deep breath, in and out. "I'm going to try it." Ash laid his hand on the cross, hesitated for the briefest of moments, and then pressed it firmly. It clicked inwards and locked into place. Immediately, another loud grating sound resonated behind them, and Gabe spun around, ready to bolt for the door. *What could happen now? Pits of death? Spears shooting from the wall?*

Instead, to everyone's relief, the centre of the floor started to drop, revealing a series of steps leading down.

Gabe walked to the top of the them, torch shining into the depths. "These go down quite a long way. I'll lead."

⚜

Nahum stepped back into the shadows of the antechamber, beckoning Harlan to follow him.

"They're annoyed. We need to capitalise on it," Nahum whispered, while the leader, a man called de Moret, argued with another.

"How? We have no weapons, and that sneaky bitch, Mouse, is somewhere around here. Besides, if we act now, they could kill Niel."

"Just be prepared. And keep an eye on Mouse at all times!"

Harlan nodded, and Nahum studied the room for what felt like the hundredth time. After they had been captured, they had been hustled down the passage and into a small antechamber that must have been where Shadow and Gabe had been earlier. It was made of smooth stone blocks fitted tightly together, unadorned except that in one wall was an arched doorframe, a stone door sealing the way. The knights had tried to open it, but it was shut tight.

They were obviously wary of damaging it, so patience had won out over their frustration. More worryingly was the sound of Gabe and Shadow's muffled shouts on the other side. De Moret had tried to communicate with them, advising them of the situation and warning them to open the door, but they had told him they were trapped. Nahum wasn't sure if that was true or a ruse. Now, they had fallen silent.

Nahum wasn't sure what that meant. They could be dead, or they could have escaped. It was impossible to know. He decided to brave a question. "De Moret. You say you are Knights of Truth and Justice. Why haven't you got any information on how to open this?"

De Moret turned his deep-set eyes on him. "Because history has not been kind to us, and our predecessors chose to hide their treasure well. But we're close now. Too close to stop."

"Do you really think the treasure is here?"

"No. We believe another clue to the whereabouts of that treasure is here. The path has been hidden, so that only the true inheritors shall find it."

"How did you know to come here? To this church? Tonight."

"Theo Carmichael and Tower Keep have been under observation for a long time, as have many other places. We heard what he found. And what your companion discovered within it."

Nahum frowned, exchanging a worried glance with Harlan. "How did you find that out? He only opened the blade up hours ago."

De Moret smiled. "I have my ways."

"You have someone in the house."

"Perhaps. It is no business of yours."

Nahum wouldn't push it, but maybe Theo had employed someone new recently. Maybe it was even Owen, the gardener they had suspected earlier. He pressed on. "And you hired Mouse."

"An admirable assistant."

Harlan intervened. "I know your name. It's a Templar name."

"My ancestors were Templars, as were many of our other knights' forebears. Our order is old, dedicated. Determined. The treasure is ours. Not Theo's."

"You know, I am not unsympathetic to your cause," Nahum said, and meant it. "You were treated badly. I understand what drives you. Let us help."

"We don't need your help."

"Actually, I think you do. And we need yours. Our friends are on the other side of that. You need to get in. We have the key, too."

"No." De Moret cut him off and turned away. "We will get the key, and if you're lucky, you'll get to live."

"At least you tried," Harlan said softly. "Meanwhile, we're at a stalemate. The night is marching on, there are dead knights in the church, and soon it will be daylight. At least, I hope it will be. This night seems to have lasted for ever."

Another flurry of activity had them turning to the doorway, but Mouse had returned, carrying a bag. She ignored Nahum and Harlan and crossed to de Moret's side. "I've got the charges."

"Everything okay up top?"

"All quiet."

"Good. Let's blow this door."

"Woah!" Harlan stepped forward, alarmed. "You could bring the roof down and kill us all!"

De Moret glared at him. "I know exactly what I'm doing. Who do you think set the bombs in the lodge?"

Nahum was beginning to hate this man and his smug smile. Now he fervently hoped Shadow and Gabe had made progress. "You nearly killed my brothers."

"But I didn't. While I would rather not do this, we have to get in there, or all is lost."

Without another word, he turned his back and started to lay charges around the door. Mouse gave Nahum a fleeting look that was almost an apology. Right now, he hated her, too. For some strange reason, Niel had felt he could trust her. He took a deep breath and looked away. Anger wouldn't help him now.

Only icy calm would do.

Thirty

A huge, iron-bound door blocked their way at the bottom of the stairs, and Shadow waited impatiently for Ash to open it. They heard the repetitive clunking sound of several mechanisms releasing before it finally unlocked and revealed another room.

For a second, as their torches swept over the space, Shadow couldn't quite work out what she was seeing. Everything seemed to glow with a golden light.

And then she realised. It was gold.

"Oh, my God!" Theo said, almost breathless. "Is that what I think it is?"

"Yes!" Shadow said, grinning from ear to ear. The golden, twinkling light beckoned her. "At last, we have actually found treasure!"

"*Wait*!" Gabe's arm shot out in front of her to stop her from walking forward. "Can we just check the place out first, before we trigger some cataclysmic event?"

As one, they all shone their torches across the floor and around the rest of the room, discovering that it was designed like a church. The walls and floor were constructed of pale grey stone, but the central walkway was lined with gilded columns that soared to a golden roof, and at the far end was a huge altar. Throughout the entire room, heaped on pews and the floor, was treasure.

"Oh my goodness," Theo squeaked. "There's so much gold! Is it gilded, or solid?"

Ash whistled. "Surely not solid gold—or at least, not all of it."

"The floor looks safe," Gabe said, gingerly testing the ground beyond the bottom step. "I think we've passed all the tests now."

They slowly made their way into the church, torches flicking everywhere. Shadow spotted a series of arched recesses with candles and lanterns, and borrowing Theo's matches, she moved methodically along them, lighting them as she went. The golden light magnified and bloomed, and as it reflected off the surfaces, the light increased, revealing the true wealth around them.

Reliquaries of all shapes and sizes were heaped on the floor and on stone plinths, displayed to impress. Gold and silver crosses studded with gems, caskets inlaid with precious metals, gold coins, jewels, goblets, and so much more that Shadow could barely take it all in. The most impressive sight of all was the enormous gold cross mounted on the wall behind the altar. It was three times the height of a man, encrusted with jewels, and absolutely dazzling. She wondered how they had managed to get it down here. She had no interest in Christianity, but nevertheless, she appreciated that the cross was awe-inspiring, meant to drive the devout to their knees.

Gabe joined her, looking troubled. Uncertain. "I didn't expect this. I thought we'd find nothing! Or at best, a bag of gold."

"But this is good, right?"

"No." His mouth was set in a grim line. "So much hidden wealth is insane. And greedy."

"But you said you were once this wealthy. A prince with palaces, servants, and endless wealth."

"I was, but eventually it left me feeling uncomfortable. However, our God liked such tributes. It exalted him. And this type of worship clearly didn't change in all of the centuries that followed our demise. This should have been put to better use."

"To be honest, Gabe," Shadow said, trying to keep the impatience out of her voice, "the other Gods are no different. I don't know why you remain so disappointed by them all. You expect too much of them. I don't." *Especially after being conscripted into Herne's Wild Hunt.* "And I am not going to apologise for liking gold."

His eyes narrowed, and he headed to a pile of weapons. He clasped an ornate, jewelled hilt, and pulled it out of its scabbard. The edge of the blade was rusted. "This place is not immune from the damp of ages. The Templars' swords, perhaps?"

Ash joined them, abandoning his inspection of a gilded casket. "Or the weapons of those they escorted to Jerusalem. Remember, they acted as bankers—for royalty too, not just pilgrims." He stared up at the ceiling. "As above as below. Another layer of meaning. Another church below the one on the ground level."

"Didn't you say," Shadow said, recalling his earlier suspicions, "that this might lead to the Emerald Tablet?"

"Yes, I did. I wonder if it's here? Of all the items present, that would be of the greatest value to us—and to JD."

"Over all this gold?" Shadow was incredulous.

"Yes, and we can't take *all* of this!" Gabe swept his arm out. "It's impossible. And besides, it should be in a museum. Theo!"

Theo was still browsing the objects in a daze. "Yes?"

"You still aim to share this, right?"

"Of course. Can you imagine this displayed to the world? Or even this very room? It's magnificent!"

"But what about the knights?" Shadow pointed upwards. "And Harlan, Nahum, and Niel. We need to bargain with them!"

"There's no way, Shadow, that they will carry out all of this un-detected," Ash pointed out. "I'm going to start searching for the tablet...just in case it's here."

Before he could say anything else, a dull boom resonated above them.

"Fuck it! What now?" Gabe asked, already jogging to the bottom of the stairs.

Shadow ran with him. "If they've blown the door, they could trigger something again!" Determined not to get stuck or half-drowned in mud again, Shadow sprinted past Gabe and up the stairs into the dust-filled room, yelling, "Stop! Don't move!"

A knight stood in the shattered doorway, sword drawn, and a grenade in his hand. His eyes glittered with fury in the pale light.

"*Stop!*" she yelled again. "If you don't want to destroy everything, I suggest you listen. We have found treasure. Lots of it. More than any of us will ever need. But if you make one wrong move, you could bring everything down on our heads."

His eyes raked over her and Gabe, before studying the room with its mud-blackened wall and floor. "What happened here?"

"A trap." She looked beyond the knight. "Where are our friends?"

His head jerked, and another knight pushed Harlan and Nahum into view. Both looked fine, but furious. A small figure was next to them. *Mouse.* "Your other friend is outside the church. Still alive. But he won't be if you don't guide me inside."

"Step only on the slabs marked with the *Agnus Dei*," Shadow in-structed. "Nothing else."

"You're lucky that blowing that door didn't set anything else off," Gabe said. "Nahum! Harlan. You're unharmed?"

"Fine, brother."

"As well as can be expected," Harlan drawled.

The knight still stood in the doorway. "Who else is with you?"

"My brother, Ash, is downstairs, and Theo. That's all." Gabe released his sword hilt that he'd been clasping. "We need to work together. There's no point in fighting now."

"*I'll* decide that. Step back!"

Bristling with annoyance, but knowing they needed to comply for now, Gabe and Shadow made space for the knights to enter.

The knight pointed at Nahum. "You first. Join your friends."

Stepping carefully, Nahum studied the floor and crossed to the stairs, finally reaching Gabe and Shadow's side. "There you go, de Moret. It's all safe!"

Reassured, de Moret crossed quickly, and at the top of the steps, stared downwards. He summoned several knights to join him, but left Harlan and Mouse guarded in the antechamber. "Your friend will stay here as insurance for your good behaviour. Now, take me downstairs."

With Gabe at the lead, they headed down the stairs again, de Moret and his knights at the rear.

⚊⟨❖⟩⚊

After a furiously intense fight, Niel killed the final knight he found at the bottom of the bell tower.

He had not intended to kill any more men; only incapacitate them. A courtesy, after they had spared his life. He had secured two of them, knocking them unconscious, and locking them in one of the church rooms, but the last knight refused to yield.

Niel was bloodied, too. His opponent, one of the most experienced swordsmen he'd ever fought, had inflicted cuts on his arms and legs, an especially deep one across his flank. He regretted the death. He would have rather spared him. Plus, killing someone in a house of God made him uncomfortable. He was under no illusions about the old God who had caused them such anguish, and he certainly owed him nothing, but for the many who treated this place with respect and reverence, he regretted sullying it. He only wished they'd come to their senses and make their own decisions, without recourse to old scripture that had no place anymore.

However, before he headed to the crypt, he stepped outside the side door and checked the graveyard. Shadowy figures were already moving through the gravestones. *More knights.*

Retreating inside, and hoping they wouldn't use any more bombs for fear of attracting attention, Niel shut and barred the door, and then wedged a pew behind it for good measure. He did the same with the main entrance, checked that the men were still incapacitated, and then headed downstairs to the crypt. He hated that they were now trapped inside, but at least they were secure. And they could escape through the bell tower, if needed.

Once in the crypt, it was clear where he needed to go. He relieved the dead knights of their weapons and dropped through the hole in the base of the tomb, landing lightly on his feet. Niel's stealth always surprised people. They assumed that because of his size he would be loud. However, all the Nephilim had been taught how to move silently. Their fathers had drummed it into them. It was part of their heritage. They might not have fey magic, but their angelic blood possessed certain unique qualities.

Progressing along the short passageway, he saw another chamber ahead and several knights facing away from him. Not knowing who or what was beyond them brought him to a halt. One wrong move now could be disastrous. He lowered himself to the ground, melting into the deepest shadows, and settled in to watch and listen.

Thirty-One

Ash was searching through the contents of one of the gold caskets when Gabe and Shadow arrived with Nahum, several armed knights behind them.

He straightened, placing his hand on his sword hilt, and moved closer to Theo, anxious to shield the old man from whatever the knights might threaten. He noted the lead knight held a grenade, and suspected they had more hidden in their cloaks. They'd be idiots to use them here, but Ash wasn't taking anything for granted.

Nahum acknowledged Ash with a nod before addressing the knights. "De Moret. You have found what you came for. There is no need for any more violence."

De Moret didn't speak. Instead, he strode down the central path and dropped to his knees in front of the altar, taking a few moments for a murmured prayer. Then he stood, hands on hips, studying the underground church. "Magnificent."

"Is this all of it?" Ash asked. "All of the lost treasure?"

"No." De Moret walked over to the nearest casket, picking up a gold cross with reverence. "There is much more hidden in other places. Somewhere in here will tell us where."

"Perhaps," Ash agreed cautiously. "Although, I think you may find the map carved into the Chamber of Truth above will be of more use."

"We will study all of it. And everything will be removed."

"You can't!" Theo clenched his fists and lifted his chin defiantly. "This is history! You can't take it all!"

"It is *our* history, and we most certainly will."

"How?" Gabe sounded irritated. "It would take a week at least to move all of this. The village would see you. And there are dead bodies in the churchyard, and a half-destroyed tomb in the crypt."

De Moret gave an icy smile. "But there is a convenient passage leading from here to Temple Keep. It may be blocked for now—oh yes, I have heard from my men. But we can rectify that. And no one visits the crypt. We will lock the door, clear the churchyard, and no one will be any the wiser."

"Except that you're talking about *my* home!" Theo said, outraged.

"If you want to live to enjoy it, you will shut up and let us work. Either that, or we'll kill you and let you rot down here. And that goes for the rest of you, too."

Gabe laughed. "Generous sentiment from a man of God. Have you lost your way?"

De Moret's lips twisted as he stared at Gabe. "I know what you are, and I do not fear you, or your fallen fathers, *Nephilim*." He virtually spat the word out. "You were cast out. You should have drowned. Perhaps I will finish all of you. Do the job the flood clearly failed at." He nodded at the knights. "Keep them quiet while we search down here, and then I'll decide what to do with them. The papers must be here somewhere."

"Papers?" Ash asked, unable to stop himself. "Surely they will have long since rotted. The swords down here have rusted. Maybe other things, too."

De Moret marched to his side and held out his hand. "I gather you have the key. Give it to me."

The key was the only bargaining tool they had at this point, and Ash hated to hand it over. However, Harlan was a prisoner, and he had no idea where Niel was, or how many other men were at de Moret's disposal, which meant the knights had the upper hand for now. Reluctantly, Ash handed it over.

De Moret held the key up. "De la More masterminded all of this, you know, but we never knew where the treasure's final resting place would be. We suspected that his close friends may have picked another spot, but it was here all along. As is his tomb."

"I thought his tomb was upstairs?"

"No. A false tomb for the uninitiated." De Moret smiled icily at Ash, before making a few swift adjustments to the key. In seconds, another key was in his hands, a small golden one that had been concealed within the first. "He was a clever man, as am I."

De Moret marched over to the huge, golden altar and started to search it, while Ash and Theo were escorted to where his brothers and Shadow were guarded by a ring of knights. Their weapons were collected and placed well out of reach, and for now, none of them resisted. Ash suspected that like him, his companions were curious as to what was about to happen.

De Moret was assisted by two men, and within a few minutes, they had success. He inserted the key into a place low down at the centre of the altar, and a section of it split into two, revealing a tomb hidden within.

Ash shook his head. "You were right about a puzzle box. This whole place has secrets within secrets."

"And there are bound to be more," Shadow said. "De Moret seems to know what he's looking for."

"Instructions that were passed down," Gabe suggested, "even when the map was lost."

A shout of victory ended their conversation, as de Moret held a package aloft and addressed his knights. "The lost papers of the Templars! The list of treasures of the ages. And this. One of the greatest treasures of all."

His companion lifted a bulky object and placed it on the altar. For a moment, Ash couldn't see a thing as his view was blocked by one of the pillars. And then a dazzling green light shimmered over the altar. Ash shifted position, heart in his mouth, knowing what he would see, and yet he still wasn't prepared for it.

The Emerald Tablet of Hermes Trismegistus was propped on the altar in its own support. A candle had been placed behind it, and the light dazzled outward, highlighting the words that had been carved into it. Ash could feel its power, even from a distance. *The block of emerald alone would have been priceless, but the information it contained...*

The men who were guarding them were a short distance away, distracted by their surroundings. They kept a cursory watch on the group, but most of their attention was on the magnificent church and its contents. Ash took advantage of it to address his companions. Keeping his voice low, he said, "We can't let them take it. It's too powerful in the wrong hands."

"But is it any better," Nahum said softly, "in JD's?"

"If we are to have any hope of understanding Black Cronos and defeating them, we need that tablet."

A hushed discussion was taking place at the altar, and furious glances were being cast in their direction.

Shadow's voice dripped acid. "We will not walk out of here alive, despite his smooth words and assurances. We have seen too much, and know too much. And he knows who we are, which suggests to me that they *are* linked to Black Cronos. We need to act now."

"You still have your knives, Shadow?" Nahum asked.

"Of course."

"They've hemmed us in well," Ash noted. They had been placed in a simple side chapel that echoed the design above them, with a low ceiling that would restrict their abilities.

De Moret finished his conversation, and one of his companions hurried back along the nave and to the stairs. He cast them a dismissive glance, and brought his hand down to their guards. It was the sign they were waiting for.

Shadow acted immediately. She jumped onto a pew, raced along it with a daring show of balance and speed, and before the closest knight could respond, placed her hand on his head and vaulted over him, slashing his neck with her knife with breath-taking speed.

Blood spurted out in a wide arc, splattering everyone as he fell to the floor, and the other knights scattered. The man heading for the stairs broke into a run, shouting to his colleagues above, and Shadow pursued him.

But that was as much as Ash could see, because the knights attacked, and he was suddenly fighting for his life.

⸺❖⸺

Harlan heard the muffled shout from below and knew exactly what that meant. The closest knight turned to him, his eyes hard in the dim candle-light.

"Your time is up, American."

Harlan reacted instinctively. He kicked him in the knee and he stumbled backwards. But there were at least another three men clustered in the antechamber, plus the highly untrustworthy Mouse.

He was screwed.

In an act of horrible, ungentlemanly behaviour, he grabbed Mouse and pushed her into the knights, trusting they wouldn't kill one of their own, but frankly at this stage not caring one way or the other, and then faced the one remaining knight behind him. He ducked and rolled as his sword slashed at him, and then watched with surprise as the knight was dragged backwards, his shout of surprise ending with a blood curdled cry as his throat was slit.

Niel strode into view, blood-stained and covered in dirt, his eyes gleaming with a battle-hardened mania as he advanced on the others. Unexpectedly, Mouse jabbed her Taser into the man closest to her, and he fell with an agonised shout, his body bucking and twisting on the floor. In the confusion, Harlan jumped on the back of another knight, punching him repeatedly in the head as Niel tackled the others. Harlan and his opponent fell to the ground, rolling over each other as Harlan tried to dodge the long blade that had fortunately become tangled in the knight's cloak.

For a few minutes of grunting darkness and confusion, Harlan couldn't work out what was going on. All he knew was to keep punching and rolling, fearing he would feel the fiery sting of a blade between his ribs at any moment. Adrenalin made him stronger, and with a final punch that made the knight's head slam into the ground, his opponent finally slumped, unconscious.

Harlan was coated in sweat and blood. His knuckles were raw, every bone in his body seemed to ache, but he was alive. Most of the lanterns had been smashed in the fight, but the remaining light revealed that Mouse was pinned in the corner, Niel's long blade at her throat. Her mask had gone, and Harlan finally saw her face.

She looked terrified, her beautiful almond eyes open wide, her lips parted in a plea, her hands up, palms outwards. "I'm sorry, Niel, I had no choice earlier. If I hadn't incapacitated you, they would have killed you."

Niel didn't speak, instead he pressed his blade to her skin, and a spot of blood rolled down her neck.

Harlan staggered to his feet, using the wall to lever himself up. "Niel, she could have used the Taser on us. She didn't. She used it on him." He toed the man lying on the floor. "I must admit, she talked their cause up well, though, earlier."

"Because she's an accomplished liar," Niel growled, "who'll do and say anything to save her skin. But that's who you are, right, Mouse? You'll act for anyone who pays enough."

"That's not true! I have my boundaries, as do you. I had to make a choice today—for you and for me. I knew I had to wait for the right time to strike. I bought us time."

"How very convenient." Niel's expression was bleak. Hard. Harlan suspected he was at war with himself. He wanted his revenge, but equally couldn't quite bring himself to kill her.

"Niel." Harlan's voice sounded harsh in the hushed chamber. "Our friends are downstairs. They need our help. Remove her Taser, and let her go."

"No. There are other knights up there, and she may let them in. Search her, Harlan. Strip her of weapons. And be careful."

Harlan held out his hand. "Taser first."

Mouse didn't hesitate to hand it over, and he quickly strapped the pouch it was in around his waist before almost apologetically searching her. He found a small dagger strapped to her thigh, and one on her forearm, but that was it. She didn't even look at him. Instead, she stared only at Niel. Harlan felt like a jerk. Tension simmered between the two of them.

Securing the knives, Harlan stepped back. "All done. She's clean."

"Good. Where now, Harlan?"

"There are stairs to another level in the next room. Let me go first," he insisted. "I heard the instructions. Stick to the *Agnus Dei*."

Wondering what he was about to find below, he started across the chamber and headed down the steps.

Thirty-Two

Gabe grabbed a gilded icon from the top of the small altar and hurled it at the advancing knight, taking advantage of the confusion caused by Shadow's attack. At the same time, he expanded his wings and charged, using his wings as another weapon.

The scene in the chapel was chaotic. His brothers were using anything handy as weapons. Icons, crosses, even the wooden pews, but the knights' long blades bought them space. Theo kept back, but added to the confusion by hurling priceless objects at their enemy.

Gabe picked up a pew and used it as a battering ram, running at the man closest to him. He pinned him to the wall with a blistering crash, and Gabe heard the knight's ribs crack. Gabe lifted the pew and slammed it into his head. It snapped back, hit the wall, and he slumped to the ground.

But Gabe couldn't celebrate yet. Another knight was already on him, his sword aimed at his gut, and he had no more room to swing the pew. Gabe swept around instead, his wings throwing his opponent into one of his companions, and they both went down in a tangle of limbs. Gabe needed a weapon. He lunged at an abandoned sword, which had slid beneath another pew.

Unfortunately, he wasn't quite quick enough. Another knight jumped over the pew, striking Gabe in his side, and he felt blood pump out, the sting of the blade like fire. Gabe scrabbled to turn, his long reach almost at the hilt, just as the man swung the blade at his outstretched arm.

—◆◈◆—

Shadow raced across the nave, dodging caskets, icons, and other treasure, and with only seconds to spare before the knight was out of sight on the steps to the upper chamber, released her knife.

Infuriatingly, it struck the wall and ricocheted to the floor, missing her target. Before she could throw the next one, running footsteps indicated that another knight was already behind her.

She turned and took aim, and with grim satisfaction, saw this weapon hit its mark. It struck the man in the throat, and he fell immediately. De Moret was right behind him, his sword raised and hatred in his eyes. In the seconds she had spare, she raced to the pile of their confiscated weapons, grabbed her sword and Nahum's, and turned to face de Moret.

—◆◈◆—

Nahum smashed at his opponent's sword with a large gold cross, using it to knock the blade out of his hands.

The irony of the situation wasn't lost on him. A Nephilim using a cross to battle the remains of a Templar order, whose knights had sworn to protect the pilgrims who wished to pay their respects to God. Would their fallen fathers be pleased at such a fight, or would they find something to fault in Nahum's actions? No doubt his own father, Remiel, would laugh. *Another point scored against the old God.*

Nahum blocked the thoughts from his mind as he swung the cross again, smashing the knight on the temple and sending him sprawling. Gabe was spreadeagled on the floor, a man looming over him, sword raised. Nahum smacked the cross into his arm, and with a grunt of pain, the knight fell awkwardly across the upended pew. Gabe grabbed the sword he'd been reaching for and immediately impaled the fallen man.

Nahum pulled Gabe to his feet. Several knights lay on the ground now, either dead or unconscious, and Ash was tackling the final one. Nahum ran up behind him and brought the cross down on his head. He crumpled to the floor.

Ash sighed with relief. "Thank you, brother." He turned to Theo. "Are you all right?"

To be honest, Theo looked a little green as he took in the bloodshed and injuries, but he nodded. "I'm fine, thank you. A little winded, but otherwise unharmed. But Shadow..."

His sentence was unfinished, his gaze beyond them, and they all turned to watch Shadow nimbly fighting de Moret, wielding both of her swords with an effortless grace and dexterity.

Gabe ran to the nave, the rest following, but it was clear that she didn't need any help. De Moret, for all his skills, was retreating. They bounded over pews, dodged around piles of gold, and leaped over caskets, the clash of their swords echoing around the church. Then Nahum remembered the knight who'd ran up the stairs. There was no sign of his body. He must have escaped.

Nahum yelled, "I'll head upstairs!"

However, by the time he'd reached the steps, a body was tumbling down to meet him, the smell of burnt flesh biting his nostrils. Nahum stepped back to watch the man's twitching body as Harlan descended the final stairs.

Harlan grinned as he waved the Taser. "I like this thing! I might have to get one."

"Looks like you already have," Nahum answered, peering past him to see Mouse, and then Niel right behind her. Ignoring Mouse for now, he said, "Niel. Good to see you."

"Brother." Niel's eyes were hard, his expression unreadable, except that Nahum knew him all too well. Niel liked Mouse, and she had betrayed him. "Is everyone okay?"

"Fine. Well, de Moret still fights, but Shadow has his measure." Nahum watched her for a few seconds, noting that Ash and Gabe circled close by her, in case she needed assistance. She didn't. If anything, she was holding back—toying with de Moret, like a cat with a mouse. De Moret knew it, too. Nahum could see the sweat on him even from a distance, and the knowledge that he was losing was clear by his increasingly desperate actions.

Nahum turned away and addressed Niel again. "Are they all dead upstairs?"

"Mostly. More were gathering outside, though."

"Then let's secure the survivors, and guard the doors. Harlan can watch Mouse."

"No. She's too untrustworthy."

Mouse spoke to the group for the first time. "No, I'm not. I told you, I'm on your side. I saved your life!"

Niel's gaze flickered and then hardened again, and Nahum intervened. "Niel, with me, now. I need you. Harlan?"

"I'm on it." Harlan gestured Mouse further into the church, the Taser aimed at her. He picked up the fallen knight's sword for good measure. Mouse didn't object. She walked, hands raised in surrender, and then took a seat on a pew, like a meek penitent.

Nahum heard Shadow's victory cry as he hustled Niel up the stairs. He didn't need to see de Moret fall. He'd seen enough bloodshed for one day.

Ash surveyed the fallen men and the blood-splattered gold, and wondered if it was really worth it. And then his gaze fell on the Emerald Tablet of Hermes Trismegistus.

This was worth it.

A splash of de Moret's blood marred its pristine surface, and Ash used the remnants of his torn shirt, damaged when he'd hurriedly expanded his wings, to wipe it clean. The candle still burned behind it, seeming to set light to the words carved on it. The chatter between Shadow, Gabe, and Theo, melted away as the words danced before his eyes. They were easily legible, and yet contained meaning that his special language skills could not discern.

The block of emerald was at least two hand-spans wide, four long, and several inches thick. The writing was cursive, ornate, and bewitching. Magic emanated from it, and yet it wasn't a grimoire. Nor was it a spell. However, it promised the secrets of the universe; the fundamentals of magic that Raziel had bound into his book, but in some kind of coded form.

Or at least that's what alchemists believed. Ash wasn't sure what to think.

Gabe's voice disturbed his thoughts. "At least we know that the count doesn't have it. It's been here for centuries. Half of me feels we should hide it again."

Ash sighed, and turned to face him, noting his bleak expression. "We can't keep hiding knowledge, Gabe. We're not gatekeepers. There's been enough of that already, don't you think?"

"I do," Shadow said, standing next to him to study the tablet. She shivered in its green glow. "Arcane knowledge is a dangerous thing. But it's even more dangerous to lock it up and pretend it doesn't exist. Besides, it might help JD, *and* help us defeat Black Cronos."

Gabe grunted. "Raziel's Book of Knowledge almost sent JD mad. Will this do the same?"

"It's a chance we have to take," Ash answered.

Theo looked dazed, but the battle seemed to have energised him. He took it all in. The room, the dead bodies, Gabe and Ash's wings, and Shadow's ethereal, Otherworldly appearance, as she had cast aside her glamour for now. "I don't know half of what you're talking about, and frankly," he gestured at their wings and Shadow, "I'm not even sure what you are, but I'm glad you're on my side. And Shadow is right. Part of me detests the Templars for the things they accumulated and then hid. They aren't custodians of knowledge, and neither are we. It should all go to a museum."

"Not that," Ash said pointing at the Emerald Tablet. "If you will grant us one request, Theo, other than your silence on our abilities, it would be to let us take this. The rest is yours to share with the world."

Harlan joined them, having ushered Mouse into a closer pew so that he could talk. They were both dusty and bloodstained, and Harlan in particular looked battered and bruised. "I've seen the defences that JD has on his house," he told them. "It will be safe with him. Anywhere else would place the tablet somewhere where the count could get it. We do not want to advertise its existence. I guess it depends," he turned to Mouse, "on what she will say, and what we do with her."

Mouse just glared at him. "You know me, Harlan. And you saw what I did up there. I was on your side!"

"Eventually. Zapping Niel has given me doubts."

"So, what are your options here? Are you going to kill me? Or lock me up forever?"

Shadow raised her still-bloody swords. "Killing you is just fine with me."

"No!" Gabe's voice echoed across the church. "No more killing." He stared at Mouse. "What about Nicoli?"

"I'll tell him that we lost." She shrugged. "It happens. I'll also tell him that everything that was found here tonight will be on the news." She lifted her chin. "I can keep secrets, too."

"Until they have a purchase price," Harlan pointed out.

"Then pay me more." Her eyes lit up. "Give me a piece of priceless iconography, and I'll keep this silent forever. I can disappear for a while."

"My blade can make that happen," Shadow muttered.

Ash smirked. Shadow was always consistent and economical. Gabe wasn't so amused. "Shadow, no. Mouse, we may need to work with you in the future, so I'll accept your terms. Harlan, choose her something, and then I'll escort her upstairs. I want to see what's happening up there. Make sure any remaining knights are retreating. I'll offer them a sweetener, too."

"Like what?" Ash asked. "They could be surrounding us even now, ready to mount another attack. And what are we going to do with all of these dead bodies? Prison won't suit any of us. We haven't got Maggie Milne or Newton to help us here."

"We'll offer them this." Gabe leaned down and picked up the package that de Moret had taken from William de la More's real tomb. "De Moret said it would lead them to the rest of the treasure—that this was just a small part of it. This should assuage them. Plus, it will be daylight in a few hours. They can't afford to keep fighting, and they will want to be out of here by then. They can take this and their fallen. I think they'll accept it. I would, if it were me. You learn to pick your battles."

Shadow nodded approvingly. "I like it. Although, I suggest we announce the discovery in another twenty-four hours. That will give us time to clean ourselves up, and all the blood, and move the Emerald Tablet to a secure location. The authorities will be so overwhelmed with the discovery that they won't question anything else. Theo? Harlan?"

Theo could barely contain his excitement. "Yes! Absolutely. I knew this would be my greatest find. *Our* find," he corrected himself. "Full credit will be made to The Orphic Guild, of course."

"Then it's a deal," Harlan said, grinning broadly. "Hopefully it will earn me the commission of a lifetime!"

While Harlan found Mouse a suitable item of treasure, Ash started to wrap the Emerald Tablet in de Moret's cloak. He felt a sense of loss as he concealed it, and the church seemed much darker.

He just hoped Harlan was right, and that JD could protect it.

—◦❖◦—

Niel's side ached from the wound he had received, and his arms felt like they were on fire from the many cuts he had sustained. He sat in the pew staring at the altar, wishing he could be anywhere but here.

He felt like a fool. The memories of his earlier excitement at seeing Mouse stung even more than his injuries. Once he and Nahum had ascertained that the church was secure and that the knights had maintained watch around the church rather than advancing, weariness had swept over him.

For a while he kept busy to keep his thoughts at bay. He and Nahum had piled the dead next to the side door, keeping the two prisoners still trapped in one of the rooms, and then Nahum left him to his own devices, keeping watch through the stained glass window.

Nahum was a thoughtful brother. His only comment was that sometimes events weren't always as they seemed, and that time would probably tell. Niel was in no mood for platitudes.

Strident footsteps made him turn around, and he saw Gabe walk through the nave with de Moret's body over his shoulder, Shadow next to him. He stiffened as he saw Mouse's slight figure between them.

"What's she doing here?" he asked, rising to his feet.

"She's leaving," Gabe said.

"Like hell she is."

Gabe placed de Moret's body with the others. "I'm not arguing with you. The decision is made. Mouse has been compensated for her time, and she will keep our secrets. There are other services she may do for us in the future." Gabe turned to her, his dark eyes looking black in the shadowed church. "I will hunt you down and kill you myself if you betray us."

"I won't. I wasn't lying." She threw her shoulders back and lifted her chin as she addressed Niel. "I made a bargain. It actually wasn't a hard call. A Taser over a blade. I would do it again to save your life, Niel."

Niel couldn't bring himself to answer. Silence would impart his feelings more eloquently than words. His throat burned with fury and shame, but he wouldn't argue with Gabe.

Not here. Not in front of her.

"Are the knights out there?" Gabe asked.

"Yes, brother," Nahum answered. "Throughout the grounds."

"Good. We need to bargain."

Mouse appealed to Gabe. "If I walk out now, they'll kill me."

"Then I'll fly you away from here," Nahum said, immediately. "From the bell tower. Gabe, have you a plan?"

Gabe held a bulky package aloft. "I have. I will trade this. Wait with me while we bargain, and then take Mouse when we're done."

Nahum nodded, already opening up the side door.

Niel stayed back with Shadow, watching the proceedings, both armed and ready to attack if needed. Mouse kept her distance, her gaze averted from Niel, but he still felt her presence. He could barely look at Shadow, either. *Her teasing earlier was bad enough, but now...* He bristled, waiting for her scorn.

"You know," Shadow said softly, her lips close to his ear, "I would have killed her, but Gabe forbade me." Unexpectedly gentle, her hand touched his arm. "She doesn't deserve your regard, brother. If she crosses you again, just say the word and I will gladly kill her." Niel's throat tightened even

291

more at her unexpected words. His mouth opened, but words refused to come. She squeezed his arm again. "I mean it."

He forced himself to speak. "Thank you, but I'll do it myself."

"I actually don't think she will betray you, for the record." Her voice lowered even more, and her breath tickled his ear. "Strangely, I believe her. I think she might actually like your well-hidden qualities." He glanced at Shadow, and saw a glint of humour in her eyes. "Us women are mysterious creatures. It's part of our charm."

His normal response reasserted itself as their banter slipped back into place. "If you say so, you wilful madam."

"I'm fey. I'm always right." She grinned and watched Gabe negotiate the deal.

Shadow never failed to surprise him with her unexpected, generous gestures. Niel squeezed her hand and whispered, "Thank you."

Thirty-Three

J ackson escorted Estelle and Barak to Lucien's makeshift cell, ensuring the door to the remote side corridor was locked behind him before they progressed.

They had arrived back in London after an early flight, and both looked refreshed. They also seemed close, as if they had reached an understanding between them. Whatever had transpired in France obviously suited them.

"You're not taking any chances, then?" Estelle asked as she watched him lock the door.

Jackson shook his head. "We can't afford to, after last night." He cocked his head at Barak. "Your call was uncanny timing. Although I might have been better off staying in bed. I ended up putting myself right in harm's way."

"Sorry. I had a feeling, and I had to call. I'm glad to see you're okay, though." Barak took in the corridor and other locked doors. "I take it that no one else is down here?"

"The great thing about The Retreat is its wealth of rooms and corridors. This one is now off limits for the foreseeable future. I hate that we're having to do this." Guilt at having gone back on his word to Lucien still ate at him. "We've turned an old office into a cell. We had to work quickly, but fortunately the tranquilliser knocked him out for hours."

"And now?" Estelle asked.

"He's fine, but chained up like an animal. We've had to draft in more guards." He pointed to the four men clustered outside a room up ahead, Miller being one of them. "I had no idea that the lab had been experimenting with tranquilliser darts. Thank the Gods they had, or things could be very different right now."

"Hold on," Estelle said, stopping him and drawing him aside. "The conversation we had on the phone was brief, to say the least. Tell us what's going on."

"Sorry, you're right." Jackson was shattered, but coffee had revived him. He hoped he sounded more coherent now. "Things were a bit up in the air earlier, but now we have a better plan. Sort of. We've stripped the room of everything except a mattress on the floor and a bucket in the corner. We've fixed chains to the walls, and Lucien is currently cuffed to them. It looks awful, but it's the only way. We've also left the door open so that we can see him at all times. I have to admit that I'm really happy to see you two. Miller was brilliant last night, but just knowing that you're here, with your abilities…" He trailed off, hoping to hear a favourable response to his earlier proposition.

Barak exchanged a wary glance with Estelle. "We can stop here for a while, but not indefinitely. Don't get me wrong, we want to help you, and it's important to us that you and everyone else here is safe, but I guess we need to know what your long-term plans are. What exactly is it you want us to do? Be prison guards?"

"No, not just that." Jackson leaned against the wall, hands in his jean pockets. They felt like they were hanging off him, like he'd lost weight, which wouldn't surprise him in the slightest. "Layla has run tests and we're waiting for the results, but we're just trying to work out what could have triggered his change. It seemed to come out of nowhere. We also can't decide whether JD should come here, or if we move Lucien there."

Estelle nodded in understanding. "But that means putting him in a van and risking him changing in there. Or he runs wild and kills JD."

"Exactly. I think the best plan is that we watch him for a few days, talk to him, try to understand the trigger. Maybe get JD to see him here, and then make a decision. If we do move him, I'd be really grateful if you helped us."

"We can do that," Barak agreed. "But have you heard the latest from Harlan or Gabe?"

"No. What's happened?"

"They've found the Emerald Tablet of Hermes Trismegistus."

"*What?*" Jackson pushed away from the wall with new found energy. "Where?"

"In the Templar treasure, beneath Temple Church by Theo's place."

For a moment, Jackson couldn't speak. "This could change everything!"

"Perhaps," Estelle said. "Or it could just add another layer of absolute confusion to everything."

"Does JD know?" Jackson asked.

"He will soon."

Wild excitement flooded through Jackson. "This is brilliant, but you're right, we can't get ahead of ourselves. We have to focus on the present." He said this more to himself than the others. "Are you ready to see Lucien?" They nodded, and in moments they were outside Lucien's room. He greeted Miller, who had refused to leave until he was happy with the arrangements. "Are we okay to go in?"

"Sure. Just keep your distance."

Lucien's feet and one arm were each attached to thick chains that were fixed to the wall. He was still dressed in scrubs, lying on the mattress and staring at the ceiling, but he sat up when they entered. Jackson felt a jolt of pity for the man. He looked haunted, and there were dark circles beneath his eyes.

"Hey, Lucien. I've brought you some visitors."

"You've come to watch the animal, like a zoo."

Estelle shook her head, her eyes full of compassion. "Not at all. We've come to help you."

"How? How do I control this?" Lucien looked down at himself, his face twisting with disgust as he looked at his tattoos. "I have no memory of last night. Nothing! It is a void!" He took deep breaths. "I was told I killed a man. I don't even remember that!"

Jackson closed his eyes briefly, as if he could block out the memory of the fallen guard, and then looked at Lucien. "It wasn't your fault. You had no control."

"But it *is* my fault. I did it! I can never undo it!"

Barak crossed the room, despite Miller's warning, and sat down on the edge of Lucien's bed. "I have killed men and other creatures. Lots of them. Some deserved to die, many did not. I will carry that always. But I cannot dwell on the past, and neither can you, Lucien. We must move forward, all the time. That is why Estelle and I are here. We will help you control this."

"How?" Lucien leaned forward to stare at Barak with doubtful, angry eyes, and Jackson saw Miller bring his rifle up. "You should have left me there! I'm a monster."

"You are not a monster." Barak laid his huge hand on Lucien's shoulder, unafraid and reassuring. "I don't know how we deal with this, not yet. And I won't lie. This won't be easy, but we will find a way. Your life will be different from now on, but it doesn't mean it's over. It's just beginning."

Jackson exhaled a breath he didn't even know he was holding, and for the first time in hours, he felt hopeful. They *would* find a way.

They had to.

———⊰◈⊱———

Harlan helped himself to a huge serving of bacon and sausages, piled scrambled eggs on top, then sat at the table in Theo's dining room that overlooked the moat.

Only Gabe, Shadow, and Theo were there, also eating large breakfasts, as if none of them had eaten for a week. Thankfully, they had showered and changed clothes, although Harlan was sure he could still smell the stench of the awful mud that had flooded the Chamber of Truth. Nahum and Niel were still in the underground church, guarding the treasure and cleaning the place up.

He grinned at everyone. "I hope you all slept well. I slept like the proverbial log!"

"You're just thinking of your commission," Shadow said, amused.

"Well, that sure helps. And you're not?"

"Of course I am. I dreamt of gold. Lots of lovely gold."

Theo rubbed his hands together, a twinkle in his eye. "I'm just looking forward to calling the British Museum. I can't wait to see their faces. This will be the find of the century! I confess, I have no idea how this works, but it will be fun."

"Well, we'd better clean all of the blood splatter off today before anyone gets here," Gabe said, grimacing. "That will be a nightmare."

Harlan swallowed a mouthful of food. "Are Niel and Nahum okay?"

Gabe nodded. "I've just got back from seeing them. Everything's fine. The church is secure and tidy, the crypt is locked, and they've made a good start on the clean-up. We'll relieve them soon. Both of them will go with you to JD's."

"You sure you can spare them?"

"Of course. I know you don't want to risk transporting the tablet alone."

"No, I really don't." Harlan sipped his coffee, looking forward to seeing JD's face. He hadn't told him the news over the phone. He wanted it to be a surprise. But then something else struck him. "You know, JD will want to come here and see all of this before anyone else does. It wouldn't take him long to get here. Any objections, Theo?"

"I guess not—as long as he knows he can't pilfer anything else."

"I'll make sure he understands." Harlan could already see the avaricious glee in JD's eyes. He contemplated Nicoli's smug face, too. "I still suspect that Nicoli might try something."

Shadow shook her head and pushed her empty plate away. "I trust Mouse will keep her word. She'll tell him virtually nothing, and she certainly won't see him in his office."

"You trust her?" Harlan asked, surprised. Shadow didn't always mix well with other women, although to be fair, she did like the White Haven witches.

"Yes. She has a vested interest in our group." She grinned, her meaning clear. "And she was well paid last night. Don't *you* trust her?"

"I hardly know her," Harlan confessed. "Only by reputation, which is quite impressive. As you know, she's done work for us before. Which, by the way, brings me to another issue that's been troubling me." He turned to Theo. "Someone on your staff has betrayed you. I think you know who."

Gabe grunted as he forked up more food. "You're right, Harlan. Someone who can come and go in the house without anyone giving them a second thought. Someone who knew about the knife, and knew that you had found the key."

Theo's face fell, and it seemed his moustache became limp, too. "Oh, no. Not Chivers. Don't tell me the butler did it!"

Harlan laughed. "I think he probably did. Who else comes and goes as much as him?"

"It wasn't Owen," Shadow said. "I was wrong about him, and I'm happy to admit that."

"But we know Chivers is a gossip!" Theo said, appealing to all of them. "All the staff say so. Any one of them could have shared the information."

She gave Theo a wry smile. "You wanted him to retire, and he refused. He begged to stay. It has to be Chivers. It's time for him to go."

"Damn it." Theo thumped his cup down on the table. "All right. I'll do it later."

"Do it now!" Gabe insisted. "Before anything else goes wrong." He pushed his plate away and stood up. "I'm going to head back down to the church. There's more to see down there, and I want to make sure we haven't missed anything before anyone turns up. We need to explore the other tunnels, too."

"I think we should leave the one we blocked well alone," Shadow told him. "Otherwise, we risk bringing the church down on our heads and killing ourselves. What worries me, is that the church may say the treasure belongs to them."

"I would contest that," Theo said. "It is *under* the church, not in it. Although, it admittedly is their land."

"Potentially the money would be split between you and them," Harlan suggested. "And you did find it. That will count for a lot."

"*We* found it," Theo said, thoughtfully tapping his cup. "I couldn't have done it without you. I think that maybe the money should be split several ways. It will be worth millions! Plenty to go around."

Harlan stared at him, not quite believing his ears. "Are you seriously suggesting that, Theo? You hired us to help."

Theo brushed his fingers across his moustache, twirling the ends in his absent-minded way, before staring at them each in turn. "Yes, I'm serious. The more I think about it, the fairer it seems. We did this together, so we should all benefit. Plus, you fended off the Knights of Truth and Justice. No doubt they are on the trail of the rest of the treasure right now. We need to get our story straight on that," he said, nodding to himself. "Of course, we have no idea how long all this will take. It has to be valued. We might have to argue with the church, but either way, there's a lot of money to go around." He smiled, pleased with his decision. "Yes. I'm completely sure."

"Herne's hairy balls on a stick!" Shadow exclaimed. "We'll be rich! Mind-blowingly rich!"

Gabe had thumped back down in his seat. "Theo. Are you absolutely sure? Because I'm taking you at your word. A gentleman's agreement. Time to back out now if you have any second thoughts."

Harlan willed Gabe to shut up, but Theo merely shrugged. "No second thoughts. Let's shake on it, now. All of us."

Before Harlan could even take it in, they had all shaken hands on it. A decision to split three ways—Theo, Harlan, and Gabe and Shadow's team. With this kind of money, he could give up work. He could buy a yacht. He could build a palace.

But would he miss all this? The thrill of the chase. The uncovering of secrets. The unravelling of mysteries.

Yes, of course he would.

He stared at Shadow and Gabe, his comrades in arms, and couldn't keep the panic out of his voice. "Does this mean you'll retire?"

Shadow rolled her eyes and glanced at Gabe for confirmation. "No! Will you?"

"No!" He shuffled in his seat. "I quite enjoy all of this. Not the threats to my life, to be honest, but the rest of it."

"There you go, then." Shadow grinned, and raised her cup in a toast. "To our next adventure!"

⋯⊰❖⊱⋯

Thanks for reading *Midnight Fire*. I'd love you to leave a review here: https://happenstancebookshop.com/products/midnight-fire-whit e-haven-hunters-book-5-ebook

The sixth book in this series is called *Immortal Dusk* and is set close to Yule. The search for Black Cronos gains pace, and then a Fallen Angel creates havoc. You can buy it here: https://happenstancebookshop.com/products/immortal-dusk-white-haven-hunters-book-6-ebook

Newsletter

If you enjoyed this book and would like to read more of my stories, please subscribe to my newsletter at https://www.subscribepage.com/tjgreens newsletter. You will get two free short stories, Excalibur Rises and Jack's Encounter, and will also receive free character sheets for all of the main White Haven witches.

By staying on my mailing list you'll receive free excerpts of my new books, as well as short stories, news of giveaways, and a chance to join my launch team. I'll also be sharing information about other books in this genre you might enjoy.

Ream

I have started my own subscription service called Happenstance Book Club. I know what you're thinking! What is Ream? It's a bit like Patreon, which you may be more familiar with, and it allows you to support me and read my books before anyone else.

There is a monthly fee for this, and a few different tiers, so you can choose what tier suits you. All tiers come with plenty of other bonuses, including merchandise, but the one thing common to all is that you can read my latest books while I'm writing them – so they're a rough draft. I will post a few chapters each week, and you can read them at your leisure, as well as comment in them. You can also choose to be a follower for free.

You can comment on my books, chat about spoilers, and be part of a community. I will also post polls, character art, share rituals and spells, share the background to the myths and legends in my books, and some of my earlier books are available to read for free.

Interested? Head to Happenstance Book Club. https://reamstories.co
m/happenstancebookclub

Happenstance Book Shop

I also now have a fabulous online shop called Happenstance Books
where you can buy eBooks, audiobooks, and paperbacks, many bundled
up at great prices, as well as fabulous merchandise. I know that you'll love
it! Check it out here: https://happenstancebookshop.com/

Substack

I now write over on Substack, and my page is called Where the Witches
Gather. I'd love to see you there. Substack has a wonderful community of
witchy writing and seasonal celebrations. You can find me here: https://s
ubstack.com/@wherethewitchesgather

YouTube

If you love audiobooks, you can listen for free on YouTube, as I have
uploaded all of my audiobooks there. Please subscribe if you do. Thank
you. https://www.youtube.com/@tjgreenauthor

Please read on for a list of my other books.

Author's Note

T hanks for reading *Midnight Fire*, the fifth book in the White Haven Hunters series. I've always been fascinated by the Templars, and couldn't resist writing a story about them—as many do! As usual in my books, some of the facts are correct, and some have been twisted to serve the story.

First, the true facts. Across Europe, the knights really were arrested on Friday the 13th of October in 1307, conspired by King Philip IV of France. Pope Clement V was initially annoyed, but then gave his blessing. They were accused of heresy and blasphemy, charges they denied. England, Portugal, and Spain all delayed the arrests. While many knights were eventually arrested, tortured, and burned at the stake, huge numbers were not. Many were forced to join other orders. All Templar land and property was seized. The Knights Hospitaller benefitted the most.

The Templars really did become the first banking system, and they amassed huge amounts of wealth and power. Eighteen ships did set sail, rumoured to contain Templar treasure, and were never seen again. William de la More was the last English Commander of the Knights Templar, and he died in the Tower of London after refusing to confess to the charges made against him. In Portugal, the Knights Templar simply changed names, and in Spain, they all joined another order. While rumours abound, their treasure has never been found—supposedly. Lots of places associated with the Templars still exist today. The Templars are also believed to have gone on to found many other organisations, the Masons being one of them. And yes, they were obsessed with religious artefacts and were indeed believed to have found the Ark of the Covenant and the Turin Shroud.

What's fiction? Temple Keep and Temple Moreton are completely fictional, although many places with 'Temple' in the name exist across the UK. They all have historical links to the order. I decided it was logical to assume that some of the treasure could have ended up in England. I made up William de la More's family too, and everything about the dagger is completely fictional.

I like to believe that if the treasure was ever found, someone would declare it, but who knows; it could be in private collections across the world already.

The Emerald Tablet of Hermes Trismegistus is also rumoured to be true. I thought it was time for it to make an appearance in this world.

I also wanted to explore and develop Barak and Estelle's relationship, so I hope you enjoyed that. I couldn't let Black Cronos go, so you can be sure that Black Cronos and the *Comte de Saint-Germain* will continue to appear. As for Lucien, well, who knows what will happen there! I'm planning on writing another White Haven Hunters book next year, so look out for that.

If you're interested in reading more background on my books, head to my website and check out my blog:

If you enjoy audiobooks, *Spirit of the Fallen*, White Haven Hunters #1, *Shadow's Edge*, #2, and *Dark Star*, #3, are all complete. *Hunter's Dawn*, #4, is scheduled soon. Please visit my website's audio page for links to all of my audiobooks:

Thanks to my very clever and skilled cover designer, Fiona Jayde Media, and to the fabulous Kyla Stein at Missed Period Editing. I owe a big thanks to Jason, my partner, who has been incredibly supportive throughout my career, and is a beta reader. Thanks also to Terri and my mother, my other two beta readers. You're all awesome.

Finally, thank you to my launch team, who give valuable feedback on typos and are happy to review on release. It's lovely to hear from them—you know who you are! You're amazing! I also love hearing from all of my readers, so I welcome you to get in touch.

If you'd like to read a bit more information about me and all of my series, please head to my website where I blog about the research I've done, among other things. I have another series set in Cornwall about witches, called White Haven Witches, so if you enjoy myths and magic, you'll love that, too. It's an adult series, not YA. My YA fantasy series is called Rise of the King, and is about King Arthur.

If you'd like to read more of my writing, you can join my newsletter at https://www.subscribepage.com/tjgreensnewsletter. When you register, you will receive get a free short story called *Jack's Encounter*, describing how Jack met Fahey—a longer version of the prologue in *Call of the King*, the first book in my YA Arthurian series. You'll also get a FREE copy of *Excalibur Rises*, a short story prequel to Rise of the King. Additionally, you will receive free character sheets on all of my main characters in the White Haven Witches—exclusive to my email list! By staying on my mailing list, you'll receive free excerpts of my new books, as well as short stories and news of giveaways. I also share other books in this genre you might enjoy.

Finally, I welcome you to join my Facebook group called TJ's Inner Circle. Please answer the questions to join. https://www.facebook.com/groups/tjsinnercircle

About the Author

I write books about magic, mystery, myths, and general mayhem, and they're action-packed!

I was born in England, in the Black Country, but moved to New Zealand for 16 years. In 2022, I moved to the Algarve in Portugal. I live with my partner, Jase, and my cats, Sacha and Leia. When I'm not busy writing, I read lots, indulge in gardening and shopping, and I love yoga.

Confession time! I'm a Star Trek geek—old and new—and love urban fantasy and detective shows. My secret passion is *Columbo*! My favourite Star Trek film is *The Wrath of Khan*, the original! Other top films for me are *Predator*, the original, and *Aliens*.

In a previous life, I was a singer in a band, and used to do some acting with a theatre company. On occasion, a few friends and I like to make short films, which begs the question, where are the book trailers? I'm thinking on it...

Why magic and mystery?

I've always loved the weird, the wonderful, and the inexplicable. My favourite stories are those of magic and mystery, set on the edges of the known, particularly tales of folklore, faerie, and legend—all the narratives that try to explain our reality.

The King Arthur stories are fascinating because they sit between reality and myth. They encompass real life concerns, but also cross boundaries with the world of faerie—or the Otherworld, as I call it. There are green knights, witches, wizards, and dragons, and that's what I find particularly fascinating. They are stories that have intrigued people for generations, and like many others, I'm adding my own interpretation.

I also love witches and magic, hence my additional series set in beautiful Cornwall. There are witches, missing grimoires, supernatural threats, and ghosts, and as the series progresses, even weirder stuff happens.

Have a poke around in my blog posts, and you'll find all sorts of articles about my series and my characters.

My primary series is adult urban fantasy, called White Haven Witches. There's lots of magic, action, and a little bit of romance.

My YA series, Rise of the King, is about a teen named Tom and his discovery that he is a descendant of King Arthur. It's a fun-filled, clean read with a new twist on the Arthurian tales.

White Haven Witches has a spin-off called White Haven Hunters, and a second spin-off is planned for the near future. It's called Storm Moon Shifters, and is about the wolf shifters who work at the Storm Moon Club in London. And of course, Hunter and his pack, the shifters from Cumbria, will pop up, too.

I've got loads of ideas for future books in all of my series, including spin-offs, novellas, and short stories, so if you'd like to be kept up to date, subscribe to my newsletter. You'll get free short stories, character sheets, and other fun stuff. Interested? .

If you'd like to follow me on social media, you'll find me here:

f facebook.com/tjgreenauthor/

𝓟 pinterest.pt/tjgreenauthor/

tiktok.com/@tjgreenauthor

youtube.com/@tjgreenauthor

goodreads.com/author/show/15099365.T_J_Green

instagram.com/tjgreenauthor/

bookbub.com/authors/tj-green

https://reamstories.com/happenstancebookclub

Other Titles by TJ Green

Rise of the King Series

A Young Adult series about a teen called Tom who's summoned to wake King Arthur. It's a fun adventure about King Arthur in the Otherworld.

Call of the King #1

The Silver Tower #2

The Cursed Sword #3

White Haven Witches Series

Witches, secrets, myth and folklore, set on the Cornish coast.

Buried Magic #1

Magic Unbound #2

Magic Unleashed #3

All Hallows' Magic #4

Undying Magic #5

Crossroads Magic #6

Crown of Magic #7

Vengeful Magic #8

Chaos Magic #9

Stormcrossed Magic #10

Wyrd Magic #11

Midwinter Magic #12

Sacred Magic #13

White Haven and the Lord of Misrule Novella

<hr />

<u>White Haven Hunters</u>

The action-packed spin-off featuring Shadow and the Nephilim.

Spirit of the Fallen #1

Shadow's Edge #2

Dark Star #3

Hunter's Dawn #4

Midnight Fire #5

Immortal Dusk #6

Brotherhood of the Fallen #7

<hr />

<u>Storm Moon Shifters</u>

Paranormal Mysteries set around the wolf shifter pack, Storm Moon.

Storm Moon Rising #1

Dark Heart #2

<u>Moonfell Witches</u>
The First Yule Novella
Triple Moon: Honey Gold and Wild #1

Printed in Great Britain
by Amazon

b8f99935-d74e-4439-9130-96970e220542R01